D1164732

BLOOD BETRAYAL

ALSO BY AUSMA ZEHANAT KHAN

THE BLACKWATER FALLS SERIES

Blackwater Falls

THE ESA KHATTAK AND RACHEL GETTY MYSTERIES

A Deadly Divide
A Dangerous Crossing
Among the Ruins
A Death in Sarajevo (a novella)
The Language of Secrets
The Unquiet Dead

THE KHORASAN ARCHIVES FANTASY NOVELS

The Bladebone
The Blue Eye
The Black Khan
The Bloodprint

BLOOD BETRAYAL

AUSMA ZEHANAT KHAN

MINOTAUR BOOKS
NEW YORK

This is a work of fiction. All of the characters, organizations, and events portrayed in this novel are either products of the author's imagination or are used fictitiously.

First published in the United States by Minotaur Books, an imprint of St. Martin's Publishing Group

www.minotaurbooks.com

The lyrics on page 120 are from the song "ICE El Hielo" by La Santa Cecilia.

Library of Congress Cataloging-in-Publication Data

Names: Khan, Ausma Zehanat, author.
Title: Blood betrayal / Ausma Zehanat Khan.
Description: First edition. | New York: Minotaur Books, 2023. | Series: Blackwater Falls Series; 2
Identifiers: LCCN 2023028816 | ISBN 9781250822406 (hardcover) | ISBN 9781250822413 (ebook)
Subjects: LCGFT: Detective and mystery fiction. | Novels.
Classification: LCC PS3611.H335 B57 2023 | DDC 813/.6—dc23/eng/20230626
LC record available at https://lccn.loc.gov/2023028816

First Edition: 2023

10 9 8 7 6 5 4 3 2 1

For Yasmin, Semina, Kamran,
Auntie Aira, and our dearly loved Uncle Munir,
from the girl who fell in love with you all
when she was twelve years old.
I will always think of you as home.

BLOOD BETRAYAL

1

Harry loved his hometown, except on nights like these. The streets of Blackwater Falls were deep indigo, the darkness blotting out the foothills and cloaking the houses at the bottom of the hills. He couldn't see much; he could only hear the footsteps he was chasing, young voices calling out to each other. He took a terrible moment to decide whether to call for backup or continue on by himself. Budgets were tight; he wasn't supposed to waste resources. And he was only on the trail of a couple of kids, young hoodlums who'd been marking up the town with graffiti. Street art, some said. What the young did for entertainment these days.

He turned a corner, feeling a twinge in his chest. He raised a hand to massage the twinge, and at the same time switched on his body cam. Best not to make mistakes, like getting out of his car when he should have radioed in. But the suspects he was chasing had disappeared down a lane where the car couldn't follow. He was a middle-of-the-road cop, never amounting to much, but he was good at keeping the streets safe at night, and was liked by the people he met.

Not by these hoodlums, though. They were shouting insults at him like "pig" and "fuck the police." It gave him a sense of who he was dealing with. There weren't many Black kids in town, except for the kids of workers at the local meatpacking plant. The ones he was chasing might not be local; graffiti artscapes had popped up all over the greater Denver area. Blackwater's gazebo had been hit, as well as the concrete wall behind the falls. Both had been cleaned up, but now a quiet residential neighborhood was at risk of being defaced.

Harry didn't like it.

"Stop! Police!" he shouted, hearing the strain in his voice that echoed the pumping of his lungs. He was definitely getting past this. It was time to talk to Sheriff Grant about retirement. The sheriff took good care of his boys—he'd often told Harry he was a credit to the department. Be nice to go out on a high note. One final collar, all violence avoided.

Harry stopped for half a second, fumbling for his flashlight. Where was it? There. His thumb switched it on, flooding the dark crosswalk.

One of the runners had sprinted away, vaulting a fence, something Harry couldn't hope to do. The other was straight ahead, heading into a cul-de-sac. The vandals had already been here, garbage bins lined up in a row, the lurid sprawl of graffiti on the cans.

"Stop!" Harry shouted again. "There's nowhere to run, son."

He gave chase, the flashlight veering wildly. He was closing in on his suspect, who was trapped between the fenced-in dead end of a cul-de-sac and the bins Harry had just passed.

The runner stumbled. Harry didn't get a good look at his face, but the runner had something solid in his hand, he saw it in the beam of his flashlight.

Gun!

"Don't do it, son," he cried. "I don't want to shoot you."

His hand sweating, and his heart thumping wildly in his chest, he slicked his own gun free, dropping the flashlight to the road. He was supposed to hold them both, he thought, but somehow he couldn't manage it. If he fired—God, if he fired, he didn't want to cause any harm.

The runner darted at Harry, his raised arm menacing. He loomed above Harry, his build disguised by the baggy hoodie he wore.

Harry fired a warning shot, a sharp crack through the silence.

"Stop now, kid! Please!" His voice shook.

The runner charged as Harry fell back, his hand raised squarely in front of his face.

Harry couldn't see a thing. He gave the runner one more warning, saw him raise his hand.

Harry's gun went off.

The runner's hand opened and the object in his hand rolled away down the street.

Then he dropped like a stone.

Harry's sweat-slicked hand gripped his radio. He fumbled through a call for backup.

A sharp voice on the other end snapped him out of his daze. An ambulance was en route.

He fell to his knees. Blood flowed over his hand, and Harry's whole body trembled.

He found the wound below the neck and applied pressure. The pulpy mass of blood beneath his fingers made him want to pass out, as doors opened, flooding the street with light. He saw the runner's face. He was far too young to die, and Harry began to sob.

People gathered around him, some with their cell phones out.

He had just enough presence of mind to order them back into their houses. They couldn't be allowed to touch anything. Not the flashlight he'd lost track of, not his gun, and not the object that had rolled away when the runner had let it fall.

Not a gun, no, not a gun.

It was a can of spray paint.

2

Inaya studied the photograph that had pride of place in their family home, the blue and gold mystique of Afghanistan, the lonely gate in the desert with its spiraled columns and interwoven *hazarbaf* decoration, patterns laid in brick. A pair of turquoise doors between twin minarets and beneath a high sandstone arch was the photograph's one note of light; the rest suggested abandonment either by God or man, and the bone-deep weariness of war. The print hung in the hallway that opened onto the Rahmans' elegantly furnished living room, where Inaya and her father were lingering over *elaichi* chai.

Inaya's father, Haseeb Rahman, had told his family that the photograph had been taken by a friend from his youth. One of many friends her father had left behind on his journey as a refugee from Afghanistan to Pakistan to Chicago, to settle ultimately in Denver, Colorado, each migration adding a new flavor to his life yet subtracting something also. Her father carried within him a profound sense of loss. Inaya considered the print with fresh eyes and asked her father, as she often did, to tell her about its history, to name the place it was taken.

Like the detective she was, Inaya surmised that if he spoke the name of the place with the derelict gate, she would be able to search out its history—a war story, most likely, the vestiges of a past her father rarely spoke of, secrets he kept to himself.

There had been a history before Peshawar, she knew. A life lived under Taliban rule in a land that her father loved. She wanted him to speak of it so the wounds could heal. She knew there was something he wasn't telling her, something that had made a profound impact on how he viewed the successive invaders of his country. He denied that it was about the Soviet occupation that had lasted a decade, but if it was about the more recent American presence, she wondered why he didn't speak. Her partner in policing, Catalina Hernandez, often shared her thoughts on harm done by traumas left untreated, a veil of shadows cast over minds in deep distress. Let the light in, and the mind could heal. Yet her father continued to deflect her questions. Some memories were better left buried, he believed. To resurrect them would be to invite a form of *nazar,* the evil eye creeping into the light with its foreshadowing of harm.

"Tell me about the picture, Baba. One day I might be able to visit the ruins of the house with the gate, and you could come with me."

"I will never set foot in Afghanistan again. I have seen too much."

His quiet certainty unnerved her.

"You can't know that, Baba."

"A flame when it starts to blaze can burn down a whole town. Don't ask me to dig up old graves, to wash my wounds with blood."

She wondered if the poetic phrase was a quotation. Her father was fond of the poetry of Maulana, or Rumi as he was known in the West, but even more so of the great Pashto-language poet Khushal Khan Khattak, whom her irreverent younger sisters had nicknamed Triple K. The verse could be one of Khattak's. She didn't have the chance to ask.

Freshening his voice, her father said, "If the Taliban should fall, then I will tell you about the country on the other side of this gate. The gate that stood between two worlds."

"Let it be soon, Baba." She pressed his hand.

He poured her another cup of tea. "You are more persistent than your mother and sisters, I suppose this is what comes of having a police detective for a daughter."

The doorbell rang, piercing the quiet moment. Inaya made a wry face.

"You jinxed us," she teased. "That's probably for me."

Inaya's younger sister Noor came down the stairs as Inaya went into the hall. Dressed all in pinks, Noor looked as fresh and lovely as a tulip.

"Wow." Inaya made big eyes at her sister. "Has someone come to pick you up?"

Noor bumped Inaya with her hip.

"I was doing a clip for my social media channels—how to judge the right shade of pink for your skin tone."

Inaya flicked on the outside lights and peered through the peephole. No one was standing on the porch. Kubo, the family cat, twined through her legs with an affectionate murmur, nearly causing her to trip. Kubo believed it was his sworn duty to be the first one to greet visitors.

"Catch the little rebel, Noor."

"Come here, darling," Noor coaxed. Inaya opened the door, stationing herself between the open door and her sister out of habit.

The heady scent of gardenias drifted in from the porch. She cast a glance around, not seeing anyone. A frisson trickled down her spine.

As she made to close the door, she heard Noor gasp. Kubo had slipped from her hold and streaked through the open door.

Someone moved in the shadows at the foot of the drive. Noor made a move to chase Kubo down. With a face like stone, Inaya shoved her back with one arm. She pulled the door closed behind her, keeping it shut with one hand.

A man emerged from the shadows, freezing Inaya in place.

Kubo was caught in his grip, huge hands clasped around his neck.

The man advanced on Inaya, who stood frozen, her hand gripping the doorknob.

"Detective Rahman?"

The man's name was John Broda. His voice rose up from her nightmares.

3

In the short time since Inaya had left the Chicago Police due to John Broda's attack on her, Broda had aged ten years. He had been a fit and muscular police officer, topping six feet, with a military haircut and blue eyes that seared. Their color was faded now, dark rings beneath his eyes, his once-chiseled face gaunt, his fit frame almost wasted.

He set the cat down on the porch, and stood face-to-face with Inaya.

She dredged up every ounce of courage she possessed. With a group of others, this man had violently assaulted her, tearing the headscarf from her hair. He'd threatened to disappear her sisters. He'd vandalized her family home, and chased her off an important case involving police accountability. She had left Chicago in disgrace, and she no longer wore a headscarf. Broda and his friends had broken her, but she wasn't broken now. She had a team she trusted, and a boss she knew would back her in her work at Community Response.

Maybe Denver wasn't all that different from Chicago, but it felt like it was, and Blackwater Falls, south of the metro area, was beginning to feel like home. She wouldn't back away from Broda again, though fear had leapt into her breast.

Her ribs had cracked beneath his boots.

She wasn't wearing her police radio or her gun, and her cell phone was inside. Nonetheless, she kept her hand firm on the doorknob, relieved that Noor's efforts to join her had desisted. She heard her father's voice in the hall, and knew he wouldn't leave her by herself. She had to act, and now.

"Get off my property, Broda."

Those faded eyes sharpened, taking Inaya's measure. He held up both hands in the classic gesture of surrender.

"I'm not here to hurt you."

"You couldn't." Contempt hardened her voice. "I've learned a few things since Chicago."

His sigh eased from his body, his towering frame diminished.

"I've learned a few things too. Please. I just want to talk. I need your help, Rahman."

She scanned the street behind him, searching for his vehicle, searching for the others who had to have come with him.

He read her actions easily. "I'm alone." He was wearing a pale green Henley, the sleeves rolled up to show a handsome blue quartz watch. He separated his shirt from his slacks and did a slow circle before her. "I'm not armed. See for yourself."

The unfamiliar humility in his voice diminished Inaya's fear.

"What do you want from me, Broda? Haven't you done enough?"

His ruddy skin blanched. What would make a man like John Broda, king of his particular castle, ever approach her again? She'd done what he wanted: she'd dropped her investigation into his friend Danny Egan, a dirty cop if ever there was one, who'd beaten a young Black man unconscious. Marcus McBride had been in a coma for months, until his mother had made the decision to turn off his life support because Marcus wasn't coming back. Six weeks had passed since then—why had Broda come here now?

"I know what I've done," Broda said gruffly. "This isn't about me. It's about my son. It's Kelly who needs your help."

"Why? What has he done?"

"He's an officer with the Denver Police. Last night, he was caught out in a raid. They say he shot an innocent suspect. Kell's been arrested for murder."

Shocked, Inaya didn't speak.

"Do you understand, Rahman? My boy's life is at stake. Kelly—" Broda's deep voice choked. "Kelly is just a kid."

Angry that he would play on her sympathy, Inaya demanded, "How old was his victim?"

Broda raised his ravaged face to hers. "That's just it, Detective. Kelly didn't do it."

Irony twisted Inaya's smile. "That's what they all say."

"That's not who my boy is. He's more like you than me. He tries to do things right, he left Chicago because of me—a friend of mine transferred him here."

It was quite an admission coming from Broda—so much so that it gave Inaya pause.

Catalina would see right through her: her sense of compassion was being nudged to life. She had to remember not to fall for Broda's tricks.

"You shouldn't be here," she said at last. She let go of the doorknob and bent to scoop up the cat. "I don't trust you, and there's no reason on earth I would help you."

Broda trailed one hand through the gardenias in their box.

"That's where you're wrong. I know I owe you, Rahman. I didn't come here empty-handed. You help me, I help you."

Don't ask, don't ask, she told herself.

"How?" she plunged ahead.

His hand slipped into his pocket. He brought out his phone and held it up.

"I've got Danny Egan's confession. I'll give you the first recording now, the rest when Kell is free. You're a lawyer, Rahman. You'll know what to do."

She couldn't speak to him at her house, and she couldn't take him to the station. So with grave doubts, she chose a place where she felt safe, the Lebanese café on Main Street. She'd be in public, she'd have witnesses to her discussion with Broda—if it was a trap of some kind, she wouldn't be caught unaware. She reassured her father and sister that she'd be home soon, keeping the news about Broda quiet. Her parents didn't need any additional worry; they'd uprooted themselves because of her, refusing to let her go off to Denver on her own.

She drove through town slowly, taking in the glimmer of lights from the foothills, the soft blues of nightfall and the glass-paned storefronts of the boutiques that lined Main Street, the lamps casting a golden glow, the scent of sage in the wind. How fresh the air was in Colorado—it restored her to herself, even as she wondered if she should call Cat for backup, or her boss, Lieutenant Seif. Both would want to know. Both would want to be there for her. Yet in some peculiar way, she still felt tainted by Broda's assault, and she didn't want Cat or Seif to know that. Cat would offer disturbing psychological insights; Seif would tell her to take it on the chin.

She found a spot near the Marhaba café under a fuchsia-festooned streetlamp. Good. Every single minute, she wanted to be in public, to keep Broda in the spotlight. He was the kind of man who could and would creep up unsuspected.

He was waiting for her inside, surprising her by getting to his feet and holding out her chair. She shifted to the other side, to keep an eye on the door. There were a couple of other patrons inside the café, there for coffee and dessert, and now Marhaba's proprietor and Inaya's friend, Cyrine Haddad, fluttered warmly to their table.

Inaya made introductions, pointedly stating Broda's full name.

"Police business," she told Cyrine, who withdrew with a look of concern.

"Show me," she said to Broda, who set his phone on the table and hit play.

Danny Egan was at a cop bar in Chicago, surrounded by his friends. Inaya recognized Schierholtz and Dixon, two of the men who had been part of her attack. There were a handful of others as well, buried in a corner. Some of them were drunk; Egan wasn't. In the thirty-second segment, he began to brag about his record. *"They call me Teflon Dan because nothing sticks."* Not even his battering of Marcus McBride. *"Kid thought he knew his rights, he said."* Egan laughed. *"I showed him his rights. I beat him to a pulp. Bet he hears my voice in his dreams."*

It was as clear an admission as Inaya could have dreamed of. It was too good to be true.

"He couldn't have known you were recording him."

"He didn't," Broda agreed. Cyrine's son, Elias, brought their order to the table. Broda looked at the little leaf of mint that decorated Inaya's tea with surprise. His cup held coffee thick enough to stand up on its own. "Egan's been getting out of hand with his successes." Broda's mouth turned down. "I thought it'd be good to have insurance." He took a sip of the rich coffee, surprised by the taste, downing the rest of the cup like he was choking back a shot for courage.

"There's more?"

"Plenty more. Enough to buy the McBrides a multimillion-dollar settlement, courtesy of the CPD. All they need is a good attorney, someone focused like you."

He took Inaya in. She'd changed into a dark gray suit so she could wear her holster—she wasn't meeting Broda unarmed. He could see the holster strapped over her pin-tucked shirt.

"I didn't think you admired me," she said coldly.

Broda set both of his hands on the table. "You think I knew Danny set out to fuck up McBride? You know the streets—what we're facing out there. I thought Danny made a bad call. It could happen to any of us any time we're out on patrol. It could have been me."

Inaya turned her head away, unmoved. "Yes. You've known your share of violence."

"Put me away, I don't care. But I don't want Kell to go down. He's a good cop." Broda paused. "Sensitive. This shooting—it's the first time for Kell. He's never drawn his gun before."

He signaled brusquely to Elias. "Same again."

She hadn't touched her tea. She wouldn't until Broda left. At the back of her mind, she considered it another weapon. Hot water to splash in his face.

Enunciating carefully, she gave Broda her cell number.

"Text the video to me."

He didn't hesitate. Inaya's cell buzzed with a notification. She checked the video and slipped her phone back into her pocket.

His blue eyes never left her face. "You'll help me?"

"I won't break the law for you. And I won't cover up your son's crime. If he's guilty, he'll face the consequences. Do you still want me to consider it?"

Broda's entire body sagged. He wiped a hand over his face, and to her shock, she saw it was trembling. He'd been hanging on to a fragile hope, not expecting a way out.

"I'm not afraid. I know Kell didn't do this. Not even by accident."

Finally, Inaya inspected her tea. "Then you'd better tell me about it."

Kelly Broda was a patrol officer in his first year with the Denver Police Department. His partner was the same partner he'd had in Chicago, a woman named Madeleine Hicks. She was Kelly's best friend from childhood, and they'd accomplished life's major milestones together. Kelly was from a law enforcement family going back five generations. Madeleine and Kell were thick as thieves.

DPD had planned a raid on East Colfax, a part of town known for drugs and prostitution with a mix of strip clubs, lounges, tattoo parlors, chop shops, and weed joints dressed up as cannabis dispensaries. An informant had passed on a tip that more than marijuana was passing through the doors of Mile High Weed. Kelly, Madeleine, and half a dozen other patrol officers had been pulled in as backup to the DPD's Drug Task Force. They'd planned to interrupt a high-stakes opioid sale, but someone had tipped off the dealers minutes before. The deal was aborted and the players had scattered, the task force in pursuit.

To muddy the waters further, civilians were in the mix, emptying out onto the street. And East Colfax residents had a long history of animosity toward the Denver police, claiming with some justification that they encountered far too much police violence, stop-and-frisk run amok. It was getting so Black folks shouldn't bother driving. Use public transport instead.

Into this nightmare the untested Kelly and Madeleine had strayed, in hot pursuit of dealers on the run. In the ensuing chaos of the chase, a suspect had been shot and killed.

"The kid was Hispanic, Latino, whatever they call it now. He was twenty-one, a year younger than Kell. All of East Colfax is up in arms—they're burning tires, breaking windows, hell—" Broda Senior broke off. "They had to call in reinforcements. To calm things down, the DPD had to say they'd taken an officer into custody."

Inaya pondered all this, sorting through Broda's version of the facts. He was leaving something out, deliberately, she thought.

"Why?"

"Because the kid was shot in the back."

Inaya took a second to digest this. "Was he involved in the drug deal?"

Broda shrugged. "No one knows yet. Madeleine and Kell intercepted him on the strip. Could be he was in the wrong place at the wrong time—you know how Hispanics are. There's a lot of them and they stick together. Could be he was part of the neighborhood."

Inaya swallowed her anger. She knew Broda's spots hadn't changed.

"What does your son say? Does he admit to shooting the young man—do we have a name, by the way, or is he destined to remain 'the kid'?"

"Mateo Ruiz." Broda's shoulders sank. "Just a kid like Kelly." His hands curled into impotent fists. "Don't know why he had to go out and get himself killed."

"I doubt Mateo intended that," Inaya said shortly. "Any more than Marcus McBride did. He was a young man too." They both knew that youth didn't count in favor of Black or brown men who came into the crosshairs of the police: if you looked like a man, you were a man, while the opposite played out for someone like Kelly Broda, whose youthfulness and lack of experience would weigh in his favor.

Shame didn't sit easily on Broda's face. "The problem is Kell's not saying anything."

"Without a lawyer present, you mean?" Natural enough. As a police officer himself, Kelly Broda would know all the traps cops set for the unwary.

"With a lawyer, without. He hasn't said anything at all. He just sits there, shell-shocked."

"He must have said something to you."

Broda looked bewildered. "He won't talk to his old man, won't say a word to defend himself. The only way I found out about any of this was because Mad called me."

"Did she see Kelly shoot Mateo in the back?"

"The gunshot could have come from anywhere, the streets were thick with cops." Broda's face set into lines of stubbornness. "Mad didn't see a thing. There was smoke from the tires, and the riot police used tear gas."

The timeline was muddied. Who'd gotten to the scene first? How long had the raid lasted? When did the protests start? How long had it taken riot police to arrive? If she was going to help Broda's son, and she didn't know that she would, she'd need a clear idea of the fallout of the raid, get someone on the Drug Task Force to talk to her. If there was smoke everywhere—

"Then couldn't it have been an accident?"

Broda smacked a fist into his palm. "That's what I'm desperate for my boy to say. Just tell the truth. If it was him, say it was an accident." Broda shifted helplessly, his big-man energy depleted. His hand curled around his cup as his empty gaze checked the street. "Kell won't talk to me, but maybe he'll talk to you. Will you do it? For the rest of the video?"

"I'll have to think it over and I'll need to clear it with my boss, *if* I decide to help you. That's Lieutenant Seif at Community Response. He might consider this a valid case for us." And there was more she wanted from Broda, though she didn't intend to tell him that yet.

A look of intense relief lightened Broda's sunken features. She thought it was premature. There were questions she hadn't put to him yet.

"Can anyone apart from his partner vouch for your son's character?"

"I don't know if he's still seeing his girl from Chicago. He might have moved on to a new one, my boy is popular with the ladies." He said this with some pride.

Inaya knew what to ask to wipe the smile from his face. "Was Kelly's gun fired?"

"No!" A knee-jerk response that didn't fool her.

John Broda had just lied.

4

On the night that Harry Cooper killed Duante Young, the Blackwater Falls sheriff's station was a scene of chaos. Lieutenant Waqas Seif strode through its doors that night with a sense of foreboding. Even Julie, the station's call-taker, had lost her composure—she was admitting visitors to the sheriff's office, left and right. That wasn't where Seif was heading. He spared a smile for Julie, another for a frazzled-looking woman in her fifties who was pacing the lobby, and indicated the interior. The bullpen was in the back. Harry Cooper was segregated there, and it was Harry he needed to see.

When Julie buzzed Seif in, the older woman grabbed his arm.

"Are you going in to see Harry? Could I come with you? I really need to see him."

Seif turned to face her, keeping his impatience to himself. He was the head of Community Response. His admittedly short temper and the behavior it sometimes provoked could rebound on his unit.

"Ma'am." He held the door open, but barred the entrance with his arm. "Are you a member of Mr. Cooper's family?"

The woman hesitated. She had a fine cloud of blond hair that was fading to gray. Her eyes were a watery blue, and her skin looked waxy, sagging a little at her jawline. She was a stocky woman wearing a cotton dress in a pink floral print that was more appropriate for a girl in her teens. She clasped the arm that was barring the door, and he noticed the dimples in her elbows, the little bands of fat around her wrists.

"I'm Harry's girlfriend." Her voice was as wispy as her appearance. "Harry called me to say he was in trouble. I don't know what to do to help him—I don't know what's happened."

Seif responded to the earnest entreaty in her eyes, asking for her name. When she identified herself as Tania Davis, he suggested she contact Harry's legal representative. He would need a lawyer of television caliber, cocksure and able to grandstand.

"If you wait here, I'll tell you what I can once I've seen him. But I understand the matter is very serious. It's in Harry's best interests if you keep this to yourself."

Tania Davis was wearing a lipstick in a bright shade of pink. She gnawed at her lower lip, and some of its shine wore off on her teeth. Seif pointed to the restrooms.

"If you need a moment to yourself."

He slipped through the door before she could delay him further. There would be a need to speak to her later, as everyone and everything in Harry's life was about to come under the closest scrutiny. On his way out, he would warn Harry's girlfriend about the likelihood of running into the less constructive members of the local press.

He checked his watch. As soon as he'd spoken to Harry, and resolved a few matters with his higher-ups, he'd call his team in. He'd already been warned about a raid on East Colfax in Denver earlier that evening that had resulted in a shooting in a largely Latinx area. The shooting Harry was involved with in Blackwater meant his unit's attention would be split. Two shootings, two separate cases. A bad night's work, all in all.

He found Harry Cooper in the back, uncuffed and in his patrol uniform, still in possession of his gun, surrounded by Blackwater deputies, offering him words of consolation. One had gone so far as to bring him a sandwich and a beer. They sat untouched on the desk beside him.

Seif took stock of the older man. He was a big man, sturdy though not overweight. He looked to be in his sixties; Seif's preliminary check of Cooper's file told him Harry was younger than he looked, his amiable features wiped clean by shock, a ghastly pallor to his skin. His eyes caught Seif's and he straightened in his seat.

Here we go, Seif thought, flipping open his ID.

"Harry Cooper? Lieutenant Waqas Seif, Community Response Unit." He glanced at the other officers. "Who's on your forensics team? Why haven't

Officer Cooper's clothes and weapon been taken into evidence? You know better than that."

This was met with predictable hostility. Seif cut through the angry response.

"All of you, step away. Get forensics in here. We'll need to swab the chair as well." His head swiveled to Harry. "Don't touch anything else."

No one moved until he barked, *"Now."*

He turned to Harry. "Where's your union rep?"

"I don't need one." The deep baritone was thready.

"You're not expecting to be charged? That's a grave mistake on your part."

Seif had already heard an earful. Harry Cooper was possibly the most liked if not admired officer under Sheriff Addison Grant. A lifer on the streets with no ambitions for promotion. He'd written none of the exams, and wasn't aiming for detective. For the past twenty years, he'd been patrolling the streets of Blackwater Falls, without a single demerit or, for that matter, a commendation. He'd never used excessive force, and though he kept up with his firearms training, tonight's shooting was the first time he'd used his gun. He wasn't inclined to the swaggering authority that characterized most of Grant's team. His reputation was that he cared about the communities that rubbed up against each other in Blackwater; he loved the outdoors, he could always be counted on to pitch in for any minor or major disaster; he'd take Sunday shifts directing traffic out at the Blackwater megachurch so other officers could spend time at home with their families. He was a level head in a crisis, and he didn't aspire to be more.

The story of the shooting was already being framed: Harry Cooper was the last man on earth who would shoot an unarmed suspect. He would only have drawn his gun in defense of himself. The body-cam footage showed as much: he'd issued all the proper warnings, and fired off a warning shot. He'd given the suspect every chance.

He wouldn't be charged. And if he was charged, it wouldn't go to trial, because if it did, Officer Harry Cooper would be acquitted within the first hour of the jury's deliberation. That was how clean Harry was.

Seif wasn't buying it. He was naturally suspicious with a deep-rooted cynicism that had been fine-tuned by his time with the FBI. Dealing with the many transgressions of Blackwater's sheriff hadn't helped.

He held his fire while the forensics unit processed Harry, having a quick word with the ballistics expert. "How many shots fired?"

Only two, an answer that tallied with the shaken statement Harry had given at the scene, where Harry had been treated for shock and brought to the station via ambulance.

When Harry returned, Seif settled him in a quiet corner of the bullpen.

"There's a woman named Tania Davis waiting outside for you. I told her to contact your lawyer, you'll be needing one."

"Please." Harry held up a hand in appeal. "Tell Tania to go home. She shouldn't be part of this."

"She said you called her." Seif straddled a chair opposite Harry, his fore-arms resting on the back.

"She was expecting me back. I guess that's not possible tonight." The helpless note in Harry's voice irritated Seif no end. Did he think he could kill a civilian and expect the matter to end there?

"Officer Cooper—"

"Call me Harry."

"Officer Cooper, this isn't your official interview. That will be handled in due course. I'm looking for your initial interpretation of events. You can wait for your lawyer or your union rep, or you can speak to me now, it's up to you."

Harry stirred in his chair. Awareness of his predicament descended on him all at once.

"You think I did this on purpose."

"Did you?"

"I was going to retire next month. I would never ever dream of or want . . ."

"A stain like this on your record?"

"To take the life of another human being. God." He buried his face in his hands, his shoulders shaking.

Seif accepted a moment's doubt. If it was a performance, it deserved full marks. Harry Cooper's remorse was unmistakable, and no one could fake that kind of pallor—the sickly gray, the pulse beating hard at his throat. He gave Seif a swift account of the events of the night, the chase on foot, the dark streets of the residential neighborhoods, the splitting up of the suspects. It didn't come out as a well-rehearsed recital. Cooper backtracked several times, second-guessed himself, but in the end his actions were clear enough.

"Did you know the victim?" he asked Harry.

Cooper shook his head, his lips slack with bewilderment, the nest of lines beneath his eyes standing out in stark relief. It was a face eloquent of misery at the outcome of his actions. Seif could more easily have believed malicious intent of any other cop. Of the sheriff himself.

As if he'd conjured him up by his thoughts, Grant burst into the bullpen.

"What the *fuck* are you doing with my officer?"

Other men pushed in behind him. The bullpen was spacious and well-designed, windows along the west side of the room opening up onto a nighttime view of Rampart Range. The room crowded with big men, all of them armed like Seif himself.

"I want you out of here, Seif."

Seif took his time standing up, unfolding his long limbs from the chair with an air of total disregard. The Community Response Unit was about as popular as Internal Affairs.

"Sheriff." His greeting was cool; he was eye to eye with the sheriff, both men topping six feet, though Grant had fifty pounds on him, part muscle, part excess weight. "I think you'll find I'm here at the request of the commissioner. Given that your officer shot an unarmed man—a *Black* man at that—I'll be taking over the investigation."

The words "you and what fucking army" were shouted from the back of the room. They were answered by a thunderous assent.

With his back to a still-seated Harry, Seif turned to face the room. He took a perverse pleasure in refusing to meet their anger with his own, though his calm was merely surface. He could hear Inaya's voice chiding him for letting his temper fly.

"No army. Just a handful of highly trained detectives. They'll ensure that the truth is served and the victim's life is weighed with care."

Grant huffed a laugh. "Duante Young was no angel. He was shot while fleeing the scene of a crime. Harry gave him every chance. You can see the recording, and then you can clear out."

That was half of what Seif had come for. The original had been checked into evidence; what Grant showed him would be a copy. And now he had a name on the victim.

A monitor flared to life in the room. With Harry's muffled sobs in the background, Seif watched the chase play out, fear tight in his gut.

Events unfolded exactly as Harry had described.

"You can see Young is about to fire," Grant told him with more self-control. The shot fired, then the room went quiet as Duante breathed his last, Harry's hands wet with his blood.

As Harry's weight shifted, the camera spun away. It veered wildly over the graffiti, coming to rest on a can of spray paint, the object Harry had mistaken for a gun.

"I thought it was a gun," Harry whispered. "I swear I thought it was a gun."

Grant gave Cooper's shoulder a hearty pat. "Nothing to worry about, Harry. You did things by the book—it's as clear as day. We've got that can in evidence."

Using the cursor, Seif rewound the video to catch an earlier segment of the chase. He played it in slow motion, then paused the recording on the flashlight flaring down the opposite end of the cul-de-sac where Duante Young's escape route had been cut off. He ran down a checklist in his head, things to put his team on, not least of which were thorough background checks on Harry Cooper and Duante Young so there were no surprises.

Seif leaned closer to the screen, his expression dangerous.

The garbage bins looked deliberately lined up; it was a cul-de-sac, open at the opposite side. Someone had blocked off the entrance to the street.

There'd been nowhere for Young to run.

5

Areesha Adams knew that the call could come at any time. She could be at home with her husband and her boys, as she was now, and she'd get that strange little forewarning, that something bad had happened and, whatever it was, it would affect them all. Her husband, her sons, her friends, their community.

That warning bell had gone off too many times in the past for her to ignore it now. Dinner was over. Her husband, David, the handsomest man she'd ever seen, had finished clearing up with the help of their sons. Now her three boys were relaxing on the well-sprung couches in the great room, arguing over which TV show to watch.

A smile touched her lips as she listened to the familiar sound of family harmony. Kareem and Clay were ten and eight, and they'd both hit a growth spurt. They'd end up as tall as David, who blew her a kiss from the sofa, one arm looped around Clay's neck. She came to join them, pulling up the Pictionary game on television. It involved drawing with a magic marker in the air while the sketch was replicated on the screen. The player could then act out clues in synch with the sketch, which led to several rounds of hilarity, as neither Areesha nor David could draw, and the boys' guesses were completely off the wall. Clay collapsed into her arms giggling after another raucous turn. Areesha buried her face in the nape of his neck, tickling him with her nose.

The sound of the doorbell was an unwelcome interruption. It was late—after ten on a Thursday night—not a time for callers, and certainly not the boys' friends.

David straightened from the couch, pulling his long-sleeved tee straight and rolling down his sleeves. His eyes on Areesha, he said, "Let me get it, baby."

She told the boys to stay put, joining him at the door.

David turned from the peephole, puzzled. "It's a woman. Not one of your friends."

Areesha double-checked, her sense of unease from earlier returning now tenfold. Whatever was on the other side of the door wasn't anything good.

When she opened the door, the woman on the other side stared into Areesha's face as if it were a guiding light. She'd been holding herself tautly; now, upon seeing Areesha, she seemed to collapse, one arm gripping the railing at the top of the outdoor steps. She was wearing a heavy coat despite the warm summer weather, a red scarf knotted around her neck. Her hair was confined in a low, textured ponytail, her unlined face bare of makeup. Impossible to guess her age, but the expression in her eyes came to Areesha on a bright, dangerous current.

"Please help me," she said. "My name is Mirembe Young. My son was killed last night."

Though neither of them worked from home, Areesha and David shared an office on the main floor for when clients came to call. They were both practicing lawyers, David in criminal law and Areesha a civil rights attorney. Their shared business premises were at East Colfax and Twentieth Street, at a cross section of a number of Black and Latinx neighborhoods, close to Areesha's clients, and a short walk to the campus of Metro State University where David taught part-time.

Now, Areesha ushered Mirembe Young into the office at home, a cozy, well-furnished space nearly taken over by David's legal tomes and Areesha's ever-expanding caseload.

She cleared one of the chairs for Mirembe to sit in, crossing to the seat beside her.

David brought them tea, Mirembe's heavily sugared, then left the two women to talk.

Areesha urged the cup into Mirembe's hand, concerned by the other woman's look of fragility. She was holding up, numbed by the news, the shock acting like a tranquilizer. The tremors would come after, the grief that would take her to her knees, Areesha had seen it too often to mistake the signs.

She leaned in close. "Tell me what happened."

Mirembe's cup clattered in its saucer. "That's just it, I don't know." Her voice was deep and rhythmic, each word measured and rounded out, the syllables like notes on a scale.

"You received a police notification?"

"Yes, they showed me their ID. They said there was an accident last night." She shook her head, catching herself. "My son Duante—he's dead. He was shot while running from police. They said he was involved in a crime, but that was not Duante. He wasn't mixed up in anything bad, he hardly ever stayed out late, unless he was at a club with his friends."

Areesha skirted around the mention of the shooting. That moment was coming. "*Was* he at a club, to your knowledge?"

"No." Mirembe's lips began to tremble. "I thought he was in his room at home. He'd said good night like he always did."

"You didn't see him leave the house?"

"No."

"How old is Duante, Mirembe?"

"He was twenty." The empty cup fell from her hand. "He wanted a celebration for his twenty-first. Some kind of street party." A sob tore through her voice. She rocked herself back and forth in the chair, a lament pouring from her lips. "He's gone, he's gone, he's gone."

Areesha reached out and took Mirembe's hands, holding them strongly in her own. She didn't speak or offer assurances. There were none to be had. This was the first introduction of pain, the first quivering note in an entire symphony of grief. Mirembe's emotions would rise and fall as they entered each new movement. The identification of the body. The quest for answers. The public outcry. The inevitable clearing of the relevant officer's name. The moralizing of the network news. Law and order, law and order. The familiar commentary: *Duante was no angel. Duante refused to surrender. Duante had a gun. Duante brought it on himself.*

She let Mirembe cry until her eyes were red and her voice had given out.

A knock sounded on the door, and Kareem's head poked around it.

"Mum, is everything okay? Do you or the lady need anything?"

Mirembe raised her head, swiping at her face with the tails of her scarf. A fine coating of moisture glazed the soft skin of her cheeks. A gesture of her hand invited Kareem close. His ten years sat heavily on his frame, his gentle eyes dark with anger. He reached for the tissue box and passed it awkwardly to Mirembe.

"It's all right, sweetheart," Areesha told her son. "Go to bed. I'll check on you later."

Kareem's baby face hardened—a suggestion of the father in the son. "Is it another one, Mum? Another boy like me?"

"It's Duante." Mirembe wept. "He'll never be twenty-one."

Areesha saw Kareem off to bed, taking a moment to warn David that their sons would need him. When protests broke out, both Clay and Kareem would want to be on the streets. Especially if they knew their mother was called on to represent another bereaved family.

"The house specialty," David had said once with rare bitterness.

She returned to the office, where Mirembe had made an attempt to regain her composure. She had moved to stand beside the window looking out onto the quiet streets.

"Tomorrow, everything will change."

It would, Areesha thought, pierced by a pang of sorrow. For this one night, Mirembe had her grief and her loss to herself. Tomorrow *The Denver Post* would run the story. Then it would go national and key figures in the movement would arrive. Duante would mean something different to them all. And when the right-wing channels got hold of the story, experts would tell them the police had acted lawfully, the Black body on the ground circumscribed by legal means.

Areesha went to stand beside Mirembe, drained of the pleasure of an evening at home with her sons. She was gearing up to fight.

"I need to ask you some questions."

Mirembe took out her phone to show Areesha a picture of Duante. A young man with a clever face and beautiful hands, poised beneath his chin. He was smiling at the camera.

"He was an artist," Mirembe explained. "I wanted to focus on his hands."

Areesha murmured a consolation. She had no pat phrases for times like these, no platitudes. Nothing she said could be right. So she did what she did best. She took on the case.

"Was Duante shot by the police?"

A question that offended with its lack of feeling. But she knew what her purpose was.

"Yes." Mirembe clasped her phone to her heart.

"Once or more than once?"

"Twice, they said. The first was a warning shot."

"Why did they need to warn him?"

"He was caught spraying graffiti on private property."

Areesha paused, thinking ahead. "What kind of an artist was Duante?"

"He painted public art."

"Could it be seen as graffiti?"

"Yes." A hard look came into Mirembe's eyes. "That doesn't justify killing him."

"No; it doesn't. Was he armed? Did he own a gun or ever carry one?"

"No!"

"Was Duante ever arrested on other charges? Drug charges or other acts of vandalism?"

Mirembe's hand gripped her phone. "What kind of questions are these? You sound like the police."

Areesha softened her voice. "That's why I'm asking. So I can prepare you, so I'll know everything they know."

Mirembe jerked her chin. "No arrests, no drugs, no vandalism. He was in art school, for God's sake. He made a living off his work, unlike some of his friends. He was popular, but there was some jealousy too because my boy had made something of himself. He'd won awards in a street-art competition. That's probably what he was doing out—working on his murals."

Areesha's gaze flickered over a photograph of her sons. She took up a notepad.

"Can you tell me the names of the DPD officers who came to visit you? Did they tell you where Duante was when he was shot—what part of Denver? Was it around East Colfax?"

Mirembe's curls were dusted gray at the temples. She rubbed a few of them free, and they sprang up like ghostly tendrils around her face.

She rested her hands on the desk, looking down at the blank sheet of paper.

"I don't know if they were Denver police. Duante wasn't killed in Denver."

"Then where?"

"Blackwater Falls. It's south of the city."

Areesha's faint whisper of premonition was now a clarion call.

Her blood leapt in her veins. She had him. She finally had Sheriff Grant.

"Did they give you the name of the officer who fired at Duante? Was it Addison Grant?"

"They said it was someone who worked for him."

No doubt. Carrying out Grant's instructions.

"Was the officer alone?"

"Single patrol," Mirembe whispered.

Areesha kept her tone firm. Mirembe wouldn't last much longer. "Describe the officers who came to your door."

"One was Latina, I think. She said she was a detective. Her partner was a young man."

"Detective Catalina Hernandez, and Officer Jaime Webb?"

Mirembe nodded, surprised. "You know them?"

Areesha came to her feet, the notepad discarded. "I know they're going to help us."

"They're saying they have footage. The police officer—his name is Harry Cooper."

"*Harry Cooper* shot Duante?"

Mirembe didn't notice Areesha's sudden start.

"He said he didn't mean to, but the police are saying Duante had a weapon. But my son doesn't own a weapon. That isn't who he is."

It was beginning, then. The cover-up of the crime.

6

Dawn came early in the summer, pale traces of color outlining clouds massed low. Areesha was at the morgue with Mirembe, where Detective Catalina Hernandez had joined them. Her compassion embraced them as the pathologist led them into the cold room to identify Duante.

Cat waited at the entrance as Mirembe held fiercely to Areesha's hand. The fluorescent lights stuttered above their heads, the large room separated in two: a glass partition with a table to one side, rows and rows of steel drawers to the other, along with the usual implements required by a medical examiner.

How many dead did Denver claim? Areesha wondered. A curtain was drawn across a partition to prevent them from seeing what lay behind it. She had already heard about another shooting that night, this one in the heart of the city, not south of it in Blackwater Falls. Was this the other body? A young Latino sharing space with Duante in death?

She didn't ask. This moment was for Mirembe and her son, and as the pure white sheet was drawn away by Dr. Stanger, Areesha looked down at the young man's face. His hair was like Clay's. Ringlets like little plumes arrayed around a delicate forehead. Eyes closed, dense lashes bunched on his cheeks. Skin a bluish gray beneath its deep brown coloring, no sign of the bullet, and if there had been arterial spray, Dr. Stanger had cleaned it up. Duante didn't look at peace or as if he were sleeping through a dream. Death hadn't robbed him of expression. His eyelids and jaw were drawn tight, as if he carried the violence of his final moments into the sterile room. She disturbed the sheet at his side. As she'd thought, his fist was clenched.

Not the hand that had held the can of spray paint for his work as an artist, then.

Mirembe was utterly still at her side except for the hand that gripped Areesha's so hard that the bones might break. Areesha swallowed a sound of pain, giving Mirembe what she needed. She released Areesha after a moment, raising her shaking hands to Duante's face.

"I'm sorry." Dr. Stanger looked it, his face grim with concern. "I can't allow you to touch Duante until we release him."

He didn't use the words "the body" and, silently, Areesha thanked him for it.

Duante wasn't a body. He was a young man who was loved. Deeply loved, dearly loved, as she saw in Mirembe's unraveling.

She wouldn't moralize this, turn it into a cause for the movement.

She would simply be with Duante in this moment, praying for Jesus to accept him into the beckoning light, where their children gathered in the white-robed ranks of a heavenly choir.

Mirembe fished out a cross from her neckline. She held it above Duante's face, then pressed it to her lips.

"My child. My boy. My hope for tomorrow."

Tears moved down her cheeks, a soft, unending stream.

"I'd like to be alone with him," she said.

Areesha hugged her, then let her go. "Give him my love. My love, David's, Clay and Kareem's. Our prayers are with his beautiful soul."

She retreated to the narrow white corridor with Cat.

The two women had met on a previous case, not liking each other at first. They had worked through their initial distrust to arrive at a place of understanding, even kinship. She saw her own pain reflected in Cat's eyes. If Catalina Hernandez could, she would gather them all up in her arms and keep them safe from the dangers of a harsh and unforgiving world.

"You all right?" she asked Cat now.

Catalina shrugged. "Things have been bad these past two nights. This is my second visit." She nodded at the curtain on the far side of the room. "There's another young man here—Mateo Ruiz. He was a student at the Colorado School of Mines. He was shot two nights ago as well."

"I heard something about that. Was it an officer-involved shooting?"

"They're keeping a young police officer incommunicado—the shooting was the outcome of a drug raid on East Colfax. Protests broke out right after. The fires are still burning and the jails are full."

Areesha grasped her elbows, leaning back against the wall.

"The same old playbook. Headlines will focus on the property damage."

"Neighborhood riots. Neither Duante in Blackwater nor Mateo in Denver will be named."

Areesha thumped the back of her head against the wall. "Is CRU on this? I know these are two different kinds of shootings but they both sound like CRU should be involved. A young Black man—a young Latino: both shootings demand the presence of CRU."

Cat looked tired and a little worried, something else weighing on her mind. "We have a team meeting at eight in the morning. The lieutenant will tell us then. We don't really have the staff to work two different cases, unless—?" She directed a questioning glance at Areesha.

"You couldn't keep me away."

"I'll see if I can get the lieutenant to invite you to our briefings."

Areesha grimaced. "He prefers me to be seen, not heard."

"Not anymore," Cat said.

They paused as a sound reached them from the cold room. Mirembe was singing to her son, her voice a low contralto. Mahalia Jackson's "Trouble of the World," now Duante's elegy.

They were as quiet as if they were in the front row of a church.

When Mirembe's song faded, they heard the murmur of conversation between Mirembe and the doctor, and news Areesha had been holding tight burst free from her.

"Duante was killed in Blackwater by one of Sheriff Grant's men. He's an artist. His mother thinks he was probably out working on a public mural—he wasn't involved with drugs."

"Oh, Areesha." Cat grasped her arm, a gentle touch, so different from Mirembe's clinging-to-life grip. "You're still on Grant?"

"He runs Blackwater like it's a sundown town. We can't hide from that fact." She put a hand to her aching head.

"There's something more?" Cat asked. "Something that doesn't fit?"

"It wasn't Grant who shot him—it was Harry Cooper."

Cat nodded. She knew Harry's reputation.

"It could be that the shooting *was* an accident."

"Areesha." They both heard the sound of the table moving on its wheels. The identification was complete, so Cat spoke swiftly. "You know those protests I was telling you about? They're about the shooting of Mateo Ruiz during the drug raid in Denver. The news about Officer Cooper killing Duante hasn't gone public yet. When it does—"

Cat didn't have to tell her—the whole situation was charged. Together, the two shootings would provoke a nationwide outcry.

"Will you help me?" she asked Cat.

"In any way I can."

Areesha drove Mirembe home through the empty streets to a small double-gabled house near the hospital quarter on 20th Street. The front lawn was neat, bordered with bright pink petunias, with three potted palms on the freshly painted porch.

"You don't need to come in, I promise to try to sleep."

Areesha had already warned Mirembe not to enter Duante's room, to leave his belongings untouched. The press would excavate Duante's life far more thoroughly than Harry's. That was part of the equation. Mirembe understood without the need for further elaboration. The irony of it was that Mirembe was a psychologist, her practice focusing on the trauma survivors of PTSD. Had the moment been right, Areesha would have communicated that to Cat, who was the CRU's criminal profiler, a psychologist herself.

There would be time, Areesha thought. Time for each moment to be weighed in isolation before it became a part of the greater whole. When Mirembe looked back on the moment she had seen her son's body, there would be much she didn't remember, and perhaps that merciful silencing of memory was the work of the Lord, allowing the brain a space to cope.

She didn't know. She was dog-tired, and she was just at the beginning. That wasn't why, of course. Her fatigue was generational, the wisdom and losses of ancestors, just as her resilience was chipped at in increments, stealing bits of herself day by day.

When she made it back to bed, David turned over, shaking himself awake. She changed into her nightclothes and slipped into bed beside him. He took her in his arms, shifting the strap of her slip aside to kiss her shoulder.

"Is it what we feared?"

"It's much worse than that." She settled into his arms, turning up her face to kiss the strong brown column of his throat. "Two dead in two separate police shootings. Two young men—one Black, one Latino. What are we going to do?"

David captured her face between his palms.

"Whatever we do, Areesha love, we'll do it together."

"I can't expect you to shadow me, David. You have a job of your own—and you'd be more at risk than I would."

His fingers tightened on her jaw. "Because men are shot dead more often than women?"

She nodded, turning her face to breathe a kiss into his palm.

"They could fill the ocean with bodies, Areesha. I'm still not letting you deal with this on your own. I'm going to cry with you, I'm going to walk with you. I'm going to *be* with you."

Her little cry was incoherent. She gave herself up to David.

7

Inaya knocked on the door of Seif's glass-paneled office, not without a sense of trepidation. Seif was bad-tempered and guarded at the best of times; their recent understanding as they solved the case of a teenage girl's murder hadn't changed that. He allowed room for intuitive leaps among the close-knit members of his unit, but his preference was always to do things by the book.

He was on the phone when she knocked. He raised a hand to wave her in as he dealt with the call. He was jotting down notes with his free hand with the amethyst pen he favored, so starkly valuable and out of place that Inaya's curiosity continued to be piqued about where Seif had acquired it. She knew better than to ask. He might tell her or he might as easily warn her to mind her own business.

He wore a suit most days, but today there was something extra about the care with which he had dressed. His summer-weight suit was a fine navy blue, flexing across his broad back when he turned his chair to the side, listening to his caller with an air of the sharpest attention. Instead of his usual monochromatic flair, he wore a shirt so white it was startling against his tanned skin, and a navy tie with a narrow red stripe. She wondered how his shoulder holster fit beneath a jacket custom tailored to his body.

He'd let his Persian-dark hair grow out a little longer, its natural wave more apparent. Just as he turned to look at Inaya, she transferred her gaze to the commendations on the wall behind him. He'd also framed the first page of the use-of-force guidelines for reasons Inaya couldn't guess, unless it was to remind him never to draw his gun.

He waved her to the chair across from him as he hung up the call saying, "We'll talk again, West."

Inaya's eyebrows shot up. Lincoln West was an undercover FBI agent posing as a member of the Disciples motorcycle club, a group of vigilantes who patrolled Blackwater Falls, often in conjunction with Sheriff Grant's deputies. They'd gotten to know him over the course of their last investigation: Lincoln West had become a friend.

"You're early, Rahman," Seif noted.

It was fifteen minutes before the team meeting at eight a.m.

For a moment, Inaya was diverted from her purpose. "Was that West on the phone? Is he working with us again?"

Seif quashed her assumption at once. "I'll brief you on what West had to say at the meeting. Now I'll ask you, Rahman, why are you taking up my time?"

Inaya's lashes fluttered down to shield her eyes. She'd been expecting a shift when it came to their professional relationship—a greater warmth, perhaps, that came from the trust they'd built. Seif was no different now from when she'd first met him: cold, sarcastic, impatient.

She dropped the friendliness from her tone.

"I need to talk to you before the others get here. Did you call us in because of the raid on East Colfax in the city two nights ago?"

Rumors flew fast and furious around a police station, and the Community Response Unit was no different. Inaya was hoping that CRU would be assigned to the shooting Kelly Broda was involved in—the killing of a young Latino. Not only would it tidy things up for her, but she'd be able to rely on Seif's insights and on her entire team.

"The East Colfax raid is the Drug Task Force's business, not ours. We need to get out in front of another incident. Catalina's already taken point on it."

Back to his preferential treatment of her partner, Cat. This time, Inaya didn't mind. It would free her up to focus on Kelly Broda.

"I have an interest in the drug raid, sir. I'd like to speak to the officer involved in the shooting that took place during the raid."

Seif sat back in his chair, the amethyst pen between his fingers.

"What's your interest?"

This was where she had to tread carefully. "The officer involved may be charged with the killing of a young Latino by the name of Mateo Ruiz. You must have heard how things got out of hand during the raid. Riot police, tear gas, the shooting. I know it's not our jurisdiction, but it seems like CRU should be involved."

"That's my call, Rahman, not yours. There's been an officer-involved shooting in Blackwater Falls that I've designated as our priority."

Inaya frowned. "Because you're still after Grant?"

Though Seif was the head of their unit, he was also working undercover for the FBI on police corruption and violence. The FBI was tightening a noose around the Blackwater Falls Sheriff's Department. Sheriff Grant ran Blackwater like his own personal kingdom—Seif had been recruited to topple him without letting Grant know. Within their own unit, Inaya was the only one who knew of Seif's undercover role. They had yet to find a smoking gun, though Seif had come close.

He gave her one of his sharp looks. "Inaya. What's your interest in the raid?"

Inaya practiced her breathing. Slow. Calm. Measured.

She looked up to meet the sparkling chips in Seif's eyes.

"The name of the officer who shot Mateo Ruiz during the drug raid is Kelly Broda. He's the son of a former . . . colleague from my time in Chicago. He says his son has the utmost respect for the law. He would never shoot a suspect in the back, as Mateo was shot. He's asked me to help prove his son's innocence."

Seif stood up and moved around his desk to shut the door. Instead of resuming his seat, he picked up the remote for the blinds and shuttered his glass-walled office.

"The 'colleague' from Chicago is John Broda?"

Inaya twisted in her chair, her stomach plummeting. "You know him?"

"You were thoroughly checked out before you transferred here, Rahman. You had to know that. I don't pick just anyone for my team."

Inaya had spent months doing routine tasks like visiting community picnics and fairs, hardly high-caliber stuff that required a team of experts. Still, she'd been useful to Seif.

"John Broda isn't your colleague—he's your enemy."

Seif gave her a slow once-over, finishing up at her hair in its customary French braid. She could feel her skin burning, knew where Seif was heading.

"Don't," she said.

Seif didn't back down. "You used to wear a headscarf, Rahman, don't try to deny it."

He turned her chair around, his hand hovering over the length of her braid.

"I've told you before not to touch me, Lieutenant!"

Seif dropped his hand like a brick. "I wasn't sure if you meant it."

Goddammit, he was right. She hadn't then, she didn't now.

"Qas." His name broke from her lips in a whisper.

Seif sat down at his desk again, his jet eyes softening as he took in her distress.

"I know about the assault in Chicago, Inaya. Broda and his friends kicked you, beat you, stripped off your scarf. They terrorized you with their threats. You were working a big case—you had one of Broda's friends in your sights for beating a Black kid unconscious. I know about Marcus McBride, too. The cop responsible for beating him to death got off. So you tell me this." He braced his forearms on his desk, leaning in. "Why would you want to do Broda any favors? Is he threatening you? Does he have something on you?"

Inaya couldn't fight her body's response. Her hands were clenched in fists. Seif reached across to take them in his own, working her fingers loose.

"Tell me, Inaya."

The coldness had vanished. His eyes were soft now, shot through with pinpoints of light.

She was holding his hands despite promising herself she would keep her distance.

"Broda has Danny Egan on tape admitting he knew Marcus wasn't a threat. Freely confessing to beating him just because Marcus stood up for himself. Broda will give me the video if I try to help his son." Her brown eyes pleaded with Seif. "I told him I wouldn't cover anything up. I said I'd talk to Kelly and see what I could do for him, that's all." She tightened her grip on Seif's hands. "It's important to me to undo some of the damage I did. I left Marcus's family without justice, now I have the chance to fix that."

Seif's thumbs stroked over her palms, the touch sending streamers of fire over her skin.

"You can't fix it, no matter what you do. Marcus is lost to his family. That's on Danny Egan, not you. You know in your gut that Broda can't be trusted—he's working an angle, and once he has what he wants, he'll hang you out to dry."

"I've spoken to him, I don't believe that's true. He's only thinking of his son. He's desperate," she admitted.

"And desperate men do dangerous things." With a complete change of voice, Seif asked, "Did you always wear the headscarf?"

"Yes. As soon as I was the right age."

"Your mother doesn't. Your sisters don't."

Seif had been to her home and met her family.

"It's a personal choice."

He nodded. "Do you want to wear it again? Did Broda make you afraid to?"

Inaya's fingers were drumming a pattern on her knees. When she looked down, her braid fell forward across her blouse. It was hair, just hair. It carried no special import on its own, was charged only with the meaning she ascribed to it—a sign of her personal devotion. Seif's words made her feel exposed.

"Hijab is a private matter," she ventured.

Seif's sympathy drained away in an instant. "Not if you're allowing Broda to involve you in a case, it isn't. If anything, Rahman, it's a conflict of interest. You know Broda personally, there's no way you should be interfering in a case that implicates his son. Especially as a member of Community Response."

She knew he was right. It didn't alter the fiery determination at her core. Though she didn't owe a damn thing to John Broda, she did owe it to Marcus to push it, even to do things in the dark with Seif left out of the picture.

She sat up straight in her chair, unnerved by the way Seif was watching her as if he could read her thoughts. She'd give him what honesty she could.

"I'm not certain if I want to wear a headscarf again. It was part of my life for years. Then it became this heavily politicized thing everywhere you looked. Laws enforcing it, laws banning it, a talking point of each conversation, a target on my back—it wasn't just the incident in Chicago. It's as if

I *became* my scarf, and there was nothing else to me. My private, personal relationship with God became everyone's business—even yours."

She knew he was totally engaged. The dent at the corner of his mouth had deepened, a quirk to his dark good looks that captivated Inaya.

"I want to, but I don't know if I can find my way back to it. My commitment is just as intense without it, and lately I've begun to wonder if there are other paths to God."

"You don't feel as if Broda robbed you of something essential to yourself?"

Irritation sparked in her eyes. She wondered why men found a simple concept so difficult to grasp.

"Broda's assault frightened me. It even made me jumpy for a while. But who I am—who I want to be—was never defined by John Broda."

They weighed each other up in the little silence that fell. At last, Seif tagged the remote again, letting the light into the room. The team was straggling in, Jaime Webb bearing a tray of coffees that couldn't have been more welcome.

"I don't care." Seif bit out the words. "You're still not working with him."

Though Jaime Webb was the most junior member of CRU, he was eager to make his mark on their new case, whatever it turned out to be. Setting the tray of coffees down, he wheeled in a whiteboard for Catalina's briefing. The four lead members of Community Response clustered around their desks, studying the outline Cat had pieced together.

Cat seemed desperately tired, he noticed with concern, her eyes bleary with fatigue, her normally pristine appearance a little ragged at the edges, her lavender blouse untucked, her loafers scuffed and lacking their usual shine. Soft, small, and round, Cat wore no makeup today. She looked young and defenseless, hefting her giant handbag onto her desk. She often brought lunch for the whole team in her capacious purse, something Jaime was always eager to claim.

Now Cat got to her feet, pacing beside the whiteboard.

Seif's voice was all consideration when he spoke to Catalina. He set her cup of coffee on her desk close at hand, inviting her to take her time.

"I was on two calls last night," Cat explained, her honeyed tones overlaid with sorrow. "Dr. Stanger has been busy at the morgue. You know there were two separate officer-involved shootings two nights ago, one in Denver and one in Blackwater Falls?"

Everyone nodded in response.

"The Denver victim was a twenty-two-year-old Latino by the name of Mateo Ruiz." Cat pointed to his photograph on the whiteboard. "The cop accused of shooting him is patrol officer Kelly Broda. He's only twenty-four, a new transfer to Denver, though he was a patrol officer in Chicago for five years."

Jaime hunkered down in his chair, a fierce scowl on his normally pleasant features. "Heard Ruiz was shot in the back."

The worst situation a cop could find himself in. You could say you feared for your life, but not when a suspect had his back to you or was on the run.

Cat pointed to additional photos from the morgue, which corroborated Jaime's statement. A single gunshot wound just below the left shoulder blade penetrating through to the heart. Entry wound, exit wound depicted in the series of shots.

"I met with Mateo's parents last night. I consoled them as best as I could."

They all knew no consolation was possible in circumstances where parents lost a child. Nothing made it better, nothing counteracted the agonizing loss.

Inaya shot a glance at Seif. "So we *are* working the Ruiz shooting?"

The lieutenant let Cat answer.

"My husband, Emiliano, got the call from Mateo's parents. He asked me to meet them at the morgue, I wasn't officially assigned by the lieutenant." Cat's husband ran an NGO called We Rise Together working with the undocumented, and serving many other needs of the vast community that relied on him. It was a calling Cat had shared until she was recruited to the CRU by Seif. "I wanted to be there with them, and I picked up as much as I could from Dr. Stanger on the chance that we'd be called in, then did a little digging on my own. It's still the lieutenant's determination whether we take on the case."

That explained Cat's weariness. She must have worked through the night.

At a nod from Seif, Cat continued with the briefing, outlining the circumstances of the Drug Task Force raid, the dispensary that was the target, and emphasizing the fact that Kelly Broda was a patrol officer, seconded to support the task force alongside his partner, patrol officer Madeleine Hicks.

Jaime raised a large hand. "They partner up in Denver? Blackwater cops don't."

"It depends on the beat," Seif said. "East Colfax, we don't send cops out on patrol alone."

"How many officers did the task force ask for as backup?"

Cat fielded this one. "Six. Along with the ten members of the task force. And yes, before you say it, all eighteen officers were on scene. Riot police too." She indicated a map of the street where the raid had taken place. "Suspects fled the scene ahead of the takedown. Someone tipped them off about the raid. Mateo Ruiz—" Catalina pointed to his photograph. "It's unclear whether he was in the dispensary or out on the streets when he was caught up in the chase and shot. His body was found in an alley close to the dispensary."

"What does Broda have to say about the shooting?" Jaime asked.

"That's just it. Kelly Broda refuses to talk. We don't yet know where the shot came from or who fired the gun."

The team pondered that for a moment. Inaya brought up the obvious question.

"What about the bullet? Won't ballistics tell us whose gun it was? Kelly Broda wouldn't have been suspended if there wasn't some evidence against him."

"It's far too soon for that. Julius hasn't done the postmortem yet, and ballistics will take a while to come in."

Each of them knew that delays now could only work in the department's favor. It would buy them time to decide on a press strategy and the right approach to take with Kelly Broda.

"So we wait," Jaime concluded.

"I don't know that we can afford to." Cat looked torn caught between the work she had trained to do as a psychologist, and her present position with

Community Response. "The residents aren't going to take this one quietly. The speedier our response, the less chance that the shooting blows up."

Seif took over, urging Catalina into her seat. He flipped the whiteboard over, and this time the face that flashed out at them was Black.

"I know you're all bound to have strong feelings about the shooting of Mateo Ruiz, but the DTF doesn't want us in their business, so right now, the Duante Young shooting has to be our priority." He quickly outlined the details of the second case. "Officer Cooper is on admin leave, while we go over the shooting."

"Grant didn't put up a fight?" Jaime's question was sheepish. He'd been drafted to the CRU from the Blackwater sheriff's department, one of Grant's protégés. It was also why he had something to prove.

"He did. That's no reason for us not to do our job." He showed them the same images he'd offered to Inaya. "On the face of it, a clean shooting, but those garbage bins are blocking off the opposite end of a cul-de-sac lined with houses. Could be something, could be nothing. We can see that Duante was on the scene previously because of the graffiti on the bins. He had the can of spray paint on him."

"We can't be sure it was Duante who sprayed those cans," Inaya pointed out. "Someone else could have set up those bins."

"There was another suspect," Seif agreed. "But he was with Duante, so why would he have done that? *When* would he have done that?"

"The graffiti could have been done earlier, the bins placed there to dry them out or get the smell of spray paint away from the houses."

Jaime made a frame of the pictures with his hands, narrowing down his focus.

"Look." He demonstrated, getting up. "It's a continuous pattern, though I don't know that I would call it art. It flows over . . ." He counted to himself. ". . . all six bins. We'd have to check how long the bins were there—unlikely the locals would leave them there if they're blocking the street. There would have been complaints."

Seif made a chopping gesture with his hand. "That rules your theory out, Rahman." He went on before she could object. "Then there's the bodycam footage."

He'd set up an oversize monitor beside the whiteboard, now they gathered around it.

Cat's velvety eyes went round. "I'm surprised they gave that up so easily."

"It exonerates their officer." They chuckled at Seif's dry tone.

He let the footage play out, once, twice, then a final time frame by frame. Inaya glanced over at the use-of-force guidelines pinned to the wall.

"It's clean," she admitted. "Everything done by the book."

"I've been with Areesha Adams and Duante's mother, Mirembe," Cat said. "That was my other brief at the morgue. Even Areesha says Harry Cooper is the last cop she'd suspect of drawing his gun because of racial bias." She studied Seif. "This seems like a case for community mediation. Release the details, apologize of course, and continue to work with the community."

"You mean 'work' the community, not 'work with,'" Inaya said.

Seif switched off the footage. "As I told Detective Rahman, we don't need any surprises. Let's confirm that Duante *was* responsible for that graffiti. I want as exact a timeline as we can construct of his movements prior to the shooting. I want to know who he was, and why, when he doesn't live in Blackwater, he ended up there that night. You've established contact with Duante's mother, Catalina, you and Rahman can follow that up." He turned to Jaime. "Your task is simpler. I want you to work your Blackwater contacts, find out as much as you can about Harry Cooper. Go all the way back. Find out if there are other incidents in his record, anything covered up or that doesn't add up, and I mean the tiniest detail."

He paused, considering Jaime's eager expression. "If you still have any pull with Grant, try to get him to talk. He'll know Cooper better than any of us. I don't want what he'll release to the press. I want to know what he *knows*."

"You think there's more to this than meets the eye?" Jaime asked.

Seif rubbed the back of his head. "I received a tip from an informant earlier warning me about deputy gangs. Any of you know what they are?"

Catalina ventured a reply. "I thought they operated only in Los Angeles. They're like a shadow government, the real power at a precinct. They act outside the rule of law: intimidating citizens, harassing whistleblowers, and the like. For them, the thin blue line is mile-wide. Our NGO dealt with several complaints from residents who came from East LA."

"Very good, Catalina. That's right. It could be that something similar is operating in Blackwater or at the DPD. If that's the case, their instinct will be to cover up anything that doesn't fit the narrative of their officer's innocence. Be on watch for that, and report to me immediately if you face any intimidation." His eyes rested briefly on Inaya. "That's why you're partnered up. Neither you or Catalina are to work any aspect of this case alone. If need be, you call in Jaime or me as backup."

Inaya spoke up. "And you, sir? What will you be doing?"

"Community response," he grunted. "Trying to convince the commissioner we shouldn't be responding to the inevitable backlash with officers in riot gear."

"Areesha could help with that," she suggested. "I can work the other case, follow up on Mateo Ruiz, reassure his parents, find out if there are other protests planned."

Seif braced his hands on Inaya's desk, aggression in every line of his body.

"I told you. You're connected to the cop accused of shooting Mateo. If there's going to be a prosecution, I'm not letting you undermine it, are we clear?"

A lovely, lilting voice interrupted this catechism. "So you're still a bear with a sore head first thing in the morning."

Four heads turned toward the voice. A strikingly attractive woman stood there. She was wearing a fashionable maxi with a print of pink and orange roses blooming against a white background. She had a fall of silvery-blond hair that framed her perfect face in waves. Her blue eyes were bright with mischief, her full lips arranged in a pout. Jaime gaped at her. She was like an orchid planted in the mud, completely out of place at their headquarters.

"Lily!"

Jaime's gaze shifted to Seif, his surprise—or was it shock—mirrored in his face.

"Darling," Lily responded gaily. "Am I interrupting?"

She waved a hand, the nails painted a soft rose that matched her dress, but his attention was caught by a ring on the chain around her neck. A brilliant marquise diamond surrounded by shining baguettes glinted from the chain. Despite the gemstone being large enough to be spotted by the space station, its setting and sparkle were exquisite.

Seif was ashen beneath his normal healthy color. "You're still wearing it?"

"Why wouldn't I?" Lily said sweetly. "You gave it to me. You said it was mine to keep."

8

Defying Seif's orders with some anxiety, Inaya set up a meet with John Broda at the falls, pleading with Cat to visit Mirembe Young without her and to rope in Areesha for backup.

"Just don't get into any trouble or Seif will have my head for deserting you."

They were making their way to their cars in the outdoor parking lot, the dry heat blistering on their backs. If she wasn't wearing slacks, the leather seat would burn her legs.

Catalina shaded her eyes with a softly dimpled hand. "I think the lieutenant is making a mistake. Mateo Ruiz should be our priority if the higher-ups want to head off disaster."

Inaya knew Cat wasn't politicking—she cared deeply about the communities she came from, Inaya took that for granted. It was their job to consider all aspects of community response, and that included anticipating the fallout from officer-involved shootings, a sanitized phrase for when cops shot civilians.

She slipped on her sunglasses. "Will there be more protests in Denver?"

Cat took a moment to tuck in her rumpled blouse. "Inaya, I wouldn't be surprised if the communities in Blackwater and East Colfax link up. The shootings of the two young men are similar. Mateo was out late, Duante was out late. Maybe each of them, for different reasons, was in the wrong place two nights ago. But in Duante's case, spray-painting graffiti isn't a capital offense."

The two women looked at each other grimly.

"Why did Duante run?" Cat sighed.

"Would he be alive if he didn't?"

There was no guarantee and they knew it.

Cat stepped up into her giant SUV, a car that Inaya teased compensated for Catalina's lack of height. She didn't feel up to their usual banter.

"Cat—?" Inaya tapped on the car window.

As it powered down, Catalina shook her head, her face soft with compassion. "You want to know about Lily?"

Bitter lines formed around Inaya's mouth. "I didn't know Seif is engaged. He should have told me."

Catalina reached across the passenger seat and opened the other door, letting the heat escape. She folded down the reflective screen on her windshield before she answered.

"Is that where you are with him? What about the fact you work together?"

"I don't know." The sun was beating down on her head. She'd noticed that she rarely saw the locals wearing a hat to protect against the heat. She was susceptible to sunstroke. "I just wish he'd told me."

Cat began to blast the AC. "You should get in the car if you want to talk."

Inaya checked her watch. "I need to get to Broda. Just tell me."

"He *was* engaged to Lily some time ago. As far as I knew, he broke it off."

"She was wearing a ring."

The sight of it had stunned Inaya. Was Seif the kind of man who played despicable games? She hadn't thought so, but admittedly she didn't know him as well as she should. He was intensely private, some hidden turmoil roiling beneath the surface.

"He seemed surprised by that" was all Cat could say. "Talk to him."

Inaya shrugged, unlocking her car. "Maybe." She shook it off. "I'd better get this done."

Broda met her at the gazebo by the falls, a short drive from CRU headquarters in downtown Denver. Inaya never minded the drive. Once the traffic was clear, it was soft green hills and open skies all the way. She drove down Main Street past Cyrine's bakery to the falls at the south end of town. She parked around the corner, shedding her blazer as she walked to the gazebo.

Bright daylight. Plenty of people about, feeding the ducks in the pond or splashing each other along the narrow walkway that passed under the falls. A warm breeze that felt like silk carried the mist to her overheated skin. She glistened like a freshly finished oil painting, making no move to wipe it off.

The gazebo was large, occupied by several families. Broda had walked down the dock that extended from it for privacy, and that was where Inaya joined him, grateful that the sun was on the far side of the pond.

Broda wasted no time. "Well?"

So he was still making demands.

"I can't do it, it's not our case. At least not yet."

She was braced for his bullying or fury, even for an act of violence, but Broda's shoulders caved in, his chin sank into his chest. Magpies shared their grating calls in the silence, winging across the pond in bands, the blue undersheen of their throats pointed up by the sun.

Broda's head swung up. "You want me to pressure your boss?"

The question made her angry.

"He's not the kind of man who can be pressured."

Broda pressed his fist to his heart. "What, then? What do I do? My son needs someone in his corner."

"He might already have that," Inaya said with care. "A club within the DPD that looks out for its own, though I don't know what the price of membership is."

Broda dropped his fist. "You're talking about gangs?"

Inaya gave him a straight look.

"Kell's the last cop in the world to join a gang."

"What about his partner?" Inaya asked.

"Maddy? Maddy's a straight arrow. She watches out for Kell when she's not busy with her boyfriend." He sounded surprised by his own admission. "Makes a change for Maddy to have someone of her own because when they were kids, Maddy and Kell were inseparable."

"Could the boyfriend be involved in a police gang and exerting some pressure?"

"He's a cop. SWAT officer, I think. Mad came out here to support Kell, but now she has a real reason to stay."

Three police officers, then. Maddy, Kelly Broda, and the unknown boyfriend. And Broda had avoided her question about the gang.

"If Kelly is as straight as you say, it might be worth it to help you."

"He is. You can't count on much in this world, but you can count on that. Ask Maddy, she'll tell you."

But Maddy was hardly likely to implicate her own partner. And if she'd been with Kelly that night, why had the raid gotten so out of hand? Hadn't she watched his back? There was also the matter of the gun. She challenged Broda on that.

"It will be clear from the ballistics report who fired the gun. Your son doesn't claim to have lost his weapon, does he?"

"No." Broda's gaze shifted away, his knuckles tight on the rail that circled the gazebo as they slowly made their way back. "His weapon was holstered."

"What does his partner say?"

"Talk to her," Broda urged. "And get my son to talk. That's what you're good at, right? That's what they said about you in Chicago." For an instant, the old sneering arrogance dominated his features. "Rahman can get the birds to sing. She can charm them from the trees."

Inaya's face closed down. "Because I cared about the people I represented, and they knew it. I worked hard to earn their trust."

Broda's expression shifted again. They had returned along the dock, and he stood back to allow Inaya to enter the gazebo before him, unmindful of the picturesque setting. His thoughts were all to one end—the trap his son was in. The trap he believed Inaya could spring him from.

"You can get it back." He held up his phone to entice her. "Egan will never see the outside of a prison cell again, if you do this for Kell."

He couldn't win her trust that easily. Broda knew something about the gun.

"What if you're wrong?" she asked. "What if it *was* Kelly's gun? What if he does belong to a gang and the reason he's not speaking is because he's been warned off. He's under their protection, which means your son is in their debt."

The strength seemed to leave Broda's body, his bones and sinews without substance.

"If that's where the evidence leads, so be it. All I want is the truth."

And all Inaya wanted was justice for Marcus McBride. If Kelly Broda could lead her there, she would talk to him, find out about the gun, and go on from there, despite the fact that Seif had warned her off. She would work on Seif, talk him around because this was exactly what the CRU was meant to do: ensure that victims like Mateo Ruiz weren't ground down by law enforcement. She could turn things around for Mateo and his family.

The only thing she wouldn't do was make Broda any promises.

9

If Broda was the man in full, his son Kelly was the merest imitation. He was well-built and attractive, his cut collarbone giving definition to his skintight T-shirt. What was interesting and unexpected to Inaya was the sensitive cast to his lower jaw and the soft wave to his hair. He was twenty-four, with five years in Chicago before he'd requested the transfer to Denver Police. In Chicago, he'd been working toward detective. His experience on rougher streets than Denver's meant that he had a great deal to offer as a patrol officer.

There were none of his father's resentments in his face, the accrued set of grievances that had molded John Broda. He had the same broad, smooth forehead without the aggressive bone structure. His wrists and hands were nearly as small as Inaya's. No calluses on the thumbs and forefingers. Either he wore gloves, or he didn't spend much time on the gun range. She sensed that it was a struggle for Kelly to hold himself still, to keep his expression impassive as she sat down across from him.

He wasn't under arrest, he was under custodial protection, the room at a motel not far from his house clean and unpretentious, with no trace of junk-food wrappers or the aroma of grease. A double bed, a desk, a flat-screen TV. A bathroom at the back, and a chest of drawers on which a duffel bag rested, gym socks spilling out of it. His feet were bare now, slender, well-shaped feet. He ignored Inaya's presence entirely, dropping to the floor to continue a series of push-ups. He might be on the lean side but it was all muscle.

She took the seat at the desk, introducing herself, explaining that she'd come on behalf of his father to help get at the truth. If he needed a criminal defense attorney, she could arrange that for him. Despite his enormous capacity for empathy, she wouldn't recommend her own father. This conversation with Kelly was the only point at which the Brodas and Rahmans would intersect. She wouldn't forget how dangerous Broda was.

Kelly let her talk herself into silence, saving his breath for his workout.

Broda had said his son wouldn't talk, but she hadn't realized that the same lack of cooperation would also apply to her.

She took a photograph out of her handbag, keeping it facedown.

"You're not expecting to be charged, so you've figured out there's no point in speaking. You've probably realized that under the surface, Denver isn't much different from Chicago. Your colleagues will protect you. Madeleine Hicks has already sworn that you didn't fire your gun. I'm sure others will back her up."

Kelly sped up the pace, his biceps bunching. Other than that, he showed no reaction.

Inaya leaned down from her chair, her thick dark braid swinging forward over one shoulder.

"Ballistics might tell a different story. It would be better for you to explain what happened that night before we get the report. Frame the story, so to speak."

She didn't sound sympathetic in the least; perhaps Kelly found that bracing, but when he spoke between push-ups he took the fight into her camp.

"You're very attractive. I get why my father was obsessed with you."

She couldn't control an involuntary shudder. "Your father hates me. He always has."

Kelly shifted onto his back, settling into a series of crunches, his T-shirt bunching up to reveal a strip of tanned skin at his waist. She didn't think he was showing off. He was trying not to let the reason for Inaya's presence penetrate his mind.

"He wouldn't ask someone he hated to fight for the life of his only son."

Some nuance in his voice caught Inaya's attention. There was something about Broda's relationship with his son that she needed to plumb. What had Broda said? That Kelly had wanted to be as far away from his father as possible. Because Broda was the kind of cop his son had no desire to emulate, or for reasons closer to home?

"You have siblings."

"They're irrelevant. John Broda's glory is only reflected in his son."

Kelly continued the crunches without pause.

"You're getting at your father, is that it? Some kind of complicated revenge? Why? As far as I know, he dotes on you—he makes no secret of how proud he is of you. He doesn't believe for one minute that you killed Mateo Ruiz."

The crunches came to an abrupt halt. Kelly vaulted to his feet, grabbing a towel from his duffel bag to wipe the sweat from his face. He moved to the mini-fridge in the room, pulling out two bottles of water, offering one to Inaya.

She took it, carefully setting the photograph on the desk.

She watched as Kelly drank from the bottle. He wiped his mouth with the back of his hand, taking a seat on the bed.

"If you think he's proud of me, you must have fallen for his act. What I don't get is why. I know about you, Detective Rahman. My dad roughed you up in Chicago. Not a little. A lot. You were in the hospital. Then you quit your job and ran away, that's how much he scared you." He took another pull from the bottle, his throat working. He set it aside and hunched forward over his knees, his face close to Inaya's so he wouldn't miss her response. "Why in hell would you want to help him? What does he have on you?" Again he didn't wait, evaluating Inaya from head to toe. It wasn't a leer. It was like Kelly Broda was trying to figure out what made her tick. "He's threatening you, is that it? He came after you to finish what he started?"

"Do you think that badly of your father? Are you worried you might be like him? Is that why won't talk about the shooting? Or is it something else—maybe a son not measuring up to his hero cop father." A series of questions aimed like bullets. He felt their impact, flinching a little at each one.

"You play hardball," he said.

"I don't play at all. I simply want to know if you killed Mateo Ruiz."

Unlike John Broda's, Kelly's eyes were a clear topaz. They suited the leonine hair that fell around his face as he ducked his head. He contemplated his knees.

"The bullet came from my gun. That's all I have to say."

Inaya turned the photograph over, forced it into Kelly's hands.

"Why, though? Don't you think you owe Mateo's family some answers? How would you feel if it was your mother who was in their place?"

Kelly studied the photograph, giving nothing away.

"Your father says your partner Madeleine is worried about your state of mind. Her report says that the shot came from somewhere else, not from where the two of you were positioned. She says you're not the kind of cop who solves his problem with a gun."

With a total lack of interest, Kelly passed the photo back to her. The topaz eyes met hers.

"Maddy's my partner, so that's how she sees me. But you know and I know, Detective Rahman, there's no other kind of cop."

When the brown cop had left, Kelly dropped the pose. He curled his six-foot-plus body into a ball on the sagging springs of the bed. One arm clasped his knees. The other shaded his eyes—eyes that burned with tears that refused to fall. Huge, convulsive sobs caught in his throat. To be in this terrible place, to have taken Maddy down with him. He'd thought to escape everything John Broda represented, his anger, his disapproval, his toxic insistence on building Kelly up in his image; instead, he'd brought his father with him.

Once, they'd done everything together. Shooting, hunting, fishing. Workouts at the gym near the precinct. Darts tournaments at their local bar, trivia nights with his father's friends, father and son an unbeatable team. Long talks about his responsibilities as a man. The younger sisters he had to watch out for. The boyfriends he'd have to look into. And if anything happened to Broda on the job, well then, Kelly would step into his shoes. He would be the man of the house, solid support for his mother, a stalwart oak for the women who gave meaning to John Broda's life. Broda didn't cheat. He'd never so much as looked at another woman, despite what Kelly had said to Detective Rahman. He was head over heels in love with the wife who had given him four healthy children, his high school sweetheart, he'd made vows to her and he'd kept them. He wasn't the kind of cop to demand a freebie from a working girl, or a hookup with an underling after a night on patrol—how would his wife ever know? John Broda had strong Christian values, and he took those values seriously.

Kelly's mother was the same. She was lively and vibrant and madly in love with John. She'd kept her figure and still dressed for her husband. She arranged frequent date nights, and didn't complain when John's work took him out on a call or caused him to miss a special night. John had worked like a dog for nearly forty years, going flat out to give his wife and children everything they deserved. Total support, even when the CPD took flak during the protests, during the nights the South Side was on fire. He did his job with a rare dedication because he had Sharon to come home to. A woman whose eyes still lit up when he walked through the door. A woman who didn't question what he did on the job, their love true blue all the way.

Kelly had tried to make her see. He'd wanted someone to share the terrible burden of their work—work that his father made seem like a holy calling. He'd tried to make his mother understand just how different he was from John's idea of who he should be. His mother wasn't hearing it. She'd told him he needed to understand what his father was up against. Every day was like going out to war, any encounter with the public could turn ugly, dangerous, or fatal. His father didn't need the pressures of wokeness; he was a good man doing an impossible job and she expected Kelly to have his back both in public and in private. Maybe Kelly needed counseling? She said it hesitantly, out of earshot of her husband, because any sign of weakness in the Broda household was an admission of failure. Men couldn't be sensitive or weak: men couldn't fail. Their backs had to be broad and they had to shoulder their burdens in silence without giving in to the strain. John Broda still used words like "pussy," though never around his girls. John went easy on his girls, but then daughters were easy to spoil, to love, and his three girls doted on him. Daddy was a hero to them all.

The only one Kelly could talk to was Maddy. Maddy with her strong shoulders and dysfunctional home, who'd barged her way into the Broda household from her house next door. She should have been his sisters' playmate. Instead, from the first moment, she'd clamped onto Kelly and refused to let go. Maddy was a tomboy, a term now out of fashion. She didn't like tea parties or playing with dolls. She wanted to play rough-and-tumble with Kelly, and she did. Her parents had split long ago: she didn't know where her mother was and she lived with an alcoholic father. She had no ambition separate from Kelly's because there was no one to encourage her, so John Broda took her on as a fifth child. Except that he didn't treat her like one of his cherished daughters. He took one look at Maddy and seemed to sense her inner toughness, the resourcefulness that meant that even with the bad hand she'd been dealt in life, she didn't much care and she didn't view herself as in any way deprived. Not since she had Kelly.

Kelly should have found it suffocating. Maddy was everywhere he was, Maddy did everything he did, Maddy shared his father's attention. Kelly found it a relief: there was someone else John Broda could focus on, someone else who had to learn how to be a man the hard way because Broda treated both Kell and Maddy as if they were brothers-in-arms. He'd often thought John Broda would rather have had Madeleine Hicks for a son.

Maddy took to it like a fish to water. She loved John and Sharon, she loved the girls, and she adored Kelly like an older brother. If Kell was going to make beat cop, so was she. If Kell had aspirations to become detective, so did she. If Kell transferred out of Chicago to get away from the influence of his father, of what his father thought of him—or maybe from his father's reputation—Maddy said goodbye without a second thought. You didn't leave your partner behind. And you sure as hell didn't ever leave your best friend and big brother alone on a new police force in a new town.

It might have been cowardly of Kell, but he was glad he didn't have to ask. He'd been relieved beyond measure when Maddy requested the same transfer. The CPD took Maddy seriously. She had a jacket full of commendations, and she acted like a bodyguard to other female officers: tough and always ready. She wore her hair scraped back in a short ponytail, she shuddered at the thought of makeup, though Colorado's dry, hot sunshine had taught her to use lip balm and sunscreen, and she spent most of her free time doing CrossFit or out at the gun range with Kell and her boyfriend, Younas. The move to Denver hadn't changed that, it had simply added Younas into the mix as someone else Maddy loved.

The best thing about Madeleine Hicks was that if he wanted to sound off about John Broda, she'd listen without complaint. She wouldn't try to offer mitigation for John. And if Kell felt like being quiet and keeping his thoughts to himself, Maddy was fine with that too. She usually made him take it out in some form of physical exercise: a 10K run, a weekend obstacle course with Younas, or cycling up the trails in the Rockies. Maddy was blooming in Denver, color in her cheeks, a sparkle in her eyes since she'd started dating Younas, a captain with SWAT. Kelly liked the man. An elite team leader, the best of the best, Younas had nothing to prove to anyone and he enjoyed Maddy's sheer physical toughness, something that scared most men off.

Denver was a new beginning for Maddy, like it was supposed to be for Kell. But here they both were in a mess of Kelly's making. He'd made Maddy follow him to Denver, and now he'd trapped them both in an intolerable situation.

He saw the bloom of blood on the suspect's back. The man fell in a series of staggering steps, the shocked look on his face quickly replaced by pain. The kind of pain that crucified and left room for nothing else, God help him.

Smoke in his eyes, tear gas choking his throat because reinforcements hadn't considered whether the officers seconded to the task force were wearing their gas masks. They weren't, and the coarse texture of the gas was caught in Kell's eyes and his throat.

He whimpered as if scenting it again.

He heard the sound of the young man's body hit the pavement through the shouts and calls and thumping boots around him.

His left ear was aching from the gunshot, the sound coming close enough to maim, his hand shaking and sweating as he checked his holster. A frantic look at Maddy, the whites of her eyes flashing as for a rare moment, she lost control and gave in to the terror of the raid.

He heard his own voice scream a high-pitched garble of sound. Only later would it resolve itself into his friend's name.

Her hand on his shoulder felt like a boulder coming down to crush him. They both hit their knees, though Maddy had the presence of mind to call in an ambulance. Someone else took control of the scene, someone worked on the body on the ground, shouting out orders as riot cops swarmed over the ground.

Maddy's arm came around his shoulders. Then or now?

Both.

He'd missed the sound of her key in the door. The bed swayed under her weight, then she was there, a strong arm bracing his shoulders.

"God, Kell, this is awful. This should never have happened."

She stroked her hand through his hair like a lioness settling a cub.

"It wasn't your fault, Kell, you have to remember that. The kid shouldn't have run. He shouldn't have resisted arrest. Hell, he shouldn't have been there at all."

A coating of ice spread over his limbs. It crept from his fingers and toes to the center of his body, his heart like a block of granite in his chest. It weighed a thousand pounds. He couldn't lift his head. All he could do was listen as Maddy whispered, "Kell, it wasn't your fault."

10

Areesha rang Cat's doorbell a little after eleven in the morning. Cat lived in a semidetached house with a shared porch, the house painted Tuscany yellows and ochers. The lawn had been landscaped, with a line of trimmed mulberry trees shading the path along the drive. Ceramic pots in a lovely dark green framed both sides of the stairs, another touch of warmth. Cat's home was much like Cat herself: well-tended and welcoming.

Catalina had asked Areesha to accompany her to Mirembe Young's police interview, which would be conducted at her home. She was surprised that Inaya wasn't joining them; she knew Seif preferred that his detectives work as a team. She suspected it was more to do with their safety, as Jaime Webb was allowed to roam around town on his own. Misplaced chivalry or chauvinism, she wasn't quite sure which it was with Seif.

The house was in a comfortable neighborhood, where she saw plenty of people outdoors on their porches in the heat, watching over children. Some shouted with delight as they chased each other through a pair of sprinklers. Others were cycling with their parents, while a winsome Black girl in a white dress drew gallant little fairies in pink and blue chalks on the sidewalk.

All in all, an idyllic scene, except for the sound of raised voices in the house. The windows were open and Areesha could hear them through the screens. They were arguing in Spanish. Areesha had a rudimentary understanding of the language, and she guessed they were fighting about Catalina's work. Areesha rang the bell again, desperate to spare Cat any embarrassment when she realized that the argument with her husband could be heard all along the street. Even the little girl with her chalks had paused her work, distressed.

Areesha smiled at her and waved. She returned to the task of adding wings to a bright blue fairy, her pink tongue poking out of her mouth in concentration.

"If you go now, you'll be making things worse," the man inside the house now said in English.

"You can't blackmail me like this, I won't accept it. I don't know what's happened to you, *mi amor*." Areesha shivered at Cat's obvious despair.

"Don't say I didn't warn you, Cat."

The man's voice fell quiet. Footsteps came to the door, and a flustered Catalina welcomed Areesha inside.

"Just give me a moment to collect my things."

She introduced Areesha to her husband, a fit man a few years older than Cat, his highly individual face set to stubbornness. His handshake was strong, and bore a trace of his anger. He invited Areesha to sit in the living room furnished in terra-cotta colors. Exquisite hand-painted ceramics covered nearly every surface in the room. A green glass art deco chandelier hung from a pendant in the ceiling, matched by lamps with apricot-colored pleated shades.

Emiliano followed her gaze.

"A gift my parents sent from Mexico."

He was sitting stiffly, and she sensed it was an effort for him to shift gears like this, exchanging pleasantries when the issue with Cat was unresolved. She began to ask him questions about the work of his NGO and the move he and Cat had made from Arizona. Did he prefer the desert climate or the mountain snows? Did he see the same kind of clients?

He began to respond to her genuine interest, the unhappiness that had shaded his eyes changing to alertness, illuminating his passion for his work. He was teak-skinned with wavy black hair that threw up hints of blue under the light. Both contrasted beautifully with his snowy-white shirt. He was an inch or two shorter than Areesha, but he would tower over Cat. When Cat came to join them, her heavy bag over her shoulder, she could see they were a good match—they seemed to fit together despite the tension in the air.

"We'll talk again?" Cat sounded timid as she put the question to her husband.

The harshness in his face smoothed out. He took Cat's hand and pressed a kiss to her knuckles. She touched a hand to his cheek.

"I'll make dinner tonight. Whatever you want, *mi amor*."

Emiliano dipped his head at Areesha. "She can wind me around her little finger with her empanadas." His reluctant grin revealed a set of beautifully even white teeth, a certain rakishness to his appeal. "You can't solve everything with your cooking, *querida*."

Areesha gave him a smile of her own. "I don't know—it seems to work on my husband."

They all laughed, but in the car Cat said, "I'm sorry you had to hear us argue." Her cheeks were flushed with embarrassment.

Areesha drove smoothly, keeping an eye out for children as she turned off Cat's street.

"It happens in all marriages, Catalina."

Cat turned to look out the window as the leafy streets flew by. Areesha was taking the back roads instead of the highway, cutting across a series of small green parks.

"I wasn't sure if it was the right decision to leave our NGO, but it was getting difficult to work with Emiliano full-time, harder to separate our professional and personal lives. It's one thing to talk out your work after you come home, it's worse when you can't retreat from it. So I thought Community Response would challenge my preconceptions, allow me to grow."

They drove for a few minutes in silence until Areesha asked, "You don't have children?"

The line of Cat's mouth went flat. Her fingers clutched the strap of her handbag.

"No."

Areesha checked her blind spot. "Stop me if you feel like I'm prying."

"If I wanted my privacy I shouldn't have been shouting down the house." She shook her head. "A man without sons? Emiliano wants a houseful of children—I have too much to do as it is, I can't take on anything more, not now. I don't want my life swallowed up."

"You think it would be?"

Cat turned in her seat, her face stamped with challenge. "You tell me."

"I know a little of what you're feeling." They moved through a series of roundabouts at a speed barely above a crawl. Even engrossed in a conversation, Areesha was mindful of her driving. She could be pulled over on a whim. "My boys are in the line of fire, the border between my work and their reality seems to be shrinking by the day. You learn not to worry for yourself, but you never stop worrying for your children. It's given me a headful of gray hairs."

Cat looked over. Areesha's curls flowed over her skull, rich and bouncy and black.

Both women laughed.

"I wouldn't change it." Areesha reached across to squeeze Cat's hand. "If it's right for you, you'll know. And yes, the sacrifices are enormous, but remember, so are the rewards."

Mirembe Young was waiting for them. The shock of Duante's death had passed, now the grief had set in. Her skin sagged under her jawline, and her voice was hoarse from a night spent in tears. The living room was crowded with women; others were in the kitchen setting up food to serve. One of the kitchen counters was stacked with boxes of LaMar's Donuts, and children would stumble into the house from the yard to be given a snack.

The house was saturated with conversation: angry, heartbroken, patient, resigned, and every flavor of wisdom that women who had lived through conflict and loss could offer. Areesha moved into the kitchen—she knew many of the women and began to ask about Duante.

Cat stayed on the sofa with Mirembe, who looked as if her bones were finding it hard to bear her weight. She began sentences, then set them adrift, until she found a point to focus on. She asked Cat about the funeral, and Cat explained the intricacies of releasing the body. Mirembe could take her son home, if she waived her right to an investigation. If she wanted to pursue the actions of the police, the body would have to remain at the morgue until the inquiry concluded. Peace or justice, Mirembe would have to choose.

From the dead look in Mirembe's eyes, Cat knew she hadn't understood. Again she asked when her son could come home. It would be fruitless to repeat herself, so Cat asked if she could sit in Duante's room. There'd been no reason to order a forensic search of his room; that would frame Duante as suspect rather than victim. Seif had made the call not to offer provocation.

She wandered up the stairs alone to the room at the end of the hall. Dominating the room was a Black Lives Matter poster with the emblem of the raised fist, black against a white background. The ceiling of the room slanted above the bed, so Duante would have been staring up at the poster whenever he lay on the bed. It couldn't have been intended as a reminder, because she doubted that Duante ever forgot.

She hadn't woken up a single morning without thinking of the first alarmist broadcast about an influx of asylum seekers at the border. It would likely have been the same for a fiery young artist like Duante.

She sat on the bed, putting her problems with Emiliano out of her mind. They weren't going away even if he'd made light of them in front of Areesha. If she was late tonight, his complaints would start up again. Fine, she'd deal with it then. For now, she let her eyes wander over Duante's walls. She was a profiler: Duante's room would speak to her.

His walls were covered with his own artwork. He had framed a mural of Black women broken into separate images. The first wore a mask that said "I Can't Breathe." The second was a grandmother who held a pair of scales in her fist. Tears escaped from the eyes of a third who looked upward to a series of doves arranged to form the words "Stop Killing Us." The fourth was a woman who reminded Cat of Areesha, her jacket emblazoned with a call to action: REMEMBER THE DEAD, FIGHT WITH THE LIVING. Next to this was a woman whose arms were looped with prison chains. The final portrait was of Breonna Taylor, with crimson flowers spilling from her lips.

The mural wasn't painted with rage. Love throbbed through each portrait, the faces exaggerated, the eyes incandescent, the lips ripe with knowing. Cat caught a glimpse of her own face in Duante's mirror. She looked like she'd long since given up the fight.

As if to echo her thoughts, she noticed two more frames on Duante's desk. One was a proverb: *Our art is resistance*. The other photograph showed a very young Duante in a family group, his mother smiling brilliantly into the eyes of a lean, attractive man with his arm around her waist, a child sitting on his shoulders. He was laughing uproariously, his small hands grasping both sides of his father's head. It *was* Duante's father, wasn't it? Both Mirembe and the man in the picture were wearing wedding rings.

Cat searched the drawers that contained sketchbooks and notepads. His laptop was in another, and she wrote out a receipt for it. Apart from the mural featuring the women, the rest of the colorful art in his room didn't showcase the graffiti Mirembe had told them about.

She collected Duante's sketchbooks and sat down on the bed again, flipping through his drawings. She ran her hand over a page. It came away clean. The drawings would have been sprayed with a fixative, which reminded Cat that she hadn't seen any evidence of spray paint. Other things she had missed in her initial search: there were no paint supplies. It could be that Duante had another space where he worked. She'd get Jaime or another team member to chase that down, though she didn't really know what she was looking for. Sketches of graffiti art? Or the work of competitors who didn't come up to scratch?

No surprises, Seif had said. Digging deep into Duante's background was a form of the cover Emiliano spurned her for, his criticism striking deep enough to hurt. Where was the gentleness that was meant to exist between spouses? For one reason or another, Emiliano had been angry at her since the day she'd joined the police. He said because of her work. She privately thought it had more to do with her being less available for his needs.

Was she being selfish in demanding a life outside of Emiliano's expectations? She didn't think so, but wasn't every woman mired in shadings of self-doubt? She wondered if Emiliano questioned himself, regretting his bouts of temper. She was beginning to feel more like a child who'd flouted her curfew than a woman confident enough to make decisions for herself. The sad thing was she'd rather have been with Mateo's parents genuinely responding to their needs, but this was where Seif wanted her, and because Seif gave her so much latitude, she tried not to let him down. He wasn't a gentle man by nature, but to Catalina, Seif had been kindness itself. If he would only show Inaya the same forbearance.

She had to admit she found Seif and Inaya's byplay quite absorbing. She was rooting for romance to bloom, for Inaya to release the lieutenant from the padlocked cage in which he lived. It was far less taxing to think of her colleagues than to worry about Emiliano.

"Cat?"

It was Areesha at the door. She'd brought up a tray of coffees and doughnuts.

"Cop food," she joked. She joined Cat on the bed, clearing a space to set down the tray on the desk. Cat showed her the first of Duante's sketchbooks.

"Mirembe wasn't exaggerating, Duante really was talented."

Cat set the book aside, reaching for her coffee. When she'd drained the cup, she picked up another book. At the top of the first page, Duante had scribbled, "Dad, the African Lion."

Page after page was filled with sketches of the lean Black man in the photograph on the desk. His face in three-quarter profile, a notoriously difficult angle to capture, his face in every possible mood, though charm and laughter prevailed, and that look of love. For Mirembe? For Duante? Each sketch was dated, ranging over a period of the last five years.

"What happened to Duante's father, Areesha? Has Mirembe told you?"

"I didn't ask. Too much else to do."

Cat considered another sketch, this one filled with images of Mirembe. Duante had titled it, "Mum, Queen of the Universe." The statement said a lot about their relationship.

Duante had captured something unique to Mirembe, a depth of wisdom in the lucid eyes, and even with the use of charcoals, the sketches were saturated with the treatment of light.

To Cat's consternation, a black *X* covered the sketch on the final page. It was Mirembe, several years younger, wearing a doctor's lab coat over her shirt and slacks. Around her neck hung a lanyard with a visitor ID. Mountains rose in the distance behind a plain occupied by rows of tents to the side of a vast complex of low-roofed buildings. Trucks appeared between the buildings, the daubs of charcoal raw and swift, the page deeply indented.

No place name; Mirembe's features partly obscured by the giant *X,* so much so that at second glance Cat wasn't sure it *was* Mirembe. Whoever the subject of the portrait was, she had done something to earn Duante's wrath.

"What do you think made Duante so angry?" Areesha asked.

"We need backstory." Cat picked up her doughnut. The sweet bite of chocolate against her tongue gave her spirits a much-needed lift. "I know it seems like cover," she said, preempting Areesha, "but it will also ensure you're prepared to deflect whatever they throw at Duante."

"It's not in question, is it." Areesha made it a flat statement. "Harry Cooper shot Duante, he's admitted as much."

"There will be a lot of mitigation," Cat warned. "Complete exoneration isn't out of the question. We have to find out what Mirembe wants."

"She hasn't had enough time. She's only just found out her son is dead." Agitated, Areesha collected the sketchbooks and set them in a stack on the desk. "As desperately as I want to respect Mirembe's wishes, the story will grow beyond her very quickly."

"You're saying Duante's death might become strategic?"

"Right now we have a chance for Mirembe to tell us how she wants us to proceed while hers is still the voice that matters. Before the media storm takes over."

"She's going to want to see the body-cam footage, but Areesha, it's deeply distressing. It might make things worse. What if *Mirembe* decides that Harry did nothing wrong? Won't that be a blow to the movement?"

"Mirembe knows what's at stake. Whatever we feel, whatever we want, we're in service to something greater." She moved to study Duante's mural of the six women. "Doesn't this say it all, Catalina? They *have* to stop killing us."

11

Downstairs, the women had spilled out into a backyard where roses ran riot in splotches of pink and gold. There was a water feature at the end of the garden, where small children splashed each other under the eyes of the women who had come to support Mirembe in her grief.

At a signal from Areesha, the rest retreated to the kitchen, leaving the three women alone.

Mirembe had made a tremendous effort to gather herself for Cat's questions. She'd drunk several cups of coffee, and some of the haze had faded from her eyes.

"What do you need from me?"

"Areesha told me you're a psychologist," said Cat. "I am as well."

"But you work for the police?"

"I work for the Community Response Unit, because the communities I represent are overengaged by the police. This is my chance to sort that out."

Mirembe nodded.

"May I ask you some questions, Mirembe? Perhaps as you answer them, you'll know how you want to proceed."

"I want to see that footage for myself. Don't let them disappear it."

"You have my word I won't."

Mirembe took Cat through Duante's movements for the past week. She hadn't known that Duante had slipped out on the night he was killed, but the rest of the week, his actions had been as usual. He spent time at a shared studio space downtown that belonged to an art collective, where he was paid for tutoring street kids in his unique set of skills. The rest of the time, he wandered the city taking photographs. When he wasn't doing that, he was filling out applications—job applications, grant applications, scholarships, and so on. He entered contests—art and photography both. He hung out with friends, he belonged to a club that promoted young musicians from the inner city. He was often recruited for cover art. Lately, Duante and a few of his friends had gotten involved in a local street-art contest that granted cash prizes. Naturally, they were all in competition for the prize.

Cat took detailed notes. The names of friends, the location of the studio, Duante's contacts in the world of art and music. All of this would be copiously checked out by other team members and funneled back to HQ. Any stone left unturned would earn Seif's rebuke. He prized thoroughness even when he had more pressing work on his plate.

"About the graffiti art," Cat said. "You said his interest in it was recent?"

"Yes. It's just a few months old. The competition takes place in stages like a video game. If you clear one level, you're invited to compete in the next, until the judges narrow it down to a single winner. It requires a great deal of imagination and flexibility, because much of street art is completed in secret. Eventually artists run out of canvases to paint."

"Meaning abandoned or derelict buildings?"

"Construction sites too. Potential locations are also suggested by the contest organizers."

"It sounds quite challenging. Why would a serious artist like Duante take time out of what sounds like a jammed schedule to participate?"

"It was the cash prize." Mirembe's voice was bleak. "Duante had already won five thousand dollars in the initial stages. The grand prize was fifty thousand. The money would have helped with art school."

Cat raised her eyebrows. "Who was offering that prize?"

"It's all in there." Mirembe gestured at Duante's laptop. Areesha had brought it downstairs. "Why does any of this matter? We know what happened to my son."

Cat changed tactics. "We can follow that up ourselves. Did you notice any change of mood in Duante? Was he worried about anything or did he seem preoccupied?"

"My son didn't shoot himself," Mirembe said icily.

Cat looked up. "Forgive me, I'm just trying to get a full picture of who

Duante was." She produced the crossed-out drawing on the final page of Duante's sketchbook. "Was this you?"

An expression of great sorrow settled over Mirembe like a cloak.

"Duante was angry when we moved here from D.C. He was happy there, he had built a reputation for his art. In Denver, he had to start from scratch."

Cat caught a slight inflection in Mirembe's voice. "There was more to it, wasn't there?"

One of the women left the kitchen and came to sit beside Mirembe, one arm along her shoulder. "I'm Charlotte Reaver," she said. "It's time you wrapped this up. Doesn't Mirry have enough to deal with as it is? You police folks have no shame."

Areesha leaned forward, speaking gently to the two Black women. "Duante will be in the news soon. If we're going to protect him, we have to know what we're up against."

Charlotte Reaver sat back, affronted. "If I didn't know your handsome husband, I'm not sure I would trust you, Reesh."

Areesha didn't take offense. She patted Charlotte's knee, nodding to Cat to continue.

"Duante being upset about the move wasn't just about being settled, was it? Young people tend to be more adventurous, more flexible than their parents, don't you find?"

She wasn't asking out of idle curiosity. She wanted to know why Duante had defaced that final sketch of his mother, the queen of his personal universe.

"D.C. was home while my husband was alive. All Duante's memories of his father are there. He viewed the move as a betrayal. He felt like he was losing his father, and he blamed me for that. But we had to go." Mirembe gave a defeated shrug. "Duante seemed to be finding himself here. I didn't think he was still angry."

Cat cut through to the question that mattered, though she couldn't see how it had any bearing on the shooting. It was all politics, a young man's life at the center of it all.

"Why did you find it necessary to move across the country?"

"I was a trauma specialist at Walter Reed. I worked mostly with veterans suffering from PTSD. The job got to be too much. For the sake of my own health, I needed to make a change. Duante found that hard to forgive."

A light went off in Catalina's mind, a piece of knowledge half remembered. Hadn't Areesha noted from the first that she and Mirembe had a great deal in common, not least their work? The work for which Mirembe was so well-known? Duante's sketches of his mother had captured the essence of the woman, the eyes that had seen too much, the deep compassion and wisdom. The seriousness and care that attended her work and sustained her reputation.

"You're *Dr. Mirembe Young,* aren't you? The author of the famous book?"

If she was, it would explain in great part Duante's political leanings, the fiery splendor of his work. Dr. Mirembe Young had written a blistering tome in defense of America's veterans, sent off to fight unholy wars in the name of defending freedom—or as Dr. Young had cast it, enriching the war machine—then cast off without concern upon their return home. She'd compared the budget available for war to that available for the care of the veterans who fought those wars, her assessment stirring up a ferocious national debate, not just on the issues, but because Mirembe was a woman speaking on this, and a Black woman, at that. The only thing that saved her was the veterans who agreed with her.

"America's Veterans, America's Victims," Mirembe said. "The book that follows me everywhere. It's the reason I made the move—I couldn't have known it would cost me my son."

Cat listened to this, quick to sense the feelings beneath the surface. Areesha beat her to it.

"It isn't your fault, Mirembe. No one can predict the future."

Or as Inaya might have said, drawing upon her faith, no one knows where the place of death will be ordained.

"What happened to Duante's father, Mirembe? Where is your husband now?"

"He died," Mirembe answered in a hard, flat voice. "All the good men die."

12

Trouble was brewing at the DPD, and Seif knew it. If he'd wanted a quiet case to follow up the mammoth complications of the last one he'd been called in to supervise, he was out of luck. He had two equally complex cases to deal with: a potentially justifiable officer-involved shooting, and the murky outcome of the Drug Task Force raid, neither of which were his biggest problem. The rumbles in the corridors of power were what concerned him, particularly as they trickled down to every cop on patrol. Blackwater cops had already thrown up a wall: Harry Cooper was one of their most reliable men, and they weren't going to allow CRU to mess him up.

He'd advocated caution to Grant. Lie low and let things get quiet. Grant had done the opposite. Jaime Webb had already reported back that Blackwater cops were bringing in young Black men, casting the net wide, to see who might have been with Duante that night. Find him, get him to admit to the vandalism, and Harry's case was open-and-shut.

They hadn't done any actual policing, no digging into Duante's friends or confederates at his art studio—they'd just gone into the communities that surrounded the manufacturing plants and picked up young men on the street. If stop-and-frisk was good enough for New York, it was even better for Blackwater.

As for the DPD and the drug raid for Mateo's case, the task force had closed ranks. It refused to confirm which officers had been called to the streets as backup, who the targets were, or whether Mateo was even part of the raid at all. Obstruction was the name of the game, and very little sympathy was offered in a statement to the public, because sympathy was tantamount to an admission of guilt. The task force's job was to keep drugs off the street, the cops had done nothing wrong. Not at all the approach Seif wanted to take.

He called Jaime Webb in to join him.

"Any luck dealing with Grant?"

Jaime flushed, a bright red glow that made his blue eyes pop in contrast. He had an inside track to Grant, but he didn't always use it wisely.

"I told him protests were brewing in Denver that could spill over to Blackwater. He said his boys could handle it, and if need be, he'd call me in."

"And how are his 'boys' dealing with things?"

Jaime searched for tact. "With a heavy hand."

Seif swore. He'd hoped for success through Jaime trying the softly-softly approach—it looked like he'd have to step in again. He could just imagine what his boss at the FBI would say: he was making it too obvious that he wanted something on Grant.

"Is Areesha Adams on the scene?"

Jaime's giant Adam's apple bobbed. "She's busy with the mother of the victim."

"Then I'd better move. Get to Grant before she does."

Though he enjoyed the sight of Grant pushed to the limit by Areesha, it wasn't fair to make her do the work in his place. Grant was his problem, not hers. He reached for the jacket he'd flung over his chair. It was a snug fit over his shoulder holster, good for the image he wanted to project, an armed and dangerous man.

A muffled knock sounded on the glass door to his office.

It was Lily. Again. This time she was dressed in a chic jumpsuit, the cut flattering her figure, the color the same astonishing blue as her eyes. She had pinned up her blond hair on one side and fastened a flower behind her ear—a gardenia, a rose, an orchid, nothing was too much on Lily. She was lightly made up, and wearing sparkling earrings that matched his ring on the chain around her neck.

She smiled brightly at Jaime, who flushed like a kid in first grade.

Her eyes met Seif's. "Do you have time to talk now?"

He'd done his best to put her off after the team meeting. Clearly, he hadn't succeeded. And if he didn't let her have her say, he had no doubt she'd be back again. Her tough-minded persistence was a quality he very much admired in Lily, except now when it interfered with the strands of his present. Lily was his ex. He thought she'd be married to someone else by now; instead she was here in his office, wearing the ring he'd given her a lifetime ago and insisted she keep out of a mix of gallantry and embarrassment. What kind of man demanded a woman return his gifts under any circumstances, let alone when he'd broken her heart?

He sent a dazzled Jaime on his way, and pulled a chair out for Lily.

"I don't have much time."

She dropped her manner of artificial gaiety, her hands folded on her lap, her legs neatly crossed to the side. They were covered up by her royal-blue jumpsuit but he knew they were gorgeous, one of her best assets, just as everything about Lily was formed to advantage. So why the jumpsuit now and the long maxi the other day? Lily's taste had always run to short dresses and skirts, the better to show off those million-dollar legs.

With an effort, he wrenched his gaze from her legs and caught the smile that curved her lips. Full, kissable lips made up with verve and glamour. Inwardly, he sighed. He'd thought he was immune to her charm and cleverness now; more, he'd thought she hated him for the way he'd broken things off more than a year ago.

You're not who the boys need.

As sharp-edged and brutal as anything he'd done in the past.

So why the sweet smile now? Why was she still wearing his ring? Was it purely out of sentiment or was it wishful thinking? Lily wasn't pushy or demanding. Nor was she delusional—she was smart and self-aware, and she'd accepted that they were over. But he'd used the twins as his way out, instead of making it about her, so maybe he'd left the door open just that little bit. And she knew him well enough to have grasped that.

"Why did you want to see me?"

Her voice a little husky, she said, "I didn't used to need a reason."

His gaze was implacable. "You need one now."

Her pointed chin tilted down. "We've both had time to think, Qas. To reconsider the past." She cast a quick glance over her shoulder, scanning the empty office. "You're not with anyone else, and I'm not either."

"I haven't been living like a monk," he told her. "There have been women."

She gripped the edge of his desk with her fingers, the nails painted a bright fuchsia.

"But have you been happy?" Those ocean-blue eyes took his measure.

"What does that matter to you?"

"You matter," she said simply. "You always have and I think—I think I can do what you want, now. *Be* who you want. Like you asked me before—to be an example for your brothers. To make them part of our home."

She gestured gracefully at her pantsuit, at the coverage it gave her. "I don't drink anymore either. I could have made changes before, if you'd been honest with me. I didn't know you properly."

"I didn't know myself."

Despite himself, he was feeling her pull again. She *had* made changes, channeled her flash into little touches like the flower at her ear, toned down her flirtatiousness, otherwise Jaime would have been toast.

But he didn't want that from any woman, he realized. He wasn't the kind of man who made demands, particularly when he had no rights to exploit. And then there was Inaya. If he hadn't exactly made promises, he'd made his interest clear.

Lily cut off that train of thought. "We have history, Qas."

Each time she pronounced his name like "Cass," he remembered Inaya doing her best to sound out the "Q" in his name. *Qaas,* long and drawn out, the Arabic "Q" harder than Lily could manage. Yet Lily was here in this moment, a warmth in her blue eyes for him.

He couldn't ignore that either.

"We have history," he agreed.

Her face brightened at once, a triangular smile on that vividly painted mouth.

"But that's what it is," he went on. "*History*. You wearing my ring doesn't change that."

She played with the chain. "I wear it to feel connected to you." She looked up. "I know you haven't forgotten that what we had was good. That kind of connection doesn't happen for everyone. I think we owe it to each other not to throw it away."

Fatally, he hesitated, and she had him.

"Please, Qas. Let's go out to dinner and talk."

"You don't owe me anything, Lily."

She moved close to him and kissed his cheek, leaving her imprint behind.

"But you owe me plenty, Qas."

There was no dodging it, he did.

He checked with Julie at the reception desk to see if Grant was free, the encounter with Lily still on his mind. They were having dinner that night, though she knew well enough that with an active case anything could happen to disrupt his schedule. She'd always accepted that with good grace, one of the reasons he'd loved her. Loved her? His ferocious scowl at the thought frightened Julie, who asked if he had indigestion. He smoothed out his expression, even managing a smile as she waved him through to Grant's inner sanctum.

He was stunned to see Harry Cooper seated on Grant's leather sofa across from Grant's massive desk. The window covers were up, and blinding late-summer sunlight poured into Grant's office, lightening the chill of the air-conditioning. The foothills shone as if scrubbed, clean and green and glistening from a drift of early-morning rain, a vista so fresh and unsullied he wished he were anywhere else to take it in. Up at Chatfield Reservoir, catching the view from the stone breast of the dam. Or at the pastures near Inaya's house.

Harry had a clipboard on his lap, and he was filling out what looked like the paperwork for administrative leave. It should have been a computerized process, everything else about the Blackwater substation was state-of-the-art, but Grant kept some of his procedural processes off the books, the reason the rumors of his corruption had been so difficult to pin down.

He'd interrupted something, no doubt. Grant telling Cooper exactly what to write, though Cooper's guileless, pale eyes seemed incapable of secrets or intrigue.

He stood to greet Seif, advanced a big and capable hand, though his handshake lacked assurance.

Grant rounded on him. "I thought I told you—you can't speak to Harry without his counsel present."

Seif made himself sound respectful. "I'm here to talk to you, sir."

Grant strode to the open door of his office, a hint of temper in the way he closed it.

"We have nothing to discuss. Your people aren't wanted here. This shooting was clean. Harry is clean. We gave you folks the footage—what more do you need to know?"

As Harry turned to the paperwork, Seif approached Grant, keeping his voice down.

"You've brought people in."

"I'm looking for Young's accomplice. You know we've been after whoever's behind the vandalism of our public buildings."

"The suspects you've brought in—"

"'Persons of interest,'" Grant corrected.

"Your cells are full of young Black men. Have you thought about the optics of that?"

Grant bristled at Seif's tone.

"Blackwater is already on the map for profiling minorities. Your men have gotten careless. What reason do you have for picking up these men? Do they have priors? Was there probable cause or anything else resembling proof of their having acted with Duante Young? Do you think they're going to sit quietly in those cells? How long before Areesha Adams is on the scene? She's a power in this community, have you considered that?"

He fired the questions at Grant. Grant colored with fury in response at the thought of Areesha, but it wasn't Areesha who knocked on Grant's door.

Julie's cheerful voice sounded from the intercom as she carefully pronounced, "David Fortunate Adams to see you, Sheriff."

The door opened to admit a movie-star-handsome Black man in his late thirties. He was dressed with a flair that would have done justice to a gala event.

"Julie said you had a minute or two for me, Sheriff."

Seif privately suspected Julie would be hearing from the sheriff for letting not one but two interlopers into the inner sanctum without prior consent. Julie's policy seemed to guarantee admission as long as she recognized the visitor.

Grant's anger cooled. He met Adams with a strong, positive handshake.

"You're here to look out for Harry?"

Adams's eyes swept around Grant's office, coming to rest on Harry, who held the clipboard against his chest like a talisman, a hopeful look transforming the wretchedness of his expression. David's melting black eyes turned to stone.

"Not at all," he said with dignity. He shot his cuff and checked his impressive watch. "To my knowledge, you've detained eleven Black men without charge. Without grounds for suspicion, other than the color of their skin. I'm here to see them released."

Behind Adams's head, Seif gave Grant a pointed look. He'd warned him. Adams was a well-known criminal defense attorney, just like Inaya's father. Perhaps he'd show up next.

"Don't you have a case in Denver to deal with?" said Grant. "That drug raid?"

David Adams was undeterred. His eyes slid from the paperwork on Harry's lap to meet the challenge in Grant's.

"Nothing is more important to me at the moment than Duante Young's life, and thus, the manner of his death."

Harry's voice quavered. "Let them go, Sheriff. I don't want harm done in my name."

David Fortunate Adams looked him over again, his judgment cast in stone.

"Further harm, you mean."

Harry broke down again. "I should never have drawn my gun."

An admission against interest witnessed by all three men.

13

Friday prayer was usually good for sorting out Inaya's thoughts, leaving her with a sense of peaceful reflection. The young imam who was visiting from Turkey spoke eloquently of the busyness of everyday life, when communion with one's Creator seemed like the last priority. He spoke of foundations. If the inner foundation was secure, the rest would be solid also.

When you go to meet God, when you take that first step, you will find that God is already there. You need not seek God in the mansions of the stars, instead turn inward to your heart.

She prayed for guidance from God with two things on her mind. The first was to see whether she could get access to the gun used to kill Mateo Ruiz. It would have been entered into evidence at DPD headquarters, where the Drug Task Force was stationed, and it would confirm a few simple facts of the case. There was bound to be resistance, however, to her outside inquiry. Tempers might fly, doors could be shut, and Seif would find out that she was acting outside his wishes, God help her. Her second concern was to meet with Kelly Broda's partner, Madeleine Hicks, and hear her version of events on the night the raid had taken place. Could she vouch for her partner with eyewitness testimony, or was she covering for him by rote, as most cops would do with their partner in the crosshairs?

In her prayer's final supplication, Inaya knew why her thoughts were disturbed. She was making these inquiries not out of any concern for the innocence of Kelly Broda—they had yet to make a real connection—but rather with her focus on bringing Danny Egan down. Her sympathies were all with the family of Marcus McBride, and by extension with Mateo Ruiz. Rare was the occasion where the taking of life could be justified, though lexicons of exoneration had sprung up in defense.

She held a paradoxical view. Nothing was as precious or as sacred as a human life. Yet from her father's experience as a man in flight from his own country, his own *people,* she also knew how cheaply life was held, how it could be taken without anyone left to mourn. Children starved in the camps where her father had spent a decade of his life. Others were sold for labor or for purposes too dark to describe. Still others gave up on a life that promised nothing beyond the boundaries of the camp. The borders that kept some safe consigned others to misery just as easily, with the moral questions remaining unexamined. Why were some lives prized beyond rubies while others were like chaff in the wind?

The fatalists would say the dead's time had come, the hour written by God. There was nothing to do but accept it, no matter what the circumstances were.

As a police detective, Inaya wrestled with the question of the sanctity of life. As an observant Muslim, she had other instincts, and reconciling the two was imperative for her to be able to have faith in the work she did.

She should be acting for Mateo Ruiz instead of Marcus McBride. But the time would also come when she would have to think of Kelly Broda—had he killed a young man in cold blood or in the exigence of an incident?

She found Maddy at her gym, not far from Kelly Broda's house. She was tall and lean, and indescribably alert. She was working on some kind of leg press, her gray T-shirt soaked with sweat, her golden face glistening with perspiration as she moved. She didn't get up to shake hands; she nodded at the machine beside her, which had a seat. It was for strengthening the upper body, clamping the arms of the machine together, then letting them loose again. Weights could be added by pulling out a steel pin at the back.

"Join me," Madeleine said. Her breathing was steady. "Beats sitting at a desk."

Inaya was wearing a long smock-like shirt over loose white leggings. She supposed her attired could pass for gym clothes, but her preferred form of exercise was an early-morning run or a swim at the local pool during women's hours. She didn't like any kind of exercise that required mechanical aptitude. She had a mental block when it came to things like figuring out how to open window sashes or latches, or managing to parallel park, and figuring out the complexities of a weight machine while the other gym rats watched wasn't high on her list of enjoyable activities. Nonetheless, she sat down on the bench, and much as she had done with Kelly Broda, she watched Madeleine go through her routine, pausing only to increase the weights on the leg press.

Maddy's muscle tone was impressive, though she was lanky rather than bulky, a Thoroughbred, not a Clydesdale, though what was Inaya doing comparing another woman to a horse? Madeleine Hicks had an open, good-natured face. She seemed approachable, and she would want to go to bat for Kelly Broda.

Two men built on the Schwarzenegger model walked by, both in tank tops and shorts. One of them winked at Inaya, who responded by flashing the badge at her waist.

Madeleine barked a laugh.

"Ms. Hicks . . ."

"Call me Maddy. Everyone does."

She pushed the bar of the leg press out. "This is a bodybuilders' gym. If you're female, you're going to get noticed. The badge won't hold them off for long."

Briefly, Inaya considered the headscarf she had abandoned. Nothing deflected male attention faster. Then again, the men in the gym weren't bothering her in any way, they were probably just keeping in practice.

"You're on leave, Maddy?" she confirmed.

"Admin leave, yeah."

Maddy sat up, freed herself from the machine, and moved over to another that seemed designed for working the inner thighs. Her long golden limbs gleamed.

Inaya began going over the events of the night of the raid with Maddy, who was eager to set the record straight.

"We were picked at random—like they could have called on any patrol officers, but I think they were impressed that we were from Chicago, so we were often sent out as backup." She looked down at her flexing thighs, a little embarrassed. "Because we had so much experience on the streets."

"You and Kelly Broda, you mean."

"Yeah." Maddy paused to wipe sweat from her forehead with a wristband, her sandy ponytail bouncing with her movements. "We're always partnered up. It works well for us because it's like we've developed our own language. Even when I can't see him, I can feel where he is, and it's the same for him. Though mostly, we're just driving around together, looking for signs of trouble."

"Had you patrolled that area before?"

"Sure." Her wide mouth turned down at the edges.

"Problems?"

"You could say that."

"As part of the Drug Task Force raid?"

"No, just part of our regular patrol. But maybe that's why we were asked to support the DTF operation—because we knew the streets."

Maybe. Inaya would have to check that out with task-force officers.

"What about Kelly's gun?"

The leg weights clanked down sharply.

"What about it?" Madeleine sat up, focused.

"Kelly said the fatal shot came from his gun."

A red tide of angry color swept up Madeleine's face. "Kell's being an idiot."

"So it didn't?"

"All I can tell you is that Kell didn't shoot that kid."

"So you had a visual on the suspect?"

Maddy faltered. "What are you getting at?"

"If you knew Mateo Ruiz was young enough to look like a kid, you must have gotten a good look at him. You would have been in close proximity. Why? Did you clock him coming out of the building?"

Maddy rolled her shoulders, thinking. "Yeah. That's what must have happened."

Inaya pounced on that. "You're not sure?"

"There were a lot of people milling about that night, and there was plenty of smoke from the tear gas. Everything happened so fast. I don't have a clear picture in my mind."

"But you *do* know that Kelly didn't fire that shot."

"I said so, didn't I?"

"How do you know that?"

Maddy's hands clenched around the gym equipment. "Because one, Kell never but never unholsters his weapon. And two, the shot didn't come from our position."

"How could you tell if you don't have a clear picture of that night, with the smoke and the chaos of the raid?"

Maddy's eyes widened, but she had her answer ready. "I pay attention to my partner. Our lives depend on each other when we're out on patrol."

"So why he did he say the shot came from his gun?"

Frustrated, Maddy shouted, "I've said I don't know, haven't I? Why don't you pay attention?"

Heads turned around the gym, and abashed, Maddy went quiet. "I'm sorry. I just don't know why he's being so bullheaded about this. It's like he's pointing a gun at himself which is such a stupid, macho thing to do. Nothing he's doing makes any sense to me."

The weapon in question would have been entered into evidence. Checking that out for herself might give Inaya a clearer idea of why Maddy and Kell had two different stories to tell.

She thought of another question. "Were you briefed on the raid in advance?"

"Wouldn't have made much sense otherwise, us being there."

Inaya realized she'd have to re-interview Maddy once she had a map of the area for Madeleine to point out exactly where she and Kelly had been positioned.

"So you chased after Mateo Ruiz upon his exit from the dispensary?"

"I think so, yes." Maddy didn't sound entirely sure. "I think it was him, but we could have gotten mixed up once we began the chase."

"What were the orders given by the DTF? Were you meant to shoot at suspects fleeing from the scene?"

There was no mistaking the censure in Inaya's voice, and Maddy scowled in response.

"They said to apprehend them," she said sulkily.

"By any means necessary?"

"No."

"Then why would any of the officers fire at Mateo Ruiz?"

"Maybe he seemed like a threat."

"You and Kelly are the ones who chased him—did he?"

"I don't know."

"Did you see your partner aim at Mateo Ruiz?"

"No!"

"Did he shoot to kill?"

"I said no!"

"Then did you shoot Mateo? You were overzealous, perhaps. Trying to make your mark, get the DTF to notice you."

"Kell doesn't want to work drugs," she said, toying with the pin that adjusted the weights.

"How is that relevant?"

Maddy faced her squarely. "Kell's like my big brother. I follow his lead so I can be sure to have his back."

"I thought he was aiming for detective."

Pride lit Madeleine's eyes.

"He's more than qualified."

"Then what happened? He's put in a lot of time."

Maddy hesitated, as if she was looking inward. After a moment, she sighed, her bony shoulders caving in.

"Kell has a bit of a complex about his dad. I think he decided to stay on the streets to make up for his dad's actions. He wants to show people that you don't have to be afraid of cops on the street, we're not there to hurt them. I'm happy to support him even if I have to go up against John."

"Why? Does John have problems with his son? With his ideas on policing?"

Maddy grunted. "He's a bit of a bruiser. But you know that already, right?"

Didn't she just. There was a lot more to dig into here about the relationship between Broda and his son. Inaya had the distinct impression that no one was being entirely forthcoming with the truth. She'd have to talk to one of the DTF officers who had organized the raid. That would clear up the matter of the gun. And if she could correlate the body-cam footage from that night, not just Maddy's and Kell's, but all of it, she would also have a clearer idea of where the shot had come from, and surely Dr. Stanger could give her some help with that, as well. She'd ask Cat to talk to him, as he'd already briefed her on the body. His report would come in soon, and when she came back for round two, she'd have Broda and his son in her sights.

Prove him innocent, Broda had said.

But what if the fatal shot *had* come from Kelly's gun? With her trigger-point awareness of her partner, wouldn't Maddy have noticed? Cops covered for other cops all the time, and Maddy had claimed Kelly as a brother, a simple enough explanation. But she was puzzled that Maddy seemed to have no idea why Kelly had made his confession. If they were close enough to have moved to Denver together, that meant she knew the ins and outs of the relationship between Kelly and his father. Was it possible that Kelly was trying to get back at his father in some way, despite the cost to himself? And would their very different ideas on policing be enough to provoke such a reaction? Wouldn't Maddy have tried to get to the heart of the matter? As his de facto little sister, maybe playing a peacemaking role. She decided to push a little more.

"Maybe that's not the reason Kelly hasn't tried for detective. Maybe it's about you."

"What's that mean?"

"You said *he* was more than qualified. What about you? If you couldn't make the cut, maybe he felt it was his responsibility not to leave you behind."

"If I wanted something more, I'd aim for SWAT, not detective. I've got an in there. Kell and I are close, but that doesn't mean I'd hold him back from something he wants. If he made detective, he'd have a whole team at his back." She scrunched up her face in worry. "I wouldn't have to be responsible for him."

Looking at Maddy, Inaya thought she seemed fearless enough for SWAT, not bragging about her abilities, just aware of her own competence.

"What's your in at SWAT?" she asked.

To her surprise, Maddy blushed. "My boyfriend is a captain there. He's keeping an eye out for an opening for me in another jurisdiction. He'll put in a word."

"Would you pursue that if Kelly made detective?"

"Yeah, why not? I don't want to be on the streets in my forties." An artless grin lit her face. "And you know how they train at SWAT, all the cool stuff they get to do, blowing shit up."

So they were close but not inseparable.

"So maybe Kelly is the one who's holding *you* back."

"I owe him a lot," Maddy said with total sincerity. "I owe the Brodas a lot as a family, so it's not hard to keep watching out for Kell. He'll work out this stuff with his dad eventually, and then I'll be free to do my own thing." She grinned again. "My boyfriend can't wait."

Inaya was no longer certain that the debt Maddy felt she owed extended to covering for Kelly. Not if Maddy had ambitions for herself, and another important man in her life.

"How does your boyfriend get along with Kelly?"

"He likes him—they have guy stuff in common, plus they're both cops. He even has a friend who set Kell up with his cousin. He wouldn't vouch for Kell if he didn't like him."

Her answer was excessive; she was trying too hard to clear one man or the other.

"What does Kelly think?"

Maddy out-and-out laughed. "You have to see this cousin. She's a bombshell and she loves the outdoors. What's not to like?"

Inaya made a note to check out Maddy's claims about her boyfriend. He could be as well-adjusted as she claimed, or he could be jealous of a man who spent so much time with Maddy. But if what Maddy was saying was true, the shooting of Mateo Ruiz was a significant obstacle to the future she was planning for herself. She might be patient but she wouldn't want to torpedo it, and she wouldn't have as much incentive to get bogged down in covering for Kelly. It was just as possible that everything she had said to Inaya was simply the truth as she remembered it in the chaos and confusion of that night.

"Did you tell your boyfriend about the raid? Say, when it was taking place?"

"Of course not. We were strictly warned against a leak." But her expression had soured, her eyes shifting away from Inaya's. "It was an accident," she stressed. "Too many people on the street, too much noise and chaos. Get the footage and you'll see. The shot came from out of the blue."

Maybe it had. But until someone admitted that, Kelly Broda was still in the frame.

14

Areesha spent a busy weekend with her husband and sons, doing her best to tamp down the instinctive rage of the young at the senseless death of a young Black man.

"Does property matter so much?" Clay, her younger son, had asked. "So much that they'd kill Duante?"

He was having a hard time grappling with the idea that defacing public property was a capital offense.

"To white folks it does," her older son, Kareem, had shot back.

Areesha didn't like how bitter Kareem had become, his normally sunny temperament given over to a sullen rage. There were two paths for Kareem to go down. He could make plans for his life, develop himself, and eventually achieve satisfaction through his chosen path while maintaining a commitment to his own community, expressed through various works of service the way his friends in the church or the Nation of Islam did. Or the cause could become his life, and everything he did would be geared toward a life of activism: Black studies, a Black college or university, a leading role as a community organizer—someone others could depend on. He often said to her that he wanted to become a civil rights attorney like Areesha, so he could take some of the load off his mother's back. She hoped that was the path he stuck to, because the cause could become all-consuming, it could be a struggle to feel either joy or hope when confronted with so much grief and anger. You could lose sight of yourself as the movement swept you up.

She was a fine one to lecture him, she thought wryly; her work-life balance was hardly ideal. If David didn't support her with such devastating tenderness, she would have sunk long ago. They'd rearranged their priorities to bring children into their world: neither one of them had to jostle for supremacy when it came to their careers, and it helped that their work was so closely aligned. Areesha was out in the community, David was armed with the law, both of them adept at using a system that so often worked against Black communities.

That was David's secret power—his thorough command of the law and of the leading debates surrounding criminal justice reform. Well, one of his powers, at least. The others were his monumental calm, his ability to keep pushing against brick walls until they began to crumble and to present himself with such competence and dignity that all attempts to demean or diminish him gave way. She loved that about David. He never made too much of himself or his own personal feelings: she and Clay and Kareem were his world. If all was right there, he could handle anything else.

She had brought Mirembe to him to help Mirembe decide how she wanted to proceed.

The question had been posed to Mirembe: Did she want Duante's body or did she want to force a reckoning with the sheriff of Blackwater Falls?

They sat across from David at his magnificent mahogany desk, bookshelves gleaming with bright legal tomes behind him, and a couple of framed family photos. One was of David with Areesha and their sons, but Mirembe's eyes settled on a photograph of David with his parents and sisters.

"Where was the photograph taken, Mr. Adams?" she asked in her low, melodic voice.

"Please call me David, Dr. Young." He sat back in his fine leather chair, dressed to perfection in a crisp tan suit with a sharp red tie. His shoes were polished, the silk square in the pocket of his blazer impeccable. All of it—the office, the baronial desk, the red leather legal tomes, David's appearance—was designed to give confidence and comfort to his clients. They could trust him. He knew what he was doing, and he was wildly successful at it.

"Then you must call me Mirembe, David."

Mirembe, too, had made an effort with her appearance. She was dressed in professional attire, in a teal-green skirt suit with a blouse patterned in white, black, and teal. She wore a light veneer of makeup, and clutched an expensive elbow bag at her knees.

David's young paralegal brought in a tray of coffees, and a hint of

Mirembe's smile glimmered through in thanks. She set her purse down carefully on a corner of David's desk.

"I want to arrange my son's funeral, that is my first concern. I also want to know . . . Do they normally shoot to kill just because a Black boy is running?"

David arranged Mirembe's coffee as she preferred it, sliding her cup toward her. His eyes rested briefly on Areesha.

"Mirembe, they won't think of Duante as a boy. Even if he had been a minor, the police would be looking to paint him as a threat. It's much easier for them if he's of age. That doesn't mean we can't fight it," he reassured her. "It just helps to know what we're fighting."

"Understood." Her voice was soft with despair.

David stretched back to the console behind him, on which his printer and a number of file folders rested. He chose one of these and passed it to Mirembe.

"These are Blackwater's use-of-force guidelines, and they're in line with the new guidelines outlined by the DPD. Take them home with you and read them—you'll see the emphasis is on de-escalation, but as far as I understand, officers mainly see the guidelines as increasing the amount of paperwork they're required to fill out if they so much as unholster their weapons." He encompassed both women in his rueful glance. "I'm not sure how strong of a deterrent increased administrative duties are." He steepled his fingers beneath his strong, square jaw. "The issue here is that Officer Harry Cooper identified himself as a police officer twice. He gave verbal warnings, and he only raised his gun when he thought a weapon was being aimed at him. On the surface, a justifiable use of force. And there is the fact that Cooper is very much shaken by the shooting. He's not known as a bully, or someone racially motivated, so there is a great deal to offer in mitigation."

"The weapon was a can of spray paint," Mirembe cried.

David nodded. "We can and will reproduce the scene. Test out the lighting conditions, see how identifiable the spray-paint can would have been under similar circumstances, if you wish. My feeling is that Cooper panicked, despite having the presence of mind to issue the verbal warnings. He would have been afraid that the other suspect was circling back."

"Yes," Mirembe whispered. "Yes, please do that."

"The other issue is the vandalism, the string of similar incidents in Blackwater Falls, with public property defaced."

Mirembe's hands were fastened around her coffee cup, oblivious to its temperature. Areesha was still waiting for hers to cool. She urged Mirembe to set her cup down before she spilled its contents on her beautiful blouse and burned her skin.

From somewhere, Mirembe gathered her inner reserves.

"Duante was *not* a vandal. He was an artist. He stuck to the parameters of the contest he'd entered. That contest did not call for defacing public property—that was a strict consideration. Abandoned sites only. He'd never created anything in Blackwater Falls before."

David made a note on his pad. "Are you certain of that?"

"Absolutely." She rounded on Areesha. "You turned his laptop over to Detective Hernandez. You can find the proof of it on there, assuming your friend can be trusted."

"She can," Areesha said calmly. "But I also arranged to have the hard drive copied."

Never forget they're police, she'd reminded herself.

"Have they found the real vandals?" Mirembe asked bitterly.

"I'm not certain they're looking, but that's a matter I've raised with Sheriff Grant."

David had also succeeded in arranging the release of the Black men Grant had arrested.

"If we could find the young man who was with Duante that night, it would help us understand why Duante used the garbage cans of local residents as a canvas. That's a point against, I'm afraid." His glowing eyes focused on Mirembe. "Do you have an answer to that?"

Mirembe glanced behind David's head to the small windows between a pair of bookshelves. The early morning light filtered through, glowing.

"I wish I did, David. I can ask around about his friends."

"Let me do it," Areesha said. "Give me a list of names and I'll follow up."

"Don't use your detective friend," Mirembe warned. "I don't want to paint a target on anyone else's back." She turned back to David. "What about the funeral?"

"I've spoken with the pathologist. He's moved the postmortem to the top of his list. As soon as it's complete, you can make any arrangements you wish. I will keep on this, I promise. They have no reason to hold Duante's body once cause of death is fully established."

"We know who caused it," Mirembe said. "But of course, he'll never stand trial."

"Is that what you wish?"

Mirembe looked him straight in the eye.

"Someone has to answer for the death of my child." She gestured at the photograph of David and Areesha with their sons. "You understand. You have two boys of your own."

"I do," David said. "We both do."

A comfortable pause settled over the room, and in the quiet, they turned their attention to their coffee, sipping in silence until Mirembe spoke again.

"I want to meet this Harry Cooper. I want to look into his eyes and ask him why, with his experience, he couldn't find an alternative to shooting my son dead."

15

Inaya's conscience was troubling her. She hadn't convinced Seif to let her work the Mateo Ruiz shooting; he'd insisted she focus on Duante Young. But Catalina was doing a fine job on that, and she'd roped in Areesha to help. An hour or two checking out a few basic facts about the Ruiz shooting wasn't really wasting her time. It was disobeying orders, but she was convinced she could get around Seif if she tried, using the attraction between them. He wouldn't see through her, would he? Even as the thought darted through her mind, she felt a pang of shame.

Might as well accept that she was disobeying orders and take the consequences. If she did good work on both cases, Seif might be prepared to let it go.

A little anxiously, she drove down the East Colfax area strip, searching for the cannabis dispensary. She wanted to get a feel for where the shooting had taken place. It was a typically seedy strip, though the cannabis dispensary was new, a squat, square, glass-fronted store with the windows of its upper story shuttered. Not blacked out but closed by painted green shutters that gave it a look of class. It stood out against its neighbors, a strip club called Shotgun Willie's, a few pawnbrokers with giant WE BUY YOUR GOLD signs, two liquor stores on either side of the street with graffiti marking up their storefronts. Right across from the dispensary was a fast-food falafel joint, and beside that a building without windows in the front. Unusually, the windows ran along the side of the building, and she saw that it was a nightclub, the name "The Black Door" stenciled in silver on an imposing black door, the "l" a stylized slash of red. She also noted that the building's main door was painted a discreet red. No lights, no silhouettes of nudes or exotic dancers, nothing flashy that drew the attention.

She nosed her car farther down the street to where a bar with the requisite neon sign was taking in its deliveries for the day. She could stop and talk to some of the locals, but if it got back to the DTF before she got clearance from Seif, she might be stepping on their toes. Better if she went straight there and introduced herself as someone acting for Kelly Broda. Then she could circle back to Kelly and his partner.

She turned down a side street to head back to DPD headquarters, where Community Response had their offices, mulling over the issue of Kelly's gun. Suppose she went down to the evidence locker before she talked to someone on the Drug Task Force. That would give her an advantage when it came to any questions she asked. Any footage from the night was probably locked down tight, but she shouldn't have any trouble accessing the evidence room. It was buried in the basement, and she knew most of the officers who worked there on rotation.

Twenty minutes later, she parked her car in its designated spot and hurried through a side door, flashing her ID with a disarming smile. She took the elevator down to evidence, praying she didn't run into Seif, who was likely running the investigation from their offices in the same building. She had to check the directory to see what floor the DTF was on—all the way at the top. Good. She'd take the stairs from the basement, and hopefully would only run into cops from other units. She murmured a prayer under her breath, fully aware that she didn't exactly deserve God's help because she wasn't on the up-and-up.

Never mind that, for now. The officer on rota at evidence was a hearty woman in her fifties with her hair in a no-nonsense buzz cut. Sharon? Shelley? Shyla, that was it!

"Hey, Shyla. Busy day?"

Shyla snorted. "Not so much." She held up a book of crossword puzzles. "Gives me time to sharpen my wits. Though I'm stuck on a clue that says 'when you know you've been satisfied and it isn't a situation.'" She waved the little blue book at Inaya, who took a quick peek at the nine-letter clue.

"Satiation?" she offered, though she didn't dare condescend to spell it. "All right if I go in to check some evidence on a case?"

"Hey, you're right!" Shyla set aside her book of puzzles, proffering a clipboard for Inaya to sign in. "What case?"

"That shooting at East Colfax." She kept talking to distract Shyla. "They're probably still processing evidence from the scene, but I promised I'd take a look and see how far we're along."

Shyla shrugged, lifting a bosom like a prow. Her foundation garments were good. "I wasn't on duty that night, but you're probably right. Those crime scene boys—girls, too, maybe—like to dot every 'i' and cross every 't.'"

"Mm."

So far, so good. Shyla buzzed her into the room's subterranean premises, after looking up the case number, and directed her to the right aisle. Inaya beamed a smile at her. That was easier than she'd expected.

Cases were assigned alphanumeric codes, and evidence was locked up in an alphabetical order that matched those codes. The DPD was going high-tech and implementing a new system where each officer would be assigned an ID for digital entry to a cage. So far, they were still on the old system, evidence neatly organized into its case cubicle with the cubicle left unlocked. The sign-in sheet and electronic entry into the room were considered safeguards enough.

Thankful for it, Inaya found the right code quickly. Her guess had been correct: there was very little evidence in storage from the raid. A few plastic envelopes holding items like the account ledgers from the cannabis dispensary, six cardboard boxes that were labeled with the chemical names for street drugs. Inaya bypassed all these. Shifting the boxes aside, she found what she was looking for in a plastic evidence bag.

Darting a quick look around, she confirmed that she was alone in the cavernous room. She slipped on latex gloves from her purse and carefully opened the bag. The weapon used to kill Mateo Ruiz was hefty and a little awkward, far too big for her hands.

She turned it over in her hands just as the door to the evidence locker buzzed again. Someone else was entering the space. She shoved herself quickly up against the cage, trying to blend in with the shadows. Footsteps moved in her direction, and, panicked, she took another quick look at the gun before sealing it back inside its bag.

It wasn't a police-issue Glock.

She didn't have time to check the label, but the gun looked like an antique piece, maybe a single-action revolver of some kind. No time to take a photo either, so she shoved the bag back onto the shelf and jerked her neat suit jacket back into place.

The evidence locker was temperature-controlled, but she was beginning to perspire.

"What the hell are you doing down here?" a cold voice asked.

Of all the damnable luck in the world, the voice belonged to Seif.

She wondered if she could bluff it out.

"Taking a look at some evidence. I wanted to make sure it was processed correctly."

"What case?"

Seif was standing too close. Now he looked beyond her to the reference code on the cage. One look at the six boxes of manufactured pharmaceuticals and her cover was blown.

"Didn't I tell you to stay away from anything involving Kelly Broda? You're not authorized to pry around in DTF business. You're going to bring trouble down on our heads."

He glared down at her from his superior height, crowding her against the cage.

Well, she'd been caught red-handed, so she might as well take a proper look at the gun. She jerked it back out and offered it to Seif for his inspection.

"This is the weapon that was used to kill Mateo. It's unusual to say the least."

Seif's voice dropped a little lower as he asked, "Didn't you hear me, Rahman?"

Inaya made the mistake of looking up into his face. Despite his proximity, he wasn't trying to flirt with her; his eyes were cold chips of ice.

"I'm sorry, sir, but it's not a huge waste of our resources, is it? I've been checking out the Brodas on my own time, and there seems to be an air of mystery around the gun used in the shooting. Kelly says it *was* his gun, but this isn't his Glock." She couldn't help the cajoling note in her voice. "Can't we dig into this? What could it hurt to speak to a member of the Drug Task Force? Find out if the gun has been printed and what else it has to tell us? Was it found at the scene or placed there afterward? What about Kelly's

Glock? Was he carrying two guns? And how does that make any sense if he—"

She was speaking quickly, the words tumbling out, because Seif's stillness disturbed her. His body was warm against her, and despite his stern expression, she didn't feel threatened. He held the pose for a moment or two; then, sighing, he bracketed Inaya with his arms, pinning her against the cage without laying a finger on her.

"Why are you so damn stubborn?" he asked. "I'm trying to keep you safe."

Thrilled by the admission, Inaya poked the bear.

"I can handle myself, Qas."

The ice in his gaze was chased out by tongues of flame.

"Like you did in Chicago?"

Inaya tilted up her chin, refusing to be cowed by his temper.

"I did the best I could. How do you think you would do facing six-to-one odds?"

His face went dark at the words; then he ruthlessly suppressed whatever he was feeling and stepped back, turning over the plastic bag in his hands.

"This is a Merwin Hulbert revolver," he said in a puzzled voice. "It's right there on the nameplate. It's a Wild West kind of gun." His black eyes caught Inaya's. "Have you seen the ballistics report?"

Inaya smiled at him, relieved, and his gaze lingered on the smile.

"Not yet. I thought I'd introduce myself to someone on the task force, and see if they were willing to share what they know about the gun."

He hefted the weight of the gun in his hands. "If this is the gun that was used, the bullet would be a cartridge—I don't even know if they make that kind of ammunition anymore. Unless the gun came preloaded. Even then, it wouldn't be guaranteed to fire."

"Another reason to speak to someone on the task force. Did they find the cartridge on the scene or on the body? I don't know anything about this kind of weapon, which begs the question: Why would anyone use a gun like this when a Glock would guarantee a kill?"

"You're saying the shooting was deliberate?"

"Why else would this gun have been used? At the very least, it raises some questions."

The first one that came to her mind was whether Mateo Ruiz had been a target.

"Fine," he said at last. "It does. Here." He held the gun up inside the bag. "Take a picture, get the evidence number, and any other information you can from the tag."

Her slim brows flew up. "In case it disappears?"

"Take the picture, Rahman. I'm already cutting you a lot of slack."

When it was done, and the package was safely put away, Seif escorted her from the room. He gave Shyla a charming smile, the kind he'd never used on Inaya.

"Thanks for the heads-up."

Shyla glanced at Inaya. "Sorry, kid. I never mess around with the lieutenant's orders."

16

Inaya rode up in the elevator with Seif, a question in her eyes.

Irritably, he answered, "Since you're not going to give up on the Mateo Ruiz shooting and how it connects to Kelly Broda, I'd rather you stay within reasonable limits." He ticked off his conditions with his fingers. "First, I clear it with whoever's in charge at DTF. Second, you keep me apprised every step of the way." He folded down two fingers, which left one raised—thankfully not his middle finger. "Third, you don't meet with Broda Senior on your own. It's all a little too easy," he warned her. "I don't believe in John Broda's sudden gestures of goodwill, and if you're anything like the cop I know you to be, you shouldn't either."

He stood back and let Inaya exit the elevator first. She was pretending to be chastened. He caught it when she grimaced at Catalina, whose expression seemed to suggest that she knew Inaya was in the process of digging herself out of a hole.

"We take this teamwide," Seif said, calling the team to attention. "The shooting of Duante Young in Blackwater Falls is still our first priority, but if Detective Rahman is determined to keep on the Mateo Ruiz shooting in Denver, I want you two at her back." He pointed at Jaime and Cat. "Can I trust you to keep her from stepping over the line?"

They nodded, Jaime with utter seriousness, Cat with a flash of her beguiling dimples.

In very short order, they traded information. Cat brought them up to speed on what she'd learned about Duante—the graffiti competition, his resentment at his move from D.C., the sketch of his mother that he'd blacked out with such rage.

"You've brought his electronics in?" Seif asked. When she nodded, he turned his attention to Jaime. "Follow that up. Work with our techs to find out more about this contest. And Catalina, see if you can track down some of Duante's friends—we have to work the vandalism angle if we want leverage on Grant." He shifted gears back to Jaime. "What did you find out about Harry Cooper's background in Blackwater?"

Jaime's eyes lit up with enthusiasm. Seif had overlooked a lapse or two, and he could see that Jaime felt like he was back in favor. He gave a succinct report. Grant hadn't lied about Cooper. His record was clean; there were no complaints against him by the public, no sign of unsatisfied ambitions. He liked the work he did on the street, and he did it well. He was also on the roster as a search-and-rescue volunteer for hikers who got lost in the Rockies. He kept himself reasonably fit, had a good word for everyone, and had been in a steady relationship with Tania Davis for more than ten years. They lived together, though they weren't married.

"That's unusual, surely." Seif looked to Cat. "For a man of his generation from a conservative Christian community?"

The specter of the Resurrection megachurch hung over Blackwater Falls, and nearly all of its residents. The church also had a vigilante arm, in the form of Christian bikers who'd named themselves "the Disciples."

Jaime passed Cat a photograph of Cooper, and now she studied it thoughtfully. She looked up with the light of battle in her eyes.

"It might not have been Harry's decision. It could be that this Tania is the one who's a little unorthodox. What do we know about her?"

"Not much. I should point out that their house is just one street over from where Duante was shot. Not on the same cul-de-sac, but in the same neighborhood." Jaime turned to Seif. "Do you want me to follow that track?"

"I don't think it's significant if Harry Cooper was on a routine shift that night—he's a Blackwater cop who lives in Blackwater, so patrolling close to home isn't out of the ordinary. But if anything else comes up, let's call Tania Davis in for a little chat. I met her briefly at the sheriff's station. She seemed thoroughly conventional to me, and very attached to Harry. Anything else?"

Jaime cleared his throat. "Cooper *was* married once. He married right out of high school, he and his wife had a son, then he lost his wife to cancer."

"So maybe he didn't want to go through that again which is why he and Tania never married." He held up a hand, anticipating Cat. "I haven't dismissed your theory, I'm just thinking aloud. What about the son—where is he?"

"He's career army."

"So he's on deployment? That's why he isn't here to support his father?"

"That's the funny thing," Jaime said. "His service record is classified."

Seif raised his jet-black eyebrows. "Interesting. Let me see what I can find out from my contacts. Send me the details, and I'll work that."

"The Cooper shooting of Duante is open-and-shut. We need to talk about Mateo now."

Seif's gaze swiveled to Inaya, his face mirroring her impatience, but he let her continue. She told them about her interviews with Maddy Hicks and Kelly Broda.

"Kelly claims it was his gun that fired, but sir, we've *seen* the gun."

She described the Merwin Hulbert to the others, telling them that Seif had called it a Wild West kind of gun, and Cat posed the same questions Inaya had raised.

"A targeted killing if the weapon was that unique—that specific. But who would be after a young man like Mateo? How would they know he was at the dispensary during the raid?"

"That's another thing that's not clear," Inaya admitted. "Whether Mateo *was* on-site and was a target of the raid. Was he a potential dealer?"

Angrily, Cat responded, "Not all Mexicans have links to the cartels."

Seif interrupted. "From what I've learned from the DTF, this wasn't cartel business. These were homegrown designer drugs that cater to the wealthy."

"We need background on Mateo." Inaya looked to her partner. "We need to get a feel for East Colfax. Do you want to work Mateo's case with me? Talk to his family and friends?"

Cat's gentle mouth firmed. "Yes. Of course I do. But we need ballistics first. We need to know about that gun—it will give me a better sense of who might have wanted to target Mateo."

Jaime raised his hand. "This might be way off track, sir, but you *did* say it was a Wild West kind of gun."

"So?" Seif crossed his arms over his chest.

"Remember the deputy gangs you mentioned? Could there be a connection?"

Seif should have thought of that for himself. Deputy gangs ran police departments like their own private fiefdoms, though Denver seemed too small a locale to be taken over by a group that insisted on total obedience to how they ran their operations without drawing unwanted attention. They were also often infiltrated by white supremacists. So with the use of a weapon nostalgic for the days of the Wild West, and a Latino victim, could there have been a sign that the shooting wasn't what it appeared to be on the surface? It wasn't outside the realm of possibility. Inaya would need to press harder with Kelly and Madeleine to find out if they'd been under that kind of pressure. Police gangs also had their own initiation rites; could a targeted killing be one of them?

Seif moved to the team whiteboard, scribbling down assignments.

"Sir, the Disciples are Christian nationalists, right?"

He looked over his shoulder at Inaya. "You're thinking they would know if the DPD is running its own gangs?"

"There are some obvious connections."

Inaya had tangled with the Disciples before, and knew their contempt for minorities.

"We're talking two different jurisdictions."

"The Disciples don't limit their vigilantism to Blackwater, even if it's their main base. Their club president lives in Boulder, remember?"

"They're branching out?" Cat asked.

"I've heard that too," Jaime said.

Seif turned around, his shoulders resting against the unmarked side of the whiteboard. "What are you suggesting, Rahman?"

"I think West could help us here, maybe even check out the area with me."

Lincoln West was the Disciples' road captain, club name Ranger. He was a confirmed Christian biker, with a reputation for toughness. He was also working undercover with the FBI. He'd aided Inaya on a previous case, and they had a certain rapport.

His eyes narrowed. "I thought you wanted to work with Catalina on this."

Inaya smiled at Cat. "I do, and I will. But West could give us an in. Give me a chance to see what he knows and figure out where it might lead."

"I want progress on both cases," Seif said firmly.

"You'll have it." There was a cocky lilt to her voice that he found irresistible, but still he took his time before granting his permission. He pointed to Jaime. "Keep your eye on Detective Rahman. Shadow her when you can." He rubbed the back of his head, where his haircut had grown out and the natural curl was becoming unruly. "Catalina, run down our priorities for me."

Cat hadn't taken a single note, but her recall was nearly perfect.

"You'll dig into the military records of Harry Cooper's son. You'll also be talking to the DTF to get us a copy of the ballistics report to confirm that the Merwin Hulbert was used to kill Mateo Ruiz, and whether there were any prints on the gun. We'll continue to keep an eye on the unrest around East Colfax, and we'll make sure Dr. Mirembe Young and Mateo Ruiz's family remain fully informed. Jaime will chase up the graffiti and vandalism angle through our techs, Inaya and I will do the same through Duante Young's friends. Inaya will check out the deputy gang possibility with West, then the team will regroup."

"You're a marvel," Seif said, and Catalina blushed.

He was adding to the list of tasks on the whiteboard when Catalina spoke again.

"Sir, there's something else. I've heard from Areesha. Dr. Young is insisting on speaking to Cooper herself. She also wants her son's body released."

His shoulders tensed.

"The first might be a problem, the second shouldn't be at all. You can speak to Dr. Stanger, confirm the postmortem is complete, and take things from there. With regard to speaking to Cooper, let me put that to Grant."

Cat nodded. "If he doesn't cooperate, things will blow up quickly. Areesha thinks local protests might go national, and we know that won't work in our favor."

"Grant won't want a spotlight on what he's been up to in Blackwater. That might give us the leverage we need."

He looked at his team members, their faces expectant, and made a wry admission.

"We can't accomplish all of this in one night. Take your time. Go home and see your families. And when you start to move on things, make sure you keep me informed."

He thought about West and remembered to caution Inaya when the others had left.

"Make sure you don't blow his cover."

West had other uses, and Seif would soon be reporting to his own handler at the FBI.

"I'll be careful," Inaya promised, utterly sure of herself now that she'd gotten her way.

What the hell, he thought. First Lily, then Inaya. No matter what his instincts told him to do, he couldn't say no to women.

17

A giant black pickup truck with Christian decals on the windows and a steel-plated fish at the rear pulled up at Inaya's house later that evening. The driver honked the horn with characteristic verve, and Inaya smiled to herself. She'd changed into a pair of skinny jeans with a thin, overlong white blouse that did a good job of covering her rear, a requirement for all her clothing. She'd freshened her makeup and brushed out her hair before scooping it up in a ponytail. She also wore silver hoop earrings and a line of hammered-silver bracelets on both wrists.

Her younger sister Noor, a ridiculously well-put-together fashion plate, cast a professional eye over Inaya at the door.

"Wow," she commented. "What gives, *baji*? Did you go to all this trouble for your smoking-hot boss?" She peered out the front window, not bothering to be discreet. "I didn't know he drove a pickup. He struck me as more buttoned-up than that."

"And you're so worldly-wise," Inaya teased. "Such an expert on men."

"Shut up." Noor punched her on the shoulder, grinning.

Inaya checked that she had her phone in her handbag, and snapped on her shoulder holster, this time without the accompanying blazer. She swung the front door wide, Noor still hanging at her side.

"Wait, *beta*!"

It was her mother, rushing to catch her before she escaped.

She took in Inaya's appearance with a pleased smile.

"*Beta,* how nice you look! Who are you going to see?"

Decidedly *not* a well-heeled Pakistani doctor, as her mother hoped. She suppressed a sigh, turning back to kiss her mother on the cheek.

"No one special," she said. "It's just someone I know."

"Ouch," a deep voice grumbled from the porch. "And here I thought you liked me."

Lincoln "Ranger" West loomed up behind her in classic Disciples gear. A white T-shirt plastered to his muscular chest, a patched leather vest over it, and low-slung, extremely tight jeans that outlined the power of his thighs. His long, wavy dirty-blond hair was partly covered in the front by a checkered bandana. He'd removed his sunglasses, and his white grin shone at Inaya through the thick stubble on his jaw. His hazel eyes twinkled at her.

"Aren't you going to introduce me to these gorgeous women?"

Inaya looked from her mother to West. Sunober Rahman was staring at West's tattoos with fascinated horror. His knuckles, arms, even his throat all bore testimony to his faith. The one at his throat proclaimed him a **CHRISTIAN WARRIOR** in bold, black, stylized letters.

Sunober murmured faintly under her breath. *"Khuda na khaasta, Khuda na khaasta."*

"Hi there!" Noor said cheerfully. "I'm Noor, Inaya's sister."

West mimed an arrow striking at his heart. "One was bad enough," he said. "But now I find out there's two of you?"

Noor answered for Inaya while their mother continued to pray. "You haven't met Nadia yet. She's the real heartbreaker."

West gave her a lazy wink. Then he addressed Sunober in a respectful voice.

"A pleasure to meet you, ma'am. I won't keep your daughter out too late."

Belatedly, Inaya made the introductions. Her mother clutched her arm, speaking barely above a whisper. "This man is your friend? He's your *date*?"

Inaya pointed to her holster, hoping it would reassure her mother because West had appeared at her door like every mother's worst nightmare. The fact that he was attractive didn't help in the least. The tattoos did his speaking for him. Thank God he hadn't brought his bike.

"You know I don't date, Ami. And if I did, I'd leave my gun at home. This is police business."

"I see." From the dismay in her expression, Sunober didn't see at all. It couldn't be helped. Inaya hadn't expected West to get out of his truck to collect her.

She squeezed her mother's hand in reassurance.

"You have your cell phone with you?" Her mother's words sounded like a plea.

Inaya sighed. She'd be thirty soon, yet her mother still kept an eye on her like she was a wayward teen. "I do. You can call me anytime."

She tapped Noor hard on the shoulder. "Take care of Ami while I'm gone, and stop flirting with every man you meet."

"How else will I get any practice?"

Inaya shook her head, shutting the door behind her. She didn't apologize to West. He had to know the impression he made.

He opened the door of his truck for her like a gentleman, and helped her to climb inside.

When he pulled out of her cul-de-sac, he gave her an innocent smile.

"Sorry about that, Brazil."

Brazil was a nickname he'd given her when she'd lied to him about her background at their first meeting. She hadn't known he was undercover then.

Inaya's lips curved up. "I think you enjoyed that."

"You look fantastic," he added.

Her heart gave a strange lift. She fought it down and said, "You're a married man, remember."

His smile dried up, his attention on the road as he merged onto the highway, headed north, the purpling peaks of the Front Range to their left.

"What is it? Has something happened?"

Inaya canvassed West's truck. It was spick-and-span, the interior scrupulously organized so that nothing was out of place, no garbage strewn about or fast-food wrappers scattered on the seats. A steel thermos with the Disciples' logo branded across it sat in a cupholder, and that was it. No sign of a woman's occupation, though she knew West's wife had been in Mexico, waiting for her papers to come through. The interior of the cab smelled of West, clean and male and earthy, with no trace of a woman's lighter fragrance.

"Did your wife get her papers?"

West's chest moved with his deep sigh. "Yeah, she did."

"That's good news, isn't it?"

West looked at her briefly, then shifted down to change gears.

"Would have been if she wanted to stay married to me. She doesn't. She was in Mexico too long, while I was with the boys up here. She met someone else. She says she's fallen in love with him, and she wants a divorce."

"I'm so sorry, West!"

She couldn't imagine how West's daughter had taken the news.

Picking up her thought, West said, "Mercedes doesn't know yet. Marisol is staying with us for now, but she already has one foot out the door."

"Did you love her?" Inaya asked softly, knowing she was getting too personal.

"Wouldn't have had a kid with her if I didn't." He shrugged his shoulders, his gaze locked on the darkening silhouette of the mountains. "But it doesn't hurt like I thought it would. Don't judge me, Brazil, but I played around on her. A woman doesn't forget when you do something like that."

Inaya fidgeted in her seat. "While you were together, you mean?"

West let a few miles elapse in a silence that Inaya didn't break before he answered. "While she was with me, she was the only one for me. But she's been gone quite a while, and I suppose I got restless."

"The Disciples would have expected you to hook up with women at some point."

"Don't make excuses for me. What you're saying is true, but when a man takes vows, he should keep them."

Inaya tried to imagine a biker-style wedding, West's wild hair tamed into a neat man-bun and a boutonniere pinned to his club vest, and failed.

"Your wife didn't do much better," she observed.

West suddenly relaxed. "You're good people, Brazil. I thought you'd consider me one step shy of the devil."

"You don't have horns, just tattoos."

She wanted to take back the words as soon as she'd said them.

West changed the subject. "You ever think about getting a tat? Your sister looks like she'd be game."

Inaya laughed. "Noor is up for anything, but my mother would kill her if she did. As for me—" She tilted her head. "I want to leave the world with my body unmarked, the same way I entered it."

"Nice," West said. He flexed the Wounds of Christ tattoo on his forearm.

"I want my Lord and Savior to recognize me as one of His own when it's my time."

"He will." With the dangerous nature of the undercover work West had undertaken, she had no doubt about that. The Disciples ran drugs and guns, and counted insurrectionists among their number. Violence was a given with their way of life. She and West had chatted on the phone when she'd called to arrange a meeting. He'd filled her in on the little he knew about the potential for deputy gangs within the DPD. He'd spoken to Boulder, the geographically named club president, who kept a close watch on the DPD. Boulder had made connections there, connections he was normally too tight-lipped to share.

When West had suggested the time might have come to work those connections, Boulder had opened up a little. There was a small subgroup within long-serving officers of the DPD that was also called the DPD. Confusing, but in their case the initials stood for Denver Patriots Division. They controlled precincts around several East Colfax and downtown neighborhoods—those with significant populations of people of color. They ran their territories much like the Disciples did, their patriotism founded on a white supremacist ideology known as the Great Replacement Theory, an anti-immigrant concept that posited that white people were being replaced by immigrants and people of color in the nations they claimed as their own. Muslims and Jews were among their targets, Muslims as foreign elements that posed the twin dangers of holy war and Sharia law, Jews blamed for their role in orchestrating the replacement. The theory had its origins in a book by a French author called *Le Grand Remplacement*—it had lit a flame throughout Europe, and had been picked up by white supremacist groups around the world. Now it was close to being mainstreamed by outlets like Fox News.

The Denver Patriots Division within the DPD believed that their state was being overrun by immigrants, particularly Mexicans and other undesirables, but most dangerously by Muslims, whose mosques were starting to multiply, and who called for un-Christian accommodations like women's hours at the local Y or private cemeteries for burial. For the present, however, their focus was on neighborhoods where Mexicans tipped the balance in demographics.

West didn't know how many officers were involved or who was at the top of the Patriot hierarchy. He did know that new recruits were being pressured to join. When Inaya had asked about initiation rites, he said the Patriots were like any other gang. You had to prove that you deserved to belong, because as with any group, membership came with unique privileges. Inaya had pushed him further and found out that those privileges could include unearned commendations, plum assignments on various police units, rapid promotions, along with opportunities to earn extra income on the side. Most importantly, cover could be given if and when it was necessary. With excessive use-of-force complaints, for example. Or missing body-cam footage or other evidence that had been tampered with.

The sooner those new evidence protocols were in place at the DPD, the better.

"Do you think the shooting of Mateo Ruiz might have been an initiation rite? Both Kelly Broda and his partner are new recruits."

"We can ask around."

"Even if we can't be seen together."

West's expression gentled. "I'll handle the white folks, you talk to the rest."

He was driving Inaya to the neighborhood where Mateo had been shot, the same strip she had driven through on her own, but in West's case, he knew what to look for. He had contacts on the streets. Inaya remembered the tattoo parlors that had caught her attention—West would fit in well there. He could chat up the artists while claiming to be on the hunt for a new tattoo or two.

A question came to her mind, and without thinking, she asked it.

"Do you have a tattoo that represents your wife?"

West reversed into a tight parking spot without using the rearview camera, his arm slung along the back of Inaya's seat.

"Wanna see it?" he teased.

Thank God for her darker complexion, she thought, as color pooled in her cheeks.

"Uh, that's okay."

He cut off the ignition, a wicked smile on his face. Then he thumped his chest right over his heart. "It's her name, Marisol, surrounded by the petals of a rose."

Inaya was disarmed by the image. "That sounds rather romantic."

His smile faded. "I was a young fool in love."

"And now? What will you do about things? Try to reconcile?"

West flung himself out of the cab with the same big-man energy he brought to all his movements. He came around and opened Inaya's door. She noticed now that the parking spot he'd chosen was off the main strip, tucked away in a dark corner. She stood before him, coming up to his heart, right where Marisol's tattoo would be.

He turned serious all at once. "I'm not interested in holding a woman against her will. There's no life for me and Marisol if she wants someone else. I need to let her go." He tapped his chest. "And if I'm a free agent, maybe I'll have her name tatted over with something else."

He looked so guileless that Inaya viewed him with suspicion.

"Like what?"

"Let's see." He pretended to consider, his devilish grin breaking. "Marisol, Marisol. Maybe I could get that changed to say 'Marry me.' We'll stamp the sun right out. Think it'll work, Brazil?"

She laughed at his bilingual joke. "Very smooth. You won't be able to keep the women away."

"Good." He started up the street, pointing with one finger. "You take the other side, we need to stay clear of each other."

Inaya looked over her shoulder.

"Any chance we were followed by a member of your club?"

West had been in this game awhile. She knew he didn't leave things to chance; still, his answer reassured her.

"Hard to keep my eyes off you, Brazil, but I managed to watch for a tail."

They split up on their separate errands, and Inaya found herself wandering down a side street that opened onto a nook made up of old duplexes and houses converted into apartments. A few residents lingered on their stoops, and down at the end of the street someone was holding a cookout. Beer bottles clinked in the distance as the smoke from the grill wafted over her. Barbecued chicken. Her mouth began to water.

She introduced herself to each resident as she made her way down the street to the cookout. The little nook was mixed. She met Somalis, Ethiopians, Mexicans, several Arabs, and a young couple from Nicaragua. Some of the residents were uneasy. She caught a break with Amro, an older man from Baghdad, who picked up on her name, and gave her a warm salaam. They began to chat, trading histories and tales of migration before she slowly brought him to the point: Had he witnessed the raid? Did he know about the shooting?

He sent her to the end of the street. "Those are all Chicano families." He said the word with care, as if someone had taught it to him. "If anyone can help you, they can, though they may not trust you, my child."

She looked into his soft brown eyes and decided to take a chance.

"If you know them, perhaps you could reassure them about me? I'm not with the police who carried out the raid." She explained about the Community Response Unit with a few carefully worded sentences. "We're here to help you when there's trouble with the police."

Amro gave her a little bow and gathered up his walking stick, accompanying her to the cookout with slow and labored steps. She matched his pace and kept the conversation light. It turned out the barbecue was organized by a youth volunteer group—mainly Black kids mixed in with a few older women. Her thoughts flew to Mirembe and the huge amount of work that still remained to be done, both for Duante Young and for Mateo Ruiz.

Amro introduced her, repeating her phrases about her unit, but it was already too late. Her badge on her belt, her shoulder holster against her white blouse had already made her known. The kids turned their backs, muttering to each other. One of the older women took her aside.

"This isn't the right place for you, certainly not now."

Inaya didn't think her Community Response spiel would be effective with this dignified woman, so she ventured, "I'm a friend of Areesha Adams, do you know her?"

A lanky youth broke from the group to stand beside the woman. He was wearing a kerchief around his neck that he jerked up to cover his face. "You keep Miz Adams's name out of your mouth. Who do you think you're playin'?"

She spread her hands in a helpless gesture of appeal. "I *do* know Areesha, but that isn't why I'm here." She searched out the faces in the circle. "I'm here to ask about Mateo Ruiz. Did any of you know him?"

The woman intervened before the boy could shout her down. She pointed out a cross street to Inaya.

"Do you see what's happening there? I'm telling you to leave for your own good."

Feeling the air around her shift, Inaya drew back at once. Against the fading light of dusk, a series of barricades had been erected at the intersection. White and red, probably stolen from the police, with a huge white banner draped over them.

She read it with a deep sense of unease.

NO COPS. THIS IS A PROTECTED NEIGHBORHOOD.

A noise shattered the camaraderie of the cookout like someone banging on a bass drum.

Thump. Thump. Thump.

As Inaya watched, a white sheet was unfurled down the side of an apartment block. The tender young face of Mateo Ruiz was painted on it with such accuracy and attention to detail that the artist must have known Mateo. Beneath the image of Mateo was a trenchant statement.

ANOTHER MARTYR FOR THE CAUSE.

Blood dripped from Mateo's soft, dark eyes, and as fireworks and flashbangs went off, Inaya knew one thing without question.

This peaceful neighborhood was imminently at risk.

18

Inaya made an urgent call to West; then, mindful of her authority to act, she dialed Seif as well.

"They've put barricades up at both ends of the street, but it's more like a street party. Please—do everything you can to avoid a police response."

She switched her phone to video and sent Seif a recording of the gathering.

"Where's Webb?" Seif demanded.

"I haven't seen him."

"Keep a lookout, Rahman. I'll alert the commissioner. Try not to get in trouble."

Now was not the time to tell him that she regretted wearing her holster in the open. She didn't expect violence from a gathering of families and students—Mateo's classmates?—but she also didn't want her weapon to be a cause of provocation.

"Will do." His next call would be to Webb, she knew, so she'd hang back.

Three words ran through her mind on a loop: *do not escalate, do not escalate, do not escalate*. Peaceful protest wasn't against the law, but if riot police showed up in militarized gear, violence could erupt in a flash.

She'd told Seif the truth. Someone had strung the barricades with tiny fairy lights, creating a festive atmosphere. Mexican pop songs sounded from a large boom box carried on the shoulder of a teen. A taco truck had pulled up and customers were lined up six deep, laughing and singing and chatting. As Inaya examined the crowd, she saw young girls with thick brown hair holding up a chain of signs they'd obviously colored themselves.

She kept moving. In the middle of the street, the mood was more serious and she could see a group of middle-aged women gathered around an unsmiling couple. Tears streamed down the woman's round cheeks. The man stood a little apart, his hands behind his back, his face austere with pride though his eyes glittered with grief. These would be Mateo's parents, Antonio Ruiz and his wife, Ana Sofia.

She edged her way toward them, expecting hostility. Instead, she was received with no small measure of relief, as if she held precious answers that would reunite them with their son. Inaya had no power to call back the dead—she offered what honesty she could, Kelly Broda's predicament the last thing on her mind.

Ana Sofia reminded Inaya of her own mother: her unconditional love for her son transformed into the bleakest sorrow. She spoke enough English to make herself understood, and her questions hit Inaya in the chest like painful little arrows.

She learned that Mateo had two younger sisters, Guadalupe and Valentina, twelve and seven years of age. They sat on the stoop behind their parents, trying not to cry.

Mateo had been a much-loved older brother, solicitous and protective, and little Valentina was his favorite. When he came home from school on the weekends and holidays, he would take the girls out for a treat. Inaya followed this up and found out that Mateo had been a student at the Colorado School of Mines in Golden, not that far from Denver. He'd won a scholarship and was studying to become a metallurgic and materials engineer. Inaya wondered if his field of study involved the manufacture of prohibited substances. There was no way she would ask them.

Ana Sofia showed her a photograph of Mateo. He was small, with a delicate build and fine features, his hair a beautiful tangle of curls, his smile a little shy.

"How could my Teo have frightened your police?" His mother's voice softened with love at the shortened version of his name. "How could you have killed him on his father's birthday? That was why he came home from his college."

Inaya had no answer. She took Ana Sofia through a series of questions. Had Mateo owned a gun? Did he have any friends the family might not have approved of? Had he ever been in trouble with the law? Had he gone to the dispensary to buy marijuana?

Ana Sofia shook her head in frantic response. No, no, no, he was a young man under the protection of Jesus, surrounded by the love of his family and friends, Teo didn't need to seek excitement from such things. He was on a beautiful, dazzling path to the future. He was planning to take care of his family so his parents could finally retire. They operated their own street kitchen and also did deliveries. Mateo's little sister Guadalupe jumped up from the steps. Her small fists on her hips, she confronted Inaya.

"You think we're illegal, don't you?"

Confronted by a young girl with a ferocious, unresolved anger in her eyes, Inaya wished she'd come with Catalina, wished she could bridge the distance with her partner by her side.

"I don't think anyone is illegal," she said. "Some people may not have citizenship, but they're still people. Just like you and me."

The tension eased out of Guadalupe's thin body. She pointed at Inaya's badge.

"Cops don't say things like that."

Antonio gently herded his daughter back. In careful English, he asked, "What do you really want to know? Are you saying our Teo somehow earned that shot in the back?"

"It could have been a mistake. The street was crowded, there were a lot of people around. Whoever fired the shot might not have seen Mateo—it could have been a stray round."

Antonio raised his chin. "Of course you would say that."

People were beginning to gather around them.

Inaya looked Antonio in the eyes. "If Mateo wasn't at the dispensary, what was he doing out on Colfax that night? Do you know?"

His jaw turned into stone. "You want to dig into him, yes? Ruin his name, tell all his secrets, bring his mother to her knees."

"No," she protested. "I want your family to find some measure of peace."

Antonio motioned to a protest sign carried by one of the girls in the crowd.

SIN PAZ, SIN JUSTICIA.

Inaya bowed her head in response.

It snapped up again at a blast of sound from the barricades.

"THIS IS THE DENVER POLICE. YOU CANNOT RESTRICT TRAFFIC ON THESE ROADS. REMOVE THE BARRICADES AT ONCE."

Inaya made her apologies to Antonio, fighting her way through the crowd. She could hear the whispers at her back, feel the mood of the crowd change, tense and angry and frightened. She walked faster, keeping her head down until she was face-to-face with the cop who held the bullhorn. He was in riot gear and he wasn't alone.

Inaya snatched the bullhorn from his hand, flashing her police ID.

"This is a peaceful gathering."

The officer raised his face shield.

"Sorry, ma'am. No permit was filed for this gathering."

"Because it was spontaneous. When would the residents have had time to file a permit?"

The officer remained polite. "I'm just doing my job, ma'am. Keeping the streets safe."

"These streets *are* safe, Officer. It's the presence of you and your friends that could cause things to escalate." She leaned over the barricade to whisper furiously at him. "This is not a good look for the DPD when we've just shot and killed a young man from this community." She indicated Antonio and Ana Sofia. "Those are the parents of Mateo Ruiz."

His gaze didn't move beyond her, and the tension in his body didn't ease. He nodded to another officer, who was holding his own bullhorn.

"REMOVE THESE BARRICADES OR THE POLICE WILL DO IT FOR YOU."

The young people in the crowd began to push forward toward the barricades.

She was caught between the press of people behind her, and the line of riot police. She spotted Black kids from the cookout gathering behind the police. All of it promised disaster.

Sirens began to sound as additional cruisers arrived. A roar emerged from the crowd.

"NO POLICE. NO POLICE."

The cops in riot gear moved and the barricades came down.

Inaya retreated to a stoop nearby and took up the horn in her hand.

"Please return to your homes and no one will be harmed. Please disperse for the night, Community Response can take your statements in the morning." She angled her horn at the barricades. "This is Detective Inaya Rahman, Community Response Unit, asking you to stand down. Your role here is finished."

The kids at the downed barricades surged toward the cops like a wave. Inaya dropped the horn and grabbed her phone, setting it to record. Her focus was on the crowd, kids shouting angrily, "No police, *sin policía*." They came up against the shields.

Behind the police, a cheer went up, as the crowd rushed the cops from behind. They were caught between the two groups, and out of the dim roar came a distinct sound.

Pop, pop, pop.

PepperBalls aimed low at the asphalt, where clouds of smoke began to rise.

"Stand down! Stand down!"

Inaya was close enough to the line to hear Jaime Webb's voice shouting. He muscled his way through the line of cops to Inaya as a row of black batons snapped free.

She drew a deep breath to shout a protest, but oddly, the crowd had fallen silent. So had the police. A woman approached the police, her head adorned by a wreath of flowers, a mask covering her face, though her body was naked.

She seated herself with the dexterity of a dancer, right in front of the police. Then she smiled and brought her knees up, maintaining perfect balance as she spread her long limbs wide.

She was a light-skinned Athena, though the Naked Athena from the Portland protests whom she called to mind had been white, and Inaya wasn't certain that this woman was Latina. If she was, no doubt the press would anoint her with her own distinctive name.

Inaya hesitated. Instinct told her to push Athena out of the way, keep her safe from violence. She was too slow to act. While their mothers wailed in the background, other young women ran up and seated themselves in a row beside Athena, their dark heads thrown back.

The officer who had ignored Inaya now looked to her for help.

Jaime stepped up in her place.

"Go home, guys. No need to make a mess. We'll clear things up here."

But that wasn't what happened.

The officer who had quoted his orders called his team back into line.

Batons raised, they advanced.

19

Follow Detective Rahman.

Those were his orders from Lieutenant Seif, and Jaime tried not to disappoint him. He'd thought the evening would be fairly routine as he followed Lincoln West's pickup. He didn't trust the Disciples, and he wasn't sure why the lieutenant did. Imagine his surprise then, when West behaved like a perfect gentleman, helping Detective Rahman from the high step of his cab. They'd stood close together, at ease with each other like friends, another big surprise. Still, he was worried, so he breathed a sigh of relief when they split up and the detective turned down a corner into a neighborhood park. He'd kept an eye on the cannabis dispensary and the pawnshops as he'd driven by. Things seemed quiet on the street, apart from a few busted-up windows from the raid. No cruisers on patrol now, the damage already done.

He tried to do good work, be a good man, like his mother had instilled in him. She'd been so proud when Sheriff Grant had taken an interest in him. And even happier when Grant had sent his dad away where he couldn't hurt them anymore. She was always ready to give the credit to Jaime when unexpected blessings came their way.

That was why policing mattered to Jaime. He owed it to his mother to do the best he could even when the job was thankless. He blamed the DTF for the hostility they faced from the public, for the headlines that pointed fingers and the cynical photographers who took pictures that made decent officers look like bogeymen. Dammit, that wasn't who they were.

Didn't people know that there was genuine evil out there? He'd seen it in his own home. Who fractured a six-year-old's ribs if he drank the last of the milk? There were plenty of wrong ones out there, it wasn't just his dad.

And Lieutenant Seif had taught him there were men who did worse than that. Men who preyed on women or who kidnapped little girls and held them prisoner in dirty basements, men who hired them out, men who beat up sex workers to steal their hard-earned profits, men who got girls addicted to blow so they could use them for sex. But Jaime wasn't that kind of man.

He looked at the girls who had joined the naked woman on the pavement and shuddered.

They needed to understand that he was here to protect them, though his brothers in blue were sending the opposite message. Who threatened schoolgirls with electric batons? Who would fire PepperBalls at naked female flesh?

His colleagues were good men like himself, men with families, with partners, daughters, children. What did they see that scared them so much that they dressed for combat? The cops had killed Mateo Ruiz, it wasn't the other way around.

The lieutenant had urged him to try to keep his head, to let his breathing slow down in a confrontation, to try to evaluate his options with a clear and focused mind. He spotted a couple of officers in the line of police who he thought might be Latino, and appealed to them for help with collecting the girls who had gathered around the naked woman on the asphalt.

The officers broke ranks with the others and he reminded himself again, *Good men*.

He could count on good men.

One tried to push the line of cops back, the other helped him scoop up the schoolgirls in the middle of the road and push them back into their parents' arms. A quick and effective conversation followed in Spanish as they attempted crowd control, and as the noise quieted down, a sad lament floated through the air.

Jaime knew songs like "Bailando" and "Despacito," like everyone did. This was a tune he didn't know, though he made out the words "*el hielo.*" He thought it meant ice.

They could use some ice to cool this confrontation.

Detective Rahman was on the phone, standing toe-to-toe with the officers in line. Jaime was moving to assist her when he realized that the naked woman hadn't retreated. She was still vulnerable and exposed.

He crouched down in front of her. If his colleagues wanted to get to her, they'd have to roll right over him. He took a closer look at her, hoping to make a connection. He was stupefied by the sight of her up close—she could be Latina, or she could be white, he couldn't tell. Was she an ally of this community or a member of it?

His gaze drifted over her again. Her brown eyes thickly fringed with lashes, the tawny curls that covered her shoulders like a cape. Her beautiful breasts with dark nipples. His heart thundered in his chest. She was warm and fleshly and made of human magic, and some inescapable fragrance from her body found its way into his lungs.

As delicate and breakable as she seemed, with her proud head raised and her eyes staring straight ahead at what had to feel like a line of marauders, her body radiated strength. He felt like he'd been seared by lightning. Because he knew what she was doing, exposing herself like that.

She was asking the police if all they did was destroy. If they'd ever offered their protection to things that were tender or creative, expressive of untrammeled joy. It wasn't her body she was laying bare—it was her humanity. "Come," her naked limbs were saying. "See that we are the same." In that same moment, Jaime knew the cops in the line didn't care. They couldn't feel the magic emanating from her core.

Jaime grabbed a blanket from someone in the crowd and spread it over the woman's shoulders, shielding her from view. He was careful not to touch her. His father's violence had taught him that you never put your hands on a woman without her consent, and when you had that consent, you were careful to measure your strength. Jaime's hands were like hams. He'd use them in her defense, turn into the Hulk if he had to, because now he knew violence *could* have a purpose. He'd heard the detectives discuss the question of righteous anger, but he hadn't grasped what they meant. This was different. It was visceral and immediate. Jaime could be this brave woman's shield, like an old-fashioned knight.

She moved to shake the blanket from her shoulders.

"I'm holding them back," she said calmly, her voice so beautiful, it sounded like the strings of an angel's harp. The hairs on his nape shivered. His tongue went dry in his mouth.

"As long as I stay here," she continued, "they won't use their batons."

Jaime was stunned by her innocence. He decided he would have to touch her, if only to move her out of harm's way.

Sirens sounded behind him, the sharp noise cutting through the lament of *el hielo*. Then a cop shoved Detective Rahman, and Jaime uncoiled like a spring, his arms a cage around her.

They were trapped between the police and the crowd of protesters. Fear churned in Jaime's gust, an acid taste in his mouth.

Blows intended for Inaya fell on his unprotected forearms.

No problem. He could take it. He was built like a tank, and he'd suffered harder punches when he'd been far more vulnerable.

Detective Rahman wasn't helpless either. She gut-punched a cop and stole his shield, a sudden noise breaking through the shouts of the crowd.

The ringing in his head wasn't from a blow. A loudspeaker blared three words.

"DO NOT ESCALATE."

The flash of a camera blinded him.

When he could see again, Detective Rahman was safely in his arms, and Lieutenant Seif was standing on top of a cruiser at the far end of the block, loudspeaker in hand, the commissioner beside him. Then Jaime heard the sound of pipes coming from west of the block. The sound grew louder in the momentary quiet—a crew of Harleys revving their engines.

As the cops stood down, the protesters who had been running to meet them dispersed.

He felt a sharp thud in the center of his chest and he realized Detective Rahman was trying to break free. Shaking his head to clear it, he obliged. He turned swiftly on his heel, searching for the angel in the blanket.

In a matter of minutes, the neighborhood had emptied. The angel was nowhere to be seen.

The cop who had helped to protect her was kneeling on the ground with a nosebleed. Jaime quickly checked to see if anyone else had been hurt. He hadn't heard a gunshot, just the pop-pop of PepperBalls, and the crunching of batons. His panic abated when he saw that the doors of nearby ambulances were still closed.

The angel hadn't been harmed. Neither had anyone else.

The sirens went quiet, the cops shifting to arrange themselves in a circle around the commissioner. Jaime was sticky with sweat, his senses roaring with tamped-down panic, on the brink of an adrenaline crash.

Seif caught his eye and beckoned him over to the cruiser—Detective Rahman was already with him—and he marveled at Seif's cool. Every cop in the city would be outraged with him; he looked like he couldn't care less. His suit was sharply pressed and his hair rose in neatly combed waves from the bones of his skull. Total cool, total poise. Jaime tried to match that poise, but he didn't have what it took. He wanted to find the angel, though he knew she didn't need him. She'd achieved what she'd set out to do: held the violence at bay for a precious moment in time.

The only noise now was the song on the boom box floating through the summer air.

His high school Spanish kicked in. He made a rough translation of the lyrics, and he felt sick at his own stupidity.

ICE is loose in these streets.

You never know when it might be your turn.

El hielo.

ICE, not ice.

20

A week later, they were still cleaning up the mess. Not the mess on the streets, but the political controversies the protests never failed to generate. Seif's boss at the FBI had called him, asking if he understood what it meant to be undercover. In a few succinct sentences, Jacob Brandt had let him have it. So be it. He'd fall on his sword if he had to; he wasn't about to become part of a machine that rolled over civilians. He knew what that was like. His father, his family—the Palestinian people knew what it meant to be crushed. But nonetheless, Brandt had kept his picture out of the papers, so he hadn't completely blown it.

He still had to explain why he'd made the cops stand down. He'd earned the wrath of the Drug Task Force, though he'd talked them around, the commissioner's presence at his shoulder an unequivocal asset. Commissioner Benson was passing the buck by turning things over to Community Response. Seif didn't care: he did his best policing under the gun, and with what he'd faced at the FBI, handling the DTF was a cakewalk.

Then he'd gotten Frank Simmons, head of DTF operations, on his own, and asked a few pointed questions. Had Mateo Ruiz been on their radar? No. Had he been on-site at the dispensary before the raid went down? No. Did he have drugs on his person? Again, no. Had the tox screen come in, and what about the bullet that had killed him? Why was he shot in the back?

Simmons tried to stall. The tox screen wasn't in yet; Dr. Stanger was backed up. They did have a match on the cartridge, though: as they suspected, it was fired from the Merwin Hulbert. The shot had pierced Mateo's heart. The young man had bled out on the street.

When asked whose prints were on it, and who the gun belonged to, Simmons looked a little cagey. Seif waited him out, a trifle bored.

Kelly Broda's prints were on the gun. Smudged, as if that made a difference. But the gun was registered to a *John* Broda, a cop who'd been suspended for excessive use of force on the job in Chicago. Why Kelly Broda had been carrying that gun, why he'd used it instead of his police-issue weapon, Frank Simmons couldn't guess.

Seif's entire body tightened to trigger point. He asked if Simmons had been in touch with Broda Senior. Did John Broda know his specific gun had fired on Mateo Ruiz?

Simmons shrugged. All he'd done was tell John to hire outside representation for his son because things looked bad, and there was only so much the police union could do.

A savage satisfaction settled in Seif's bones.

He'd been right all along. John was tipped off about his son by the DTF.

In her eagerness to act for Marcus McBride, Inaya had been played.

He'd stop over at her house and tell her that after he checked in at home. He'd promised his twin brothers he'd make it home for dinner tonight.

He walked out of the building, ignoring the stares that followed his departure. Epithets were flung at his back, and a cold smile touched his lips. He'd heard worse at the FBI, where the hazing had been insane. A few insults from rednecks who ran a cow town weren't worth a second thought.

Despite telling himself that, Seif was tired and out of sorts when he arrived home. He'd bought his family a sleek, modern construction in a Wash Park neighborhood. Three stories high with huge Palladian windows, the house gave them all plenty of personal space.

A low stone wall fronted the property and their cubicle of a lawn. The front of the house to the right was a tall wall made of smooth brick laid in a herringbone pattern, with a black wrought-iron balcony that cut through the center of the wall. He had his coffee there sometimes, because the balcony led out from the main bedroom. His brothers' bedrooms were on the opposite side of the house, giving them their privacy. Making up for the smallness of the lot, there was a rooftop patio with patio furniture to lounge on, a games section where the twins could usually be found, and a state-of-the-art grill.

He could smell something good coming from the kitchen as soon as he let himself in. Alireza had a fondness for Persian food, their mother's legacy, and the fragrance of *shirini pilau* drifted through the house. There had better be *koobideh* as well. After the week he'd had, he couldn't survive on rice alone, no matter how tasty it was.

His brothers bumped fists with him, and from his spot at the stove, Alireza gave him his sweet smile. Mikhail had set the table with their mother's Iranian ceramics and the Palestinian-embroidered place mats his grandmother had sent them from Jerusalem. The table looked festive. It also looked like home: the unique home of the three sons of a Palestinian father and an Iranian mother, mixed and vibrant and as full of warmth as their mother had been.

They exchanged salaams, and Seif went to wash his hands, dropping his laptop off in his office on the way, proud of the way his brothers were growing up, smart and handsome and strong—his sacrifices had been worth it. He wondered if they would move out as soon as they could to escape his supervision, but he didn't think so. When they'd lost their parents—their mother to cancer, their father to political murder—the three of them had become a tight little clan with no outsiders allowed.

He'd noticed that Mikhail's salaam was on the sullen side, and tension splintered through his calm. He'd take the problems at his job any day over trying to wrangle the twins. He splashed cold water on his face and returned to the kitchen to do battle.

He got soft drinks from the fridge and set them on coasters on the table beside the glasses. Alireza brought the pilau to the table on a platter. The three of them settled in their usual places and offered their bismillahs before tackling the meal.

They ate with the swiftness and enthusiasm of three hungry men while Seif asked questions about the twins' day. They weren't back at college until after Labor Day, so for now, both of them had jobs on the side. Mikhail had wanted to make money off activist TikTok videos, but Seif had shut that down cold, so instead he'd joined Alireza in a web-design company that paid reasonably well. The twins loved poking around on computers, so it was a win-win.

"What about you?" Alireza asked. "Arrest anyone today?"

Seif snorted, reaching for his glass. "It was almost the other way around."

The twins knew he'd been getting heat for intervening at Colfax the other night. They hated the fact that he was a cop, but were glad he'd stopped the police from intruding into a grieving neighborhood, conceding there might be some point to Community Response, after all.

Seif was still wearing his suit, so Alireza asked him, "Bro, don't you ever sweat?"

"I have to go out again," he explained. He waved his spoon at the spread on the table. "What gives? *Shirini pilau and* kebabs? This was a lot of work."

Alireza looked smug. "Can't we do something for our big brother once in a while? Why do you always think that we're up to no good?"

"Because I know you." Seif took another bite of pilau, the sweetness of shredded carrots and warm raisins melting against his tongue. The twins exchanged a look.

He knew that look. He dabbed his mouth with a napkin and set his spoon aside.

Mikhail's spoon clattered against his plate. He set his jaw. Both the twins had grown out their curly hair and their beards. Mikhail had a Palestinian kaffiyeh wrapped around his neck. Alireza wore an Amnesty International bracelet with the image of barbed wire carved into its side. Not only were the boys his personal headache, they were perfect targets for racial profiling.

"Speak up," he said. "I have to head over to Detective Rahman's soon."

Wide grins cracked the twins' serious expressions.

"Good," Alireza said with some satisfaction. "Don't lose sight of that sister."

As part of the Muslim student etiquette they'd embraced, they only referred to Inaya as "sister."

"I don't see how I could." Seif found the humor in the situation. "I'm her boss. I see Detective Rahman at work every day." He laid a slight emphasis on Inaya's title that was entirely lost on the twins.

"Dude," Mikhail protested. "Tell me you don't call her Detective Rahman."

"I bet she'd like it if you called her Inaya," Alireza added. "Try it."

They were trying to mess with him, catch him off guard so he'd give in to their schemes. They also cut Inaya way more slack for doing the same job than they afforded him.

"This isn't about my detective. As far as I know, neither of you is angling for a date."

"*Your* detective." Alireza's face was bright with mischief. "We're making progress."

"'No woman, no cry,'" Mikhail sang out.

Seif didn't respond though he wanted to laugh, and eventually Mik came clean.

"Listen, bro. You're going to see a charge on my credit card bill that you might not like."

The twins' credit cards were supplementary to his. They could have gotten their own, but he didn't want them to. It was one of many ways that he kept an eye on what they were up to.

Seif raised an eyebrow and Mikhail hurried on. "It's for plane tickets. We'll pay for it, you know that, but I needed to use my card to book our seats."

A stone lodged in Seif's throat. He'd been over this subject with Mikhail what felt like a thousand times. They'd argued it into the ground.

"Where do you think you're going?"

Mikhail scowled at him. "You know where we're going. We're going home."

"This is your home," Seif said coolly. "This country has given you everything."

"Except a sense of belonging."

"That's up to you. *You* have to make the effort."

"Like you did at the FBI?" Mikhail asked with a sneer. "You forget that time they ran you through the dryer?"

Seif never forgot anything. He'd been ruthlessly hazed at the FBI before he'd made the cut. His trial by fire had culminated with an incident where he'd been caught in the shower after physical training, then tossed into an industrial dryer. He'd made the cut and never looked back.

He looked at the twins with utter seriousness. "If you don't think you belong, then nothing I've done has meant anything. None of it has been worth it."

Alireza, the habitual peacemaker, intervened. "Mik's not saying that, Waqas. We know what you've done for us—"

"Because you never let us forget it," Mik cut in.

Alireza elbowed his twin. "That's not true either. The thing is, we *need* to go. We want to find out what happened to Baba."

"How?" Seif's calm façade didn't alter. "If I couldn't do it with the resources I have at my disposal, how do you expect to find out what happened to our father?"

Mikhail leaned forward. "By asking questions."

"You think I didn't ask? You were just kids when he died, what do you know about it?"

"We know we have the right to go home. We also have the right to protest the killing of our people. They murdered Shireen, just like they killed Razan. She was a medic, for God's sake!" Mik was shouting at him now.

Shireen Abu Akleh, a journalist, and Razan Al-Najjar, a medic, had been shot and killed by Israeli forces in the not-too-distant past.

Seif gave Mikhail a moment to rein in his temper. Right at this moment Mik hated him.

"So you both want to go?"

Alireza gave him a pained nod. "I couldn't let Mik go on his own."

"All right. Give me a moment."

The twins looked surprised by his capitulation. He went to the office to retrieve his laptop. He set it on the kitchen island, booted it up, and logged in to the FBI. Next he called up his personnel file. When it was on the screen, he summoned the twins to the island.

"Have a good look at what they have on me."

He waited while the twins read the notes on file, the explicit cautions about his background and connections, and the languages he spoke. The final note had been written by Jacob Brandt and was permanently attached to his jacket: "*Keep under surveillance*."

"Fuck." This time Mik's rage was on Seif's behalf.

Seif pulled up the deep dive the FBI had done into his background. "Now read this."

This part of the file was on Mikhail and Alireza's activities as young activists: their ties to Iranian activists, their links to BDS, the Boycott, Divestment, Sanctions coalition that targeted the state of Israel. It also included a thorough list of their activities and contacts. He let them read to their hearts' content, and when they were finished, he showed them another note on his file: PROHIBITED FROM TRAVEL TO THE MIDDLE EAST.

"You're booked on a flight into Tel Aviv, right? Your names will be flagged because of me. You'll be detained for interrogation. The Israelis might put you right back on a plane and send you home." He shrugged. "Or they might come up with charges against you. I'm sure there's plenty of provocative material on your laptops and phones."

He logged out of his account, leaving the twins sullen and silent.

"You're half Iranian," he told them, watching their faces. "Maybe you're agents of the Iranian regime. Maybe Mossad can use you in some way." Before the twins could think of a response, he added, "They'd separate you first, of course. Keep you away from each other."

Neither of the twins spoke, so Seif went on. "We have a grandmother in Jerusalem. She has other grandchildren, and you could bring trouble to their door. Are you prepared for that?"

He put his laptop away, slinging an arm around each of the twin's shoulders, their three heads close together.

"You're trying to scare us," Mik accused.

Now Seif attempted to soothe him. "It's not that, Mik. I fought this battle while you were just a kid. It was hopeless then, and it's far worse now."

Alireza knuckled tears from his eyes. "So you're giving up on Baba?"

"Doesn't your faith tell you that Baba is at peace? Trust God to take care of him. This closure you want, it's for yourselves. Nothing can hurt Baba now."

They stood there huddled together, so quiet he could hear the sound of the enameled clock in the hallway ticking over the passing minutes.

"Would you think of going to Iran?" he asked softly, knowing they wouldn't. They'd be forced into military service, and that was if their support for revolution against the current regime didn't come to light. If it did, well, Iran specialized in executions.

He knew it was just a matter of time before the twins got their second wind, so he said, "Get those tickets refunded. I'll give my detective your salaam."

He'd hoped the teasing would divert them—he hated being the one to have to deny them their dreams. He was well-acquainted with the longing for homeland. He'd cut off his roots with a machete to get the pressure off his chest. The way he looked at it, he had one of two choices: suffer the weight of dispossession until they put him in his grave, his hopes and questions unresolved; or make himself over from scratch, and embrace his adopted country as the only home he'd ever need. Don't look at the old photographs, don't maintain ties that could only dig the knife deeper. Both Palestine and Iran were lost to them. Unless the world was made over in some kind of fucking United Nations fairy tale, those dreams of homeland were dead. The twins would never know how much strength it took to accept that.

Come back to us, my son, his mother had said to Seif with such yearning.

He couldn't. He'd killed that part of himself, a cold-blooded execution.

One of these days, he wouldn't be able to control the twins' actions, and their activities *would* get him fired, but he knew better than to mention how much he valued his job. The good he felt he was doing, the milestones he'd achieved. And for now, at least, the FBI still considered him useful. He'd been the biggest, baddest operative in town, *and* he was fluent in Arabic and Persian, a fucking wet dream for the FBI.

He was saved from further argument by the ringing of the doorbell.

Opening the door to the beautiful woman standing outside, Seif grimly acknowledged that tonight wasn't going to be his night.

21

It was Lily. She was wearing a long dress in a Pucci print, a gorgeous swirl of colors from one of her favorite designers. She was also carrying a bag filled with goodies from the Central Market in LoDo, one of their favorite haunts when they'd been together. No bottle of wine this time, just an undeniably beautiful woman smelling of some delirium-inducing fragrance and trying to win him over with his favorite kind of food.

If he hadn't just eaten shirini pilau, he might have fallen at her feet.

He glimpsed his ring at her neck. The canary diamond he'd bought her flashed up at him, as perverse as a middle finger.

"Who is it?" Mik demanded.

"Not a good time, sweetheart," he said to Lily, the "sweetheart" just slipping out.

She beamed at him. "Trouble with the boys?"

He didn't answer. He took the bag from her hand, and set it down inside the door.

Using his body to crowd Lily out, he closed the door behind him, calling to the boys, "Leave the cleanup for me, I won't be late."

"We're going out?" Lily breathed. She wasn't acting. She was thrilled at his proximity, and he felt an undeniable surge of response that he cursed himself for. As if his life wasn't difficult enough, he was giving two very different women mixed signals. And if Grant or the FBI didn't shoot him, one of them probably would.

"*We're* not going anywhere." He tried to frown at Lily, sidestepping her on his way to his car. "I have a meeting with a member of my team. And I asked you to give me some time."

The door to the house was flung open by Mikhail.

Unable to beat Seif at his game, Mik turned his anger on Lily, thrusting the bag she'd brought as a gift back into her slender arms.

"We only eat halal," he told her. "We don't need whatever this is." Taking a breath he added, "My brother cooked today, and guess what, you weren't invited."

"Mikhail." Seif snapped out Mik's name with the cold precision of a bullet. His brother paled. The paper bag slipped from his hand, sending plastic containers tumbling onto the drive. "You know better than to speak to any woman that way, let alone to Lily."

Lily touched his arm, the muscles tight beneath her light, feminine grip. "It's my fault, Qas. I should have called before I came."

Mik collected himself. "I'm sorry," he said to Lily. "*Cass* and I are having issues, it's nothing to do with you." He did sound penitent until he delivered the blow, saying to Seif, "I don't want to keep you from Inaya. I know she's waiting for you."

When Lily looked uncertainly at Seif, Mik went on, "Didn't my brother tell you? He's been seeing someone else. She's gorgeous, and she's crazy smart. Best of all, she works with my brother. We call them the Dream Team."

Fury began to seep through Seif's enforced calm. Of all the stupid things to say—Mik had boxed him in. He could deny it and give Lily an opening when he hadn't figured out what he wanted. Or he could confirm it and raise the boys' hopes. He'd be pushing Lily out of his life for good, and God, he needed time to think.

"Who's Inaya?" Lily was hesitant with the name.

The tension headache that had been simmering all day blazed through Seif's aching skull.

"A detective at Community Response."

Lily looked into his eyes, her own shimmering with tears.

"She's like you?"

Meaning from the Middle East or Muslim, he didn't know.

"Yeah," Mik answered for him. "The sister is just like us. We think the world of her."

Seif narrowed his eyes at Mik, the first sign he was about to loosen the tight rein he kept on his temper. The twins had met Inaya exactly twice: once at a town hall meeting, once at the Blackwater mosque. He'd thought they were mildly infatuated with Inaya's younger sisters, who were just as happy to stir things up as his own siblings were. He knew these grand pronouncements were for Lily's benefit.

His voice dark with threat, he told Mik, "It might be a good idea if you left us alone."

"Whatever, bro."

Mikhail stalked back inside, banging the door after him.

"You're going to see her?" Lily asked.

"It's work." Seif rubbed his aching temples.

"Let me do that." Lily stretched up on her toes and pressed her silken palms against his forehead, massaging in a circular rhythm.

A groan escaped his lips. It felt good because while she did, her breasts were pressed against his chest, and he was inhaling her perfume like a man dying of thirst.

God, he was a ruthless bastard. He wanted what Lily was offering, yet he was impatient to get to Inaya, and work was just an excuse.

Lily kissed his throat and he knew he had to put a stop to this now.

He eased her hands away from his face with a gentle hold on her wrists.

"I'm fucked up. I'll take what you have to give without giving back. No promises, no future. And all the while I'll be thinking about someone else. You deserve better than that."

Lily's delicate jaw firmed. "I can be what you want, Qas."

He shook his head, her entreaties deciding him. "You can't even say my name."

All the lovely color drained from her face at the cruelty of his words.

"I'm not worth it," he told her. "I've never been worth it, and you shouldn't have to change who you are because what I want right now, I might not want tomorrow." He unlocked his car, head down, not wanting to see her face. "You're a casualty, nothing more. Get out while you're still in one piece."

"You won't get another chance." Lily's voice trembled.

"I don't want one, babe."

She slapped him hard across the face.

No, it wasn't his night.

The headache was back in full force as he sped through the silent streets of Blackwater like a torpedo aimed in one direction, Inaya Rahman's house. Like him, she lived with her family, whom he'd met.

Inaya's mother had taken one look at him and her warning bells had gone off. She'd been quicker to see through him than Lily, but what the hell, he had to discuss the case, tell Inaya about the gun.

He sought some kind of inner calm before he tangled with Inaya about Broda. The twins had hung a *misbaha* over his rearview mirror, along with a *khamsa* to ward off the evil eye. He let the *misbaha* run through his fingers, murmuring a phrase in Arabic he was surprised he remembered. It didn't help. It made him think of Jerusalem, of his father, of Mik's angry, contemptuous face and Alireza's shamefaced tears.

"God help me," he muttered.

He pulled up on Inaya's drive at the end of a cul-de-sac that was part of one of Blackwater's many gated communities. He liked the land out here, the open space; the suburban planners who'd organized the development had done well. The houses weren't crowded together; they sat like graceful ships on a dark and silent sea, the foothills stacked up like thunderclouds. Behind the development was pastureland, and one of Inaya's neighbors kept horses. He wondered if Inaya and her sisters liked to ride.

He put the *misbaha* away and honked the horn twice to alert Inaya to his arrival. He hadn't texted her in advance—the scene with his brothers and then with Lily had caught him off guard and unprepared, which was unusual for him.

The outdoor lights came on at Inaya's house. He rang the bell, Inaya's father answered the door, and they exchanged polite greetings. He was offered the usual Afghan hospitality, warm and insistent, but this time he declined. He'd rather speak to Inaya on her own in case things got a little heated.

Haseeb Rahman agreed to call his daughter and send her out to the porch, chatting with Seif while they waited.

Inaya came down the stairs at a sedate pace, her brown eyes wide and questioning. She was dressed in a pair of hunter-green yoga pants with a matching velour hoodie, though the hood was down and her hair lay long and loose around her shoulders. He made his regard as cool and professional as possible, sensing that Haseeb Rahman was quietly weighing him up.

He felt awkward saying salaam to Inaya, so he didn't. He simply told her he'd found out about the gun. She slid her feet into her patio slippers, kissing her father on the cheek.

"I won't be long."

"I will wait," Haseeb Rahman said. He closed the door after them, and Inaya indicated the patio loungers on the porch. They were side by side looking out over the beautifully maintained front garden, flowers spilling over every corner.

Good. He wouldn't have to look at her. Hell, he wanted to look at her. He was dazzled by her hair, a silken cascade that unraveled over her shoulders. He could only see the woman, not the detective, with that dark hair tumbling loose down her back. He wanted to touch the silky strands to judge whether they were as soft as they looked.

Mateo Ruiz, he reminded himself. John and Kelly Broda.

She'd picked up on one fact about the gun with the sharpness she was known for.

"So Kelly's prints are there, but his prints are smudged. What does that suggest?"

"You tell me."

"He could have used the gun, or someone wearing gloves could have used it after he did, and that's why his prints were messed up." She continued to think aloud, and Seif was content to listen. "Why would he be carrying his father's Wild West relic on a DTF raid? If he was going to shoot a suspect, he'd have used his Glock. I'd be amazed that anyone would think a gun that old could be counted on to fire. Or that the shooter could find the right ammunition. Did you find out if the cartridge was found on the scene?"

"Yeah. The cartridge was custom-made, the shot was through-and-through." He shot her a narrow-eyed look. "Don't even think of going back to the cage. Shyla is onto you."

She laughed and his own lips teased up.

"Did John Broda tell you that Ruiz had been shot with his gun?"

Inaya shook her head, and a long lock of her hair brushed his wrist. Softer than silk, answering his question. With a blush, she drew it away.

"John didn't know. He wouldn't have come to me if he did."

That goddamned optimism of hers. It made him want to growl.

"He knew his son was implicated, even if he didn't know how. The DTF tipped him off. He hasn't been straight with you, Rahman. You need to cut ties with him. We investigate on Mateo Ruiz's behalf. We don't give quarter to John Broda's son just because he came to you with a sob story. He's not done with you," Seif said bleakly. "He has something up his sleeve. I'm not letting you end up in his crosshairs."

"I'll talk to him," she insisted. "Confront him about the gun. It doesn't make sense," she went on, skating over his warning. "If the gun is registered to John, why did Kelly have it? *Did* Kelly have it? And if he didn't, who else had access to that gun? Could John have been at the scene? But if he was, why would he leave the gun knowing it would implicate his son?"

Seif sat up straight in the lounger. Ignoring the rest of her questions, he gritted out, "Didn't you hear a damn thing I just said? You are *not* talking to Broda."

She studied his face. "You're in a sour mood. I thought you were working on that."

He sighed like a grandmother whose cat had unraveled her knitting.

"I had a run-in with the twins. It's left me a little raw."

"Huh. They seemed like such angels. So polite and well-behaved."

"I'd say they'd rank right up there with your sisters for getting themselves in trouble, except your sisters haven't decided they're desperately in need of a homeland."

Her response was as compassionate as he'd known it would be. "Young men never listen to warnings about danger—they thrive on the excitement."

"Not unlike a certain detective I know."

She waved that off. "So what will you do? How do you plan to stop them?"

The tension headache was back, and he rubbed his temples again. Inaya didn't offer to soothe his savage beast, he noted. Not like Lily, who touched him every chance she got, all too aware of the spell she cast with her beauty.

Inaya was very much hands-off. In fact, he thought wryly, nothing was guaranteed to cool a man's ardor more than a woman telling him she was accountable to her Creator. She was staunch about her faith, while Seif had given up on God long before he'd joined the FBI.

His life was a tangled mess. His thoughts were a jumble and he was spending maybe one per cent of his time focusing on his work. Mateo Ruiz, Duante Young, they were the ones who mattered, not his complicated love life.

"I scared them straight, but that won't last for long. Listen, Rahman, I've been thinking about the Merwin Hulbert. The shooting *had* to be about Mateo Ruiz. We need to find out more about Ruiz, we need to place him on the street that night. Where was he coming from? What was he doing out of the house on his father's birthday?"

"He was working on a project at college over the summer, his parents said. He came home most weekends to spend time with his family."

"He must have had friends. No man that age wants to hang out at home at night."

"Maybe not. I'll dig into that. He was studying to be a metallurgic and materials engineer. Could that be connected to designer drugs on the street?"

"It doesn't sound like it, but I don't know." Science wasn't his strong suit. "I'll put Webb on that. You focus on Ruiz. Why would he have been on either Broda's radar?"

She ignored his question. "Something's up with Jaime. He was shaken by the scene at Colfax. That's not like him. I think it has to do with that woman the press are calling Naked Altagracia. He was fascinated by her."

"She was naked, enough said."

Inaya clicked her tongue. "Give Jaime a little credit."

He could tell Inaya was embarrassed by the turn of the conversation. He wondered what she'd made of Altagracia's decision to bare herself to the police. Inaya kept herself covered at all times, her style of dress chic but conservative. To see a woman give every last bit of herself like that—had Inaya found it vulgar? Was she given to judgment? He couldn't ask. He didn't have the nerve. Then he remembered that the parents in the crowd had been horrified when their daughters had emulated Altagracia's pose, quick to drag them from the scene.

What did he know about any of it? He wasn't an idealist like Altagracia or his brothers, and he wasn't imaginative, except when it came to investigating crime. Broda Senior was linked to Mateo Ruiz. His gut told him that much. What he didn't know was why Broda had drawn Inaya into his web when he'd succeeded in driving her out of Chicago, or why Inaya was oblivious to Broda's machinations.

"You're right about the gun. I'll need to re-interview both Brodas. Qas—" She anticipated his protest. "It doesn't make sense that the gun is tied to either of the Brodas. Maddy Hicks told me the shot came from out of the blue. She was as confused as we are."

"Hicks could have been lying."

"Why would she bother? She knows at some point we'll be able to pull footage from the street that night. The camera doesn't lie."

"Though the angles might confuse us." He considered something else Frank Simmons had told him. "The cameras outside the dispensary were vandalized right before the raid."

"Someone tipped the dispensary off," she guessed.

"Or . . . someone knew Ruiz would be there, and planned to shoot him in cold blood."

"That takes us right back to the Brodas. Because the gun is the one element neither of us can explain. John owes me an explanation, and I won't let him get away without one."

Seif's temper shot straight to red.

"Will you get off the fucking Brodas? I told you—you're not to contact them again."

Inaya got to her feet. "It's my case."

"And I'm your *boss*." His roar could have shaken the rafters, he'd packed so much rage into it. He towered over Inaya, furious at her. "What will it take to get that through your head?"

They froze as the screen door opened. Haseeb Rahman joined them on the porch, gently guiding his daughter behind him. Though he was in control of himself, his eyes were like hard bits of flint.

"You dare to raise your voice at my daughter?"

"No, I—"

Rahman refused to entertain his excuses. "You are welcome at my home any time, but if I hear you shout at my daughter again, you will have me to deal with. Do I make myself clear?"

Seif's blood throbbed in his ears, stained his face a dark red. He couldn't speak, couldn't think of a response, scrupulously aware all the same of Inaya's stricken silence, embarrassed on his behalf, not her own. Her respect for her father was immense, and nothing Rahman did could embarrass her. Seif struggled to pull himself together. He hadn't been told off by someone's father since he'd been a headstrong teen, wilder at heart than either Alireza or Mik.

"Forgive me." He said it to both father and daughter. "I have a temper and it gets away from me. That's no excuse. I shouldn't have turned it on Inaya. She deserves my respect."

Rahman's nod was austere, his face quiet and watchful.

Seif was under notice.

He knew Inaya didn't bring her troubles home to her parents. She was intensely private, just like Seif, but more than that, she would want to spare them any worry. So it was Haseeb Rahman who would be keeping a sharp eye out.

Inaya murmured something to smooth out the situation, and Seif made his excuses to them both, driving away in the dark, a strange ache in his chest at what he had just discovered, the loss as sharp as the day he'd received that phone call from his mother.

This was what a father was.

This was what a father did. Protect his child at all costs.

22

Late-night meetings were Jaime's favorite time for working with the team. The lieutenant had called them all in on Tuesday night, after they'd put in a hard day's work with no breakthroughs, mind you, and Jaime had kissed his mother and made his way back downtown. The techs had reported in and Lieutenant Seif said it couldn't wait.

The atmosphere of a live investigation hummed along much like the percolator in the break room, as coffee was passed around and everyone reviewed their notes. Detective Hernandez had brought in a box of miniature sopapilla cheesecakes, and Detective Rahman, never one to be outdone in this department, had purchased a box of a sticky but delicious confection known as *dil bahar.* Expecting something of the kind, Jaime's mother had sent two boxes of cannoli, and one of the techs had saved them from an onset of diabetes by rounding their snacks out with a platter of cheese, crackers, and nuts. Seif's offering was homemade by one of his younger brothers: a giant pot of pilau that was warming on the hot plate in the break room. It made Jaime forget all about the cornucopia of treats on hand.

They ate and talked and worked, Inaya and Cat sitting side by side and trading quips, though if someone had asked him, he would have said Detective Hernandez looked a little strained. She kept checking her watch when she thought no one was looking.

A bowl of pilau, two *dil bahar,* and four sopapillas later, Jaime got up and washed his hands. Cautiously, he dipped his head and asked Cat if she'd been able to track down Altagracia.

"She might have gotten hurt," he said. "I feel responsible for her."

Cat didn't tease him. "I've put out the word," she said, and with that he had to be content.

Seif glanced over at him and nodded, and Jaime took control of the whiteboard, running down the techs' reports for the benefit of the team.

"First, on the Duante Young case. The graffiti contest he entered is called Streets of Hope. There've been about fifteen entrants—we have a list of names, correlated with addresses. So far, two prizes have been awarded at the lower level—the contest works as a series of challenges, and the grand prize is awarded with the final challenge. Duante won the first two prizes, totaling five thousand dollars. There are three challenges left. No one has won them yet."

"Why so few entrants?" Catalina asked. "Who puts up the money?"

"I don't know the answer to your first question yet. As for the money, it's awarded by a corporation called The Wonder of Life, incorporated in Blackwater Falls last year. This is the corporation's first known charitable grant." He looked down at his notes. "The principal positions in the corporation are held by the same person, which isn't that unusual for a small concern. A person called Tanangelo Thompson, who we're looking into. Our tech team did find out that the corporation hasn't reported any income, so it seems on the surface at least that its sole purpose is to administer this grant."

"They could have incorporated as a nonprofit, if that's the case."

Jaime had thought about that. "Nonprofits have to meet a high standard of proof to earn that designation, turn in proof of mission, financial statements, and so on. Corporations only need to file articles and submit tax filings to the IRS. Could have been this Tanangelo was feeling philanthropic and wasn't that invested in the tax breaks."

"Is there an entry fee?" Seif questioned. "Could that have discouraged other entrants?"

"None at all. If I had to guess, I'd say there's a shortage of available surfaces that lend themselves to public art. Or it could be that the artists didn't want to risk a confrontation with the police. Entrants qualified by their personal income, not family income. Whoever set up this up is trying to help kids who were transitioning to independence."

"So Duante wasn't disqualified by the fact that his mother has an excellent job."

"No," Jaime said to Seif.

"That's funny." Catalina collected their attention. "When I spoke to Mirembe she said Duante entered the contest to help pay for art school. Maybe she's not as well off as we thought."

Seif had the answer to that. He was putting his brothers through university, he explained, their scholarships made it possible for him not to go into debt. "If Duante was applying to an out-of-state school, the tuition could be north of fifty grand a year. And that doesn't include the cost of living out of state. Maybe Duante wanted to give his mother a break."

Seif told Catalina to follow up on that, and Jaime turned over the list he'd obtained of Duante's regular contacts. They had patrol cops out speaking to the other entrants of the contest; if anything interesting turned up, they'd send that back up the chain.

Detective Rahman raised her hand. "How were the payments made?"

"Wire transfer from Wells Fargo."

"How did they get Duante's bank details?"

Jaime was glad he'd already considered this. "It's part of the contest regulations. Along with the entry, the participants have to include a void check."

Banks had security cameras. Jaime would visit that specific branch in the morning; it was in Arvada. Seif signed off on that, and Jaime turned the meeting over to the lieutenant.

Seif had gotten hold of the service record of Harry Cooper's son, and now he pinned a photograph to the whiteboard. The young man in it had a clean-cut, smiling face that resembled his father's, solidly hewn without being hearty. His eyes were the same color as his father's, and Seif knew without a doubt that the photograph had been taken before Cooper's son had seen any fighting. His half-smile was sunny, his eyes bright with pride because he'd answered the call to fight for his country.

"This is Huxton Cooper, Harry Cooper's only son. He enlisted in 2008 and saw quite a bit of action in Afghanistan. He was a member of the Third Platoon, Bravo Company. I found out why the file is classified. From the parts

I was permitted to see, it's apparent that the war was getting to Huxton—I'm afraid he *wasn't* killed in action." Seif made a few notes on the whiteboard under Huxton Cooper's picture. "The Third Platoon was based out of the Ramrod Forward Operating Base in Kandahar, and that's where Huxton committed suicide." His eyes flickered over Inaya, who kept her head down. "The war has been hard on our troops."

Inaya's head came up from her laptop. "It's been a picnic for Afghans, of course."

So the subject was sensitive. He didn't know much about Haseeb Rahman's journey to this country. The man was an attorney here. What had he been in Afghanistan? An interpreter, perhaps? If so, the Taliban would consider him a traitor, and many of his compatriots would likely view him as a collaborator.

"Was the *mission* classified?" she persisted. "Or just Private Cooper's cause of death? Harry Cooper needs to be re-interviewed, if I'm allowed to interview anyone on this case."

Seif picked up the challenge Inaya threw down. "On the Young case, yes. On Mateo Ruiz's case, I'll let you know who you can speak to."

Let her stew on that. Members of the team silently raised their eyebrows. Seif didn't care.

Sounding unsure of herself, Cat offered, "Mirembe Young did a lot of work with veterans—maybe there's a connection."

Maybe. Except that Huxton Cooper hadn't served out his commission. Dead at the age of twenty, he hadn't lived to become a veteran.

"He's been dead a decade or more. How could his time in Afghanistan have any connection to Duante? When would they have crossed paths? No." Seif spoke decisively. "As tragic as Huxton Cooper's death is, I think the only point of interest here is how Duante Young ended up in Blackwater that night. We can look into how Grant's rota is assigned, but there's no way Harry Cooper could have known Duante would cross his patrol. And if he wanted to kill Duante, he wouldn't have warned him twice—he would have fired. So let's not waste any more time on Cooper's background."

Inaya didn't contradict him, though she did have something to say. "For what it's worth, I think you're right. I can check the roster at the Blackwater substation to see if Harry was on his routine patrol." She'd rolled right over him, and he smiled at the thought. "Just out of curiosity, sir, where is FOB Ramrod? What part of Kandahar?"

Of course she wouldn't drop it. Her tenacity was his personal nightmare. To cut the discussion short, he gave her Huxton Cooper's file.

"I've never heard of it. It's a place called Maywand."

23

When Catalina got back home, Emiliano had gone to bed. He'd shut the house down: the doors were locked, the security system was armed, and all the lights were off, a passive-aggressive move to communicate his displeasure. He didn't approve of the irregular hours she worked, and he hated having their evening routine disrupted. He hadn't even left dinner out for her, not that she needed it after that feast at the station. Still, she knew how to read his moods, and the fact that he'd stowed the food in the fridge but left the dishes he'd used in in the sink let her know she could expect another heated discussion when she joined him in bed.

She'd pulled back her hair in a messy bun, and now she let it spring back into its natural wave, the cut emphasizing the roundness of her face. She was wearing a pantsuit that felt uncomfortably tight around the waist, and the same coral lipstick she'd started using at fifteen. She confronted her image in the hallway mirror and grimaced at herself. She hadn't made an effort in a long time. She dressed like she was fifty instead of thirty, and no one could say that her hairstyle was flattering. She looked used-up at the end of a long day, and she seldom had the energy to meet Emiliano's needs.

Setting her laptop bag down, she unsnapped the button of her waistband and breathed out in relief. What did he expect anyway, she thought angrily. She had a full-time job with the police, and the rest of the time she worked pro bono on cases sent her way by Emiliano, who argued there was always someone who needed their help, and oh how her priorities had changed.

Cat grabbed a beer from the fridge and popped the cap. She sank down on the sofa instead of going up to bed, pressing the bottle against her neck to cool it. Even the August nights were hot, and these damn pantsuits didn't help. Why did no one make women's clothes in breathable fabric? Everything was see-through chiffon, sweaty polyester, or other unnatural fabrics that kept the summer heat trapped close to her skin. She'd give her right arm for a few weeks off when all she did was lounge in her backyard in cutoffs and a crop top.

She couldn't remember when she'd last had a moment to herself. Even in church, her thoughts circled back to a case, a strategy she could try, a question she'd forgotten to ask. And when she did have a day off, Emiliano would drop a new case into her lap. "If you can help the police," he would say, "you can do something for your own."

She was tired of feeling guilty, tired of the fact that instead of her husband, her main source of comfort came from the women she worked with: first Inaya, and now Areesha. And Jaime, of course, God bless him. If she so much as sneezed, he'd run out to get her tea with honey. If she rubbed her eyes from staring at the computer, he'd take a few files off her desk.

So if everyone around her at work was so thoughtful, what the hell was wrong with Emiliano? Why did he have this constant need to have her pacify his temper?

She took a long, satisfying sip of her beer. She wasn't doing it tonight. She'd grab a T-shirt from the laundry room, dig out that delicious little treat of a book by Mia Sosa that she'd never had a chance to finish, and read herself to sleep in the guest room. She'd roll over as much as she wanted, and she wouldn't have to whisper her apologies when Emiliano complained.

She set the beer down on the coffee table, watching a ring of droplets form around the bottle. She wanted to grab the bottle and smash it against the wood, but what would that achieve?

A sickening thought struck her. She loved her husband, but these days she didn't like him much. He took too much without giving in exchange, and he was doing nothing to nurture their marriage. She couldn't keep justifying every decision she made. She needed room to be herself, to do work that *she* thought was important. And more than anything, she needed Emiliano to support her, not to measure her against an impossible standard.

They would have to talk and soon.

She groaned as she remembered the call Seif had asked her to make.

Well, at least Julius Stanger was unfailingly polite, and it wasn't too late to call him.

He answered on the first ring, as if he'd been waiting for her.

"Am I disturbing you?" she asked.

"Not at all."

They spent a few minutes exchanging pleasantries before Cat put her questions to him. He confirmed that tests had been completed on both Duante Young and Mateo Ruiz. He had authorized the release of the bodies to the respective families. The toxicology report was also in. He'd found traces of dextromethorphan and phenylephrine in Mateo's system. Cat's brain wasn't working, so Julius explained that the chemicals were ingredients in most over-the-counter cold medications, and the amount in Mateo's system was consistent with the standard dose.

Cat tapped a fist against her head. Of course. If a cold remedy like Day-Quil was purchased at a local store, Colorado law required the purchaser to show their license. Even then, it was rare that someone could purchase more than a bottle or two without being flagged, because the ingredients could be broken down and reformulated into meth. If Mateo had stockpiled cold meds, his license would be in the system, and he might be on the DTF's radar. But then he wouldn't be taking the medicine. Maybe that was why he'd gone out to East Colfax that night. There was a convenience store just off the main strip.

"He has none of the signs of a drug user," Julius continued, his voice warm and sympathetic in her ear. "No injection sites, his nails aren't bitten down, his color is healthy, and there are no other toxins in his blood. I checked his medical records—he had an MRI done last year after a car accident where he sustained a concussion. Everything was normal on the scan."

"Would a scan tell you whether someone was an addict?"

"I'm not saying it's exact, and I'm no expert in reading brain scans, but a scan can show disturbances within specific cognitive domains—in other words, we would see some of the effects of drug use, and scans might also predict drug relapse and possible treatment response. To put it simply, addiction changes the brain's structure, and there are different ways that MRIs can read those changes. There's a long way to go in terms of using this technology to help treat addiction, but what I can tell you concretely is that the radiologist who read Mateo's scan noted none of the abnormalities we expect to see with addiction."

"Could he have been an occasional user? Would that have an impact on the scan?"

"I don't know." Julius sounded upset with himself for not being able to give her a definitive answer. "If we hadn't released the body, I could get someone on staff to take a deeper look, but as it is, I think you stand a better chance of finding out through routine methods."

"Your best guess?"

"You know physicians hate to be pinned down."

"We won't put you on the stand," she reassured him.

"My estimation is that Mateo Ruiz was a clean and healthy-living young man. His muscle tone was well-developed, even athletic. None of his organs were diseased, and I looked in some unusual places for signs of self-injection."

Cat's curiosity was piqued. "Such as?"

"Between his toes, for a start."

"So he wasn't doing drugs," Cat concluded. "He could have been at the dispensary that night, but it's starting to seem unlikely."

"The choice of weapon was strange," Julius commented. They chatted for a few minutes before he said, "Are you all right, Catalina? You sound a little . . . weary. The death of young Latinos must hit you hard." He cleared his throat. "Ah . . . should I have said Latinx or Latine?"

Despite herself, Catalina grinned. "'Latine' might be the right word for our times, but if you used it on my *abuela,* she'd accuse you of torturing her native tongue." Latino, Latina, Chicano, Chicana, her *abuela* refused to recognize any new construction of the language. But the term "Latine" was meant to be more inclusive, a word that worked in both Spanish and English, and in time, Cat hoped they would all catch up. "It's kind of you to ask, Julius. It's been a while since someone asked if I was okay."

Cat was the giver of comfort, rarely the recipient. She took another sip of her beer, settling in to talk because it didn't sound like Julius intended to rush her off the phone. He was divorced and she knew his ex-wife had custody of their children, so he had more time to spare.

"They should ask you all the time," Julius said. "The kind of work you take on—it has to have an impact on the soul. Are you expected to counsel the family?"

"And profile them, probably."

Somehow Julius knew without Cat having to explain that her contradictory mandate was chipping away at her equilibrium.

"You do these things to help people," he reminded her. "To rule them out of danger."

That was true, she supposed, but she'd rather drink her beer then wallow in self-pity.

"My head knows that. My heart isn't as easy to convince."

"Has someone been having a go at you? I know you've been helping Areesha Adams."

"No, not Areesha. I like her, actually. Whatever she has to say, she says it to your face."

She couldn't speak about Emiliano; it wasn't in her nature to be disloyal.

"You can talk to me, you know. It won't go any further."

Cat's tired senses came to life. There was something about Julius Stanger's manner that went beyond that of a colleague. He liked her though he'd only ever seen her as a frumpy, boring, too-tired-to-take-care-of-herself detective.

"I appreciate that." She made herself sound brisk. "I should let you go, unless there's anything else you can tell me about either body."

"I've emailed in my report," he said, falling back into the role of medical examiner. "I should warn you that the bullet from the Merwin Hulbert did a hell of a lot of damage. I had to stitch Mateo's torso back together."

Catalina set down her phone and buried her head in her hands.

In the morning, Emiliano left for work before she did, without knocking on the guest room door. He'd left the dishes in the sink, added to by the clutter of breakfast, and Catalina did the same. She'd worry about the second phase of the cold war he'd initiated after she'd talked to Antonio and Ana Sofia Ruiz. She had to make sure that they weren't exposed to the sight of the damage done to Mateo's body, and she still had to follow up on Mateo's friends.

The Ruiz family were glad to see her when she pulled up at their apartment block, a house broken down into six apartments, two on each floor. The space was small and crowded with family and guests who had come to offer their condolences. Red carnations were thick on every surface of the room, the air filled with their faintly astringent scent, offset by the dozens of small vanilla candles that were lit despite the heat. Someone had strung a garland over a framed photograph of Mateo, happy and handsome and young. Cat walked to the bedroom with Ana Sofia and helped her choose a suit for Mateo to be dressed in for the funeral, begging her to leave the preparation of his body to the funeral home.

"Keep your memories bright. Remember your son as he was."

She also told both parents about the toxicology report. "He wasn't using drugs. He might have had a cold?"

Ana Sofia motioned to Valentina, and the little girl brought a bottle of Mateo's cough medicine to Cat. She dropped it in a plastic bag in her purse, thanking Valentina for her help.

Mateo had caught his cold a few days before he had come home. It wasn't anything serious. He'd bought the cough medicine because he wanted to get better quickly. When Catalina asked if there was any special reason for that, one of his cousins in the room spoke up, a girl of about eighteen with a lovely velvet mole between her eyebrows.

"One of his favorite bands was playing at the club. He was here for Tío Tonio's birthday party, but he left a little early to catch the band."

Cat's heart rate sped up. This was their first solid lead.

"Do you know the name of the club?"

"The Black Door," the girl, Graciela, said promptly.

A hush fell over the room. Ana Sofia turned a wide and pleading look on Graciela.

The elders in the room were perturbed, but Graciela didn't notice.

"Mateo loves—loved music. He'd catch any club he could. He was there most weekends. I bet he had a sweetheart there, maybe in one of the bands?"

A sob tore through Ana Sofia's chest. Two of her sisters hurried her into the kitchen, though one paused to give Graciela a tongue-lashing first.

Mind your own business! Mateo isn't here to defend himself from your gossip.

Catalina studied the younger faces in the room. She'd have to get them on their own. What could be so worrisome about Mateo enjoying some music or having a crush on a girl? She glanced over at Antonio. His dark eyes were swimming with tears as he took Graciela's hand.

"There is nothing you could say about Mateo that would be to his discredit," he said to her in Spanish. "It is true, my boy loved music. His heart was in his hands."

Now Cat noticed a guitar on a stand beside Mateo's picture. It was draped with strings of carnations, a stunning black and tan *bajo sexto,* a twelve-string guitar set in six double courses. The body was deep and wide, with beads of white decorating its perimeter, and a cutaway at the neck to allow easier access to higher positions for the left hand. It was used in norteño and Tejano music, and wasn't commonly played, except at weddings and on festival days.

Antonio raised the guitar from its rest and kissed the fretboard with an air of reverence.

"He was teaching Valentina to play. Her hands are still too small, I fear."

The sad strains of the song "Te Vas Ángel Mío" drifted into the room, and Antonio sank into a wooden chair, bowed his head over his knees, and began to weep.

Grief was a gift to the dead. Whatever had happened the night of the shooting, Mateo had been loved, and now he was mourned with the fullness of that love.

Like the other visitors, Cat respected Antonio's grief.

A little over an hour later, Cat found herself on the stoop beside Graciela and several of Mateo's cousins. Someone passed her an ice-cold Coke, and she downed it gratefully.

"Is there something bad about that club?" Graciela asked her.

"Not that I know of." Cat thought it might be a strip club. With Graciela's revelations, she moved it up her list of priorities.

"Is any of you over twenty-one?"

A young man with an Edgar haircut gave her a noncommittal look. She asked him to walk her to her car. His name was Vicente and he was related to Mateo on his father's side, the son of the brother who resembled Antonio. He also looked quite a bit like Mateo, though his features were fuller and more hardened.

"Did you and Mateo hang out at the club?"

Vicente shook his head. "I work the night shift at a tow-truck company. When I do have a night off, I want to be with my girl."

"Have you ever taken your girl to the club?"

"She's a good girl," he replied, confirming Cat's suspicion that The Black Door was a strip club. "Her parents would kill me if I tried."

"What can you tell me about the club?"

Vicente's gaze darted down to Cat's left hand, then back up to her face. He'd been checking for a wedding ring. When he saw it, he went a little pale.

"Nothing. I don't go there."

"So you don't know what the attraction was for Mateo? Did you ever meet his girl?"

Vicente's face went hard, and suddenly he looked much older than twenty-one.

"Mateo kept himself private. Maybe he thought we weren't good enough for him."

"Chicanos, you mean?"

"Mexicans, Chicanos. He never dated a girl on our block. He spoke English more than Spanish, and he didn't like to do things with any of us except his sisters."

Was Vicente trying to tell her that Mateo had worked a little too hard to assimilate? Had he needed to because he was at the School of Mines, and had been trying to fit in? She made a mental note to check out how many Latine kids were registered at the school. But if Vicente was suggesting that Mateo disparaged his own heritage . . .

"He played the *bajo sexto,*" she pointed out. "It must have meant something to him."

Vicente shrugged. "Maybe. But he was into fusion, you know." A faint contempt underlined the word. Catalina didn't understand why.

"Was that so bad?"

"You can't play American pop songs on the *sexto,* though Teo thought he could." Vicente made a scoffing gesture. "Our music is just fine the way it is."

"You and Mateo didn't get along?"

Vicente gave her a moody look. He was a few inches taller than her, but he looked like he needed a hug. She refrained. She had to see her line of questioning through, even if her maternal instincts had kicked in.

"You have any kids?" Vicente asked.

She couldn't hide her sadness at the question, and Vicente patted her hand.

"*Lo siento.* If you do someday, then don't play favorites. It makes the other kids mad. It was 'Mateo this, Mateo that' like he could no wrong. 'Mateo is in college, why aren't you?' 'Mateo has made something of himself, and look at you, working the night shift.' 'Mateo plays the *sexto,* Mateo respects his roots.'" He snorted. "If they only knew. Besides"—he drew himself up, adding a couple of inches to his height—"it's good, honest work that I do, I'm not ashamed of it. I'm not ashamed of where I come from, that's the difference between me and Mateo."

Catalina absorbed this in silence, wondering what was really behind Vicente's envy. It was too bitter to be explained away by sibling rivalry. Could he have been the one to fire on Mateo that night? But how did that tally with the use of Broda's gun?

Lost in thought as she was, the touch of the hot metal of the car door burned her hand. Vicente instantly checked it, pressing his cold bottled drink across her dark golden skin.

"Vicente. What did you mean when you said 'if they only knew.' Did Mateo have secrets that his parents didn't know?"

His reply was oblique. "They know, and they don't know. I can't tell you anything else, on Tío Tonio's orders." He jerked his chin at the opposite end of the street. "Ask about him at that club. Their precious Mateo wasn't the angel he seemed."

24

The club was Cat's next stop. She checked her phone. Emiliano hadn't texted her, and she admitted to a niggling sense of worry. Her messages were from Areesha, asking to meet at Mirembe Young's house when she had time. A group text from Jaime informed her that Seif had leaned on the DTF a little harder, and the footage from the drug raid was in. Good. If the club stonewalled her, she'd be able to go back with more ammunition.

She flashed her ID at the camera at the club's front and in short order found herself seated at a booth with an icy soft drink at her elbow. Waiting on the manager, she took a few moments to check out the club. It was much ritzier than she'd expected, given its location. The outside was effectively a cement block; the interior space was tastefully decorated in shades of gold and red with a stunning black centerpiece on the table at each booth. The tables formed a C around a dance floor. A dozen or more very expensive Murano glass chandeliers hung above the floor, and recessed into the back wall was a midsize stage with a comprehensive sound system to the side. The large amps to the back of the stage were unplugged, and the central microphone was presently draped with a burgundy-colored feather boa.

The walls were covered with plush red-buttoned fabric that would dampen the sound somewhat. This didn't look like a place given over to heavy metal or grunge or whatever the taste for live music was now. There wasn't a piano either, so she didn't think it was a jazz club despite the classy décor. She strolled across the dance floor for a look at the gold-framed posters cordoned off to one side. They depicted a few local bands she had heard of—the Gatecrashers, the Seven Suns, Naomi Westlake and the Jaybirds. One jazz group, at least. The Gatecrashers played country and folk, and she would describe the Seven Suns as purveyors of "metal lite." There were other groups whose names weren't familiar, musicians with painted faces, others in black leather vests that reminded her of the Disciples, and one piquant redhead who gave off a Celtic Woman vibe with a cello cradled in her arms.

As Cat drifted back to the banquette to wait for the manager, three young men came in. They went straight to the stage, where they began to fiddle with the equipment. They were all in their twenties with chic haircuts, dark-wash skinny jeans, and slim-fit dress shirts. One untangled the feather boa from the microphone and carried it off the stage. He looked like a corporate clerk except for the silver eyeliner that shadowed his eyes. One of the other roadies was more rugged. The third wore a pocket calculator, defying Cat's attempts to herd them all into a group.

She was about to approach the trio of young men when the manager arrived. Also young, also irresistibly chic with a dress sense Cat wished she could emulate, she introduced herself as Harper Jensen, and Cat put her age at around twenty-six. Her body was boyishly slim; her fingers were covered with rings, each with a design that seemed to suggest some significance. The cuffs of her shirt were turned back at the wrists, and a tiny, colorful dragon tattoo peeped out, green and red and gold. The tattoo was a work of art.

Music began to play and Taylor Swift's "Love Story" filtered through the club.

"The club has theme nights," Harper Jensen explained. "Tonight is Taylor Swift night."

Cat absorbed this in silence. The club didn't appear to have any particular identity.

"The younger girls must love that."

Jensen gave her a quizzical look. "I mean, middle-aged women love Taylor too, but I have to admit we don't see a lot of girls in here."

"You don't?"

Then who had Mateo come to meet?

Jensen pointed to the sign the roadies had mounted at the back of the stage, a stylized neon depiction of the club's name.

"The slash doesn't give it away?"

Cat fought the urge to smack her own head. For an experienced detective, she'd missed a lot of clues. The hush that had fallen in the Ruizes' parlor when Graciela had mentioned the club. The broad hints dropped by Vicente. Ana Sofia escaping into the kitchen. Even Antonio's statement that there was nothing about Mateo that was to his discredit. A stylized red slash removed the "l" from the word "black," suggesting the club's name was really The *Back* Door.

"This is a gay club."

Jensen gave her a professionally whitened smile.

"We cater mainly to people of color." The professional smile wavered. "You'll find our membership is almost exclusively non-white."

"Meaning white gay men aren't welcome here?"

Jensen shook her head. "Not at all. The makeup of our membership is more a reflection of the local population. Our location is convenient, so this is a place they've made their own."

Cat tried to think of a tactful way to phrase her next question. If the club was about exploring one's sexual orientation . . .

"Would you call this a sex club?"

"Not at all," Jensen said sharply. "It's a place for people who enjoy all kinds of music, a place where friendships are formed, and if that leads to romance, then that's all to the good." She pursed her lips in a grimace of distaste. "Not that I'm against sex. But we know the law as well as you do." A grin transformed her pointed face. "Too bad Coloradans are more uptight about sex than they are about weed."

That got Cat off a subject that would have sent her *abuela* spinning in her grave.

"Are drugs allowed in your club?"

It made sense. The dispensary wasn't that far away on the other side of the street.

"Not in any official capacity. We don't search our members, so sometimes they do get through. But we want to keep our license, so if members are caught with drugs other than marijuana, they end up banned for life. I think the policy has worked. This place is too valuable to our patrons to risk their membership for a chance to get high. They can do that off-premises."

Cat thought she was probably right, but she'd check with the DTF anyway, see if any arrests were stacked up. Drugs hovered at the periphery of the story, yet somehow she thought they had taken her off track.

She produced a photo of Mateo Ruiz on her phone and showed it to Jensen.

"Was he a regular here?"

Jensen brushed her long blond bangs aside to see more clearly. "Teo Ruiz? Boys, come over here. This is Detective Hernandez, she wants to know about Teo."

The one with the eyeliner responded. His name was Finn Parker, and his face immediately assumed a funereal expression.

"Teo was popular here. For such a shy kid, he was magic onstage."

Cat smiled at him. "Teo was a performer?"

"The kid played a mean guitar. He sat in with most of our bands, and he was famous for his signature song, he played it as an encore. 'Te Sentí' by Juan Pablo Di Pace, do you know it?"

Catalina didn't. She made a note to look it up.

"Was Teo here the night of the raid that you remember?"

"He didn't play that night because he didn't know the band's music, but yes, he was here on the floor. He loved to dance and he danced a lot that night. He was never short of partners. He was just so beautiful," Finn said wistfully. Perhaps afraid that Cat would find him shallow, he added, "A beautiful spirit too."

"Was Mateo officially out?"

Jensen fielded that one. "To us here at the Door, yes. We're one big family. I don't know about how things were with his relatives."

Cat would have to ask Mateo's parents, but she'd wait until after the funeral. From the iconography in the Ruiz home, she knew the family was Catholic, and whether they had been able to reconcile their faith with their son's homosexuality, Cat would have to pry to find out. From what she'd seen of the Ruizes, and knew from her own extended family, it would have been a difficult thing to accept. Not for the younger generation—who generally refused to sit in judgment on others and didn't just tolerate difference, they celebrated it—but with Mateo's parents and elders, she'd have to tread with care.

"Did Mateo have a boyfriend? Someone he regularly met up with at the club?"

"Lots of guys hit on Teo at the club. He wasn't interested," Finn said.

"Why?" Cat asked. "Did he have a special someone?"

Jensen and Finn exchanged a look, but stayed silent.

"What?"

"How does this have any relevance—wasn't Teo shot by a cop?"

"He was," Cat said calmly. "Why don't you want to tell me the answer?"

"Love Story" was no longer playing on the sound system. The next Taylor Swift track that dropped was a song called "Clean."

"Was Mateo getting over someone?" Cat persisted.

"We value our members' privacy," Jensen said stiffly.

Cat suddenly realized that the club might require members to swipe in with membership cards, and then she'd have a list of possible friends of Mateo, people she and the team could interview to see if Mateo's degree had translated into a career manufacturing drugs.

What did it matter? She was feeling despondent; she didn't want to be the one to damage Mateo's reputation, to squeeze him into a cage, or to cement the suspicion running rife through the DTF that all Mexicans were likely to have cartel connections.

It was within her power to threaten a search and seizure of The Black Door's records, to demand names, identities, and force interviews down at the station. She thought there might already have been too much of that in the lives of the clubs' members. If the club was a safe place for young gay men who shared her background, why would she want to harass them?

So she was honest with Jensen and Finn, even though she knew they couldn't understand at heart. They were progressive, they were sympathetic, but they were still white.

"There's been some suggestion that Mateo might have been a target of the drug raid. I thought if Mateo had a boyfriend or lover, he could help me clear Mateo's name."

Jensen studied her thoughtfully. "I'd like to help you, Detective, but I simply don't know. The club has three hundred members, I can't keep track of them all."

Finn filled in the blanks. "There *was* a guy. He never came in with Teo, and they didn't leave together either, but they would meet up here and dance, or sometimes head into a corner and make out. A few times I think this guy came just to watch Teo play guitar. They were into each other, like, *really* into each other, but that's all I know."

"How long would you say they'd been seeing each other here?"

"Not long. Six months at most."

"Could you describe him for a police sketch?"

"I think so," Finn said. "He kind of stood out. Not because he was built—a lot of the members are—no, because he was white. And he was rather tall."

"Would he have been a member or could he have been a guest?"

Jensen had the answer to that. "You can't get into the club unless you are a member."

"So his name would be in your records."

"Yes."

The two women looked at each other. Jensen tapped her turquoise nails on the glass surface of the table. Catalina didn't speak, though it cost her to stay silent. Finally, Jensen said, with a surprising flash of intuition, "I won't turn over records without a warrant, but if you want to have a look on the computer, just to see if you recognize any names, I won't tell if you won't."

A straightforward compromise and more than Cat had a right to expect. "Please. I'd be very grateful."

And once Jensen had taken her into the office on the second floor of the club, she knew she wouldn't be needing Finn Parker to help her with a sketch.

One name stood out among hundreds, stole the breath from Cat's lungs.

A killing blow to the DTF.

The name was Kelly Broda.

25

On Wednesday morning, Areesha received a call from Inaya Rahman. She was trying to sound professional and to the point, but Areesha caught the suppressed excitement in her voice.

"We have a break on the case. Someone called in a tip to the Blackwater police. We have a name on the man who was with Duante the night he was killed. I'm headed out to pick him up. Do you want to come?"

Areesha cautiously asked for the name, and found it meant nothing to her. Willie Reynolds, twenty years old; he was a member of Duante's street-art collective.

"Any word on who gave you the tip?"

"It was from a public phone at the Y on Franklin. It could have been a member, or someone could have walked in off the street. The Y doesn't have cameras."

"I would hope not," Areesha said tartly. "The last thing we need is more surveillance."

The Y on Franklin was in a Black neighborhood, and was generous enough to offer two days a week to the homeless for the use of their showers and bathrooms. A good pastor was a member there, and he was behind the Y's outreach.

"Do you want to come?" Inaya asked again patiently. Areesha hated feeling like she was being handled. She held on to her temper as she said, "I'll be ready in ten."

Willie Reynolds shared a loft with five other members of the street-art collective. Inaya would probably want to interview them, and Areesha intended to head that off. Associating while Black wasn't a crime. She was still fuming at the sheriff for pulling Black kids off the street.

Willie didn't seem as wary as she'd expected, most likely because of her presence. In the car, Inaya had told her that Seif had warned Grant that the case was in CRU's hands now, and Blackwater deputies were not to go near Willie Reynolds, or release his name to the press.

"The only thing that kid is guilty of is running down a street at night."

There might be a hint of genuine human feeling to Seif after all. Their earliest interactions had been fraught with mutual dislike, but then they'd worked on a Blackwater case together, and Areesha had decided to withhold further judgment. She'd evaluate Seif on a case-by-case basis. She knew he thought of most younger people as kids, though his twin brothers were in fact in their early twenties. Most cops tended to age up young Black men to make them seem more dangerous; she had no objection to Seif thinking of Willie Reynolds as a kid.

Willie was working on a canvas the size of a bedroom wall, throwing splashes of paint on it, then shaping the way the paint dried with a small handheld dryer. It should have looked like a mess. Somehow, under Willie's expert hand, the dark amethysts and blues took on the shape of a sailboat listing in a storm. She clapped her hands and said, "Okay, genius."

Willie shoved a paint rag in the back pocket of his low-riding jeans, first using it to clean off his hands. He turned the dryer off to let the paint settle, then shifted his stance to face both women, his ancient eyes giving the lie to his youth.

Willie was a high school graduate whose family didn't have the resources to send him on to community college or university. Whatever he'd learned about painting, he'd picked up here and there or under the tutelage of the street-art collective's mentors. They encouraged talent when they saw it, and tried to develop it further.

Willie's skin was a rich, dark brown with an interesting arrow-shaped scar on his face that gave it added character. He spoke with ease to Areesha, and was more formal with Inaya.

When Areesha asked him about the night Duante was killed, he got up from the table and went back to his canvas, picking up a plastic tub stained with a carmine pigment. His long, flat paintbrush broke thin lines of carmine across the amethyst storm.

"I was with Duante." His broad shoulders tightened up as he searched for a spot on the canvas to daub with another streak of color. "Don't know how I'm going to face Mirry."

"Mirembe Young?"

"Yeah."

"So you know Dr. Young?" Inaya asked him.

He flicked her a glance over his shoulder, the paintbrush clenched in his hand. Areesha was afraid that if he added to the painting now, he would end up destroying it.

Willie asked his own question. "Where you from, Detective?"

Inaya didn't hesitate. "My father's from Afghanistan, my mother is Pakistani."

"Thought your people look white." It was a comment on Inaya's dark skin.

"Some of them do," Inaya answered equably.

"Didn't figure you folks like the cops any more than we do. Unless you're one of them—shit, what do they call it—oh yeah, 'a model minority.'"

Inaya explained the responsibilities of the Community Response Unit again. "You've seen the headlines, Willie. You know they're saying Duante was guilty of vandalizing public property in Blackwater Falls. That's quite far from here."

"We aren't vandals, Reesh." Ah. Areesha might not have caught Willie's name on the streets, but he'd certainly heard of her if he was acquainted with her nickname. "We're artists." A charming smile cut across his sober face. "A lot of folks don't get that. You in your gorgeous clothes with your sense of color, you look like someone who knows what it's all about. Heard good things about you, Reesh. Maybe you could return the favor."

Areesha was wearing a fuchsia-colored minidress that stopped around midthigh. The neck, arms, and hemline had a silver-worked turquoise border. Her heels weren't ridiculous but they were high. She wasn't a cop, she didn't try to dress like one. She liked to look good for David and she didn't mind if her appearance was a bright spot in people's day.

"I didn't think you or Duante were vandals. I just want to know why you were in Blackwater that night. We need to get a sense of what led Duante there."

Willie paused to add a hint of white to the red to lighten the streak of color in the sky.

"Don't know why it matters. That cop shot him plain as day."

"We want to make sure he's held accountable. For Mirry's sake. For Duante."

"You're trying to reverse the process—cleaning up the victim."

Willie's observation was astute. That was exactly what Areesha was trying to do.

"You know how the system works. Can you help me, Willie?"

He set the tube of pigment aside, dipped his brush into a jar of turpentine, and came back to the table, his chin at a tilt.

"There was a big prize in that Streets of Hope contest. Duante and I planned to paint a mural together and if we won, to split the winnings. It had a Black Lives Matter theme."

He got up again to fetch a sketchbook from a cabinet jammed up against the wall, skirting a pile of painterly objects. In the process, he knocked over a row of spray-paint cans. One rolled in Inaya's direction. She picked it up and studied the label, then passed it to Areesha. It was the same type as the can confiscated from Duante. The object Harry Cooper had taken for a gun.

Willie slapped the sketchbook down in front of Areesha, flipping it open to show her a sketch similar to Duante's portraits of Black women. This time the portraits included victims of police violence: George Floyd, Elijah McClain, Breonna Taylor, and others.

"I have three questions."

Willie glanced up at Inaya. "Go for it."

"When you say you planned to paint a mural, did you mean a graffiti type of mural? Using spray paint?"

He nodded. "What else you got?"

"Why in Blackwater Falls?"

"The contest rules," he explained. "The phase of the challenge we were on directed us there, and suggested a number of sites. Duante and I settled on a noise barrier near the subdivision where we were chased by that cop. It's between the houses and the highway."

This information diverted Inaya from her third question. "Did you know about the vandalism in Blackwater? Police there were on the alert."

"Do I look stupid?" Willie challenged her. "If we knew about it, we'd never have headed south. It's almost like someone set us up to take that fall."

"The real vandals?" Areesha wondered aloud. She had a feeling she'd missed something critical in Willie's answers. She didn't want to spook him, so she wasn't writing things down.

"Those all your questions? I got work to do."

Inaya didn't patronize him. "I'm sorry for interrupting, it should be a crime to disturb an artist. The piece you're working on is stunning."

Willie was nonplussed by this, and Inaya took the opportunity to establish his whereabouts on the occasions when property in Blackwater had been vandalized. She didn't hesitate to take notes, and Areesha became aware again of the difference in their roles, and in their perspectives.

"When the police officer in question was chasing you, why did you and Duante split up?" said Inaya. "Why not stick together?"

All the confidence seeped from Willie's face. He was a decade older yet he reminded Areesha of Clay and Kareem—young and vulnerable, confused by a world where they weren't free to be themselves. A corrosive emotion overlay the vulnerability. Guilt, deep and stark.

"Mighta been the better course," he mumbled. "Safety in numbers and all that."

Areesha shook her head. No matter how you cut it, how you balanced your actions, safety in the presence of police was never guaranteed for them. She said as much to Willie, then going further, she added, "You're not to blame for what happened to Duante."

He shrugged off her sympathy, his eyes fixed on the sketchbook, his strong hand covering the portrait of Elijah. "Shoulda been me. I got no one to miss me. Duante had Mirry." He avoided Inaya's gaze.

"You would be missed just as much as Duante." Areesha put every ounce of conviction she could into her voice, and Willie's head snapped up. She flung out a hand at the painting. "And not just because you create beauty out of nothing." She covered Willie's hand. "These hands are a gift. Don't ever think you don't matter, because you *do*."

"Geez, Reesh." His tone was affectionate, his big hand shifting so it was holding hers. "No wonder you got a following, if you go to bat for an outcast like me."

"You're not an outcast. You're part of us. I wouldn't lie to you."

She made a mental note to connect Willie with a teacher at an art school. He might have mentors in the street-art collective, but an opinion from a professional would go some way to boosting his self-confidence. She knew Inaya would be following other leads—she had her own work to do.

"Can I ask one more question, Willie?" Inaya put in softly.

He let go of Areesha's hand. "Sure."

"Did anyone else know that you and Duante were going to be in Blackwater Falls that night? Other artists or competitors, maybe?"

Willie studied her gravely. "You think it was a setup?"

"I don't know. But I have to consider the possibility."

"The only one who knew was Raze."

"Raze?"

"Another street artist. A competitor. Fifty thousand dollars is nothing to sneeze at. We all had our eyes on the prize, but Duante liked to talk his ideas out with Raze."

"But you were only planning to work on one mural with Duante, right? Not all of them. How would you split the money if it was Duante who won the grand prize?"

Willie didn't speak. Now his face became guarded, his eyes narrowed and probing.

Inaya tried again. "Did you have an arrangement with Duante?"

"I know what I'm worth." He set his jaw and defiantly turned away.

Areesha didn't like where she thought this was headed, but Inaya asked another question before she could redirect her.

"Where can we find this Raze? Is he part of your collective?"

Inaya was crossing a line, asking for that information. Willie wasn't about to snitch, and Areesha was torn over the question of whether she wanted him to. She could find Raze through other sources, she didn't have to ask Willie to compromise himself. Or dirty herself by pushing Inaya's questions.

Willie's face was somber. "Can't tell you that, Detective. All I'm saying is that Raze was Duante's girl. I'm not speaking for her, and I sure as hell won't tell you where to find her."

Areesha's mind flew over the art they'd collected from Duante's room, the photographs he'd mounted, the poster above his bed. Inaya hadn't shared about his cell phone or laptop yet, but there'd been no pictures of a girlfriend in Duante's room, nor had Mirembe mentioned her.

"They were keepin' it quiet," Willie added. "Raze isn't anyone's trophy. She's a serious artist, she wants to be known for her own work."

"Then wasn't she after the prize?" Inaya jumped in.

Willie pressed his lips together. "Can't say for sure. She has a cousin who lives in Blackwater. He's been harassed before down there. He warned her the cops in Blackwater were trouble, and she should stay away. That might have put her off."

"Does Raze have a last name?"

"I've already told you too much."

He'd gone as far as he could, Areesha recognized, as far as she wanted him to, so she pulled David's card from her bag and passed it over to Willie.

"Don't talk to any other police. If they come to you, call my husband."

When Willie looked at her doubtfully, she said, "You know those young men who were caught up in the sweep after Duante was killed? My husband got them out."

"Power couple," Willie teased.

Areesha smiled her glamorous smile. "Happy to hear you think so."

26

Inaya was expecting a phone call from Broda with a sense of dread. She'd started something here, made promises to John Broda in exchange for information that would put Danny Egan away and allow her to make amends to the McBride family. The thought of it was like a shiny golden apple, an endlessly tempting offer of redemption, yet she told herself it was about righting a catastrophic wrong. Jenella McBride had made the decision to take her son off life support: Marcus McBride was dead. His justice would come in the *Akhirah,* she knew, but that wasn't something she could hold out to Jenella in consolation.

Headquarters was buzzing as they made progress on both cases. Jaime gave her a thumbs-up from his desk, meaning Willie Reynolds's alibi for the vandalism incidents had checked out. He hadn't been anywhere near Blackwater. The next step was for Seif to call Grant and tell him to stay clear of Willie—any harassment would be wrong and unfair, an argument that would hold no sway with Sheriff Grant, but maybe the question of optics would. She knew Areesha would call up a journalist in a heartbeat. She'd felt such warmth and compassion flowing from Areesha to the young artist that she'd finally understood how important Areesha's work was. She was the heart of her community.

She'd go over her own notes on the interview later. There was something Willie had said that niggled at the back of her mind, something she'd missed that could be important. At the moment she was worried about the impending call from John Broda.

She cast a wary glance at Seif's office. Jaime had gone in to meet with him—good. He'd be distracted, and she could slip out, which was no doubt a foolhardy plan given Seif's anger the other night. They hadn't spoken about it. She couldn't bring herself to—the interactions between Seif and her family had been mortifying to date. She wasn't ashamed of anything her father had said, she simply knew that if her boss had been anyone other than Seif, she would be out of a job. The boundaries between them were blurred. He wasn't just her boss: he'd become something more. He didn't want her anywhere near Broda, and she had to ask herself if that was the reaction of the man or the officer. If it was the former, she'd ignore it. If Seif was acting as her boss, she'd have to convince him about the necessity of re-interviewing the Brodas. She reconsidered slipping away on her own. Usually, Seif could be softened up if she took Jaime along. No reason she couldn't do that now, though Jaime had just stalked out of Seif's office looking like he was staggering under the weight of the world.

Her eyes met Seif's through the glass walls of his office just as her phone rang. It was John Broda. She turned her back and tried to look nonchalant as she wandered into the hall.

"What have you learned?" was the first thing he asked her. He sounded like a man torn apart by his own demons, but was Kelly the demon in this case?

"Quite a bit. We need to meet."

"I'll pick you up," he said. "I'm on my way to see Kell. Between us, we have to convince him that his silence isn't helping anyone."

"Is Kelly still at the motel?"

"He went home. He said he's not scared of the public. He said he deserves their anger."

"So he's speaking to you now?"

There was a long pause before Broda said on a sigh, "Maddy filled me in."

"I'll be bringing a colleague with me."

"No! That's guaranteed to put Kell off. Bad enough that he has to see me, he'll shut right up if there's an official police presence."

"Those are my lieutenant's orders. I'll take my own car. We can catch each other up at Kelly's house, outside on the street, if we must."

"I don't think so." At the cool voice behind her, Inaya jumped. Seif took the phone from her hand and identified himself to Broda.

"My detective is not a convenience for you to use," he said brusquely. "We do this officially or it doesn't get done at all."

He listened to the phone for a moment.

"Sorry, that doesn't cut it. Our way or not at all."

Broda's angry rumble came through loud and clear as Seif held the phone away from his ear. He waited, his black eyes sharp with accusation as he cut a glance at Inaya.

She held up her hands to placate him.

Finally, Seif said, "Good. She'll see you in ten."

He disconnected the call and handed the phone to Inaya.

"I was going to take Jaime with me."

"Jaime's on the footage from the raid, he doesn't have time to waste, and neither do you."

He wasn't as angry as he'd been the previous night, so Inaya took advantage.

"Who's coming with me, then?"

"For my sins, Rahman, it seems you're stuck with me."

He was just as brusque with Broda in person as he'd been on the phone. They met in the parking lot, a fine white glare beating down on their heads. Late August meant it was still ninety degrees, and the warmth would continue, on and off, well into the fall, dropping off around November.

Heat radiated up from the pavement into Inaya's black shoes. She was wearing a blazer over her shoulder holster, and two minutes out of the air-conditioning she was perspiring.

"I'll be the one asking the questions," Seif told her as they waited.

She held on to her temper. "I know how to do my job. I don't need to be protected."

"That's not what your father thinks."

A swift and accurate shot across the bow. Inaya drew in a breath.

"You had that coming," she said.

"I did."

"That doesn't mean I need you to stand between me and Broda."

"You know him better than I do. I'll talk to him, you pick up on what he doesn't say."

She bit her lip. "There's only one real question, isn't there?"

"The gun," he agreed. "The rest has to come from his son."

Broda's car pulled up. Inaya whispered a warning to Seif. "Don't bring up the past. I'm handling things with John."

He shot her a glance of pure exasperation, which she chose to ignore.

Broda pushed out of the car. Pain and worry had taken its toll on him. The bravado that was an essential part of his persona was absent. Lines of strain creased his face. He was wearing a short-sleeved shirt with a collar, and the underarms were damp.

"Let's go," Broda said.

"Not so fast." Seif directed them to a door at the side where there was a little bit of shade. "Did you know about the gun? The murder weapon?"

Broda's shoulders bunched, aggression pumping through his veins. Inaya froze. She was well-acquainted with Broda when he was in a rage. Seif edged Inaya a little to the side, his body angled in such a way that Broda couldn't lunge at her. She wasn't frightened of Broda, yet she was. That little frisson of memory kept flickering down her spine. It wasn't conscious. It was her own brain working against her, keeping her in fight-or-flight mode.

"It wasn't murder," Broda said through his teeth, watching the maneuver. "It was an accident. An accidental discharge."

"From a Merwin Hulbert revolver registered in your name." Seif's disbelief was palpable.

"What?" Broda stared at them.

Inaya wasn't sure what made her give him the benefit of the doubt. She was still fine-tuning her reactions. "You didn't know about the gun? You didn't know that Mateo Ruiz was killed by your revolver?"

If Broda was feigning his shock, it was quite a performance.

"It's an antique. It doesn't fire," he whispered.

"It did," Seif corrected him. "With a custom-made cartridge. The bullet went through with a hell of a lot of power. Now, what was your gun doing on the streets of Denver, Officer Broda? Were you there the night of the raid? Maybe covering your son's back?"

Broda fell silent, though his eyes were working. He was trying to think things through, trying to come up with an answer that wouldn't implicate Kelly.

"I don't know," he said finally.

Seif wasn't having it. "Where do you keep the gun?"

Inaya looked down and saw that Broda's hands were trembling. A flash of light illuminated her thoughts. He wouldn't have come to her if he'd known the gun in question belonged to him. There was no walking it back, so he stood mutely before them.

"Your silence isn't helping your kid." Seif's voice was no kinder, but the sharp edge to it had smoothed over.

"What would you know about it?"

"I know." Seif crossed his arms over his chest and waited.

Inaya didn't try to unruffle Broda's feathers. Let him deal with Seif. If Seif was right, and Broda was playing her, this would flush out the truth.

She took a tissue from her handbag and wiped her forehead.

When Broda kept quiet, Seif nudged Inaya. "Let's go. We don't have time to waste."

"Wait!" A tormented cry from Broda. Seif gave it another second and Broda folded.

"It's a family gun, like I said, an antique. It gets passed down to each son when he turns twenty-one."

Seif pounced. "So the gun belonged to Kelly."

Broda gave them a miserable nod.

"Why would your son be carrying that gun out on a raid? For that matter, *how* could he carry it without his partner noticing? He was in his patrol uniform. It wouldn't fit his belt, and I checked with DTF—he wasn't wearing a shoulder holster."

Broda revived a little. "That's right."

"Did he have a gun safe or locker?"

Broda straightened up from his weary slump. "Every good cop does. I trained him from when he was young. Check your weapons frequently and make sure you keep them locked up."

Inaya and Seif did the same, so they couldn't fault him. It was common sense.

But his answer wasn't comprehensive, so Inaya followed up. "Then you would have expected Kelly to keep that gun locked up, not have it with him on the street. But if you were estranged, as you said, why did he bring the gun with him from Chicago?"

An expression Inaya could only describe as cagey chased over Broda's face.

A cold "Out with it," from Seif.

Broda's eyes narrowed to thin slits of blue.

"The gun has never been loaded," he said to Seif. "We kept it on display above our fireplace. When I gave it to Kell in Chicago, he did the same."

"And here?"

Broda's face twisted with misery, and that told them enough.

They were following Broda's vehicle when a call came in from Cat. Seif told Inaya to put it on speaker. When Cat told them what she'd discovered at the club, Seif's face hardened. He knew there was more to the Brodas, father and son, than John Broda had shared. Catalina gave them a full briefing, and when Inaya hung up, she was biting her lip. Seif resisted the urge to make her acknowledge what he'd known all along: Broda couldn't be trusted.

Inaya didn't disagree. All she asked was that he not jump to conclusions, and let her ascertain the facts. They had talked things through by the time they reached the house, a duplex just off Twentieth Street downtown, close enough to the hospital to hear sirens. The duplex was old and run-down, though Kelly had begun to do some work. The paint had been stripped from the porch, and the front railing sanded and primed, waiting for a fresh coat of paint.

As Inaya and Seif stepped from Seif's car, the sun would have cooked them were it not for the old and shady beech trees that laced both sides of the street. A small group of protesters were gathered outside the duplex, mostly young Latinos holding painted signs that reminded Inaya of the protest the other night. The scene then had been hot, quick and immediate. Here it was languorous, the protesters in shorts and tank tops or shirtless, chatting and milling around, seeking the shade for relief.

They heard the sound of a lawn mower coming from around the back. Scant attention had been paid to a front lawn choked with weeds. Perhaps the back was in better shape. They rounded the house, Broda taking point, Seif allowing Inaya to precede him.

Kelly Broda was pushing a heavy-duty mower over two neat squares of lawn at the back, mowing his neighbor's as well. Both lawns were bordered with perennials, one of the beds waiting to be planted with lavender and white petunias, but Kelly had taken a chunk out of his lawn to set up a barbecue area. The massive steel grill reposed on stone slabs beneath a pergola that also contained an oversize patio set in cool shades of gray. A cooler held a six-pack buried in ice. Two of the empties sat on the floor. The back of the yard was fenced off: on the opposite side, Kelly's neighbor had planted wisteria that blossomed from a set of neat white lattices.

Kelly was shirtless, his pale skin red at the shoulders, his back gleaming with suntan oil, a baseball cap jammed on his head, beneath it a giant pair of Beats. He nodded along in time with the music, biceps flexing and relaxing as he cut another square across the lawn.

When Broda yanked the plug on the mower, Kelly's head jerked around. He paused as he took them in, his face going dark at the sight of his father.

He shut off his headphones. "I don't want you here," he said to Broda. He glanced over his father's shoulder at Inaya, and he shoved his baseball cap up. "What the fuck are you doing with him?" A sharp look at Seif. "And who the fuck are you?"

Seif cut Inaya off neatly. "One, don't swear at my detective. Two, I'm the cop who's going to bust you for killing Mateo Ruiz."

Kelly's big body went still, his large hands gripping the bar of the mower.

"We know about the gun," Seif added.

"Kell?" Broda asked in a voice colored with pain. "Son, did you know the kid was shot with the Merwin? Why wasn't that gun at home?"

Kelly's face closed down. He yanked the cap down so they couldn't see his eyes.

"I'm not talking to you." He looked at Seif as if measuring his physical strength. "Get that man out of my yard. He's trespassing."

"I'm your father." Broda's voice broke. "No one loves you like I do, Kell. I'm here for you. I'll do whatever it takes to clear you."

Father and son stared at each other, and to Inaya's shock, tears rolled down Broda's leathered face. He didn't try to hide them, he simply stared at his son.

Kelly's lip curled. "Whatever it takes? Yeah, that sounds just like you, Dad."

It was an insult, a jab at Broda's reputation as a cop, but all Broda heard was his son calling him "Dad." His expression cleared, and he took a step toward his son.

"I know I've disappointed you, son. I can change. I *will* change." He gestured at Inaya. "I'm making amends for the past. Ask Detective Rahman."

Kelly's head swiveled to her.

Quietly, she said, "It's true."

"It's too late, Dad. You refuse to accept that I'll never be a cop like you."

"It's not too late," Broda protested. "Don't throw your life away because of me. Your ma, your sisters, they can't take this. It took everything I had to keep them home. Don't damage them because you're angry at me."

There was a lot Inaya could learn from the interaction between father and son, but the heat was getting to her. Her dark head was unprotected, she couldn't stand there much longer. Casually, she walked over to the patio seating under the shade of the pergola.

She signaled Seif discreetly. "Could I have some water, please?"

Seif followed Kelly into the house.

Broda went and sat on the steps that led into the house, his face buried in his hands.

When Kelly and Seif returned, both carrying two glasses, Kelly paused at the sight of his father but didn't stop. He gave Inaya her glass and drank deeply from his own.

Seif wandered over to the unplanted petunias. Removing his blazer, and setting it on a chair, he rolled up his sleeves, and got to work with a trowel. A moment later, Broda joined him, leaving Inaya to her interview.

She pointed to Kelly's headphones. "What were you listening to?"

"White Strike. A death metal group," he explained.

His T-shirt was lying across a chair. Inaya passed it to him. She didn't feel comfortable with a half-dressed male.

He wiped his forehead with it, smirking. "Not interested in the view?"

Seif's head whipped around. Inaya kept her eyes on Kelly's face.

"This is a police interview," she told him. "You need all the protection you can get."

He scowled, jerking the shirt over his torso. "Better?"

She ignored that. "Tell me about the gun. Did you bring it with you from Chicago?"

He took a moment to consider his answer, his gaze drifting briefly to his father. "Yes."

"And did you keep it locked up?"

Another pause. "No."

"Then where?"

"In the living room on display. I can show you."

"No need. I checked it out," Seif said over his shoulder, his hands deep in the soil.

"Was it loaded?" Inaya continued.

"Hell, no. I don't even know where you'd get ammunition for a gun that old."

"Do you lock your house when you go out?"

"Yes."

"Does your father have a set of keys?"

"No."

"Could anyone else have accessed the revolver?"

Kelly hesitated. "When I have friends over, I leave the front door unlocked so they can come and go while I'm at the grill out back."

"Did you notice the revolver was missing?"

Kelly didn't speak.

"So you did?" Inaya persisted.

His jaw set. His large hands palmed his knees as he remained silent.

"Why won't you tell me?"

"Nothing to tell, Detective."

Inaya considered another angle. "Did the shot come from your position that night?"

"I don't know." A fine line of sweat dripped down his jaw from the corner of his eye.

"I think you do know." Inaya set her notebook on her knee, flipping to her first interview with Kelly. "You told me before, and I quote, 'He was killed by my gun.' If you didn't shoot him, if the shot didn't come from your position, how did you know it came from your revolver?"

Kelly shrugged. "Must have heard it on the grapevine. From someone with the DTF."

He wasn't going to budge on this, so Inaya lowered her voice so his father couldn't hear.

"You knew Mateo Ruiz."

His big body jerked in his chair as if he'd been shot. His skin flushed red before all the color leached from his face. He jumped from his chair, grabbing Inaya's wrist. "Come with me."

Her notebook fell to the ground as she jerked her hand free, but she followed him to his neighbor's yard, where he led her to the lattices laced with wisteria vines.

To prevent them from following her notepad to the ground, Inaya had grabbed Kelly's headphones and now held them in her hand. Across the lawn, Seif stood, stretched, checked out Inaya's position, then, satisfied that she had things in hand, returned to his task.

"How the fuck do you know that?" Kelly whispered.

"A colleague spoke to Mateo's family and she also checked with the club."

"Their records are private." He was unsteady with shock. He was crushing the blooms where he leaned against the fence for support. A vulnerable look came into his eyes. "What did his family have to say?"

"I think his cousin Vicente guessed."

Kelly's face closed down again. "There was nothing to guess. I was at the club some nights that Mateo was there, that's all."

"You weren't involved?"

"Fuck, no. Where the hell did you get that idea? I'm not gay." He leaned down, crowding her, six foot four of pure masculine aggression.

Inaya held her ground. "But you're saying Mateo *was*? How did you know that?"

"I don't know that he is, but most of the members are," he said impatiently. "The club serves that community."

"Then why are you a member?"

"I go on death metal nights. You can check my membership record. The nights they had a band in, that's when I was there."

"A witness placed you there with Mateo."

His sandy eyebrows arched in surprise. "Did they specifically identify me?"

They hadn't. A man with Kelly's general build had been described, and Cat had made the connection from Kelly's membership record.

"You stand out in a crowd," she said.

"I don't care what they told you. I'm not the only straight white guy who's a member of that club. You need to dig deeper."

They would. But Kelly wasn't off the hook.

"The Black Door has over three hundred members yet you noticed Mateo at the club."

Again, he flashed her that look of impatience tinged with irritation. "Because most nights I was there, Mateo Ruiz was onstage. He opened for a lot of bands. He played guitar—some kind of Mexican-American fusion. I have no reason to lie because you can check that out."

Inaya watched him steadily. "It's not ideal for a cop to frequent a gay club."

"I never identified myself as a cop. I was just there to hear the music."

"I don't mean from the club's point of view, I'm thinking of your colleagues."

Perhaps unintentionally, Kelly flexed both arms. "They don't bother me."

Inaya thought of what West had told her about the deputy gang, the DPD or Denver Patriots Division.

"Did the Patriots send you in there? Was it an initiation?"

Kelly backed away from her, his gaze shifting to the headphones in her hand.

"White Strike." Inaya echoed his earlier words. "That's a white supremacist band, isn't it? They sing about hunting down immigrants. Why would they play a gay club?"

He reached out for his headphones. Inaya swung away, keeping them out of reach.

"Did you kill Mateo Ruiz because he was gay and Mexican, a perfect Patriots target? Was that the price of admission to the Denver Patriots?"

"You can think what you like." Kelly reached for the headphones again, and this time Inaya put them to her ears and listened.

Her eardrums were pounded by noise. Electric guitars, a voice shouting about the noise, the bass banging around her skull like the beginnings of a migraine. She handed them back.

"The Black Door likes this kind of thing?"

Kelly shrugged. "They set up a website asking for suggestions, probably not expecting to be flooded by requests for White Strike. But like any business, they went where the money is."

"That seems disloyal to their membership."

"Why is that my problem?"

Her earlier suspicions about Kelly's sexuality had just been turned on their head. The way he'd checked her out, his choice of music, his explanation for how he'd recognized Mateo.

A troubling thought surfaced. What if it wasn't an accident that the site had been flooded by demands for the band White Strike? Could the Patriots have played a role in sabotaging the site? And if they did, did that point to a stronger connection between Kelly and the group?

Just then, the neighbor's screen door banged open. Bursting with energy, Madeleine Hicks tumbled into the yard.

Inaya caught the surprise on her face. She turned back to glance at the trellis and the carefully maintained lawn.

Maddy Hicks lived on the other side of the duplex. She was the neighbor whose lawn Kelly looked after, whose flowers shared a border with his. Inaya didn't have time to ponder this before a tall, well-built man with dark coloring and deeply tanned skin followed her into the yard. He, too, was shirtless, and he caught Maddy by the hand, slowing her rush to Kelly.

His eyes swept Inaya and he said not to her but to Kelly, "I've told you before, Broda. I can take care of anything Maddy needs to have done."

This, Inaya guessed, was the SWAT captain, Younas.

27

Raze wasn't as hard to track down as Areesha had feared. The young woman was exceptionally thin, with fiery dark eyes and artfully gathered locs. Her arms were covered in tattoo sleeves—a whirl of design and decoration—and she wore a trucker's hat over her locs and was dressed in an orange tank top paired with khaki overalls. With her plethora of dragon-head rings and piercings, and her ice-pick smile, Raze was immensely chic.

A friend of a friend of Areesha's worked at a business downtown where Raze came in for her daily cortado before setting off for her day job as a welder on a construction site. Areesha learned she was a mixed-media artist. She sculpted, she painted, and sometimes she did both. Areesha was hoping for a quick look, but with a tight little smile, Raze closed the door of her small studio behind her and slung herself down on the stoop of a derelict brownstone. Areesha joined her there, both women looking out at the street, unaffected by the heat. It helped that a leafy oak extended its branches over the stoop.

As she lit a cigarette and leaned forward, Raze's tank top gaped, revealing a patch of red just above her heart. A new tattoo: Duante's name was stenciled there, not festooned in curlicues as Areesha expected. Instead, each letter was distinct and dagger sharp, reminding her of the band AC/DC's logo.

"So you were with Duante."

"I loved him," Raze said without emotion, flicking ash onto the pavement.

Two teens skated by on their boards, reaching out to bump fists with Raze as they passed. She put out her cigarette and extended her arm. She was known in this neighborhood.

"Tell me about the night he was killed."

"I hear you're working with the cops now."

Areesha sighed. "Not with the cops. With a couple of friends who are cops."

"There's a difference?" The hoop in Raze's feathery eyebrow danced as she arched it.

"If there wasn't, I wouldn't be doing it."

"Slippery slope." Raze's arm swooped like a skier racing downhill.

"Don't I know it. I'm helping to make sure they don't dirty up Duante."

"Too late for that, I'd have thought." Raze sounded empty.

"Don't quit before the fight is over."

Raze turned her head. "Heard about you and your man. Bulldogs. Don't let anything go."

"Not if it's important. So you want to do this for Duante, or not? I don't have all day."

"Walk with me." Raze bounded to her feet like the limber twenty-something she was. Areesha fussed with the hem of her pencil skirt, rising more sedately. It was snug across her bottom, and earned her more than a few whistles as Raze led her to the neighborhood park. The jungle gym there was packed with children from the neighborhood, and there was also a splash pad that kids stood under, waiting for the buckets at the top to tip over and drench them with icy water. Parents gossiped at park benches, keeping an eye on the play, and Areesha smiled. This was everything she loved best about summer: joy without constraint, community without unwanted intrusion by a police force that kept encroaching.

Areesha trailed her to a set of flat wooden swings near a grove of intertwined aspens. When they had settled on the swings, Areesha again asked about the night Duante was shot.

"Our crew had dinner at the Chicken Shack before Willie and Duante took off."

"You knew where they were headed?"

"To Blackwater, yeah. It was the third challenge out of five, and D was teaming up with Willie on a mural. D was so quick with his hand on the trigger." She mimed the use of spray paint. "The art was in him, you know? It flowed from him like a river."

"You weren't competing that night?"

There was a long pause before Raze answered, and she looked away from Areesha when she did. "Too many Black folk in Blackwater Falls is never a good thing."

"You know about Sheriff Grant?"

"Yeah. It might look real nice on the surface, but Blackwater Falls is a sundown town. Black folk aren't safe after dark."

Areesha pushed off on her swing, collecting her thoughts. If she got Willie and Raze on record, it would make for the headlines, and that could change the narrative about Duante as a vandal. But there was something about how both Willie and Raze had deflected questions about the contest and the prize that worried her. It wasn't a worry she planned to share with the police, but it was there at the back of her mind. The question was whether she should pursue it.

She took Raze through Duante's movements that night, pressed her on the question of vandalism, and, reaching a little, asked if Duante might have known Mateo Ruiz.

Raze's swing moved in a pendulum arc before she dug her toes into the dirt.

"That poor kid was shot in the back, wasn't he?"

Areesha slowed her swing, as well. There was nothing quite as comfortable as a flat-bottomed swing. "He was."

"They didn't know each other that I know of. Do you think the shootings are connected?"

"I don't see how," she admitted. "What about Officer Cooper, the cop who shot Duante? Did they know each other? Did they have run-ins in the past?"

Raze clenched the chains of her swing. "You're saying it wasn't an accident? Cooper did it on purpose? They're calling him a hero on the news."

"I'm trying to rule it out," Areesha explained.

"D didn't have a record. He wasn't a vandal. He'd been to Blackwater before, he thought the falls were cool."

So even though Willie had claimed that Raze stayed out of Blackwater, her own words suggested she knew something about the town.

Raze smirked, her pointed face brightening. "We made out in that little passage beneath the falls. Romantic as fuck." Her smirk faded. "Can't even do some kind of memorial in Blackwater. The cops would just mess it up and the papers would say they were justified."

Areesha didn't tell Raze she was seeing things in black-and-white.

Some things *were* Black and white.

"Why didn't Dr. Young know you were with Duante?"

Raze turned her head so swiftly that her locs whipped against her thin neck.

"D didn't want her to know."

Carefully, Areesha asked, "Did he think you wouldn't pass muster with his mother?"

Raze's bony shoulders bunched up, signifying embarrassment. Perhaps she'd wondered if that was why Duante had kept her away. She tried out an explanation with a break in her voice. "He was angry at Miz Mirry, he didn't want me in the middle of that."

Because of the move from D.C.? Even after he'd found his place with the collective, made friends, found a girl? It didn't add up for Areesha.

"Do you know why he was so angry at his mother?"

"Some shit to do with veterans. They plagued Miz Mirry after she wrote that book. D kept getting into fights with them on Miz Mirry's behalf." Raze sounded more confident now.

Areesha breathed out. This was news. It was also something Mirembe hadn't shared.

"Dr. Young was a huge supporter of veterans. Why would vets attack her?"

Raze didn't answer immediately. She wandered over to the splash pad, joining the children standing under a bucket. It reached the tipping point and the burst of cold water drenched her tank top and overalls. She didn't flinch. She turned up her face like a goddess who worshipped the sun. She could have been buying herself time to work out the best answer.

"You ever read that book of Miz Mirry's? *America's Veterans, America's Victims*?"

Areesha shook her head.

"I did." The piercing in Raze's eyebrow had come loose under the impact of the water. She adjusted it with steady hands.

"It's about veterans' rights. At the same time, it takes the military-industrial complex to task for holding the lives of veterans so cheap, and doing so much psychological damage by having them fight what she calls these 'profit-making' wars. One of those TV channels flipped the script, said Miz Mirry was trivializing the sacrifices made by our troops, calling their courage into question." Raze sighed deeply. "No one who watches that channel bothered to read the book. They took a few quotes out of context and they came after her." Her fingers traced Duante's name on her chest. "D couldn't stand it. He fought every fight, wouldn't back down. He had plenty of enemies, not just the cop who shot him."

"You're saying a far-right veteran might have set him up to get shot?"

There was a weariness in Raze's expression that echoed in Areesha's gut.

"He wouldn't have to be far right. Fringe views have moved to the center."

"Was there a racism element to all this?"

"Isn't there always?"

"Then why did Duante blame his mother?"

Raze began to squeeze water from her locs, her hands surprisingly strong.

"Who else could he blame? She was fighting the wrong battle. The military is just cops with more firepower. He said that was the wrong side."

"Did he know that minorities make up more than a third of the military?"

"Yeah?" Raze looked surprised. "Don't think we knew that. But if Black folk are signing up, it's probably because they need a way to pay for college. The military is a trap, and if D knew about those numbers, he'd be even angrier."

So Duante's anger at the harsh realities of life had blown back on his mother. But Areesha wasn't convinced that that was reason enough to keep the women in his life apart.

"And you're certain that Duante hadn't tangled with Blackwater police before?"

"Straight up," Raze said.

Areesha decided she had to ask. "You're a street artist too, right? Didn't you want the money? Your studio, your projects, they can't be cheap. Did Duante ask you not to compete?"

Raze whistled in surprise. "You think I'd have listened if he did?"

"I don't know," Areesha said. "That's why I'm asking. It seems like the opportunity was too good to pass up. A perfect fit with your skills."

Raze dodged an answer again.

"I didn't shoot Duante—a cop in Blackwater did."

Deeply conflicted, Areesha said, "You knew what Duante had planned. You knew not to be there that night."

Raze pointed her finger and thumb at Areesha like a gun. "You're trying to pin this on me? Don't know what you're telling yourself, but you're no different from the cops."

Was her fury justified or had Areesha hit a nerve?

28

"You're not supposed to talk to Kelly without a lawyer."

Madeleine Hicks ranged her long, lean body beside Kelly Broda's, her strong face set in stubborn lines. She was wearing a sundress with wedge-heeled sandals, but the way she shifted her body was all cop.

"Babe," her boyfriend said. "Broda isn't your problem." He pulled her back, tucking her into his side. She looked up at him, undecided, worrying her lower lip between her teeth. The man turned his attention to Kelly. "Isn't that right, Broda?" His stance made it clear he was claiming Maddy in the face of a potential rival.

"Hey." Maddy nudged her boyfriend in the ribs. "Kell's my big brother, Younas, you have nothing to worry about. You saw his girlfriend at our barbecue. She's a bombshell." Maddy's hands sketched a voluptuous figure.

Ignoring his audience, Younas nuzzled Maddy's neck. "*You're* a bombshell, Mad, so I gotta keep an eye out." His eyes flicked to Inaya. "You a cop? Because if you are, you need permission to enter my yard, and this is my yard, by the way, not Broda's." He added that his name was Younas Medrano.

Inaya introduced herself, monitoring Maddy's and Kelly's body language. They were tense and a little uncertain—because Younas was keeping Maddy contained? Or because of what Younas might know about the shooting and the gun? She invited Younas into the discussion, even as Maddy tried to send him back into the house.

She provoked them by asking Kelly, "You and Maddy live next door to each other?"

Kelly's thumb absently caressed the edge of his music player.

"Younas owns the building. When Maddy moved in with him, he offered me the other side. We know each other from work and cops tend to hang together."

"So the three of you are friends?" Inaya sounded skeptical.

Younas answered her. "I don't want my girl getting mixed up in Broda's mess. She had nothing to do with it, and she doesn't have to answer your questions."

He was pulling back now, but his jealousy was written all over his rugged features. He wasn't sure of his ground with Maddy, and even though he'd rented one side of the duplex to Kelly, he didn't view him as a friend. But just how far did his sense of competition go?

"That's up to her," Inaya said. She indicated John Broda, on the other side of the lawn. He and Seif were standing near a midsize shed at the end of the garden, where Seif was attempting to stow away Kelly's tools. Broda's bulky shoulders shrugged as he showed Seif the padlock on the door. Then he bent his head to Seif and began to speak to him at length. With one corner of her mind, Inaya wondered what he was up to. "Kelly's father wanted to speak to him, to find out about the use of a particular gun in the Mateo Ruiz shooting." She switched her attention to Maddy and Younas. "Did you know about the Merwin Hulbert? Did Kelly keep it on display?"

Younas wrapped one arm around Maddy's chest. "We've seen it," he answered for them. "Like Broda said, we socialize. Why does that matter?"

Inaya focused on Younas. "I take it you know about the raid."

"Every cop in the city knows about the raid," he shot back.

"But not every cop knows that the gun used to kill Mateo Ruiz was the Merwin Hulbert."

He didn't look surprised. Neither did Maddy.

"You knew," Inaya guessed.

"Cops talk," he confirmed.

"And you both had access to Kelly's side of the house?"

Maddy looked puzzled by the question. "Well, Younas does maintenance when it's needed, and I pop over to see Kell now and then. We do dinners, barbecues, that kind of thing. We help each other out." Not by Younas's choice, from the look of things.

His arm tightened around Maddy's shoulders. He understood what Inaya was getting at even if Maddy didn't.

"The gun wasn't locked up," he pointed out. "Anyone who visited my house could have taken it—we both have plenty of visitors. You find Maddy's prints on that gun? Or mine?"

Younas was smart and intuitive. She could see how he'd made SWAT.

Seif came to join Inaya, introducing himself. "No. We found Officer Broda's, though."

"He owns the gun," Maddy put in quickly. "He mounted it on the wall."

"Don't let's talk about the gun," Kelly cut her off.

"That choice of revolver did a lot of damage," Seif pointed out. "It ripped Mateo apart."

"Sounds to me like someone wanted to put Kell in the frame." She leaned back against Younas. "Kell wasn't carrying that gun during the raid, he had his Glock, and if you check with the DTF, you'll see the Glock wasn't fired." She held up her hands, anticipating the next question. "Neither was mine."

Broda left the steps and joined them. "Stand down, Maddy. No one's accusing Kell. And no one's accusing you either. It was a raid gone bad, that's all."

Inaya looked around the circle of faces. Did Broda really believe that? Could he be that naive? Or had he become desperate in his quest to save his son?

She had quite a few things she wanted to follow up on with Maddy, but not in the presence of the Brodas.

"When was the last time you saw the revolver at Kelly's?"

John Broda's breath hitched in his chest. Maddy was merely impatient.

"We're always in and out of each other's places, I stopped noticing it."

Seif wasn't impressed. "Think harder," he warned her.

Kelly tipped his head at Maddy. "You don't need to lie for me."

Her brow puckered, Maddy replied, "We geared up at Kell's place late afternoon. I'm not sure if I saw it on the wall then. We were in a rush when we got the call. I do remember that Kell didn't lock up the house when we left. This is a safe neighborhood so he never does."

So there was no way to confirm that the gun had been in the house the night of the raid.

"What about you?" Inaya asked Younas. "When did you last see the gun?"

His answer was quick and precise. "Broda had a barbecue on the Fourth of July—that's the last time I was inside his house. I noticed it because a bunch of the guys were standing around asking about the gun. Where he got it, shit like that."

"DPD officers?" Seif asked.

Inaya was reminded of the Patriots' subversion of the acronym. Denver Police, Denver Patriots. It would be worthwhile to check the names of Kelly Broda's guests.

Seif was thinking along the same lines—he asked for the guest list. Kelly nodded.

"I'll get it together and send it over to you. But it wasn't them. No cop would steal another officer's gun."

Unless it was to implicate him. Inaya's gaze drifted back to Younas.

"Where were you the night of the raid?"

"You're putting me in the frame?" he fired back. "You think I killed an innocent kid because of Broda?" His contempt was obvious. "I was on the fucking roster that night."

"Keep it civil," Seif ordered. "We're looking into anyone who had access to the gun."

"Seems to me like you have your answer if Broda's prints were on the gun."

"I explained that," Maddy said. "That doesn't mean it was Kell."

Kelly's unspoken response was so complex that Inaya couldn't break it down. Feeling flickered in his eyes, subtly tightening the skin over his cheekbones, sighing out through his lungs. He stood a little apart, like a vessel unmoored from its dock, drifting away on the sea.

"It was my gun," he said. "That makes it my fault."

29

"Come home with me." Seif deliberately lengthened the gap before he clarified the invitation. "For dinner, I mean. It'll be leftovers, but Alireza knows his way around Persian food. And I know the boys would like to see you."

This wasn't meet-the-family stuff, he assured himself. Inaya had met the twins, this was just a catch-up in a different setting. There was plenty to deconstruct from their session with the Brodas, Younas Medrano, and Madeleine Hicks.

Inaya hesitated at the door to Seif's car. "You're sure the boys will be home?"

Seif's attractive smile lit his face. "I'm not trying to have my wicked way with you."

She glared at him. "As if I'd let you."

"That's decided, then."

She couldn't help it. She laughed, and he joined in.

"You'll have to drive me back to the station first."

"I'll drop you off after dinner."

He wasn't risking her changing her mind. He drove smoothly from downtown to Wash Park, hoping like hell one of the twins was home. They wouldn't be expecting family dinner night again so soon, and he had no idea why he'd issued the invitation.

Like hell he didn't, he scoffed. He was building bonds, testing things out, and maybe he wanted to show off his house, show her what he'd achieved through backbreaking work and sheer dogged persistence.

He didn't realize a smile was playing on his lips until Inaya asked, "Share the joke. What are you finding so funny?"

He didn't dare say he was happy again, not after she'd warned him off, but he could admit the truth to himself. He had two major police shootings to deal with, his brothers were miserable because he'd laid down the law, Sheriff Grant was up in arms against him, and Jacob Brandt at the FBI had warned him his job was at risk when he'd called to sound him out on his brothers' plans. And he hadn't figured out what he wanted to do about Lily. Yet here he was, grinning like a fool because Inaya had agreed to share a meal with him.

He hit the jackpot. The Bronco the twins had bought and fixed up was sitting in the drive, and even better, Alireza had decided to try his hand at *maqluba,* a Palestinian dish cooked in one pot with layers of rice, vegetables, and chicken or other meat, and then flipped upside down. He could smell the ginger and cumin in the air, and it evoked a sharp sense of nostalgia, a yearning he swiftly tamped down.

The table settings had been taken up a notch—all Palestinian ceramics this time—with an embroidered tablecloth their grandmother had sent to them, a confection of red, black, and gold, and small votive candles that dispersed a soft glow. If there hadn't been the customary three settings in place, he would have suspected that the twins were having girls over behind his back. He suppressed a chuckle. They wouldn't have to do it behind his back, and the kind of girls the twins hung around would refuse the invitation. Large groups were okay, intimate dinners were not. So yeah, he'd definitely hit the jackpot when he'd brought Inaya home.

"Why you looking so chirpy, bro—?" Mikhail's voice trailed off at the sight of Inaya at Seif's shoulder. The frown he'd had in place for Seif broke into a delighted smile as he gave her salaam. She responded in kind, a twinkle in her eye at Mikhail's obvious pleasure.

"Team meeting," Seif said before Mik could embarrass him.

Mik set a place for Inaya. He murmured to Alireza at the stove, "Team of two, Rez." He was loud enough for Seif to hear, but Inaya, thankfully, was preoccupied by a study of the embroidered tablecloth, the precious cloth slipping through her slender fingers.

"Mik" and "Rez" were how the twins abbreviated their symbolic Muslim names. Seif could handle "Mik," but he detested "Rez." Alireza was named for the seventh descendant of the Prophet Muhammad, and the eighth of

Shia Islam's twelve imams. Broken into its components, the two names Ali and Reza were accorded the accolades of "brave" and "kind" in homage to famous heroes of Islam, and either by fluke or divine guidance, Alireza's heart was solid gold. Mikhail's name was no less meaningful: he was named for the archangel of Islam tasked with dispensing God's providence, second only in stature to the angel Jibrail or Gabriel. Mikhail and Jibrail were said to have purified Muhammad's heart before the Night Journey and the Ascension, two touchstones of Islamic history. Seif's given name could be construed to mean "warrior" or "defender"; it was also the surname of a noted companion of the Prophet. Somewhat shamefacedly, Seif added the salutation that was spoken after any mention of the Prophet.

No matter how he tried to sever them, Seif's roots still ran deep.

Inaya interrupted his thoughts by asking Mikhail if they had a space where she could pray. Seif glanced at his watch and judged the time—the sky was darkening, it was time for *maghrib*. The heads of both twins turned. They looked first to Seif, then to Inaya.

"Absolutely, sis. You okay to pray in *jamaat*?"

"Of course," Inaya replied. "Is there somewhere I can wash up?"

Alireza showed Inaya the powder room, while Mik focused on Seif.

"Will you be joining us, bro?"

He saw the answer in Seif's eyes. His disappointment was obvious, but it changed to a hard kind of contempt that Seif found difficult to swallow. His brother was quick to judge him.

"Didn't think so. A man who doesn't heed the call to Jerusalem must find it easy to ignore the call to prayer." Mik jerked his chin at the door of the powder room. "If you want to keep her, you need to start making some changes."

"I don't do religion," Seif said flatly, though his chest ached at Mikhail's scorn. In the twins' eyes, walking away from their faith was the same as abandoning them, even when he'd proved otherwise. It wasn't fair to Seif for his brothers to hold him in contempt, but he didn't want to tread the same old ground again with Mik.

"Then you might as well take up with Lily again, seeing as you gave her your ring."

Alireza's sudden stillness at his back told him that Inaya had overheard the very last thing he'd want her to think. She'd see him as a man who used up women like Kleenex, and maybe he deserved that, but up until the end, he'd treated Lily with consideration and respect, and she'd always had his loyalty. His brow like thunder, he snapped at the twins, "Hurry up and pray, and while you're at it, try and cleanse your hearts of judgment."

He heard Inaya murmur to the twins as they moved off to the prayer room. He brought the food to the table, intent on seating Inaya to his right. The left side of his chest contracted as the pure tones of Mik's voice rang out, raised in the *adhaan*. Or *azaan,* as his mother would pronounce it. FBI-Seif didn't give a damn, but the Seif his mother had raised cherished her Persian heritage, and the softness the Persian language had given to Arabic words.

When the three returned from prayer, the twins looked a little shaken. It was Alireza's turn to whisper as he said, "Qas, the sis prayed *beside* us."

Seif hid a grin. If Mik gave the *adhaan,* Alireza led the prayer, and vice versa. Typically, women's rows were formed behind men's rows in congregational prayers. Some mosques, however, left a gap between men and women's spaces so that both groups prayed side by side as they did at the Kaabah in Mecca. It was a highly controversial matter for some, while others regarded it as more respectful and more equitable.

"Welcome to the twenty-first century," Inaya answered with a smile. "Don't worry, you won't melt from the encroachment."

With utter seriousness, Alireza said, "May all your prayers be accepted, sister."

She told him to call her Inaya, and his shock deepened. Full of mischief, Inaya continued, "You don't need your brother's permission, you have mine."

Somewhere under that beard Seif was sure Alireza was blushing. Inaya took pity on him and addressed herself to her food, which she complimented so lavishly that Alireza regained his composure. Nonetheless, the tension between Seif and the twins was hard to miss, and eventually Inaya showed her puzzlement by posing a question to the twins.

"Is everything okay? You seem a little out of sorts."

Mik opened his mouth, and Seif flinched at the thought of his criticism laid bare before Inaya. He knew she felt the call of her roots, and that she cherished her heritage—he'd rather not have Mik call him out again. Alireza beat Mik to it.

"We want to go to Jerusalem, see our grandmother, cousins, find out about our father. Our brother doesn't think it will be safe for us."

"Our prison warden," Mik corrected bitterly, the flames bright in his eyes.

Holding on to his temper with an effort, Seif said, "It isn't just unsafe for you. I've explained that to you both."

"What do you think?" Mik challenged Inaya.

"It's not my place—"

Seif dropped his hand to the table. "Just say it."

Inaya took him at his word. She gestured to the airy kitchen and great room, her gaze coming back to Mik. "Gaza is a prison. This is a palace. I don't think the comparison is apt."

Seif was surprised. He didn't know she followed events in the Occupied Territories. Because of him? Or because of that tie of faith that made the question of Palestine a defining marker of identity for most believing Muslims, despite the fact that a significant segment of Palestinians were, in fact, Christian. The Occupation reminded the *ummah* of the colonial conquest of Muslim lands in the Middle East and North Africa. The situation in Palestine was a provocation, and an ever-present wound. Strangely, he felt buoyed by the thought that Inaya might respect the heritage he himself denied.

"If I were you," Inaya continued, "I'd check the travel advisories for the region. You might have trouble entering Israel. I suspect it might also pose a problem for your brother's job." She turned to Seif. "Didn't you explain that?"

Seif tried not to smile at being taken to task.

"He did." Mik's anger deflated that brief moment of levity. "But ask him why that job is more important than his father's parents. Why it matters more than doing his duty."

"Well, if you still want me to comment on something that is none of my business, I would say keeping that job *is* doing his duty." She gestured at the spacious room again. "How else would you manage this house?" She pinned Mikhail. "Do you pay your own tuition?"

He had the grace to blush. "That doesn't give Qas the right to cut us off from our roots."

"I sympathize," Inaya said gently.

"How could you?" Mik shot back. "You don't know anything about it."

"There are many things my father loved that he left behind in Afghanistan. Roots, history, people. A town he can never return to, family he will never see again."

"We still have that choice!" Mik had raised his voice.

"Mikhail!" Seif instantly checked Mik's outburst. "Detective Rahman is a guest."

Inaya briefly touched his arm, a gesture meant to soothe.

"I'm not offended. These are difficult questions. I'm twenty-nine years old," she told the boys. "If I tried to return to Afghanistan, my father would still do his best to stop me."

"It's different for women," Mik said sulkily.

Seif wouldn't have let her go either, though he knew very little about the current state of affairs in the country.

"Why do you really want to go?" Inaya put the question to Alireza. "All you're likely to experience is humiliation, and you may not even step foot in Jerusalem."

In his gentle way, Alireza said, "Even that would make us a part of the resistance. It would legitimate our identity."

She nodded. "And the cost to your brother?"

Mik pushed his plate away, stood up. "What about the cost to us?"

When the boys had cleared out, the discussion unresolved, Seif and Inaya moved to the great room to discuss the case. But first, an apology was in order.

"I'm sorry. You didn't come here to get tangled up in my family quarrels."

"Is it hard?" she surprised him by asking.

Tension shaped his shoulders, made him draw away.

"Is what hard?"

"Hiding it from them how much you want to say yes. How you'd like to go yourself."

He'd heard the expression that in shock, blood drained from the lips. This was the first time he'd felt it. He couldn't find a defense to throw up, his agitation severe.

She took pity on him.

"I'm sorry. I had no right to say that."

She was gaining rights by the minute, the second, though he refused to let her know it. He wasn't ready for an excavation of the dark places of his soul.

He motioned her to the sofa, took the leather chaise himself, and changed the subject. Or rather, got back to the point of his invitation. The chance to discuss the case.

"What did we get from that interview?"

He passed Inaya a glass of *falooda* he'd brought from the kitchen, which she declined with an apology.

"Much to the shame of my ancestors, I really can't stand the taste of rose water."

"You're missing out."

She smiled. "I'll treat you to mango *lassi* one day."

Heat flushed through his body, though he kept himself cool as he accepted.

He rose, fetched her a glass of sparkling water, then settled back in the soft leather chaise. Inaya had taken the sofa opposite, and she sat primly with her notebook on her knees.

"What did Kelly Broda tell you when you were on your own?"

"For one thing, he's not gay. You heard what Maddy said about his girlfriend."

"Could be a cover."

Inaya mulled this over, her concentration palpable. "It doesn't make much sense to lie to us, even if he'd been wanting to keep it from his father. All I have to do is show his photograph to the leads Cat identified at the club. There might also be video—I have to check that with Cat."

"Webb has the film from the raid. We can also comb through that."

"That's what I mean—catching Kelly in a lie would be so easy that he must have been telling the truth. John told me earlier that Kelly had a string of girlfriends in Chicago. Kelly's attractive and in shape—he wouldn't have trouble getting the kind of attention he wants."

Seif edged forward in his seat. "If that holds up, then we need to find Mateo's lover. And we still have to ask why that gun if Broda isn't involved?"

Inaya leaned closer too. If he reached out his hand, he could touch her knee. Mindful of her warning, he didn't.

"Access to the gun just opened up. And maybe even a motive for other players," she said.

"Maddy?"

"Maddy might cover for Kelly if pressed—they're practically family. But I don't think her boyfriend would let her. He kept pointing us back to Kelly."

"Maybe for his own reasons."

Inaya raised her delicate eyebrows. "Younas implicates Kelly in a random shooting purely out of jealousy? If Younas was there during the raid, the cameras would catch him in action. It seems like a stretch to me."

"Suppose he got his hands on a regular patrol uniform—he might even have his old one."

They both knew you had to have years of experience before you could qualify for SWAT.

"He'd blend in, you're saying." She shook her head. "All that to keep Maddy away from Kelly? Why rent him the other half of the duplex, in that case?"

"Keep your friends close?" Seif suggested.

"Or maybe Maddy pressed him to do it because she felt obligated to keep an eye on him. She calls Kelly her big brother, but in my interview with her, she came across as feeling deeply indebted to the Brodas. She'd probably apply for SWAT if Kelly wasn't still on patrol."

Seif's eyes caught hers. "Shooting Mateo Ruiz would get him off the streets."

Inaya disagreed again. "Too messy. You don't get to SWAT like that. Worse, she could be accused of *not* covering her partner by failing to stop him from shooting Mateo in the back."

"It would have been open-and-shut if they thought they were pursuing a DTF suspect, and simply made a bad call. Cops do it all the time."

"Except for the gun."

He smiled. "Why do you always find the weak point in my logic?"

She blushed a little, sitting back to gain some distance. "We need to check out Younas's alibi. And start digging into Kelly's girlfriends. Other than that, we have to rely on body cams and the club's footage for corroboration. Then there's the Patriots. We should cross-reference that guest list, but how do we find out which DPD officers also belong to the gang?"

"I'll put out some feelers. Maybe West can give us a read." He waited for her to state the obvious, and when she didn't, he put it forward himself. "What about John Broda? Don't overlook his history with the gun."

Inaya met his gaze and held it. She wasn't unaffected by their proximity, he could see the pulse tapping away at her throat, in the tiny vee of flesh her blouse exposed. It was all he could see of her skin, because her dress code meant she covered everything except her hands. He wanted to see more, wanted to have that privilege.

"You really think John would set up his own son?"

"No," he said, when he'd gotten his breath back. God help him, he wanted to kiss her. "That grief he expressed was real, but there's something we're missing about how they relate to each other. I don't buy the idea that their estrangement is due to Broda's style of policing, as repugnant as that is. There might be more to it than that."

"It's hard to say from just two interviews." She showed him a page of her notebook, the touch of her fingers sending a spark up his arm. "Kelly doesn't like who his father is when it comes to his job, but beyond that he didn't confide in me, and Madeleine didn't say much more. Broda groomed her to join the police force, so there could be a conflict of loyalty there as well."

Seif looked down at the notebook without taking in a word. He tried to think of a follow-up when all he was taking in was her light, summery fragrance as she got up to pace.

She ran a hand over her ponytail. "We're right back where we started with the gun."

Seif moved close to Inaya. When she tried to retreat, he caught her around the waist.

"Not quite," he said. "We may have work to do but the picture is coming into focus."

30

They had a team meeting the following morning to review the film from the raid. Inaya was going to be late. West had called her from the Disciples' clubhouse in Blackwater. He had a lead on the Denver Patriots, and she had to meet with him first. But before that she wanted to spend some time with her parents, particularly her father. He was with her mother in the family room, and with her sister Noor beside them, they were paging through their wedding album. She'd forgotten about it after dinner at Seif's—it was her parents' anniversary. She didn't have a present, and she hadn't made any plans.

She entered the room and kissed them both.

"You forgot, didn't you?" Noor teased her.

"Nope. I'm taking you all out to dinner tonight." She smiled at her father. "Unless you and Ami have some romantic plans of your own?"

They protested the idea vigorously. "Without our children? Impossible."

"Where are we going?" her father asked.

Noor stepped in and saved her. "Reservations at seven tonight at Surena."

Perfect. Her parents looked pleased. Inaya mouthed a thank-you to her sister.

"Dress up, all of you. We'll take some pictures too."

Nothing pleased Inaya's mother more than family photographs. She was adept at the use of Photoshop, which she used to crop out everyone except Inaya so that she could show potential marriage partners flattering pictures of her eldest daughter. Inaya did her best to blink or otherwise ruin these photos to protect herself from her mother's maneuvers, but tonight her gift would be playing along and posing in *shalwar kameez,* quite likely draped against a pillar like some love-starved Bollywood heroine batting her eyes at the hero.

The prospect brought a bright smile to her mother's face, just as she knew it would.

"No gifts, please! Especially, no flowers. Give *sadaqah,* instead." She followed that thought to its natural conclusion. *"Beta,* save your money. These restaurants charge too much. I will make a beautiful dinner and we can take pictures in the garden. There's a family that wants to come and meet Noor. We can ask them to come for chai."

Inaya laughed at Noor's desperate expression. Noor made a pleading face at their father.

"Absolutely not," he said. "The heart of my heart is not cooking tonight. Besides, the public should see us out and about with our three beautiful daughters. And what about the new suit I bought you? Won't you wear it for me?"

Oh, he knew how to play their mother, all right. With the way her father doted on her mother, it was hard to believe their marriage had been arranged by elders on her mother's side.

"Close one," Noor whispered to her, and this time Inaya did laugh.

The photograph album was open to a picture of her parents. They had been married in the refugee camp in Peshawar, where they had met. Her mother had been a young and eager social worker, her father had been acting as a multilingual translator. He'd completed his legal education in the United States, once his immigration had been approved.

The red clay walls of Kacha Gari camp were visible in the background of the photograph, the ceremony and wedding clothes simpler than the lavish affairs of today. Her father had had no elders to vouch for his character and prospects. He'd had to rely on the goodwill of one of the imams in the camp to speak for him.

"Do you have a minute, Baba?"

Her father graced her with a smile, the loving look in his eyes her talisman against the troubles she faced in her work.

"Shall we go to my office?"

"Actually, can you come into the hall?"

He followed Inaya down the hall until she stopped at the photograph mounted on the wall. The turquoise gate in the desert. Her conversation with Seif's family about their heritage had reawakened old questions. Where had the picture been taken? Whose home did the turquoise gate represent? Why was her father so reluctant to speak of it when he clearly treasured the memory of the abandoned gate?

And why did the photograph make her think of Harry Cooper's son? The young man had taken his own life in her father's country, another victim of the war. What had Huxton Cooper seen that had preyed upon his mind? What actions had he taken as a soldier that he could no longer live with?

It was her father who had taught her that intuition was a gift of memory. Of pieces of past and present experiences melding together to warn the body of things the mind failed to remember. She needed to heed that inner voice.

"Will you tell me about the gate, Baba? Did it lead to your family home?"

His green eyes rested on her face. "Why do you want to know, my precious child?"

She let him see her restlessness. "I'm not really sure. Part of me wants to know why you're keeping it from me."

"The detective part," he put in with a twinkle.

"Yes, that. But also, part of me wants to know what this place means to you, and why it means something to me."

He looked surprised. "It does? You've never been there."

"I can't explain it," she said. "It's like a phantom place in my mind, a place I came from in a way. Maybe somewhere I need to return to?"

Grief cast its shadow over her father's face, deepened the green of his eyes.

"You were never there. You won't be able to return."

There was a hidden meaning behind the words.

"Why not, Baba? What happened?"

He touched the turquoise doors, a tremor in his lean fingers. His breath sighed out like a long-forgotten prayer.

"It was my home. My parents' home. The home of my brothers and sisters. Many years ago, it was burned by the Russians."

Her father had told them very little about his life before he arrived in Kacha Gari.

"When?"

He shook his head. "Please don't ask me."

He patted her hair, the tremor still in his hands.

"I'm sorry, Baba. I didn't mean to upset you."

He turned to her, pressed his forehead to hers, and let her go.

"You have the right to know, but I don't have the heart to tell you. Or to remember it myself. And much more terrible things have happened in the country since the Russians left. The American presence eased some things, yet also caused so much harm. The things I have witnessed on behalf of my people—my child, the horrors have been vast."

Inaya gave her father a hug, feeling terrible that she had reopened old wounds.

"I wish I could remember with you, so you wouldn't be alone."

Tears slipped down her father's cheeks.

"I have found that it is better if I forget Maywand."

Maywand. Her need to demand answers from her father was burning through her mind when she met West outside Anarchist Ink on East Colfax. Maybe a coincidence, but it felt deeper than simply Afghanistan being on her mind. Huxton Cooper had been stationed in Maywand, where he had died. The itch had resurfaced. She'd missed something. She should have followed up on Harry Cooper, but Mateo Ruiz was her priority. There was only one customer inside, a man nearly as big as West was, but much better groomed. He was reclining in a plush leather chair that looked more comfortable than the one at her dentist's office, the sleeve of his navy uniform rolled up, his badge on the tattoo artist's table.

"Give us a sec, sweetheart," West said to the girl who had set out her tools to begin.

"Sure thing, Ranger." She disappeared behind a curtain decorated with stars.

West's club name drew the attention of the man in the chair. He was young and clean-cut, his hair neatly shaped on his skull, his patrol uniform pressed. He noticed Inaya's badge and gave her a polite nod.

"Can I help you folks?"

Inaya introduced herself, and the young cop gave his name as Oliver Scott.

West was in the summer version of his club gear, the leather vest with its numerous patches slung over a skintight T-shirt and paired with even tighter jeans. It couldn't be comfortable to dress like that on a bike, Inaya thought, but this morning West had brought his truck. The other man must be wondering what she was doing with a character like Ranger.

"Brothers gave me word," West began. "You run with the Patriots."

Scott jerked up in the chair, shifting it out of reclining mode. He focused on Inaya, not West. "Don't know what the hell you mean."

"Yeah, you do."

West kicked the lever, upending the chair. He lunged at Scott, his arm at Scott's throat.

"We can do this easy, or we can do this hard."

Inaya hadn't been expecting West to resort to force. He grimaced at her. "Don't have time to make nice, Brazil. Got other heads to break today." He leaned into his arm, an easy grin on his face as Scott changed color. "Now you with the Patriots or not?"

"Fuck man, all right."

West eased back a touch. "Good. Now answer the lady—she has a couple of questions."

Scott swore, and West went in heavy again. Scott's hands scrabbled at West's arm.

To cut things short, Inaya said, "This is about Kelly Broda. Did you recruit him?"

Scott glared at her. "That pansy-ass? Said he was from Chicago, but he didn't pass the test. The Patriots didn't need him."

He struggled under West's arm. "Heard different from my club. Playboy says you went after him hard. Wanted Chicago muscle to back you up in the hood."

Scott turned his glare on West. "His partner brings the muscle. We recruited her."

Inaya's lips went numb. So Madeleine had lied. *She* was the one tagged by the DPD.

"*Hicks* signed on to the Patriots?"

Scott coughed. "Mad's true blue all the way. The pair of them were fresh meat down here, she came to us for protection. Proved she could handle herself."

"How?" West demanded.

Scott's hand scrambled for his gun. West put his knee on it. The chair shook as another skirmish took place.

"You can choke me to death, I'm not giving Mad up."

"Initiation," West said to Inaya, who was growing more uncomfortable with his tactics by the minute. It was the kind of intimidation she'd fought against ever since she'd joined the police. And apart from her qualms of conscience, there was also the fact that Community Response was a vulnerable unit within the Denver Police, and the Patriots would want payback.

"Stop," she told West.

"What did you make her do?" West insisted.

Ugly pictures formed in her mind—she'd heard of another kind of lineup, where a woman was required to service a line of men.

Scott's eyes narrowed. "No one abuses Mad," he spat at her. "She can handle herself."

"What then? A drive-by shooting? Harassing minorities while you're out on patrol?"

She got a reaction to her second suggestion.

"She taught us a few things she learned in Chicago."

"She must have wanted her partner to join up too."

"That was her test," Scott admitted. "To bring Broda in. But no one could have brought that fucker in, so we set up something else for Mad."

His foul language was at odds with the vibe he gave off as a straight-as-an-arrow cop who did things by the book.

"Where do you patrol? What neighborhoods?"

West had to lean on him hard to get the answer. She wasn't surprised to find Mateo's neighborhood among them, but he'd also included the part of town that housed the street-art collective. Her mind skittered over the possibility that the Patriots had coordinated the two shootings, a dead Black man and a dead Latino on the same night.

"Ranger, enough." A question in his eyes, West let the other man go.

Scott fixed the chair, lunging to his feet. Inaya didn't block his escape. Puzzled by that, he swung around at the door.

"You always give up that easy?"

She shook her head. "I don't want to become like you."

He sneered at that. "You'd never make the cut." He jabbed a finger at her. "You're no better than me, in bed with the Disciples."

West closed in on him, towering over Scott.

"She plays nice, I don't. Come after her, and you'll have a war with us."

Scott didn't back down. "You'd do that for a fucking wet?"

"Wet" was a shortened form of "wetback," Border Patrol slang for Mexicans who attempted to cross the river at the border.

West's fist slammed into Scott's jaw. He went down like a sack of bones.

West leaned down and jerked him up by his collar. "My wife's Mexican, asshole, so that's your free one. I hear that again and you're out for the count."

He thrust Scott away from him, rubbing his fist on his jeans.

Scott stared up at them, his hand at the sore spot on his jaw as he lurched to his feet.

"Have you ever been to Kelly Broda's house?" asked Inaya.

The corner of his mouth was bloody. He dabbed at it with his sleeve.

"What if I have, Detective?"

"You'd have seen the gun on the wall."

"So?"

"That was the gun used to shoot Mateo Ruiz."

The red mark stood out against his sudden pallor.

"So?" he repeated. "A bunch of us were there."

"Kelly Broda refused to join the Patriots. He was against everything you stood for. So I'm wondering if you used that gun to pay him back somehow. Or to get him in line."

He backed away from her, eyes wide. She wasn't done.

"There's another possibility," she added. "What was the test Maddy Hicks had to pass to prove herself to you?"

"You're fucking nuts, lady. This isn't the Wild West." He jerked up his chin at West. "We got a beef with the Disciples?"

"Not if you weren't responsible for the death of that boy. The detective will need proof."

Scott looked through Inaya to negotiate with West. "I'll talk to the boys, see what I can do." His hand formed a fist, but when West strode forward to push Inaya behind him, he thought better of the threat.

"Watch your back," he told her. "The Patriots don't forget."

West went one better. "You touch her and we roll out."

Scott paused at the threat. "I don't fucking get you, man. You and me—we're the same."

West made a sound of disgust. "I'd put a bullet through my head if I thought for a minute that was true."

31

Cat's doorbell rang late at night. Emiliano was in his study, preserving the cold war between them, and she was feeling both fed up and despondent, so she tried to distract herself by working up a profile on Mateo's shooting. It was proving to be an effort in vain, because the shooting might simply have been a question of Mateo having been in the wrong place at the wrong time. Based on her recent conversation with Inaya, the use of John Broda's antique revolver might have been specific to Mateo, or it might have been an act of the Patriots to frame Kelly Broda for refusing to join their ranks. Whatever the motive behind the shooting, Cat was no closer to an answer.

Her curly hair was rumpled, she was wearing sweatpants and an old Jenni Rivera concert T-shirt. What did it matter what she looked like? Emiliano didn't see her anymore, unless she was working a case for him. He wasn't moving from his office either, so she got up to open the door.

A woman she didn't recognize was standing on her porch. She was tall and slender, with well-defined muscles in her arms. She too was wearing a T-shirt, but the hem was tied at her waist in a chic knot, baring several inches of her toned midriff. With it she wore a pair of low-slung capris in a deep shade of green. Her eyes glowed a deep brown, and her long spiral curls fell nearly to her waist. Her nose was broad, her cheekbones were low and wide, and her full curling lips with a dip in the center were set in an ageless smile.

Cat didn't know her. Or maybe she did, a twinge of recognition tugging at her mind.

"Are you here to see Emiliano?"

Emil often saw clients at home. They maintained an open-door policy when it came to the needs of their community. It was late for a meeting, but Cat politely invited the stranger in.

Her name was Luna Clyde, and she had come to speak to Cat.

"Because you're with the police," she explained, as Cat led her through to the kitchen and offered her a glass of wine.

They sat at the island in the terra-cotta-and-gold kitchen chatting comfortably until Cat asked Luna if she was in some kind of trouble.

Luna put her hand on Cat's, gazing deep into her eyes with a soft look of concern.

"I'm here to warn you that we're working with Mirembe Young to arrange a protest against the killing of our young. I'm hoping you can do something to stave off the riot police."

Her gaze settled on a picture of Emiliano and Cat picking apples at a local orchard.

"We know about your NGO work. Some members of our community might see your role in the police as a betrayal, but I'm not one of them."

"Why not?" Cat asked simply. She had heard every possible criticism about her work from Emiliano already.

"I've met members of your team. I know what you're trying to do." Luna pointed to the stacks of files on the kitchen table. "You're trying to do more than just change the face of policing." Her long curls slipped forward to cover part of her face. "I wish that were possible."

That twinge of recognition resolved itself into an image. A photograph in the paper, the day after riot police stormed a Latine neighborhood.

Her visitor was Altagracia.

"That was a brave thing you did, but very out of character for a woman from our community. You had to know there was very little chance of not being assaulted."

"Why?" Luna asked softly. "Because the police can't restrain themselves from violence even in the face of a naked woman? Why would they think I was a threat?"

Cat continued to study her, curious. Luna's surname was Clyde. "You're speaking from a place of privilege," she guessed.

Luna shrugged. "My parents are white, but one of my grandmothers was Mexican, and my father named me after her." Her easy confidence dimmed. "I'm part of this community even if I don't speak Spanish."

That wasn't for Cat to decide. But what Cat did know was that a Latina would not have assumed she was safe in the presence of police once she'd made herself so vulnerable. Nor would she have exposed her body in front of her community.

Cat didn't agree with Luna's tactics, yet she hadn't found her diminished by her actions, even as she understood they were rooted in a sense of privilege Catalina didn't share.

Cat raised her glass for a sip of wine to find she had already drained it. There wasn't enough wine in the world to sort out the problems she faced. The glass clinked against the clay tile counter as she set it down with some force.

"You can't stop the protest, Catalina. Even if we'd taken down the barricades, the cops wouldn't have left without a fight. That's why we're taking a stand."

When Cat didn't speak, Emiliano's voice cut across the silence. He was still in a mood.

"Why don't you correct her, *mi amor*? Could it be because you know she is right?" He clicked his tongue. "It's a tragedy that my Catalina has planted her feet so firmly on the wrong side of the line. Your police force *cannot* be reformed."

Cat refused to engage. It would turn into a fight, and she could argue herself blue in the face—what a sad little pun—and the outcome would still be the same. She wouldn't allow Emiliano to put her in the position of arguing *for* the police. Things weren't that simple, and he knew it. He'd humiliated her in front of Luna, so she didn't bother with introductions. Instead, she asked Luna for details about the protest.

"Don't tell her," her husband said bitterly. "They'll be waiting for you when you come."

Luna regarded him gravely. "I came to your wife to advise her that the protest will be peaceful. The police have no excuse for violence, and Catalina can make them aware of that."

Maybe Luna was right. Cat's intervention might ease tensions in advance.

With the lieutenant, Inaya, and Areesha at her side, she could convince the higher-ups.

She saw Luna to the door, offering her own advice.

"Wherever you plan to protest, make sure you get a permit first."

Husband and wife faced each other across the kitchen island like two soldiers on the opposite sides of a trench, neither giving an inch.

"You think a permit will make any difference?"

"It will allow the protest to go forward. If I were them, I would turn it into a vigil."

He looped both thumbs in his belt, the position he took when he was ready for a fight. "Like the vigil for Elijah McClain?"

"There will be greater numbers this time."

"That just means more police. Will you be with them? With your baton and face shield?"

She stared down at the counter, feeling tears sting her eyes at his contempt. She couldn't change his mind. She wasn't going to try.

She came around the counter, taking one of his hands in her own. She looked up into his proud, angry face.

"How have we come to this place, *mi amor*? Don't you know the damage you're doing?"

He jerked his hand free, turning away from her.

"Why don't you ask yourself that question?"

"If you would try to come down off your high horse—" she began.

"If you would try to climb up out of the gutter," he rejoined, throwing the words over his shoulder, so cutting that she gasped.

Her words slow and heavy, she said, "How could you say that to me?"

He picked up her badge from the table in the family room, thumping it down on the counter. He flicked it in her direction. Cat caught it before it slid past her to the floor. Her palm closed over the badge, a weight pressing down on her heart.

"How could you join the police? How could you do this to us? We worked all our lives to fight *La Migra*—and look at you now, Catalina. You've run from the fight. In fact you've run so far, you're now on the opposite side."

They stood there breathing heavily, brown eyes flashing into brown. She looked at the man she had loved and cherished for a decade. She had known him since she was a child. She had fought every battle at his side, and now—now Emiliano was a stranger. He wasn't the man she knew, gentle, tender, with depths of compassion she had never fully plumbed.

She'd thought her work as a detective with the Community Response Unit had become a point of conflict. Instead, it was a moral line. One she'd crossed. Now, he stood on the opposite side of a continental divide.

"So this is where we are."

"This is where we are. You're not the girl I knew, the woman I would have died for." His body shrank from hers. "When *La Migra* killed our child, they killed the part of you I love."

She crumpled from the blow, one hand gripping the counter. The pain burned her womb. One of her hands was bleeding where she clutched at her badge. She looked down to find it colored red. How fitting. She wasn't just tainted in his eyes, she was knee-deep in blood.

"And if I quit the police?"

Hope flared in his eyes, his clenched muscles easing.

"Then you will be my Cat again."

She stood up straight, took her badge to the sink, and rinsed it off. She wrapped it in a paper towel and said, "That's too bad. Because you won't be my Emiliano."

32

On Saturday, Areesha, David, and their sons walked behind Mirembe's family, following them to the graveyard. The exuberance of the service was over, the open casket revealing Duante in a state of grace in his navy-blue suit with a sheaf of roses on his breast. Though many of the women had sung out, shouted, or clapped as music was played, Mirembe had stationed herself beside her son, her hand resting on his forehead. Her grief was quiet, and might have seemed unmemorable, but as "Trouble of the World" played, her smooth face crumpled. She didn't sob out loud, and she chose not to wipe away her tears. They were a gift to her son, and mother and son were bonded together in a painterly tableau.

The gathering at the grave site was somber. Areesha noticed the presence of Willie and Raze, but both stood some distance away, Raze with her phone held up as if she was filming events. She ignored Areesha, as did Willie, and it stung, but she also noticed that it was as if the pair didn't exist for Mirembe. Mirembe had cousins and other family there, yet it was Areesha who stood at her side, Areesha who watched as another Black man was lowered into the ground before he could tally up the great occasions of life. Mirembe's hand was like a claw gripping Areesha's. The veil that descended from her hat trembled with the force of her grief.

"Let go," Areesha said into her ear. "Let yourself feel it all."

Later, the main group left the small cemetery and moved back up the street to Mirembe's house, where a meal had been prepared. Eventually, when they'd all gone, Areesha joined Cat and Inaya under the protection of an oak tree at the center of the cemetery.

They talked quietly about the funeral, Inaya sharing what she had learned about Huxton Cooper's death at FOB Ramrod. Inaya had gone out to dinner with her family the previous night, where she had pressed her father about the last time he had visited Afghanistan, and any knowledge he might have of the American base. He'd turned her questions aside. An anniversary dinner wasn't the time to speak of the past: it was a moment to celebrate the present.

Inaya looked troubled by her inability to get answers from her father, but Cat's expression was one of utter devastation. Her eyes were pinched and hollow, her shoulders slumped. Inaya was wearing a sober suit with a long, fitted jacket and held an umbrella to guard against the light drizzle. By contrast, Cat's slacks and blouse were rumpled, and her untidy hair was scraped back in a style that didn't suit her. She looked like she hadn't slept in weeks.

Areesha nudged Cat gently. "You okay?"

She had to do it twice more before Cat took notice.

"Oh, of course. I'm fine."

"You don't look fine."

"Late nights on the case. Both cases," Cat amended. "I can't seem to work up a profile. Both shootings seem like a case of wrong time, wrong place."

"And Duante and Mateo paid for that with their lives."

Areesha stared across the lawn to the grave, inhaling the fragrant scent of the earth. To walk, to live, to dream, to paint, to come to the grave in the end. It hollowed out her heart, made her fear for her sweet, sensitive Clay and for her fiery Kareem. It made her tense up if David was late coming home. And it made her sweat beneath her quiet calm when she was pulled over on the road by cops, whether it was night or day.

Duante had lived the final moments of his life hunted down and terrified, the end nasty, brutish, short. The well-known words had a rhythm to them, an altogether different meaning when applied to lives truncated by violence.

She unpinned the white rose on her lapel and let it drop onto the coffin.

"How loved you were," she told Duante, holding the tears inside. "How much you'll be missed, even your mother doesn't know."

She looked up to find fat, hot tears rolling down Cat's cheeks.

She signaled Inaya with a lift of her brows.

Inaya's arm crept around Cat's shoulders.

"Come on. Let's go pay our respects at the house, then we can meet up at Cyrine's."

Inaya conferred with Seif, who'd waited by the grave before following Cat and Areesha.

It was late in the day by the time they were able to meet. David had taken the boys home, and Cat seemed disinclined to leave. She lingered at Mirembe's until the gathering was over and helped clean up after the repast put together by Mirembe's friends.

Inaya drove them both to Cyrine's, where they were greeted like long-lost friends, though they often stopped by to visit the Marhaba café. Cyrine took one look at their faces and judged that they were overdue for Mayan hot chocolate and dessert. No one disagreed.

They talked over the case in a desultory manner.

"I didn't know the service would be so joyous," Inaya observed. "Like a celebration."

"Homegoing," Areesha explained. "It's a reason to celebrate when you return to the Lord. It's how we make sense of our collective grief."

Cat wasn't listening. Inaya prodded her gently. "When is Mateo's funeral?"

"Hm? Oh, we don't know yet. They're ready to bring him home, but there's some resistance by the DTF." Cat examined her hands, toying with her ring.

"To do with the bullet is my guess," Inaya said. "That doesn't explain why you look like someone ran over your dog."

Cat stared at her, bewildered. "I don't have a dog." Her sob caught them by surprise. "I don't have a husband either."

The whole story tumbled out, and as Areesha listened, she found herself growing angrier and angrier at Emiliano. If anyone had the right to distrust the cops, she did. She'd put in her time in the trenches, she'd tallied up the losses. She didn't know Cat or Inaya as well as they knew each other, but their unexpected sensitivity in handling a case involving the disappearance of two Black girls had won her over. On a personal level, she'd grown to like them, and as they were getting closer, and more involved in each other's lives, she began to appreciate the bonds of solidarity that bound them.

Where the hell did Emiliano get off? Why was he sitting in judgment on his wife? David would give up the world to fight in her corner, why had Emiliano made this about his ego?

She didn't speak a word of this out loud. Spouses fought. It was a healthy part of marriage, particularly when both parties were strong and independent. But spouses also reconciled, and friends remembered your criticism once everything was sunny again.

She listened, she commiserated, she offered suggestions from her own experience.

Inaya was a person of deep faith, so her advice ran along those veins. She asked for God to grant patience to Catalina, and to offer wisdom to the stubborn man Cat was devoted to.

"Marriages can't be built on ultimatums," Cat said sadly.

Their dessert came and they fell on the offerings as if they hadn't eaten all week.

"Listen," Inaya said when they'd polished off their food. "I have this crazy thing I do."

Showing signs of revival, Cat raised both brows. "You mean the rose garden?"

"Yes! Isn't this a perfect opportunity?"

Areesha smiled as Cat smacked Inaya's shoulder. "No!"

"Spill. What about this rose garden?"

Inaya grinned at Areesha, dipping her spoon in the mound of whipped cream that topped her hot chocolate.

"Well, sometimes when people make me crazy or I think they've done me wrong, I bury them in my rose garden—metaphorically speaking." She waved her spoon in the air. "I take on candidates that my sisters and friends suggest should be buried too."

On a day when she thought she couldn't even smile, Areesha laughed out loud.

"Who's in this garden, ladies?"

"Sheriff Grant," Cat supplied.

"Naturally. Who else?"

"Seif but I excavated him recently, though he might end up there again."

Seif and Inaya's working relationship had been fractious from the start.

"Some guy who's been bothering my sister Nadia," Inaya went on. "John Broda, my nemesis. Some random men my mother thought I should marry." With a glimmer of mischief, she assured Cat, "There's space for Emiliano under the Honky Tonk Blues."

Cat let out a watery chuckle. "I'm not joking, Reesh. The Honky Tonks are the roses Inaya planted in her imaginary garden."

Inaya giggled. It couldn't be described as anything else. "I buried these people for a reason. I figured I'd be happy when I did, and country music makes me happy."

"You two are trouble," Areesha chided them.

Cat snorted through her whipped cream, and all three women laughed.

When the merriment died down, Cat said, "Thanks, I needed that. Things will settle at home, I have to give it time."

Inaya wasn't satisfied with that. "Well, if you're not going the rose garden route, at the very least, give Emiliano the *Lysistrata* treatment."

"The silent treatment, you mean?"

"No, Cat. The no-sex treatment. Drastic measures are called for here."

Catalina sighed. "I'm afraid he wouldn't even notice."

Areesha's phone pinged. Cat and Inaya wandered over to chat with Cyrine. She frowned at the unknown number, and when she opened up the text message, a video began to load.

It was from Raze's perspective at the funeral. She focused on her own face before she captured the departure of the mourners from the grave site, including the police officers. Then the camera panned around to the trees in the background. In the far distance between a pair of oak trees, the hazy outline of a man and woman could be seen. They were huddled together under a black umbrella that further hampered visibility. Raze zoomed in with her phone.

The couple in the distance was white; an older woman with frizzled hair was sobbing into the man's shoulder. His meaty hand patted her back, and Raze set the lens to maximum zoom, zeroing in on the man's features, pale and puffy and white.

Areesha couldn't tell who it was. His head was bent to console the woman, and she wondered who else mourned Duante. Who knew him well enough for such a display of grief?

As if someone had warned him, the man's head came up. He looked straight at the lens.

And his full lips curled.

33

The lieutenant had given them the rest of the weekend off. Rested and refreshed, Jaime was raring to go. Someone had dumped a couple of boxes of LaMar's on the center of the desk in the conference room, and Jaime had ordered coffee in for everyone on the team. The morning was off to a fine start, not least because Cat had told him she thought she'd found Altagracia. Luna Clyde. His relief that she was unharmed was enormous, and he remained in awe of her courage. Cat brought them all up to speed on Luna's warning about a joint protest. Seif motioned to him.

Jaime set up his computer. He'd studied the videos from the DTF raid exhaustively, and he'd put together an edit that compiled the recordings from eight different body cams. He'd also added graphics pinning each officer's name to his body cam, and he then compiled a simulation at the end that plotted the officers' positions on a map. There were four cops unaccounted for out of the twelve seconded to the DTF, but none of them were Maddy Hicks or Kelly Broda, who'd both had their cameras on.

His reel ran the footage four times, twice with sound on, twice with sound off, and then the simulation, first in real time, then in slo-mo, and finally, second by second. He could tell the team where each of the eight cops had been positioned when the shot went off, but even with the full ballistic report in from Dr. Stanger, he couldn't tell them exactly where the shooter had stood. He explained the working parameters, then pressed play without further comment. They needed to make up their own minds about what had happened that night.

The team watched with total focus. The doors of Mile High Weed burst open and bodies tumbled out. DTF officers followed in hot pursuit. The cops waiting outside joined the chase. PepperBalls detonated in the chaos, followed by the explosive sound of flash-bangs. The light from streetlamps was muzzy under the haze of smoke. Shouts and cries sounded, running footsteps, voices calling out, the static of a cop's radio. The chaos ratcheted up by several degrees when patrons spilled from the club up the street as the concert at The Black Door ended. Civilians began to mingle with the cops involved in the chase.

Two minutes into the hunt, a single shot rang out.

The detectives jumped at the sound. Four officers had chased suspects down the opposite end of the street. Their cameras tracked their route far from the alley where Mateo Ruiz had been shot around the corner of the dispensary. Two were across the street, one facing the dispensary, the other facing away. The first of these two belonged to an officer named Singleton. His body twisted as the shot was fired, the camera swinging from where he was tackling a suspect to the sound of the shot. Close to the alley but not down it. From his body-cam footage, it was clear that the shot had been fired from somewhere near the dispensary.

There was an instant of total silence after; then the noise surged back as a dozen different voices called out questions. Cops doubled back toward the sound of the shot. Singleton's camera captured the sight of senior officers locking down the dispensary, while he himself ran to the alley, crying out, "Oh God, oh God."

His was one of three cameras to focus on the body on the ground. It captured the sight of two cops—Maddy Hicks and Kelly Broda—bent over the body. Ruiz had fallen forward, his arms thrown out in front of him, one leg curled up at the knee. He was lying on his stomach, and besides Singleton's, two other voices could be heard.

Madeleine Hicks, trying to stop Broda from interfering with the body. And Broda's tortured response, as he cried, "Maddy, Maddy." He fought off his partner, and could be heard saying, "God, we have to help him!"

Both Hicks and Broda turned around as Singleton entered the alley.

"Who fired? Who fired?" He sounded hysterical.

Maddy Hicks gathered herself. "We thought one of you did." She stood up, her head turning this way and that, as she searched the alley in the direction Singleton had appeared from. "We were closest, we got here first." A senior officer appeared and the body cam went off.

Now the reel Jaime had compiled switched to Madeleine's body cam. She was stationed across the street from the dispensary, her camera aimed at the double doors. She angled her body so that she was looking up the street in the direction of partygoers spilling from the club.

"Shit," she said into her radio. "Sir, we've got trouble. Civilians in the mix. Kell, you see them? Should we set up a cordon?"

Calm and controlled, Kelly urged her to pull back. He seconded the warning to the DTF captain, asking for confirmation on the cordon.

A garbled voice shouted into his radio, and Kelly could be heard to say, "Affirmative."

Maddy's body cam swung back—not to the dispensary but to Kelly Broda, stationed ten yards away on the same side of the street.

"Go, go, go," he mimed, pointing to the club.

Maddy turned again. For a few minutes, nothing could be seen through the smoke and the crowd, the only sound that of Maddy's heavy breathing and her running footsteps. Then the shot rang out. This time the sound was multiplied by ten, the shooter nearby in the shadows. The camera pointed down, then shifted to the alley. Pounding footsteps sounded. They reached the utter dark of the alley. "Maddy, Maddy," came the cry, and the camera stopped on a fallen Ruiz, then jerked around to Singleton. Apart from that first brief interchange outside the dispensary, Broda didn't appear again on camera. Again the body cam cut off when the senior officer appeared. All Jaime could tell was that the senior officer wasn't the member of the Patriots whom Detective Rahman had questioned.

The last part of the reel comprised Kelly Broda's footage. His body cam was rock steady, its focus on the dispensary doors. Even when Maddy could be heard warning him about the club, the camera remained on the doors of the dispensary.

His camera picked up Maddy saying, "Kell, watch out for the club!"

Only then did his body shift, angling in such a way that he could cover the door and the sight of patrons exiting the club. The camera veered between them, his footsteps giving chase before jerking to a stop when he cried, "What the fuck?" Shock sounded in his voice.

His hand covered the camera, the audio and video muffled. For moments that stretched out, there was darkness. The shot rang out through the smoke, so loud that it suggested the shooter's position. Broda's camera began to work again, the footage jumpy and unclear until he was crouched beside Ruiz's body, fighting with his partner, and screaming, "Maddy, Maddy!"

The reel dwindled down to slo-mo, then the freeze-frame version, ending on the graphic that time-coded the officers' positions at the moment the shot rang out.

Seif turned the lights back up.

"Where does it look like that shot came from? My best guess is from Broda."

No one disputed his take. Kelly Broda's camera had gone dark at the critical moment. If that didn't convince them, the gunshot had been excruciatingly close. Unless another officer had been positioned behind Kelly, the likeliest explanation was that Broda had fired that shot.

"Maybe he thought the Patriots would keep the footage from coming out," Cat offered.

"And then his partner could claim the shot came from somewhere else," Jaime suggested. "Madeleine Hicks lied too, and now we know why. She was covering for him. But I don't get why Broda would shoot that kid. If Broda refused to join the Patriots like Oliver Scott said, it couldn't have been an initiation."

Seif took over the meeting. "Let's see if we can figure that out." He'd put each member of his team on something different. He'd assigned Jaime the body-cam footage, and asked him to follow up on the Patriots, fleshing out the information West and Inaya had gathered during their interrogation of Oliver Scott. He'd put Inaya on suspects who might have set Duante Young up the night he'd been shot, keeping her away from the Brodas—not that that had always worked. And he'd asked Cat to do a deeper dive into Broda's connection to the club, while Seif himself had done some checking into Younas Medrano.

"Up first, Mateo Ruiz. Then we'll get to Duante Young. Catalina, you have the floor."

The pinched look of distress that had been on her face of late perturbed him. Something was up with Catalina; he'd get to the bottom of it once they'd dealt with Young and Ruiz.

She spoke with less energy than usual but made up for that with her clarity.

"I took Kelly Broda's picture back to the club and showed it to Finn Parker and the manager there. The manager confirms the nights he was there, and each entry coincides with a death metal night, just as Kelly claimed. Neither the manager nor Finn were able to confirm that Kelly Broda was involved with Mateo. The club was too dark and too crowded. Also, Kelly was right about something else. He wasn't the only white male on the club's membership. I saw a few myself when I stopped by to follow up."

Seif made notes on the whiteboard. "So Broda could be telling the truth. About himself at least. That leaves us with two problems: The first is Broda's motive. The other is the question of who was with Mateo at the club, if it *wasn't* Broda. Who might have been involved in a lovers' quarrel with him, and if by some remote chance Broda *didn't* fire that shot, why would they implicate him? We'll need to get a warrant for that membership list."

Catalina raised her head. "If we're still looking at other suspects, I should point out that I didn't get a good vibe from Vicente—he was jealous of Mateo. It could be he was angry at his cousin for acting like the golden child when he was covering up the truth about who he was."

Seif took a moment to think this over. "That opens up a Pandora's box of questions, Catalina. Would jealousy alone have led Vicente to murder? What did he have to gain from Mateo's death, apart from an end to the comparisons between himself and Ruiz? Why involve Kelly Broda? And how would he have gotten access to Kelly Broda's gun?" He glanced at Cat. "Does Vicente have an alibi?"

Catalina shook her head. "He said he was working the night shift at his job. They confirm that Vicente was on call, but it's an eight-hour shift and he only brought in two cars."

"Did you track the plates on his truck?"

"I have a tech on it, but apart from speed cameras, it will be hard to confirm either way."

Jaime raised his hand. "They have to enter mileage figures at those companies. We could check how far Vicente drove that night—see if the numbers add up."

"Do that," Seif agreed. "But tell me this, Catalina—could Vicente have been threatening Mateo with exposure? Would Mateo's sexuality be considered a scandal?"

Catalina sighed. "For the older generation, perhaps. The world is changing, sir. We're all changing with it, and the young are more accepting than their parents."

Seif noted that Inaya seemed as concerned about Catalina as he was. Her expression could distract him from the matter at hand.

"By that logic, Antonio Ruiz was a more likely candidate to have harmed his son, but again, we're ignoring the gun. Right?" His dark eyes grilled Inaya.

"Antonio also said there was nothing about Mateo that wasn't to his credit," she admitted.

"Do you think he knew about this?"

He knew she didn't like giving in, but she wasn't his best detective for nothing. "I'm quite certain he knew, as did Mateo's mother. She grieved the fact that her son was gay, and maybe Antonio did too. But they weren't ashamed of him, and I don't know if they could have harmed him. Cat could tell you more."

But Cat was listless and had nothing more to add, so Seif focused on Inaya.

"We'll dig into those angles, but let's get back to the obvious first, From the body-cam footage, it's clear that Madeleine Hicks pointed out the club to Broda. Mateo was there that night. If they were involved, Broda might have seen him and gotten distracted. There's a period where his video is off but we can hear his footsteps. He could have cornered Mateo in that alley. The gun went off so close at hand it nearly deafened us. Then we see Hicks trying to pull Broda off Mateo's body—a crime of passion, maybe, that he instantly regretted."

Inaya came to the whiteboard and made a note of her own, taking the marker from his hand. She looked up into his eyes at close quarters and he felt himself falling through air.

"There's a flaw in your theory," she said. He focused on her lips, and a smile came into her eyes. "Uh, Lieutenant?"

"What?"

He heard a weak chuckle from Catalina. It took him a moment to gain the presence of mind to look away.

"If it *was* a crime of passion, why was Kelly carrying that revolver? And if it wasn't Kelly, who else had access to that revolver? What about Younas Medrano?"

Goddammit, she had him. She pulled the rug out from under him like no one else could.

"I asked SWAT about Younas. He was on roster that night. They also said it was a quiet night, and their officers take breaks when nothing is going down. They can't confirm his specific hours, one way or another."

"So he could be involved, we'd just have to dig to prove it," Jaime said.

Seif had to agree, but they had more ground to cover. He pointed to Catalina.

"This is your case now. Talk to Antonio Ruiz. Find out about Mateo and Broda—find out if they were involved, and whether they had a reason to fall out. Maybe Mateo broke up with Broda and Broda couldn't handle the rejection on top of everything else. Or maybe Mateo was threatening to out him. If he was being hassled by the Patriots for not falling in line with their harassment of minorities, exposing his sexuality would serve him up to the Patriots. No matter how you cut it, Broda had plenty of reason to keep Mateo quiet. If he knew Mateo was playing at the club that night, the raid would have given him excellent cover, especially as he knew Madeleine would cover for him."

He turned to Inaya. "Love or money. It always comes down to one of those two motives. Whether we're talking about Younas Medrano or Kelly Broda."

Something flickered in her eyes. "You're right," she whispered.

"Say that again." His smile mocked her for the benefit of the others, but he felt a swift lick of concern. "What is it?"

She searched over the whiteboard, her gaze coming to rest on the picture of Duante.

"I don't know. It was there, then it slipped away."

"Sir?" Catalina put up her hand, her eyelids drooping. She needed to be excused so she could go home and rest. She could follow through on her assignment later. "What about the missing body cams?"

Did she think Broda *hadn't* deliberately masked his actions? That someone had been standing behind him—Medrano or someone else whom everyone had missed?

"Catalina—"

"There were twelve officers with the DTF that night. We're missing the recordings from four of those cameras."

Shit. Catalina was right.

Jaime's hand shot up eagerly.

"I have their names. I think they might be affiliated with the Patriots."

Good. Another lead. And the Patriots would have ample reason to cast the blame on Kelly Broda, while clearing themselves. "Check that with West, and if necessary, get him to chase up Oliver Scott, though that's not my preferred route."

If the Patriots became a real power, the Community Response Unit would move up their list of targets, and Seif couldn't allow that. He'd spoken to Jacob Brandt about expanding his investigation into Sheriff Grant to take on the Patriots as well.

"You want to come home to those brothers of yours, don't you?" Brandt had said in response. "No need for all of Denver to have you in their sights."

But at some point in the future, the Patriots would have to be rooted out. When Seif had time, he'd dig. He wouldn't place a target on Jaime's back.

He strolled over to Jaime's desk, leaned down into his face.

"You do *not* get on the Patriots' radar, that's like putting your hand in the fire. I know you want to impress me, but leave things like that to West."

Predictably, Jaime flushed. He pursed his lips. "I can handle them, sir."

Now, Seif eased up on the reins. "Hell no, you can't. I'm not even sure I could, and I have responsibilities to my family, just like you do."

He glared at Inaya. "Detective Rahman didn't exactly let me know how she planned to tackle Scott, or I'd have put the brakes on her."

"The Patriots haven't killed anyone that we know of," she said loftily.

"Let's not make you the first. Get back to West, find out if he can confirm links between those officers and the Patriots Division. And if there is footage out there, Webb, find out why the DTF held it back. That's something you can handle, and handle well."

He strode back and flipped the whiteboard around.

"Okay. Enough on Mateo Ruiz. We either have to prove Kelly Broda did it, or we have to prove that someone else had a motive to carry out the murder. Now, where are we on Duante? Let's start with you, Rahman. I want the rundown on that art contest and on whoever might have lured Duante to the scene."

He sat down and let Inaya run the show. She put two new photographs up on the whiteboard under Duante's name. One was of a girl with locs. The other was of a young man at work on a painting in a studio. He recognized both from Duante Young's funeral. Inaya identified them as Willie Reynolds and Raze, real name Rosamunde Zambezi. She went over her interviews with them, hitting on the salient details.

"Willie says he can't forgive himself for leaving Duante that night. They planned to work on the mural together and split the proceeds. He didn't strike me as a man who would set up a friend to die, even assuming he knew the cops would be on them that night. I think it's the same for Raze—she loved Duante. But she does know Blackwater Falls. She'd been there with Duante." Inaya hesitated. "Areesha vouched for them, but I have to say, she didn't seem entirely convinced. No matter what Willie and Raze said, they might have coveted the prize money. You can do a lot with fifty thousand dollars, particularly if you don't have much to begin with. We can't discount that. I also had someone look into where Raze was that night. Her phone was off and no one can confirm her whereabouts."

Seif looked up. "I agree, we should follow that up. I'll need a favor from Grant."

Inaya frowned at him. "What kind of favor?"

"We know Willie was with Duante the night he was killed. We don't know where Raze was, and we also don't know where she was on the nights the vandalism took place."

Inaya followed his train of thought. "That suggests the kind of preparation you put into a long con. If they set Duante up to eliminate the competition."

"He did win the first two prizes." Seif flicked a hand at Jaime. "Check for their prints on those bins. The bins should still be in evidence."

Still miffed about Grant, Inaya said, "Unless Grant had some reason to release them. Like getting Harry Cooper off."

"We *know* Harry shot Duante," Seif chided her. "What we don't know is if someone else made sure Duante would run afoul of the police. Is there anything else on these two?"

"No, but there's been a development. Maybe one that widens the field." She picked up her phone from her desk and pressed a button on it. Each of their phones pinged. "Take a look at this video Raze sent Areesha. She was filming people at the grave. This is at the three-minute mark."

Seif watched with some discomfort as the video captured him in an unguarded moment gazing at Inaya when he should have been watching the crowd.

He heard Cat's murmur of surprise and realized he'd missed it, lost in his own worries. He quickly replayed the video. Raze had zoomed out to the perimeter as the rain came down in a drizzle. A man and a woman could be spotted standing beneath a pair of trees. The man was tall and broad, and he was comforting the woman who huddled under his arm. Raze zoomed in on the faces of the pair. With the rain and the zoom distortion, the picture wasn't clear.

The man's face was round and indistinct, but what was unmistakable was the chilling smile on his lips. He hadn't come there to grieve like the other mourners.

No, he'd come to see Duante buried, cold and dead in the ground.

Seif's gaze pinpointed Jaime. "Get that video over to tech and see if they can clean it up."

Inaya wrote a name on the board. He found he couldn't disagree.

The man hiding in the distance could well be Sheriff Grant.

He was about to dismiss them when Inaya wandered to his side. She didn't approach him with her usual bulldog tenacity; she looked tentative, trying to read his eyes. He deliberately closed off any sign of weakness. He didn't want to be played.

As usual, he underestimated his detective. She might have been worried about his reaction, but she was up-front about what she'd come to ask.

"I know you'd rather Cat dealt with the Ruiz family, but we're the leads on Kelly and Madeleine. We should be the ones to see this through. We don't have to tell John."

He bent his head a little to keep his face out of view. His instinctive reaction was to shoot her down. But hadn't Mikhail accused him of refusing to consider any point of view except his own? And how Inaya wanted to proceed wasn't out of line. With another detective, he wouldn't have thought about it twice.

He looked up, surprised to see a gentle expression on her face, as if she could read his mind. Hell. Maybe she could. They talked strategy for several minutes, relying on their instincts about the body-cam footage and not just the theories they'd floated with the team. They'd check out every angle, but they now had a definite suspicion.

"You're not going to Broda's house."

Inaya waited him out. He sighed and she began to smile.

"After we've checked out other leads, we'll be better prepared for Broda. There's no use pinning him down until we do."

"And I'll be on that interview?"

Her face was soft with entreaty, and like a sucker, he went down.

34

Catalina went home. She couldn't leave things with Emiliano the way they were. She knew he had a break in his schedule this afternoon between seeing clients. She would corner him and insist they talk this out. If need be, she would swallow her pride, her determination to do things her way. She would reduce her hours at the police, take up NGO work again at least two days a week. She would refuse late-night assignments—she knew Seif was desperate to keep her. Either because it made sense to have a Latina on their unit, or because he valued her insights as a profiler, or because he was playing some game of his own. She sighed. Maybe he just thought she was good at what she did and, unlike Emiliano, saw her role as a valuable one.

Seif and Emiliano had never met, and she didn't want them to. Seif would size up her husband with one swift look and see that ego had overtaken his common sense, while Emiliano would dismiss Seif as a man who had betrayed his heritage.

The house was quiet but she could hear Emiliano moving around upstairs. She would ask him to go with her to speak to the Ruiz family. His family might be able to confirm that Mateo and Kelly had been in a relationship, and whether Mateo had put pressure on Kelly to make that relationship public. She would frame the discussion with care, making sure Emiliano understood that this was about getting justice for Mateo. She would be open with him as well, about their conclusion that Kelly had fired the shot that killed Mateo, despite his denials. Perhaps a softening on her side would help Emil climb down from the position he had taken.

She set her purse on the table and leaned in to the mirror for a closer look at herself. Was she still the Catalina who had taken on ICE agents in that deadly conflict at the border? The Cat who would not allow any member of law enforcement to put their hands on a woman or child? Who would fight to the death instead? Could Emiliano penalize her for the incident that had had such catastrophic results, and then be angry at her for giving up on the fight? Was he being fair to her? Was there any way to change his mind?

Sighing, she released her hair from her ponytail and brushed the bouncy curls into order. Reaching into her bag, she found her cherry lipstick and applied it to her mouth. She also added a touch of topaz eyeliner to bring out the flecks in her eyes. She had a change of clothes in the laundry room. Her dry cleaning had been delivered, and she slipped into a cheetah-print sundress that was a little tight around the waist but that plumped up her breasts invitingly. She arranged a lock of hair so that it fell into her cleavage.

That was it. That was the best she could do.

No, wait. She had a pair of golden sandals in the closet in the hall. She slipped those on, spritzed her wrists and her cleavage with her Narciso perfume. She felt a little foolish doing it, but she needed all her weapons to win Emiliano back. She was moving up the stairs to their bedroom when she heard him call out.

Her skin went cold. God, was something wrong? He'd been under so much stress, and now fighting with her—was he having a heart attack?

The rough sound came again. Overcoming her panic, she flung the bedroom door open. At first, she couldn't comprehend the sight that met her eyes. Emiliano was on the bed, propped up by a stack of pillows. He was naked, his handsome face gleaming with sweat.

His partner was naked too; she was kissing her way up his body, her nails raking his skin.

Cat's gasp of horror was audible. Emiliano's eyes shot open, his face a dark red. He let out a weak groan, his hands going to Altagracia's waist. He lifted her off his body and set her aside, covering her with the sheet. He was wearing his boxers.

Cat's lips were numb, her hands and feet like ice. She couldn't speak, couldn't move.

The woman raised her head and Cat realized after a heart-stopping moment that it *wasn't* Altagracia, and some secret part of Cat gasped in relief at the thought. The woman in their bed worked at We Rise Together. Cat cast about for her name. Was it Maria or Ximena or . . . no, no, it was Eva. Beautiful, sleek Eva with her tiger eyes and cruel, complacent smile. The smile that mocked Cat's efforts at making herself look nice, her cherry lipstick a wound across her mouth.

"Cat, *mi amor,* I can explain—" Emil's voice resounded with terror.

Cat spoke with icy calm. "Perhaps first you could ask Eva to leave our bed."

She turned away as the two conspirators hurriedly found their clothing.

"I will call you," Eva said to Emil as she brushed past Cat.

Cat grasped her arm in a steely hold. "Call my husband again and I will find a reason to arrest you." She stared into Eva's eyes, willing her to see that nothing would make her back down. "And find yourself another job."

Eva looked at her with pity.

"That won't keep your husband from my bed."

Cat discounted Emiliano's agonized protests. "No?" She arched a brow. "If he still wants you, I'll make you a present of him. Now, get out of my house."

They ignored the crash of the front door, staring at each other in a silence fraught with pain. Emiliano's guilt and the horror of Catalina's loss, her love and trust severed in an instant.

"How long?" she asked.

He didn't pretend not to understand. "I swear to you, this has never happened before! After the other night, I needed someone to turn to—someone with time for me. Eva thinks like me, she is committed to the work. I didn't plan it, *mi vida*. It happened, but it *didn't* happen."

Cat's heart was beating so hard in her chest, she couldn't make sense of his words. She didn't know which of those statements to settle on, so she grasped at the one that mattered least.

"*She's* committed to the work? *I* built We Rise Together, *I* brought you on board. Now suddenly, you are the hero, while I've become the enemy." She forced herself to go on. "You tell yourself these lies to justify reaching for her after I have given you my life."

"What life?" he cried in desperation. "I wanted our child, and your recklessness killed it."

Cat weathered the blow by wiping her lipstick off on her wrist, a crimson gash against her skin. She absorbed the words, wondered how the man who loved her could stoop to that accusation when he was fully aware of the truth.

"I didn't have an abortion, Emiliano, I was assaulted in a detainment facility while you were out at dinner. You didn't want to know. You treated our child like he was disposable, like he could easily be exchanged for another when I was the one to feel his life bleed from my body. He was a *person* to me. No one could take his place."

"We could have tried again! You had no right to decide the issue for us both!"

"I couldn't!" Despite herself, her voice rose. "Not while I was working in the field exposed to the same danger! And yet you want to push me back there without once stopping to consider why I had to leave. I left the work for him," she said sadly. "So I could mourn my Sebastián. That doesn't mean the door was closed for good. I just needed time."

Emiliano sat down on the corner of the bed. He was wearing only his trousers, his chest strong and muscular, marked by another woman's hands.

"I came up here to make my peace with you, to give you the concessions you want. To change myself so you could have your sweetheart again. And what did you do, *mi amor*? What was your contribution to helping us find our way?" Cat's eyes filled with tears. "You have betrayed me in every possible way."

He rubbed the back of his head, then tucked his chin into his neck, a weight descending on his shoulders.

"I am only a man, and I have been alone for so long." He sank to his knees on the floor, her tears mirrored in his eyes. "I have no right to ask for forgiveness, but I swear to you it will never happen again. You are my life, Catalina. Please don't throw us away!"

An hour ago, she would have been thrilled to hear him pleading for another chance. Now all she could see was Eva taking her husband in their bed.

She dropped to her knees before him, letting the tears fall, letting herself cry out her anguish at her loss. First Sebastián, now Emiliano. She'd never been so alone.

His arms gathered her close. "You stopped me from doing something I'll always regret." He bent his head to her ear. "Even if you forgive me, I will never forgive myself."

She could demand he accept her as she was now, if she chose to believe him. If it didn't matter that he wasn't quite guilty of the final betrayal. With the trained eye of a detective, she had noticed the unopened condom on the bedside table, and the fact that he was still in his boxers. Perhaps he was telling her the truth. Perhaps his regret was sincere. Perhaps now that he was losing her, he had finally opened his eyes.

He didn't smell of Eva's perfume, so she let him hold her, and all the while her thoughts burned and her stomach roiled. She wanted to throw up. She wanted to give up, but she would never let him go. Not her childhood playmate, not the boy who had courted her so sweetly, not the man who had stood beside her until she had joined the police.

She couldn't forgive him.

Yet she couldn't face life without him.

He continued to nuzzle her ear, holding her tightly to his chest, murmuring apologies strewn with love words, offering the promise of a full confession at their church.

"Give me another chance," he begged her. And then more earthily, he added, "A chance to dig my head out of my ass."

She didn't want to laugh but she did, her lips pressing against his chest.

He tilted her face to his, sealing his apology with a kiss. She let him kiss her though she was repulsed by the thought that he'd just been kissing Eva.

She drew away, wiping the tears from her face with the back of her hand. "It's too soon. I can't decide this now." A spark of terror made her add, "*We* can't decide this now."

He nodded. He rose to his feet, pulling her up with him.

"But you won't leave me? You won't throw me out?"

"I came here to ask you to come with me to talk to Antonio and Ana Sofia. I will go alone, now." She waited for his anger to flare. He caught her hands with his own, turned them up and kissed both palms.

"Take the time you need," he said with such sweetness that Cat wanted to cry. "Just come home to me, *mi amor*. Promise me you will."

She thought about it. Wondered where she could go instead. Maybe to

Inaya, maybe to Seif. That spectacular house of his must have a guest room or two.

She couldn't be weak now. Couldn't give in to him when she'd barely processed the pain.

"I can't promise you anything right now." Her gaze flicked past him to the bed. "Wash yourself and burn those sheets. And remove Eva from my organization. Do it right away, and we can talk more later. Let the matter go and you'll be letting me go."

"Never. I will never let you go, Catalina. I swear this on my life."

His promise was an hour too late.

The scene was still on her mind when she found herself at Mateo's. His parents welcomed her in, and she gave them what she could about the investigation, promising them that a resolution was near, but she needed to ask them some questions—sensitive questions, did they understand?

With a cry, Ana Sofia fled the room. That left Antonio with his grief-stricken face and his proud Mexican bearing. Cat's careful warning hadn't dented that pride. He wasn't ashamed of anything about his son, Mateo *was* gay, that was simply who he was. He'd known it since Mateo was a child. Teo didn't advertise his identity, but he didn't hide it, either, except out of his concern for his mother's feelings.

"Ana Sofia couldn't accept it?"

Antonio's callused hand touched the bowl of pink carnations on the table. "God tells her it is wrong, so it is wrong. But Mateo is her boy, her pride, the deepest joy of her heart, she could never deny him. The struggle was hers, and it was made more difficult by our families. You understand this." His gaze met hers, neither defiant nor boastful, but with the self-assurance of a man whose integrity couldn't be impeached.

Catalina did understand. This man hadn't killed his son because he'd discovered he was gay. His grief wasn't because the burden of his actions was intolerable. His boy was his boy, his love for him wasn't conditional.

"What about the kids in the family or Mateo's friends? Did they know?"

"The older cousins knew," Antonio admitted. "They tried to bully him but Teo's heart was so big, he could easily disarm them. It was hard for anyone to be cruel to my boy. He wouldn't accept it. He would push and push until you saw him as he was."

"Was the bullying recent? Or serious? I know Vicente resented him."

A surprising look of compassion eased the stark pain that had overwritten Antonio's features. "It isn't easy to be the one who is left behind, the one who doesn't chase his dreams." He selected a carnation and passed it to Catalina. She broke off the stem to tuck it behind her ear.

"Maybe Vicente's dreams were simpler to achieve."

"Maybe. No one thinks less of him. There is dignity in doing your best. That's how I think of Vicente." He grasped the essence of her question, because he added, "No matter his complaints, it didn't affect Vicente's love for Mateo. He loved him like we all loved him." Antonio pressed a hand to his heart. "Right down to the bone. He grieves like we all grieve."

Antonio's instinctive sympathy for Vicente made her respect him more. This man was grounded, decent, sure of his place in the world. He carried himself with a dignity that respected the dignity of others. He wasn't looking to point fingers, though perhaps he didn't know Vicente as well as he thought he did. For now, he trusted her to find justice for his son. Which made the questions she had yet to ask him even more difficult.

"Antonio, do you know if your son was involved with anyone? Could he have been in love? He seems like he might have been a romantic. I understand that he often played his own music at the club on Colfax."

"We all like to have fun when we are young," he answered gravely. "I took his mother to many a dance when I was in my prime. Chaperoned, of course." A small smile edged his lips. "Much to my dismay. My beautiful Ana Sofia is an endless temptation."

Catalina's heart hurt at the proof of such devotion. Antonio and Ana Sofia had weathered a lifetime together, one without betrayal from the steadiness of the man who spoke to her with such honesty, even when tempered by grief.

"There *was* someone," he added. "Mateo was happy, buoyant. He was busy at college but he came home so often—every weekend. That wasn't just for us," he said wryly. "I know when a boy is in love. He wrote new songs on his guitar. He even made a recording, but he played the songs for us live. They were so deep with meaning, they touched the heart. Even his mother's."

"Ana Sofia listened to him play the songs for his lover?"

Antonio smiled at her, remembering. "She pretended Teo was in love with a girl. She handled it better that way, and my son with his angel's heart, was very patient with his mother. He didn't let it hurt him, you know how we feel about our mothers. We would do anything for them, but that part of himself couldn't be changed, so he told her he was God's child too."

Cat gazed unseeingly at the portrait of Mateo in the corner.

"Do you believe that, Antonio?"

"It's true," he said without evasion. "If anyone was a child of God, it was my son."

Her eyes swollen and red from weeping, Ana Sofia reentered the room. She was holding a CD, which she placed near Cat.

"I should have given him my blessing."

Cat picked up the CD. She would listen to it later, but for now she examined the cover.

Mateo posed with a decidedly *un*angelic look in his eyes, sultry and seductive, a touch of mischief in his smile. He was flirting with whoever had taken the picture. She opened the plastic case to see if there was a photo credit or any liner notes.

A small paper inset listed the names of the songs, love songs, one and all, a few with suggestive titles, a handful in Spanish. She peered at the minuscule print on the bottom. There was no photo credit but it wasn't needed. The album was dedicated to Kelly Broda. *My soul, my savior, my life.*

35

It took another two days before they were ready to bring in Kelly and Madeleine. During that time, they'd followed up every lead, received a report from Grant on the vandalism in Blackwater, delved into the Patriots, and clarified several important questions. Now Inaya and Seif stood behind the glass partition watching Kelly and Madeleine in the interview room. Neither had requested the presence of a lawyer, and it seemed neither one had tipped off John Broda that they'd been asked to attend an interview at DPD headquarters.

Out of courtesy, Seif had informed his contact at the Drug Task Force. They hadn't put up much of a fight, not that they could when the body-cam footage raised so many questions.

Seif considered the suspects. Their body language was strange for two partners and friends. Kelly's chair was angled away, Maddy staring at his back with a plea in her eyes. They didn't speak, probably because they knew they'd be overheard, but the absence of an attorney puzzled Inaya—Kelly couldn't possibly think she was acting for him. He should have called in outside help. At the very least, he should have notified his father, who would swiftly have removed Inaya from the interview.

"Let's go."

She followed Seif's lead, seating herself across from Maddy Hicks, while Seif stood behind her, leaning against the wall. They'd made the decision to confront Maddy and Kelly together. Seif would observe Kelly while Inaya focused on Maddy. They had discussed their insights from the body cams, and from Cat's call bringing them up to date, and agreed on an interview strategy. Inaya now raised their first question with Madeleine.

"How long have you known that your partner is gay?"

Maddy's head flew up. "Kell's not gay. He told you that himself."

"Really?" Inaya slid a CD across the interview table. Cat had brought it to the station. "Could you read the dedication for me?"

Maddy squinted at the tiny print, her lips mouthing the words.

For Kelly. My soul, my savior, my life. Your Matty.

She floundered for a moment; then a thought came to her, and she said, "So maybe the kid had a crush. Kell's not gay, he's a cop."

Inaya's eyebrows went up. She couldn't quite believe in Maddy's supposed naivete.

"And cops can't be gay?"

Maddy pushed the CD back at her. She slouched in her chair. "Not much fun for them if they are," she mumbled into her chest. "If you're gay, you're not macho, and cops pride themselves on their masculinity."

Inaya left Maddy's definition of masculinity alone.

"It sounds like you know why your partner might have been targeted by the Patriots."

"No—"

"Oliver Scott told us about you. He admires you. He says the Patriots recruited you. Did you go along with them so they'd leave your partner alone? Kelly would've been easy prey."

Kelly buried his head in his arms.

Maddy's teeth worried her lip. "Scott's a good cop. We're friends, that's all."

Seif tipped his head at Inaya and she went in for the kill. "So it wasn't an initiation into the Patriots? They didn't ask you to target Mateo to get Kelly to fall in line? You knew about the gun." Inaya paused, giving Maddy just enough time to see the trap. "You were at his house all the time with your boyfriend, but you don't remember the gun?"

Maddy's eyes were working.

Seif changed position to stand behind Madeleine, a maneuver designed to catch her off guard. She didn't even glance at him. Her hand clutched Kelly's elbow. His head stayed buried in his arms. He gave no appearance of listening to their interrogation.

"That's a nice shed the two of you share on your property," Seif observed. "I noticed it was padlocked. My officers are executing a warrant to search that shed as we speak."

Kelly slowly raised his head. "Why?"

Inaya took over again. "We're wondering what you keep there, what kind of hobbies you indulge in when you have a little time."

Kelly's body went solid. Maddy patted his arm. He flinched from her touch.

"Everyone has hobbies," Maddy said. "Why do you need to search his shed?"

Seif zeroed in on Madeleine again, this time off to one side. "The question is what are *your* hobbies, Madeleine? Did Oliver Scott tell you that the only way you'd get your partner under the protection of the Patriots was if you carried out the equivalent of a drive-by?"

He braced both hands on the table, capturing her gaze.

"Did you get to choose your own target or did they choose it for you?"

"I am not a Patriot." The muscle in her jaw flickered. "I would never allow them to use me against Kell. No one gets between us."

It was the admission they were waiting for, a way to get to Kelly.

"Mateo Ruiz did." Inaya tapped the CD.

Her control frayed, Maddy snapped, "I've told you and told you—Kell *isn't* gay! Stop making him out to be something that he isn't!"

"Is that right, Kelly?" Inaya pushed the CD at him. "You lied to us before. You didn't go to that club for the music, though that was a good cover. The two of you were involved."

Kelly's fingers traced the contours of Mateo's face.

"Did you take that picture?" Inaya asked.

"Yeah." He kept his attention on the CD. "It's good, right? It captures those parts of him that he tried to hide from everyone."

"Except you."

"Except me," he agreed. "Because he loved me. Because he knew he could trust me."

Maddy jumped to attention in her chair, her posture military-straight.

"Kell, don't tell them—"

He raised the CD to his lips and kissed the picture of Mateo. "It's time to tell the truth, Maddy. I can't hold it back any longer."

Inaya leaned in on her elbows, watching them both. "Did you return his feelings?"

"Hell, yeah. Didn't you listen to the songs? He was someone special."

Beside him, Maddy was breathing so rapidly she sounded like she was having a panic attack. "Kell, no!"

Inaya ignored her. "I thought the song called 'He's Not Free to Love Me' was somewhat of a giveaway."

"Yeah?" Kelly stared at her, unflinching. "Why is that?"

"Because you weren't free, were you? You were trapped by your father's expectations. By what he wanted you to be instead of who you really are."

"Dad tried to beat it out of me. Mad could tell you—he sure as hell didn't understand what it means to be bisexual—if I was into women, I should stick to women—and he tried to pound that message into me. Not once or twice, but regularly. In the garage, where my mother couldn't see. He called me a disgrace, kicked me out of the house when I turned seventeen. He couldn't accept that his big brass balls created a son like me." He let his hand dangle from his wrist. "Limp-wristed, pansy-assed, whatever you want to call it, and believe me, I've heard it all. Here and in Chicago. He served me up to his crew when his lesson wasn't getting through." He gave her a piercing look. "I think you know Dixon and the boys. They know how to send a message."

Inaya looked down.

"Dad rode me so hard, I had to transfer to Denver. It wasn't just that I wanted to get away from him to protect myself. I didn't want to *become* him, I hate who he is as a cop."

"He followed you here for a reason." They needed to know what he thought that reason was. Broda wasn't the type to make amends, and if she was right about that, John Broda had been putting on one hell of an act.

Kelly looked askance. Whatever he'd told them, he hadn't meant to implicate his father in a crime that involved the gun John Broda had given him.

Seif followed up her line of questioning, coming away from the wall. "He kicked you out of the house at seventeen, yet he gave you the family revolver? Explain that one to me."

"I talked John into it," Maddy said, voice low. "I told him he would regret it if he didn't give Kell the gun because he would lose him for good."

"He had the gun delivered, so he wouldn't have to see me," Kelly said.

"Who suggested you bring the gun with you to Denver?"

Kelly's gaze moved from Seif to Inaya and back. "He did. That doesn't mean—"

Seif began to hammer at Kelly Broda, trying to break him down. "He knew the gun was in your house. He came here to see you. To beg for your forgiveness. Or so you made it seem. Were you trying to set your father up, as a kind of revenge? You denied being gay, you didn't mention you were bisexual, you denied knowing Mateo Ruiz, you denied being involved with him because you thought you could make use of him in your plan for revenge. Once your father followed you here, the raid gave you the perfect opportunity to take your father down."

"That doesn't make any sense! My father didn't come down here until *after* the raid. He didn't know about me and Mateo."

"I thought you wanted to tell the truth," Maddy said, unexpectedly. "Of course he did."

Kelly leapt to his feet. "What the hell are you saying, Mad? Did *you* tell my father? After you knew what he did to me?"

Seif cut him off. "Watch this. I think you'll find it interesting."

Seif played the recording through his computer, with Inaya turning up the audio. All four police officers watched those three minutes play out. The screen went dark for the critical period, then came back to life with the gunshot, the camera panning to the alley. Seconds later, Kelly was crouched over Mateo's body.

"Maddy, Maddy!" he cried.

Seif played it again.

"You killed Mateo Ruiz with the revolver because you knew the gun would implicate your father. And then you got your partner to cover for you."

They hadn't restrained Kelly or Madeleine, and now Kelly leapt for Seif's throat. He was packed with more muscle than Seif, but Seif was by far the more agile of the two. He dodged Kelly easily, pivoting on one foot to shove him up against the wall, his hands twisted behind him, Seif's knee raised high, digging into his back.

"You of all people *know* I'd never hurt Mateo," Kelly shouted.

"Shall I play the video again?" Seif returned. "Don't you want to watch yourself shooting your lover to prove what a badass you are? With big brass balls like your father? A dirty cop taking down an unprotected civilian?"

"My father had nothing to do with this!" Kelly twisted free. Seif hauled him back.

"I know he didn't." He restrained Kelly with the cuffs Inaya passed him. Then he pushed him back into his chair, bringing his head down to Kelly's level. "I know that because *you* did."

Inaya pressed play on the video again, skipping ahead to the gunshot.

Kelly's whole body jerked, his face and neck covered in perspiration.

"For God's sake, stop it! I didn't shoot Mateo—I *loved* him." Great, tearing sobs ripped through his body. Maddy jumped up to shove Seif back. Seif didn't budge an inch, so she wrapped herself around Kelly like a protective shield.

"No," she crooned to Kelly. "Don't lie to them to protect your father. Tell them who you love! Tell them why you never held on to one of your girlfriends. It wasn't about Mateo."

Inaya played the gunshot again. Kelly roared out a wild denial.

"Matty's death *destroyed* me. Mateo Ruiz was my life! I couldn't have hurt him!"

Maddy's strong fingers dug into Kelly's shoulders. Her nails scored down his arms, leaving a dark trail of red.

The gunshot sounded again, followed by Kelly's cries.

And Madeleine Hicks broke, shrieking her rage to the skies.

36

Cat joined Inaya in the room. There wasn't much left to say, but she wanted Cat's insight into Maddy, who had calmed down when Seif removed Kelly from the room.

Madeleine shrugged off their offer of legal counsel. Kelly's confession had destroyed any desire she had left to protect herself.

"Kell never loved me. He should have, but he didn't. I tried everything I could think of to get him to change his mind."

"He was in love with Mateo," Inaya pointed out. "His sexuality couldn't have come as a surprise."

"He's slept with women before," she said defiantly.

"Only with women?" It was a pointed question, and Maddy's face fell. She knew why John Broda had taken to beating his son.

"Your partner is bisexual, Maddy. He just told us that himself. You can't pretend you didn't know."

"Then why not me?" Maddy cast a despairing glance at them. "I followed him to Denver. I had his back. So why couldn't he see me?"

Cat tried to redirect her. "You live with your boyfriend, and you asked Younas to let Kelly move in next door, isn't that right?"

"You think Younas put Kell off? Because he thought I'd given up on him?"

"How could you be in love with Kelly if Younas is your boyfriend?" Cat asked.

Maddy clicked her tongue. "I thought if Kell saw me with someone else, he'd eventually wake up. He'd realize it was me he wanted all along."

"He didn't want you." Inaya tried to shake her certainty. "He's never even kissed you."

Maddy glared at her. "Kell likes to take things slow."

Their careful measures weren't cutting it, so Inaya nodded to Cat, who produced a video from a club night at The Black Door.

"He kissed Mateo," Cat informed her, letting the video play.

A tall figure could be seen leading Mateo off the dance floor. They moved to a booth, where the man pulled Mateo onto his lap and began to kiss him. Within seconds, the two were deeply entangled, oblivious to the presence of others.

Maddy let out a scream.

"Turn it off!"

Cat shut the video off, watching Maddy. "You can't pretend you didn't know."

A mulish set to her lips, Maddy said, "Kell lives next door. And *Matty* was like a dog with a bone—he wouldn't let Kelly go. He came over all the time."

Matty.

The nickname Kelly had given Mateo had tipped Inaya off. She'd watched the video with the rest of the team and remembered what Seif had said. There were only two motives: love or money. And if Kelly had been in love with Mateo, why would he have killed him? The only answer that made sense, given the presence of the antique revolver, was that Kelly hadn't—it was the love he'd expressed for Mateo that had gotten Mateo killed.

Once she'd accepted that premise, the one viable scenario pointed to Maddy Hicks. She had access to the gun. She was in and out of Kelly's house. She had been the one to alert Kelly to the partygoers exiting the club. Most importantly, the footage from her camera had been obscured by her deliberate decision to forge ahead into the smoke-filled haze around the club. She'd spotted Mateo in the crowd and chased him toward the alley.

Kelly had called out in shock on his body cam. The only explanation for his bewilderment and alarm was that he had seen Madeleine cock the revolver, too late to stop her from shooting Mateo in the back.

Madeleine kept up her practice. She was a crack shot.

Matty! Matty!

Kell hadn't been calling Madeleine for help. He'd been crying out in agony to the man he loved. The man Madeleine had shot in cold blood with no more excuse than that Mateo was her rival for Kelly Broda's heart. Except there had been no rivalry, because of a truth that Maddy had refused to accept, a refusal that became lethal for all the players involved.

Love or money. In this case, a twisted love.

Catalina picked up the threads of their interrogation. "You wanted to punish him, didn't you? That's why you used the revolver. To let him know you'd killed Mateo with his gun. He'd never forget. He'd have to fight his way through a wilderness of guilt and self-blame."

Maddy's anger deflated. "He wouldn't fight back. Kell wouldn't fight."

"I'm not sure what you mean," Cat said.

"He could have tried to fight the attraction. He could have tried to want me, but he just gave in. He gave in to that boy."

Inaya marveled at Maddy's self-delusion. Why couldn't she accept the fact that Kelly had been deeply in love with Mateo?

Catalina's expression was full of pity, but her question was sharp and to the point.

"Is that why you killed your rival?"

"Kell couldn't see me with Mateo in the way. He would have seen me," she whispered.

It wasn't the confession they needed, so Inaya tried again.

"Did it work?" she asked. "Does Kelly see you now?"

Madeleine stared at them as if she couldn't believe how oblivious they were.

"Kelly saw me use the gun. He knows I killed Matty." She spoke with no true awareness of what she had just confessed. "His life is on the line, and still he won't turn me in." She held up her open palms. "If that isn't love, what is?"

37

God, what a terrible mess. The only point of consolation was that they had done their jobs. They'd found out the truth, a truth they could give Mateo's parents. It wouldn't ease them, but it might pull them back from utter desolation, the black hole of never knowing why. There *was* a why, even if it was too painful to absorb.

Inaya pulled up outside her house. The machinery of an arrest had begun to churn; she wasn't needed at the station now. Seif had talked to Kelly, who had broken down and wept like a child. He'd still refused to open his mouth to condemn his childhood friend. Seif had spoken of his reaction with a rare depth of compassion.

"He's slowly being poisoned by a cocktail of emotions—rage, grief, guilt, loss, and a profound sense of betrayal. He'll have to quit the police, but how he'll put his life back together, I can't even imagine."

Inaya left her car on the drive, startled when she saw John Broda waiting for her on the steps. He was seated on the top step, his legs bunched together to provide a lap for her cat Kubo. Like the traitor he was, her sunny-natured tuxedo was purring away in John's lap, as the big, broad hands brushed over his shiny coat.

"You didn't call me," he said. "You didn't show me the footage or I could have told you what went down."

He sounded contemplative, not angry.

"How did you know?" She stayed some distance away, keeping her voice calm so as not to alert her family inside the house.

"My boy called me. He *called* me. He's coming here to see me."

Warily, Inaya glanced over her shoulder. "Why here?"

Broda's hands stopped stroking Kubo, who meowed in protest. Broda began petting him again, showing Inaya a side of himself she hadn't guessed at.

"He trusts you," Broda said simply. "He doesn't trust me."

A car pulled up to the side of the road—Seif's car. He had brought Kelly to her house, but he and Jaime had come along as backup. Warmth spread through her at his concern. He wouldn't leave her to handle the Brodas on her own.

Kelly's face was ravaged, his eyes swollen, the skin beneath them puffy and tender.

He bypassed Inaya, going straight to his father.

Kubo leapt from Broda's arms, disturbed by the new arrivals. He now had his choice of humans to coddle him. He opted for Jaime Webb, brushing against his trousers with a series of plaintive cries, until Jaime gathered him up in his arms and hoisted him on his shoulder. To thank him for these efforts, Kubo immediately shoved his rear in Jaime's face.

Broda remained seated, Kelly facing him one step down.

"Dad." His voice was broken, ragged. "I didn't say anything because I couldn't put Mad in the frame, but also because I thought—I thought . . ." His shoulders began to shake.

"You thought I put her up to it because of how I am—how I treated you at home. You knew I didn't want you with that boy."

The thought had nearly destroyed him, the proof of it stamped on his face. A man so prone to violence, to his place as an apex predator, had been felled like a mighty oak at the thought that his own son could think he was capable of causing him such harm.

Kelly couldn't speak, so he nodded.

His knees trembling, Broda stood up, tentatively reaching for his son. When Kelly didn't reject him, he wrapped his arms around Kelly's shoulders, pulling him in close.

"I should have accepted you, Kell. I should have been proud of everything about you. I haven't been the father you deserve."

Both men were crying. "We've lost our Maddy, Kell. It's my fault. I poisoned her, I poisoned you both. That's why she took my gun. She thought she was acting for me."

Kelly buried his face in John's neck like a child in need of protection.

Broda kept speaking. "I steered you wrong. I steered you both wrong, but you're a better cop—a better man—than I'll ever be."

Kelly wrenched away in protest. "It's too late for you to say that now. You can't wash away what you did."

"You have to let me try, son."

Kelly didn't answer, refusing his father's attempt to embrace him again.

Devastated, John Broda turned away, searching for Inaya. "I did wrong by you, Detective. I know I can't ever make it right, but you'll have what I promised you to thank you for what you did for Kell." He gazed after his son, who had staggered away across the lawn.

Inaya met his eyes. "Anything I did, I did for Mateo Ruiz. And for Marcus McBride."

Seif stayed with her after the others had left. They sat side by side on the steps, the night air fragrant around them. Kubo had nuzzled his way onto Inaya's lap, his tail flicking her arms.

"Hell of a day," Seif said. "Did it give you any closure on Chicago?"

She took her time answering, as if she had to think it through.

"I don't know. If I can take down Danny Egan—if the McBrides forgive me for abandoning their cause—then maybe I'll get there."

"What about Broda? Are you still afraid of him?"

He nearly missed the twitch of her brow. She patted Kubo absently. "There will always be men like Broda on the force, and the bosses to back them. The whole barrel of apples is rotten, at least in Chicago. And now with the Patriots, maybe in Denver too."

She didn't seem disconsolate. She sounded like she could beat men like Broda at their own game, hands down.

"Is it?" Seif's voice was soft, deliberately seductive. He was determined to win her any way he could. "There's you, Cat—there's Jaime." He paused. "And you also have me."

He moved in closer, his shoulder brushing hers. His fingers strayed over the cat's back, but it was just an excuse to touch her. He turned to her, his lips a breath away from hers.

Her rueful smile surprised him. "You're my test from God, aren't you? You and your playboy moves."

He touched two fingers to the center of her full bottom lip and stroked it.

"Is it so hard to accept that I want you? Or to admit that you feel the same?"

He thought she might have kissed his fingers, but she could just have been trying to evade him. She dented his confidence like no one else. So much for being smooth.

"It's not hard, it's easy. But you know who I am, Qas."

He did. She'd made it clear that she wouldn't compromise her values. She didn't do affairs, and she wouldn't give herself to any man without a divine blessing, Goddammit.

"And another woman has your ring," she noted.

He wanted to laugh, except he couldn't do that to Lily, so he said, "I couldn't ask for it back." It took more guts than she knew for him to add, "And that's not where I want it."

He watched the silky arch of her brows.

"You'll hurt her," she said.

"I know."

"And what about me? Will you hurt me too?"

He answered her question with one of his own. "Does it matter so much that I'm not like you? You know I don't believe in God."

"Except when you need Him, right?"

The cat leapt from her lap, and Inaya turned to him, her doe eyes warm and compassionate. He didn't need pity—he needed lust, love . . . hell if he knew what he needed.

"I think you're at war with yourself."

He watched her lips move. "What makes you say that?" He didn't care about the answer.

"I've seen you at home with your brothers. And I know you tried to distance yourself from the Elkaders when their daughter disappeared."

He scowled as she reminded him of the case he was trying to forget. The way Fatima Elkader had enfolded him with tendrils of the Arabic he loved.

"I know why you put on a show."

Her voice was so sweet he could almost pretend that she wasn't taking him apart.

She raised a hand to his cheek. "It hurts, doesn't it, to be in your skin, to be in a job you love when everything about you paints a target on your back. You know they see you as the enemy, so you work hard at reminding us just how American you are, as if there's nothing more to you. As if the pride of your history isn't bred into your bones. You carry those traditions forward, and you're blessed to be connected to such a beautiful heritage. Rejecting it must feel like tearing out pieces of your heart. You must want to hear the sound of Arabic—of Persian—spoken in your own voice. There must be times when you want to lead your brothers in prayer."

He moved away from her, his face still and cold.

"If you want to be with me, I won't let you disavow yourself. I'll call the truth out of you. I'll make you walk my path." A curl of mischief touched her lips. "I'll give you every part of me, but I'll also demand everything *you* are. So the question is, Lieutenant Seif, can you be that man? Can you reclaim the pieces of yourself you've tried so hard to throw away?"

The wound was struck without a weapon, with only soft words to assail him.

He wanted her, he might even love her, but he didn't want all this. He loved his job, it was the mainstay of his life and the source of his brothers' security, but just how much did he love it? And was he deluding himself that he could keep going as he had? Cass Safe, all-American boy, not Waqas Seif with the closely held secret of the surname he had spurned, when the twins were pushing him hard to take back his father's name?

Fuck! Why did she think she had the right to force him to face himself?

Goaded beyond endurance, he told her how he felt in ferocious Arabic, swept by a savage satisfaction when she didn't understand. Of course, he didn't sound like a lover. He sounded like a man grasping for the last bits of his sanity.

With a smile he wanted to kiss off her lips, she said, "That doesn't answer me, *habibi*."

God. Maybe she did understand.

She gave his tortured feelings a break when she ventured, "If I make my peace with what Broda did to me—if I come back from feeling so exposed—I might start to wear my scarf again. How would you feel about that?"

Dressed, undressed, covered, uncovered, God, what difference did it make? He would still be her slave. The strangest image played through his mind. He thought he'd be focused on getting her into his bed, but instead, he saw her rising from the prayer mat in his house, a look of love in her eyes for him. The image filled him with a rare tranquility.

This wasn't some angel-whore dichotomy he'd cobbled together in his mind. The feelings he'd had for Lily had been real, as had his respect for everything Lily had to offer. No, this was like calling to like.

The tense line of his spine relaxed, admitting he'd lost this fight.

"We'll have to take this slow," he warned her. "I can't be reckless about this."

"If you can stand it, so can I," she teased, and suddenly he was filled with a glowing, golden vitality that he would have recognized as happiness if he hadn't been in hiding for so long. If he'd listened to the twins. If he'd acknowledged the crushing attraction he'd felt for her from that very first day.

His cell phone buzzed insistently. He took the call, viewing it as a reprieve, even though he knew it had to be about Duante, the case that was still ongoing.

He didn't know that the call from Jacob Brandt, his boss and his mentor at the FBI, would bring his hopes crashing down.

38

Areesha was meeting Mirembe in Blackwater Falls. Mirembe had wanted to visit the place where Duante had been shot, and after that they had walked down to the falls. They paused at the lookout from the gazebo, Mirembe reaching out a hand to touch the mist from the pond. The small enclosure was festooned with flowers, vines of wisteria trailing down from the gazebo's octagonal roof. Scrolled benches were placed at intervals around the pond, and between them were heavy planter pots from which colorful blooms spilled, an idyllic scene.

"I haven't been here before. I didn't realize there was an actual waterfall."

"There's a path behind the falls too," Areesha said. "It's the perfect way to cool off when the weather gets to be too much."

"I'd like to see that."

Areesha showed her the way.

A pair of teens waved at them from their paddleboat in the center of the pond. Areesha recognized Cyrine's son Elias, and Mercedes, the daughter of Lincoln West. She waved back, checking to make sure they were wearing life jackets in automatic mom mode. When she turned back to Mirembe, there were tears on the other woman's cheeks. She dabbed at them with a handkerchief.

"Duante loved to be out on the water. He was a good swimmer, and he taught most of the kids in our neighborhood back in D.C."

Areesha leaned her elbows on the rail, watching the progress of the paddleboat. She'd been thinking about what Inaya had told her about Huxton Cooper, and realized that Mirembe might have insights into Huxton's state of mind, or of other young soldiers she would have encountered through her work.

"What was it like to be a Black woman working at Walter Reed?"

"There are a lot of Black people in the military."

"But you're a psychologist. Someone very well-known."

"My patients didn't care about my fame."

"What about your book? They must have cared about that."

Mirembe shrugged off her jacket as if she needed room to breathe.

"Like everything, there were two sides to the story. Vets who knew I was on their side, advocating for more support for those wounded in mind and body. They made appointments with me, they were honest, letting it all out, even though they knew I hadn't seen combat up close."

"Just the aftermath," Areesha said.

"Just the wreckage." Mirembe's lips thinned. "So much wreckage that no one can heal entirely. Soldiers just learn to adapt."

Or, like Huxton Cooper, they didn't, Areesha thought.

"And the others? You said there were two sides."

"The others thought I was attacking their record of service because I questioned the motives behind sending these young men off to fight without adequate preparation."

Areesha faced her. "Our military is among the best-trained in the world."

Mirembe shook her head. "That's where the criticism came in. They thought I was impugning that somehow. Yes, our soldiers are well-trained, no one denies that. And the military is happy to spend money on arming them to the teeth, but there's more to war than that. These young people need to know something about the countries they're deployed to. They need to understand the people they have to engage with, if they're to win hearts and minds. There was no preparation for that. We didn't learn about the people of Afghanistan. We crossed lines we shouldn't have, and all that achieved was to harden the people against us."

"War isn't about winning hearts and minds. That's not why we got into Afghanistan."

Mirembe sighed. "Those *were* the mission parameters at one time. If we lost the support of the Afghan people, we would become an occupying enemy just as General McChrystal warned, and that was where we ended up."

"I don't know enough about it to debate this with you," Areesha mused. "Detective Rahman might. Her father is from Afghanistan. I still don't understand why that turned members of the military against you. You were doing your best for our soldiers."

"I'm a strong critic of war, Areesha. I've seen the damage, and it's catastrophic. You teach young people to be relentless in the face of the enemy, to strike before they can strike, to dehumanize them utterly, and what are you left with when they get back? How do they return to normal life? So people manipulated that. They said I was attacking their service. Being anti-war had to mean I was anti-vet."

"Reducing things that shouldn't be reduced."

"There's that," Mirembe agreed. "There's also the fact that some people should never have served in the military. The majority of soldiers are honorable, dedicated—they think they're doing good out there in the world, fighting for our freedom."

"It's possible to *believe* you're doing good while achieving the opposite."

A bitter smile edged Mirembe's lips. "That's what many Afghans said. Though many were also desperate for our forces not to leave."

Areesha straightened away from the rail. "I feel like I'm missing the point."

Mirembe picked up her jacket, letting the mist cool her face.

"There are some people with incipient sociopathic tendencies who should never be recruited to positions of armed authority. We see that with the police, and it also exists in the military. You give a young man a gun, you tell him he's a god, king of all he surveys, and that kind of young man is positioned to do real damage. When that happens, the military has two choices: cover it up or prosecute their own."

Areesha still hadn't gotten around to reading Mirembe's book. David had told her it was an immensely powerful read, and had left a copy on her bedside table.

"Unless you're a sociopath, you can't kill innocent people without experiencing the blowback. In this case, the severe mental trauma at the heart of PTSD." Mirembe changed the subject. "Come on. Show me the passage behind the falls."

Areesha followed her out of the gazebo, her hand catching at Mirembe's sleeve.

"Why did this matter to Duante? How did your work have such an impact on him?"

The grief that had never been absent surged through Mirembe like a wave. Her body swayed under the surge, and Areesha had to catch hold of her to keep her away from the water. Elias called out, concerned. "You need help, Miz Adams?"

Mirembe covered her face with her hands, her whole body trembling. Areesha held her tightly. "No, I think we're okay," she shouted back.

Nonetheless, the teens began to paddle in. Mirembe sucked in a breath.

"I spent some time at a base in Kandahar in 2010, providing clinical services to men who were fresh from combat. The idea was to ensure they began to talk about the impact of engagement while their memories were fresh."

"Engagement?" Areesha pressed.

"The killing of insurgents."

Of course, the army's priority would be the welfare of its own servicemen, yet it never failed to strike Areesha that the entire debate was framed as the resultant trauma for American soldiers and not for the Afghan people, who were, if anything, a side note.

"Were the soldiers willing to work with you?"

Mirembe stood still. "The atmosphere on base was tense. We were in the center of a Taliban stronghold, and instead of a straightforward engagement, our soldiers were ambushed by suicide attacks. The majority of coalition casualties were suffered in the area where the base was established. The soldiers coped by using drugs—hashish in particular."

"What was the name of the base?"

"Forward Operating Base Ramrod. It was later renamed Sarkari Karez. The soldiers stationed there were frustrated, they wanted to strike back, especially after one of their squad commanders was injured."

"You learned this from counseling them?"

"They made all the right noises," Mirembe said wearily. "But something was definitely off with soldiers from the Third Platoon. Reports began to filter in of the killing of unarmed civilians. Preliminary investigations were conducted, but they ended up going nowhere. I pressed several of the soldiers I was asked to counsel on this point. I told them that if they were involved, not admitting the truth would have an impact on their health."

They had reached the curtain of the falls now and moved into the passage behind them, the roar of the water making it hard to hear what Mirembe was trying to tell her. Areesha's intuition had lit up like a fire signal. She remembered what Inaya had told her about Huxton Cooper after Duante's funeral. He'd served in Maywand. That couldn't be a coincidence.

"Did you counsel Huxton Cooper? Harry Cooper's son," she reminded her. "He's dead now, so there can't be an issue of doctor-patient confidentiality."

Mirembe plunged her hands into the curtain of water. The spray fell into the tunnel.

"Huxton Cooper? That's an unusual name. I would have remembered it. No, I never saw a soldier by that name. Besides, I wasn't getting anywhere with the Third Platoon, so I decided to speak to the brass. Commanding officers give a lecture to the troops every other week as a means of touching base, so I asked for a few minutes to speak at the end of one of those lectures."

"I'm sensing what you had to say was . . . explosive."

Mirembe grimaced. "I told the soldiers on base they had a code to uphold—if anyone on base was involved in the killing of unarmed Afghan civilians, they were risking not only military consequences, but also their mental health. I warned them that not turning in soldiers who were killing civilians effectively made them accomplices in the murders that took place in the Maywand District."

"Holy Lord." As always, the words were a prayer.

"They cut off my mic but the damage was done. I was shipped out the next day and never asked to return."

"What about your trauma counseling?"

Mirembe's answer was in quotes. "'Coddling soldiers doesn't help.'"

Areesha mulled this over. "It sounds like you did your best, Mirembe. I still don't understand how any of this affected Duante. Why was he angry at you?"

Mirembe slumped against the wall.

"My son read about Maywand in my book. He said I should have done more to bring those soldiers to trial." She stifled a sob. "Black bodies, brown bodies. He saw us all as the same."

The Blackwater Falls library had spectacular views. Areesha's heels were high and growing more uncomfortable, so she took the elevator up to the second floor, where the computers were.

She tried to find a copy of Mirembe's book first. The librarian, a woman named Freya, gave her a helpless shrug. "The copies keep disappearing. Library trustees refuse to spend more money on this particular book. There seems to be some controversy around it."

"Which is precisely why you should keep it in stock."

"Do you know anything about Blackwater Falls?" Freya Kovar cast a nervous glance around. "Sheriff Addison Grant is on the board of trustees. What he says goes." Defiance sat oddly on her placid features. "He can't do anything about our computers though."

That was as good a tip-off as any, so Areesha slung her Fendi bag onto the worktop, and settled in to do some digging. The first thing she did was type "Maywand, Afghanistan" into the computer's search engine. She sat back in her chair, mouth agape at the number of results that popped up, all with some variation of the title "Maywand District Murders."

The most helpful—and likely the most authentic—of these results was the army's own military case study of things *not* to do on deployment, and how the chain of command had so abysmally failed not only the soldiers on base, but the people of Afghanistan.

Everything Mirembe had described to her had been accurate. The rumors that had infiltrated FOB Ramrod had been substantiated, though it had taken more than a year to do so after the killing of an Afghan boy, followed by other unprovoked attacks on civilians. Men from the Third Platoon had strategized the killings: they would collect off-the-book weapons and drop them on the scene to make it seem as if they had responded to a legitimate threat or attack. In police terminology, this would amount to planting evidence. Staff Sergeant Calvin Gibbs of the Third Platoon collected trophies from the victims, and others did the same. A finger here, a piece of skull there. The soldiers involved even posed with the bodies, sharing their kills with other soldiers on base. A soldier who had reported excessive use of hashish by one of the men involved in the killings was beaten badly by Gibbs and his cohorts.

When the abuses were reported, investigations by senior officials had been cursory or stalled in their tracks, despite the complaints local Afghans brought to base through their community leaders, men who were well-respected among their own. Far from winning hearts and minds, the Third Platoon was provoking the very insurgency it feared.

After a medic examined the soldier who had been beaten, the leaks on base multiplied. By May of 2010, a full investigation was launched, and eleven soldiers were prosecuted, with seven of these, including SSG Gibbs, convicted of serious crimes including premeditated murder.

Areesha read report after report until her vision blurred. She began to appreciate just how big a stir Mirembe's lecture must have made. There was no mention of it online, either because the army had found it insignificant or because they had chosen to suppress it as an internal matter. Possibly keeping it quiet had been an act of kindness.

She made some notes on a pad, trying to consider other points of view. American soldiers had been under attack by insurgents in 2009. Men trained to lethality were bristling with frustration at the enemy's guerrilla tactics, unable to pin them down. Counterguerrilla tactics were encouraged. Couldn't Gibbs and his men have seen their tactics as valid? No, because if they had they wouldn't have attacked noncombatants. But in the heat of battle, how could they distinguish between civilians and soldiers, particularly as suicide attacks were a common tactic?

But a guerrilla war by its very nature defeated the notion of "the heat of battle." The counterattacks carried out by Gibbs and others were rationally thought out and premeditated, as witnessed by the collection of off-the-books ammo meant to implicate the innocent.

If the army had prosecuted, that meant there was something worth prosecuting.

She took note of the fact that a popular squad commander had been seriously wounded, necessitating his replacement by SSG Gibbs, which was the turning point. In the army's own words, "An imposing NCO and combat veteran with a reputation for his tactical competency, SSG Gibbs led Third Platoon's descent into murder and brutality in the following months."

She read over her notes again, aware that she was missing a critical detail. Huxton Cooper's name wasn't mentioned anywhere in the reports, only those of the soldiers convicted of serious crimes. Could he have been involved in those crimes? Was that why he'd taken his own life? The connection between his suicide in Afghanistan and Mirembe's brief stint at FOB Ramrod was tenuous, at best. The rogue soldiers' killing spree had begun in 2009. Mirembe had arrived the following year—Areesha made a note to track down the dates. Perhaps she would find them in Mirembe's book.

She considered another angle. Even if Duante had resented his mother for not exposing the killings in Maywand, how did that tie into the art contest that had placed him on the streets of Blackwater on the night of his death? A vital link was missing. Or there was no link.

Duante had been drawn to the fight for justice. He would know that the U.S. military recruited heavily in Black and Latinx neighborhoods because it offered lower-income residents a chance at a free education. The toughness embodied by the military was also a selling point. Young men, in particular, craved being seen as tough, or macho, as the case might be. Put a machine gun in a young man's hands, and presto, instant transformation.

But Duante was an artist, his mind both subtle and supple—he would have been impervious to that kind of appeal. Like Cassius Clay/Muhammad Ali, whom Areesha had named her son for, Duante wouldn't be in any hurry to target those he identified with.

She had the Cassius Clay quote at hand, though Clay's words reflected his refusal to enlist in the army to fight in Vietnam. Had Duante believed the same thing? That he too wouldn't have gone "ten thousand miles from home to help murder and burn another poor nation simply to continue the domination of white slave masters of the darker people the world over"? Because the real fight and the real enemy were here at home?

Areesha's head drooped on the slender column of her neck. The library's lights were flicking on and off. She had overstayed her welcome. Mirembe had taken a cab home earlier, and she had to collect her car from where she had parked it. She stuffed her notebook in her purse, and as she did so, a shadow fell across the screen. A man's beefy arms boxed her in as he bent to take a look at the article still open on her computer.

"Now, how about that." Her nemesis, Sheriff Grant. "Afghanistan seems a little out of your jurisdiction." She clicked the computer off, and he moved to let her up.

"How did you enjoy the funeral?"

A despicable question.

"Didn't I see you there with your wife?" she demanded. "Were you using her for cover?"

He didn't take offense. "If I was there, it was to pay my respects like any decent cop."

The opening was too easy to pass up. Areesha charged in where angels feared to tread.

"And how would you know what a decent cop does?"

39

When Seif left, Inaya checked her phone. She had six missed calls. Two from Jaime, four from Areesha Adams. She called Jaime without listening to her voicemail.

He sounded happy and relieved. "Got a break on the Duante case. Could be nothing, boss, but my gut says it's big."

Inaya settled into a lounger on the porch. "Fire away. What's gotten you so excited?"

"Tech tracked down the person behind the prize offered to street artists. Remember The Wonder of Life? The company filing named Tanangelo Thompson as the president."

"I remember."

"Well, Tanangelo Thompson is actually a person named Tania Angelo-Thompson."

Should the name mean something? Memory flickered, too elusive to capture.

"And Tania Angelo-Thompson is the former married name of one Tania Davis."

Inaya caught her breath. Wasn't Tania Davis—

"Harry Cooper's lady friend," Jaime finished triumphantly. "She put up the money for the contest. And she set the stage for the challenge in Blackwater Falls."

Inaya swallowed her shock. A twist in the case. Another reason to suspect hidden depths to Harry Cooper.

Areesha had relayed Raze's observation about Blackwater: *It's basically a sundown town. No Black folk after dark.*

"Can I come with you on the interview tomorrow?" Jaime asked hopefully.

It was his lead. He deserved to come. Unfortunately, Inaya needed Cat's insight.

"I'm sorry, Jaime, I have to take Cat. And I need you to distract Sheriff Grant. If he finds out we've asked Ms. Davis in for an interview, he's bound to throw up roadblocks."

"I can do that," Jaime said. "But you don't need to ask her in. You could drop in on her."

"I have a feeling Grant's got her under surveillance. As a favor to Harry."

"I checked her schedule. She goes to the rec center every morning at ten. There's an exercise class that involves the lazy river. You might need a swimsuit."

When Inaya paused, Jaime fell over himself with apologies. "I didn't mean—that is, I know you don't—ah, that is to say, I wouldn't be there—"

Inaya began to laugh. "Cut it out, Jaime. You don't have to tread on eggshells with me. That's a great tip. I'll show up there with Cat."

"I dug up something else about the contest. About possible sites the artists could use for their designs," Jaime volunteered. "It was on The Wonder of Life website."

And when he told her what it was, the pieces of the puzzle finally came together.

It was steamy inside the swimming pool area where Cat and Inaya chatted on a bench, waiting for Tania Davis to finish her class. She hadn't caught sight of them yet. She was moving with the other middle-aged swimmers in a balletic flow through the twists and turns of the lazy river, part of an aquafit class, her movements unhurried and untroubled. That changed when she rounded the bend and caught sight of Inaya and Cat. They had taken off their jackets, and their badges gleamed on their belts. Cat wasn't armed but Inaya was wearing her shoulder holster.

Tania's flushed cheeks turned pale. She stumbled on the lazy river's track, blocking another swimmer's path. She made some excuse, and laboriously climbed the steps out of the pool, fishing for her towel from a pile on a nearby bench. She wrapped it around her waist, the ends of her wet brown hair dripping into the neckline of her swimsuit.

Sliding her feet into a pair of poolside slippers, she approached them.

Inaya asked if there was somewhere they could talk. She sensed the interest of the other members of the aquafit class. Her hand clenched on her towel in a death grip, Tania Davis led them to patio seating outside. She didn't wait for them to speak.

"Is it Harry? Has something happened to Harry?"

"I'm sorry, we didn't mean to alarm you. We're here to ask you about the corporation you set up—I believe it's called The Wonder of Life."

Tania looked uncertainly from Inaya to Cat. "Was it wrong to use my former name?"

Inaya made a show of checking her notebook. "If it is, that's not what we're concerned with. We're more interested in why you set it up."

Cat took her cue. "Why did you use your former married name, Ms. Davis?" She glanced at Tania's unadorned ring finger. "I understand you're divorced now."

Tania's hand fluttered weakly at her side. "Yes, yes, I'm divorced. I suppose I'm still in the habit of using my ex-husband's name."

Inaya's pencil scratched over her notebook. She was thankful they were sitting in the shade; it was more than ninety degrees outside.

"You divorced him ten years ago, is that right?"

Tania's fingers began to pleat her towel into folds. The skin at the neck of her swimsuit was finely ruched, and with pity, Inaya saw that she was trembling.

"Yes, that's right." It came out as a whisper.

"The Wonder of Life was incorporated earlier this year. Your house is in your own name, so is your car—we checked. Why isn't the corporation?"

"I didn't—I didn't want publicity. For trying to do good." Her eyes skittered away from theirs. "Charity is what the right hand gives," she whispered.

Cat spoke to her warmly, a contrast with Inaya's blunt approach. "It was a generous thought. Why street art, in particular?"

Tania blushed. Several members of her class sauntered outside, taking up a patio table nearby. They had purchased soft drinks from the vending machine. One of the women strolled over to Tania to offer her a Mountain Dew.

"Everything okay, Tania?"

Tania grabbed the can like a life preserver. "Yes, all good here. I just need a moment."

The woman returned to her table. She took out her cell phone with a frown.

"You were saying . . ." Cat encouraged.

Tania's lips were so dry, she had to pry them from her teeth with her tongue. "Harry—Harry took an interest in disadvantaged youth."

"That was kind of him," Cat said easily. "Why didn't Harry set up the charity himself?"

"Conflict of interest. It wouldn't have looked right."

Cat nodded like she believed it. "That makes sense. So Duante won both challenges?"

Tania dropped the soft drink can. It rolled away and no one moved to collect it.

"The entries were blind. I didn't know who won. I just signed the checks. If I hadn't chosen Blackwater as a location, he might still be alive."

"*You* decided on Blackwater?" Inaya confirmed. There was a sudden commotion by the doors, where a tall bluff man in uniform was swarmed by the women in Tania's class.

"Did I do wrong?" Tania whispered. "Am I the reason why that boy is dead? I thought he might use the space behind the falls or the back of Adventures in Mountainland." She named a ski boutique at one end of Main Street. "There's a nice brick wall there, and the owners are easygoing about things like street art."

"But Duante was shot closer to where you live, isn't that right, Tania? Nearly next door to you. What was the attraction in your neighborhood?"

Tania began to cry, but Inaya didn't let up.

"I'm going to have to insist on an answer."

Sheriff Grant was headed her way. She only had another minute.

"The noise barrier," Tania sobbed. "Between the planned community and the highway. It made a perfect canvas, so I put it on the list of possible Blackwater entry sites."

Cat rose to her feet to deal with the sheriff, buying them a little more time.

"Harry Cooper lives with you, doesn't he, Tania?"

Tania dabbed at her eyes with a corner of her towel. "Yes. Why?"

"Was he with you that night before he went on shift?"

"Yes," she said again. "Why?"

"Did you know Duante had chosen the site that bordered the highway, next to a neighborhood where there had been several episodes of vandalism?"

"No!" Color flooded back into her face. "How could I?"

"Was there anything odd about that night?"

"About Harry, you mean? Harry didn't know there would be an incident that night. I swear on my life that's true. It was his normal shift. It wasn't out of the ordinary."

"But you were disturbed that night, weren't you?" Inaya watched her. "You made a report to the police. You said you were awakened by a loud noise, shortly after midnight."

"I thought it might be the vandals," Tania admitted. "I found out later I was wrong."

"Because you'd learned Duante Young had been shot?"

Tania stared at her, a befuddled expression on her face.

"I didn't know there'd been a shooting. I didn't know Harry was involved until later."

"Then why did you call the police?"

"The garbage trucks had come by," Tania explained. "When I went to collect my cans, they weren't there. The trash collectors told us it was the same for the whole street. All our garbage cans were gone. I figured that must have been the noise I heard after midnight, just some kids playing a prank, rolling our cans away."

"The cans were one street over. Not hard to get them there from your place. And we only have your word for it that you heard a noise that night."

Tania blinked rapidly. "What are you saying, Detective?"

"I think you called the police to cover up the fact that you moved those cans yourself."

Tania gaped at Inaya. "Why on earth would I do that?"

Inaya kept at her. "You were behind the contest. You chose the contest sites. *You* placed Duante in Blackwater that night. The only question is why."

Cat couldn't hold Sheriff Grant back any longer. He was with them in three angry strides, putting an end to the interview, making no secret of his displeasure.

"You don't come near Tania or any of the residents of my town, Detective. I'll be putting in a call to your boss about your harassment."

Inaya put her notebook away without rushing. "I was asking Ms. Davis about the report she filed with the police."

Grant looked over her head to Tania, who had blushingly gathered up her towel to cover up the abundance of her figure.

"What report? If you had a problem, Tania, you should have come to me."

Tania dropped her head. "It was just a neighborhood prank, Addison. It had nothing to do with Harry, or I would have come to you."

Apparently, the sheriff knew Tania. He held his peace and she rushed in to answer his expectant silence. "It wasn't about the shooting of that boy—some kids stole my garbage can. You're far too important to bother with trivial things."

The flattery came easily to Tania, as if she'd had a lot of practice.

Grant jerked his attention to Inaya. "How does a prank in *my* jurisdiction merit a follow-up by two of your detectives?"

"We're following up on a tip about the charitable organization that awarded the prizes in the street-art contest. The reason why Duante Young was in Blackwater Falls that night."

Grant folded his arms across his chest, Tania's complaint forgotten.

"Young was a hoodlum. If he'd stopped when Harry asked him to, twice I might mention, he would still be alive. There's no dealing with that kind."

"Young Black men?" Inaya clarified.

Grant wasn't to be caught out. "Criminals. Their age doesn't fucking matter, pardon my language, Tania. Now you'd best be on your way because Tania's told you all she's going to."

Grant couldn't frighten her. Not after she'd survived Broda.

"Perhaps you could help me instead, then."

"Go ahead." He was in her space, refusing to back up. Inaya produced her notebook, thumbing the pages right under his nose.

"What was the relationship like between Harry Cooper and his son?"

Grant scratched his head, puzzled. "A damn fine one, I'd say. Harry worshipped that boy. He was killed in action, so you sure as hell won't be asking Harry about his boy."

Catalina was there before her.

"We don't need to talk to Harry. Not if Tania will tell us what she did."

40

The stalemate between Grant and the Community Response detectives ended with Seif's arrival. He took a folded piece of paper from inside his jacket and placed it in Grant's hands.

"Warrant," he said briefly. "To search the home of Harry Cooper and Tania Davis. We have officers there now."

"Where the hell is Harry?" Grant erupted. "You have no grounds to hold him."

"We aren't. Because we can't find him. Perhaps you could assist with that."

"Oh no!" Tania cried.

Grant went alert. "We told him to keep out of sight until the issue was resolved."

"The funeral was two days ago," Seif noted. "You know about that, right?"

The white-hot glare of the sun was beating down on their heads, adding heat to the confrontation. Grant slipped on his sunglasses, the perfect shield if he didn't want to be read.

"What the hell are you on about, Seif?"

"Were you at Duante Young's funeral on Saturday? With your wife perhaps? Or accompanying Ms. Davis?" He nodded at Tania, who seemed about to faint with terror.

"What business is that of yours?"

"Someone who looked like you smiled over at Dr. Young as her son was being buried. It certainly wasn't an occasion for levity—the smile was a taunt."

"It was a greeting," Grant snapped. "It's called being polite."

"Then it *was* you?"

"I don't answer to you." And he didn't. He shepherded Tania Davis out from among their midst, sending her off to change.

Inaya looked over at their audience. Several of the women in Tania's group were filming the confrontation on their phones.

Seif stalked over to them, his tough-cop persona firmly settled in place.

"Release that publicly and you'll get your friend arrested before the day is out."

Seif sent Cat to join the search at Tania Davis's house. He had his own agenda. Areesha Adams had called him and told him to read the chapter in Mirembe Young's book that dealt with events in Maywand. Once he'd finished, he'd put a call through to Brandt at the FBI. He'd guessed at a conclusion, but he still needed proof. Instead, Brandt's answers had blown the case wide open, taking him down a tangent he didn't want to explore. But if he didn't follow it up, Brandt would make sure that someone who was a lot less restrained than Seif would.

He pulled Inaya aside.

"Did you come here in Cat's car?"

She nodded.

"Good, you're driving back with me. We need to make a stop."

He didn't tell her where or why, and thankfully, she didn't ask until he'd parked his car on her drive. Then she turned to him, eyebrows raised.

"Were you missing my cat?" she asked lightly.

He stared straight out the windshield. "I need to speak to your father. We both do."

He heard the soft catch of her breath. "My father isn't involved in this."

"It's possible he can help us. I need to ask him about Maywand."

Her whole body went stiff. "Why?"

Keeping the air-conditioning on and to hell with the environment, he recounted his conversation with Areesha. He also told her about the chapter in Mirembe Young's book, filling in the details. She was tense and silent as she listened, and his chest began to ache.

"Inaya. I don't want to do this. I wouldn't if there was any other way."

"I don't understand why you're so upset. My father's memories of Afghanistan are . . . distressing for him, but he doesn't have anything to hide."

Seif turned to face her. The least he owed her was to look her in the eye. His voice softer than he'd ever made it, he asked, "Do you know where your father was in May of 2010?"

Fright leapt into her face. She stammered a little as she said, "He was visiting family in Pakistan."

God help me, he thought. "He was in Kandahar in May. At FOB Ramrod."

She shot out of her seat, slamming the door of the car.

Seif met her on the driveway, catching her by the arms as she tried to struggle free.

"He absolutely was not. I don't know where you get your information from—"

"From the FBI."

"You're *spying* on my father?"

"Brandt investigates everyone I come across on assignment. It was necessary for me to do my job." He hesitated, then plunged in. "The job I was assigned by the FBI."

"You came here because of Grant! How does that concern my father?"

"He was a force to be reckoned with during our last case. I had to pass that on to Brandt."

She struggled in his grasp. He narrowly avoided her knee, so he let her go. She didn't run away, as expected. Nor did she spit in his face, as he deserved.

Instead, she became calm, assembling facts in her head.

"My father wasn't involved in Huxton Cooper's death, any more than he had anything to do with Duante Young. You're pulling this out of thin air."

"Your father is from Maywand. He was one of the elders called upon to approach senior officials on base to protest the killing of Afghan civilians." He gave her time to grapple with that, adding with great reluctance, "He knew soldiers from the Third Platoon were responsible."

He had shocked her with the news. She hadn't known anything about it, and he wondered if that was a lie of omission on Haseeb Rahman's part, or if Inaya's father had a more disturbing reason to conceal the truth.

"I can show you proof if you need it," he said now.

"My father doesn't lie. If he said he went to Pakistan, he did."

"What if he decided on a last-minute extension to his trip and didn't tell you?"

"Why would he do that?" It killed him to witness her confusion.

"Maybe it was painful for him to approach an American base. Or to speak about the murders in Maywand."

She flared up at once. "So you think my father bore some kind of grudge and managed to maneuver an American soldier into killing himself?" Her eyes narrowed. "Or are you daring to suggest my father was involved in his death?"

"Did you tell your father anything about the Duante Young case?"

"How dare you ask me that! I never discuss our cases. Anything my father knows is something he heard on the news."

He didn't think she knew she had raised her voice, but behind her the screen door opened and her father came out. He put his hand on Inaya's shoulder, and steadily met Seif's gaze.

"I thought you might come to see me. As always, I am ready to talk."

41

Inaya sat beside her father in the formal living room in a firm display of loyalty. She spoke to her father in fluent Urdu, and Seif had no idea what she might be telling him. He recognized the words "Maywand" and "Afghanistan," and nothing else. She shouldn't be warning her father—they needed answers that hinged on Rahman's time at FOB Ramrod.

"Your case concerns Afghanistan?" The mild question came from Inaya's father, who sat very much at ease, one leg crossed over the other at the ankle, wearing an expensive suit and groomed as if he were entertaining a client at his law firm. The pleasant chill of air-conditioning meant Seif could keep his jacket on, his gun hidden from the other man's gaze. Inaya had removed hers, along with her holster, which she'd placed on the two-tiered coffee table in the center of the room. The size of the table was meant to display an exquisite collection of books. Giant picture books called *The Art of the Qur'an* and *Mosques of the World* lay open on the upper tier, alongside books from notable museum collections. The lower tier was dedicated to travel books on places like Morocco, Turkey, and Uzbekistan, and as such a visitor's feet at the level of the books would cause no offense.

He appreciated the subtleties of the room's décor, the plush white sofas, the blue, green, and white Usmanov porcelain, the silver-worked *paandaans* like a treasure trove of jewelry boxes displayed on a single shelf. Ayat-ul-Kursi, the Verse of the Throne, hung brilliantly illuminated on one wall, matted and framed in gold. The room possessed every kind of luxury to delight the eye and the spirit, but he guessed it wasn't a place where Inaya spent a great deal of time. It was the room of a woman who favored a chilly kind of perfection, reminiscent of Inaya's mother, a peacock on her own small throne.

He knew Inaya cherished her faith and her connection to both Afghanistan and Pakistan, but she balanced out her love for the glories of the Islamic civilization with a very real praxis forged in the fight for social justice. The room reflected only the former, unless the Verse of the Throne stood in for a stern kind of warning.

He read the nastaliq script hoping for but not expecting to gain enlightenment.

"Inaya—Detective Rahman—must have told you about Huxton Cooper. He was a soldier with the Third Platoon, part of the Fifth Stryker Brigade, based out of FOB Ramrod, which is where Cooper died. You know the base, I believe. I'd like to hear about your time there."

Rahman said something to Inaya that caused the tension to seep out of her shoulders. She'd been holding herself stiffly, her posture communicating her sense of outrage at Seif; now she relaxed against her father.

"Inaya's mother and I—we didn't tell our children about my visit to Afghanistan as we didn't like them to worry. The girls were all quite young at the time, and subsequently—" He raised a hand and let it fall, the gesture self-explanatory. "There was too much pain to return, even if only in memory."

"Did you meet a soldier named Huxton Cooper at FOB Ramrod?"

"I spoke only to two senior officers—the ones in charge of the Fifth Stryker Brigade—about the conduct of their men." He named the officers, and Seif wrote down the names. Normally, Inaya would have taken notes, but, he realized, she wasn't about to help him with this interview.

"You were there, when?"

"On May tenth."

"You remember the date?"

"There was quite a commotion on base the day I was there."

"What was the source of the commotion?"

"An internal investigation was launched when a young soldier was beaten by his squad. I believe he was being pressured to remain silent on the subject of his platoon's activities."

"Was the soldier Huxton Cooper?"

"I do not know. I heard rumors, but no name was mentioned. It was a busy day. The two senior officers were called away."

"Do you know why?"

"A speaker had come to the base to address the issue of the well-being of the troops. They were suffering from killing us, you see."

A hint of contempt seeped through the calm explanation.

"Who was the speaker?"

"It was Dr. Mirembe Young." And as if he hadn't just set fire to the room, Rahman continued calmly, "I am aware that Dr. Young is the mother of a young man who was recently killed, but I have not discussed the matter with my daughter."

"You sound as though you are familiar with Dr. Young." Seif tried to ignore Inaya tugging at her father's arm, cautioning him to silence.

Rahman remained unperturbed. "I have read her book. I am interested, as you may imagine, in matters that relate to the occupation of my country."

"Do you view the American presence in Afghanistan as an occupation?"

"What would you call it?" Rahman returned.

Seif watched Inaya take her father's hand in hers.

"The necessary rooting out of an enemy who would see us destroyed."

Rahman gave him a curious look. "Like the enemy in Iraq with its weapons of mass destruction? Like that enemy?"

Seif waved this away. "I'm not here to debate the war—"

"The invasion," Rahman interrupted.

"As you like—the invasion. I *would* like to know why you felt the need to visit FOB Ramrod that day."

"I was carrying out a promise. I was asked to participate in a jirga regarding the American forces who patrolled the villages in the area. I am an elder, I am a foreign-trained lawyer, and I speak the Americans' language."

"You are also from Maywand." Seif said this like he'd scored a point.

Rahman bowed his head. "From a place destroyed by the Russians when *they* were the invading army. Yes, I am from the area, otherwise I would not have been asked to have my say on the jirga. It is like a town hall meeting that decides important matters."

"And the matter in question?"

"The murder of civilians by American forces. By your Third Platoon. I was asked to represent the interests of a boy named Gul Mudin. You must have read the story in Dr. Young's book." He squeezed his daughter's hand. "No wonder the good doctor made so many enemies, the speech she described in her book must have alarmed the base."

A reasonable response, but Seif couldn't accept it at face value. "So you just happened to be on base when Dr. Young was there? Yet you didn't see her or speak to her?"

"There are thousands of people on an American base. My access was not unrestricted—I couldn't wander at will. I was there to represent my people. In some ways, it would seem, Dr. Young had the same task. But is that the question you really wanted to ask?"

It wasn't. Yet Seif didn't want to proceed, not with Inaya looking so disillusioned.

Taking a deep breath, he said, "You view American soldiers as the enemy, don't you?"

"Let us say rather, I understand the complexities of the occupation."

That wasn't an answer. He could see from Inaya's face that she knew it too.

"You must have been angry when you learned why you'd been asked to join the jirga."

"Wouldn't you have been?" Rahman pinned him with his gaze. "Your soldiers carried the fingers of our children as trophies. Do you wonder that we consider you an occupying army?"

"What happened in Maywand was an isolated incident," Seif responded. "American forces also built schools, they sent women back to work. The murders don't represent the entirety of our engagement."

"No?" Haseeb took a bone china cup from Inaya's fingers, sinking back into his seat. "Your soldiers fired on unarmed civilians during your cowardly exit."

Seif stiffened. "American troops died in that encounter. How did you expect them to respond to a Taliban attack? Don't Afghans share any blame for the state of their country?"

"Shouldn't American soldiers have to answer for the murders in Maywand?"

Seif's reply was terse. "They did. They were prosecuted."

"Not all of them."

And here he was at the crux of the matter. At the question that could destroy his hopes.

With great care, he said, "Huxton Cooper's death was recorded as a suicide. But why would he take his own life when he wasn't involved in the Third Platoon attacks? Unless someone spoke to him about those attacks and made him feel responsible. Someone who was angry about the American 'invasion.'"

Seif took a file from his case and passed it to Inaya without making eye contact.

"Look at the picture in the file. Brandt sent it to me."

She shivered a little as she opened the file, and he wanted to take her hand.

It was a picture of Huxton Cooper in an empty room. He had hanged himself from a high beam in the soldiers' quarters: the photograph reflected the desolation of his choice.

Rahman murmured a prayer for the young man in the photograph, who would have been in his early thirties now, had he lived. When the prayer was finished, he took the picture from Inaya. His finger pointed to a date stamp.

"The matter is easily resolved. I spoke to the commanders on base, then I returned to the jirga to explain the outcome of my visit. My role ended that night. The next morning I returned to Pakistan. The border between our two countries is closely monitored. It is also heavily patrolled. There is an exit stamp on my passport that verifies my departure. I was nowhere near the American base when this young man took his life."

"I would like to see that stamp," Seif said. But even as he made the concession, he knew that didn't mean that Huxton's path hadn't crossed Haseeb Rahman's. He couldn't establish that as fact, any more than he could prove that Inaya's father hadn't spoken to Mirembe at the base. But even if Haseeb Rahman was lying, he couldn't see a clear throughline to Duante's murder.

He winced when Inaya set down the file with a thump on a small glass console.

Like a dragon, she blasted him with fire. "I can't believe you came here thinking my father was involved in Huxton Cooper's death. I shouldn't have let you past the door!"

"Inaya, *jaan,*" her father began.

"No, Baba." She got to her feet. "I appreciate why you didn't want me to bring up the past. No one should be forced to return to such darkness. I'm sorry Lieutenant Seif made you do that. But this case has nothing to do with Maywand. It's about Blackwater Falls." She hugged her father, who pressed both her hands, before turning on Seif. "Now can we get back to work?"

His phone rang as he bent to retrieve the file Inaya had set on the console. She took it from his hands as he answered. It was Catalina calling from Tania Davis's house. Something had turned up in the search, a box Tania Davis kept hidden under her bed. Its contents had stunned her.

He listened to Catalina, conscious of Inaya's barely contained anger. With an effort, he made himself focus, ushering her into the hall.

"Wait, Catalina," he said. "Send it through to my phone, and flag it for Inaya. We need to see it for ourselves. We'll meet you back at HQ."

He brought Inaya up to speed on the way to the car, dodging the issue of his interrogation of her father, though he knew he wasn't off the hook.

"It appears Huxton Cooper wrote to his father from the base. Catalina has been through his letters. She's sent us a picture of one. Read it to me while I drive."

A cold silence persisted as he drove out of her neighborhood. Then she reached for her phone, Brandt's file resting on her lap. She pulled up the image Cat had sent, then settled in to read Huxton Cooper's letter.

"'I told you things are bad with my platoon, but these days they're fucking terrible. I know you'd never do what I'm about to do, you'd never let yourself down. But Dr. Young knew about the murders . . . said we have to come clean. You told me to keep my head down, but you have to know I can't live with that. I can't dodge the platoon, and I can't make you happy, so it seems I'm out of options. There's no coming back from this. Please forgive me. Hux.'"

Her voice trembled at the end. Seif took hold of her hand.

"Hell of a suicide note," he said.

"So now we know he was at Mirembe's lecture, but he doesn't mention my father."

She tried to free her hand from his but he wasn't having that.

"I'm sorry. If I hadn't talked to your father, Brandt would have sent someone else."

"It was a stupid distraction," she muttered.

"It was the timing of it—the coincidence. I couldn't just let it go."

With her free hand, Inaya paged through the file in her lap, pausing over the photograph.

"That poor kid."

"Yeah," he agreed.

"Did you read the whole file?"

"I didn't have time. Why?"

She showed him a clear white page where none of the print was blacked out. "I think your friend at the FBI sent you the unredacted file. This looks like the final report." She frowned to herself. "It's classified. But it doesn't say why."

She flipped to the final page just as he pulled into HQ.

"Oh God," she whispered.

His head snapped around. He brought the car to a stop and she held up the picture of Huxton Cooper in the empty room.

"Take another look at this picture. Tell me what you don't see."

42

Jaime was the only one at headquarters. He'd watched the footage of Duante's killing enough that he was numb, and he hated feeling numb. A man younger than he was had been killed, and support had rallied around the officer who had shot him. He knew Harry was a good one. He'd still done a terrible thing.

There was a knock on the glass doors that led into their bullpen. When Jaime saw it was Dr. Stanger, he bounded from his seat, shaking the doctor's hand. He wished he could dress like the other man, who was turned out in a lightweight fawn suit with a green tie and matching pocket square. He'd told Jaime once that too many mothers cried over their dead, so he came prepared to console them.

His green eyes were kind behind his steel-rimmed glasses, and Jaime had taken to Stanger from the very first day.

"I've been trying to reach Detective Hernandez," Stanger said in his low, well-modulated voice. "She doesn't appear to be answering calls at present."

"She's in the field. Can I help out instead?"

Stanger laid the blue folder he was carrying onto Jaime's cluttered desk.

"I emailed this to Lieutenant Seif this morning, I haven't had a response, and I can't imagine this is something you'd want to overlook."

"Ballistics report on Mateo Ruiz?"

Stanger's pale gold hair was so neatly arranged, it didn't move as he shook his head.

"Your detectives already have that. I finished up with the Ruiz case because your lieutenant moved it to the top of his list. But two days ago he asked me to put a rush on the evidence collected at the scene of the Young shooting. I've confirmed that Duante Young was killed by a bullet from Officer Cooper's gun, but there are a couple of anomalies."

"With the gun?" Jaime's big hands shuffled the pages in the folder.

"Not with the gun. With the spray-paint can that Officer Cooper mistook for a weapon."

Jaime's heart jumped up into his throat. "It was modified?" he whispered. "Weaponized? There *was* just cause, after all?"

Stanger pointed Jaime to his written report. "You see?" His finger trailed down the page. "And there's also this about Officer Cooper's clothing. He'd run into those garbage bins when the paint was fresh."

Jaime read the report, then he read it again.

His frightened eyes met Stanger's. "This means—"

"—that you'd better find your lieutenant."

Inaya checked her phone. It had been buzzing for the last ten minutes, but she hadn't wanted to abandon her father to Seif's interrogation. She was still outraged that he hadn't told her about the background he'd gathered on her father, or that her father had been under FBI surveillance.

She couldn't trust him. The thought was so painful, that she stepped out of their offices to take Areesha's call.

She'd seen Areesha face down cops at a demonstration without breaking a sweat, but now Areesha sounded frazzled.

"You need to get to my house now. Mirembe's here with me, and we're in trouble!"

Inaya was already moving, grabbing her holster and her jacket. Seif came to his feet at her agitated movements.

"Call 911," she told Areesha. "I'm on my way."

"No! He said no other cops, just you."

A name flashed through Inaya's mind, a glaring neon sign. JOHN BRODA. Seif had warned her that Broda would have an endgame. But why strike at Areesha?

"Is his son with you?" she asked. "Are they holding you hostage?"

A horrified sound came from Areesha's throat, as if she'd been prodded by a gun.

"Inaya, no, it's just him. He came to deal with Mirembe. He's holding my boys hostage. Please, get here, now! His patience is running out."

Inaya nearly dropped the phone. She'd known. Hadn't she known all along?

She signaled to Seif. To Cat, she mouthed, "Call Broda's wife. She can talk him down."

They were out the door, in the car, tires screaming as Seif peeled away from the lot.

"Stay on the phone, Areesha."

"I can't." Areesha was crying now. "He won't let me."

The phone was wrenched away, the line went dead. And even with the siren, it took them twenty minutes to get to Areesha's house.

A police cruiser was parked outside, the interior dark. It didn't belong to the DPD. It had a Starling County decal on the hood. A cop from Blackwater Falls.

The fog in her mind cleared. John Broda had never planned to take revenge. His promises had been sincere. She should have made the leap from Broda, known that at its heart this case was about one thing. Fathers and their sons.

"It's Harry Cooper," she told Seif. "Not John Broda."

"I know. That's why I needed to interview your father."

"Qas—"

"Later, Inaya. Let's deal with Cooper first."

They approached from the side of the house, circled around to the back, trying to see through the windows, but the blinds were drawn.

Inaya's phone rang again. This time it was Harry.

"Just you," he said. "Tell him if he enters, I'll shoot the boys first."

He hung up.

Seif had heard it. "No way in hell," he told her.

"I have hostage-negotiation training. You have to let me try."

"I said no."

The sound of a gunshot shattered the quiet, followed by high-pitched screams.

Inaya raced for the door. "You can't stop me," she said.

"I'm giving you a direct order." Seif's face was pale and clammy. He knew she had to go. Abruptly, he pivoted. "Come with me."

He dragged her back to the car and popped the trunk. He gave her a second gun to tuck in the small of her back. He also handed over his lightweight armored vest. In her panic, Inaya had forgotten to bring her own.

"Keep your cell on, open a window if you can, and let me hear what's going down." He glared down at her. "Don't take stupid risks."

She fingered the vest. "Don't you dare come inside if you're not wearing a vest."

"We'll have backup soon." He touched her cheek. "Keep him talking as long as you can."

The front door opened onto a shadowed hallway. Seif hauled her up and kissed her hard on the mouth, then gave her a little push up the stairs.

Her heart thumping wildly in her chest, she murmured a *dua* to herself, entering the house, gun drawn.

"Close the door and drop the gun."

The voice came through an intercom. There was no one in the hall.

Inaya obeyed instructions, though she left the door open just a crack.

"Lock the door."

She looked around. There were no cameras in the hall, so Harry Cooper was likely listening to the sound of her actions. She went to the door and loudly turned the lock. It didn't matter because the door was still open. He wouldn't be able to tell.

"Come into the dining room. If you pick up your gun, I'll know."

She passed a closet in the hall whose handle was jammed up with zip ties. The door shook and she heard the pleading cries from inside. Areesha.

"It's all right," she said calmly. "I'm here now, Areesha."

"My boys," Areesha sobbed.

Inaya stepped into the dining room. Mirembe sat at the far end of the dining table, her golden eyes wide with horror. Harry sat in a chair at an angle to her in his patrol uniform, his shiny badge on his pocket. His chair was pushed back because Areesha's two boys knelt awkwardly at his feet, his gun within his reach on the table before them.

"Good," he said. "You're here."

Seif was right. She'd been so preoccupied by the Brodas that she'd missed the bread crumbs on Cooper's trail.

"Is anyone hurt?" She took a good look at Areesha's boys. Clay was crying, chills shaking his torso. Kareem's eyes were on fire, his fists clenched at his sides. She didn't see any blood.

"What did you shoot at?" she asked Harry.

He pointed to a hole in the ceiling.

Her body shuddered in relief.

"We're all right," Mirembe said quietly. "I don't know why he wants these boys."

"Hostages," Harry said.

"Could I trade you?" Inaya asked. "The boys are terrified, and terrified kids are unpredictable. We don't want anyone hurt today, do we? Let them go and take me instead. I'm much more valuable to you as a hostage. I won't get either of us killed."

He considered this.

"They're so young, Harry," Inaya continued to urge him. "They have time to learn the hard lessons of life, don't make them face those lessons now. Kareem is only ten, Clay is eight. Please, Harry, think about what you're doing."

In a voice utterly devoid of expression, Harry said, "My boy was young too. Wasn't he worth as much as the sons of Dr. Young?"

A flash of realization burned through Inaya.

"Harry, these aren't Mirembe's boys. They're the sons of David and Areesha Adams. Mirembe only had one son. Duante. He's dead now, remember?"

The gun stayed on the table. Harry would have researched Mirembe, he would know about her family.

Inaya pushed her advantage.

"Why do you think their mother is so frantic in that closet? These are Areesha's boys. Please. Just let them go."

"She's telling you the truth," Mirembe said. "You killed my only son."

"You killed mine," he returned.

"I want to hear all about that, Harry," Inaya promised. "But first, let these boys go."

"Come here," Harry said. "Closer."

Oh God, she thought. *Ya Rub, protect us all.*

She advanced step by step until she was right in front of Harry. He picked up the gun and placed it against her heart. It was beating so hard she wondered that he couldn't hear it. Moving slowly so as not to spook him, she raised both hands to Kareem's shoulders. With a look of reassurance, she urged him to his feet.

Harry didn't move.

"Can he go now, Harry? I'll stay here with you."

Kareem jerked in her grasp. "Not without Clay," he sobbed.

She shushed him gently. "You go now, honey, and I'll get Clay. Is that all right, Harry?"

Harry shrugged, the gun prodding her ribs.

Inaya turned Kareem around and told him to head to the door. It seemed like a lifetime before his careful steps advanced. He paused beside the closet, crying out to his mother.

"Kareem," Inaya said firmly. "Go now, so I can get Clay."

When Kareem was outside, she guided Clay to his feet.

"What about Clay, Harry? Can he go too?"

"Do you want to die so badly?" He moved the gun so it was up under Inaya's chin. Its cold steel burned her skin.

"That's what good cops do, right Harry? Good soldiers, too. They take a bullet for the innocent. That's what happened to Hux, isn't it? Don't you want to be like Hux?"

The gun slammed into her jaw. Clay shook beneath her hands. She didn't dare touch her face, but the pain from the blow was excruciating.

"Don't talk about my son!" Harry thundered.

She gave Clay a gentle shove out of the way, keeping her body between his and Harry's.

"I think you want to talk about him, don't you? Go on, Clay." She nodded to the boy. "I think that's why you came here. To talk to Dr. Young."

She gave Clay another little shove. He paced down the hall to the door and disappeared.

The gun was back at her heart but still she called out to Areesha, "Areesha, the boys are out. Both your boys are safe."

The frantic cries from the closet subsided.

"Do you want me to kneel?" she asked Harry. "You can put the gun to my head."

"Leave her," Mirembe said wearily. "It's me that you want, and I don't care if I die. You took the only thing that had any meaning for me."

Harry's lethal attention shifted from Inaya for a second.

"I know. Because that's what you did to me."

"What about Tania, Harry? Doesn't she mean something? She'd do anything for you."

His attention shifted back to Inaya and she cursed herself for not finding the time for an interview. She would have known if she'd seen him. His eyes were dead, his expression flat.

Another image clicked in her mind.

"That was you at the funeral, smiling into the camera."

"Sit here." He pointed the gun at the chair to his right, Mirembe on his left. She sank down into the chair, the gun still aimed at her heart, but now his attention was split between her and Mirembe. She didn't want another civilian in the mix, but if Areesha managed to free herself from the closet, the odds would change.

"Was that Tania with you?"

His lips twisted. "You're right. Tania would do anything for me, but there's only so much she could hide. I knew the minute you talked to her about The Wonder of Life that you'd be on to me. You'd know I set that contest up to draw Duante out."

When Mirembe moved to speak, Inaya silenced her with a movement of her hand.

"You needed Dr. Young to suffer, didn't you?"

"An eye for an eye, a son for a son. Hux deserved to live," he suddenly shouted. "She stole his whole life from him."

"How? I don't understand how. She never met your son, never spoke to him or treated him as a patient. How could she have hurt him?"

"He was Third Platoon," Harry said bitterly. "And Third Platoon was a gang of psychopaths. Hux didn't belong there, he didn't want to be there."

"Yes." Inaya leaned across and patted Harry's knee. "I've read his letter. I know he wasn't involved. He had a good heart, Harry. He wanted to do right. He was a son to be proud of. You must have taught him to be that way, so why are you so angry at him?"

For the first time, he lowered the gun, resting it on his other knee.

"He gave up on himself." He aimed the gun at Mirembe. "He killed himself because of you. He wrote to tell me what he was planning to do. He said it was because of you."

"You're wrong about that, Harry." Inaya said it with conviction.

"The only thing that's wrong in all this is that my boy took his own life."

Inaya quickly put her phone on the table, calling Seif. It was on speaker, and she'd turned the volume all the way up.

"Are you so sure that he did? You think Huxton's conscience wouldn't let him cover for the platoon, so he took his own life?"

Harry nodded, the pain behind his eyes so deep, Inaya had to look away.

"You misunderstood him, Harry." Her voice was soft with compassion. "He was planning to report his squad to commanders on base. *That's* why he asked for your forgiveness. He knew he was breaking ranks—something you would never do."

Harry's jaw went slack. "No. That isn't right."

"It's in his unredacted file," Inaya continued. "And we can arrange for you to speak to your son's CO. The army covered it up at the time, but Hux didn't kill himself."

"Then how did he die?" Harry's face was white with shock.

"My guess is he was murdered by his squad. Take a look at this picture."

She took the photograph from her jacket pocket and placed it in his hand. It was one of the hardest things she'd ever had to do.

Harry stared at the picture like a man who was staring into hell, face to face with the unspeakable truth of a blood betrayal.

Inaya pointed to the space beneath Huxton's body. To the empty room.

"If Hux killed himself, how did he sling the rope onto a beam that high? Look, Harry. Even if he kicked it away, there would still be a chair. But there is no chair, do you see? The room is empty. Hux couldn't have done it, which means someone else did. The army has reopened the inquiry into Huxton's death. You should have answers soon."

Mirembe raised her head. Her bleak eyes met Harry's.

"You killed my son for nothing, Harry. For nothing at all."

They stared at each other for endless, empty minutes.

Then before Inaya could react, Harry raised his arm and fired.

His brain matter and thick hot blood splashed across Inaya's face.

43

Areesha didn't let go of her boys until David arrived. His arms were broad enough to embrace them all, and he squeezed her so tightly she thought her bones might break. She didn't care. She needed him, needed the security of his presence, and at the same time she was fervently glad he had been at work when she'd opened her door to Harry Cooper.

She hadn't seen the officer's face through her peephole. She'd only seen his badge, and foolishly she'd let him in. Time had collapsed. It felt like she'd been locked in the closet for hours, though only minutes had elapsed as she'd sobbed for the lives of her boys. She would never forget that Inaya had traded herself for Areesha's sons.

She'd walked into this case unable to imagine that it wasn't about race or that Harry Cooper would stand trial. She would have done her best. She would have called in her allies and fought as hard as she could, but this was one time that she wouldn't have to fight. This one time she could think about her husband and her children—backed into a corner not because they were Black, but because of one man's vendetta against an innocent woman. Duante had paid for that vendetta with his life. He would never return to his mother's arms—they wouldn't have the chance to repair the things that had gone wrong.

She looked down at Clay's and Kareem's innocent faces and tucked that lesson to her heart: to take every chance to let them know how much she loved them, because God knew she couldn't anticipate the random cruelties of life.

David read her mind. "Baby, there's no way you could have known. Help Mirembe now. That's all you can do."

She brought his face down to her own and kissed him deep and long. Their boys didn't interrupt them; nothing made them feel as secure as their parents' love for each other. They huddled together against the storm, thanking God for another day.

Cat watched them with a curious sense of flatness. She hadn't done Areesha or Mirembe any good as a profiler. She'd been so distracted by her own heartache that she hadn't seen through Harry's facade. The good cop, the grieving cop, the one who would never shoot an unarmed man. But between the four members of their team, and with Areesha's help, they had made the chain of events make sense. Jaime had also shown her Dr. Stanger's report. If they'd had to build a case against Harry Cooper, the report would have clinched it.

Unwittingly, Tania Davis had reported the theft of her garbage can to Blackwater police. Harry Cooper had set up those bins to block off an escape route, knowing Duante would head to the wall to paint his mural. Tania had posted the Blackwater Falls site as an option for the next phase of the contest. She'd said the entries had been blind, but Harry had maneuvered her to choose Duante's work each time, whetting the young man's appetite. He had lured Duante to the place where he'd set up the kill, ostensibly doing everything by the book—the chase, the two warnings, right down to the spray-paint can in Duante's hand. The design on the bins wasn't anything fancy: it was just enough to suggest it wasn't a random act of vandalism. Even from the minimal flourishes Harry had sprayed, a trained artist would have recognized that Duante hadn't sprayed those cans. But because of who Harry was, they had failed to look beyond the immediate facts of the shooting.

What Harry hadn't taken into account was that Willie Reynolds would tell the police that they'd planned to paint their mural on the barrier, not on a set of bins. He'd failed to notice that the spray paint on his uniform was a different brand than the can in Duante's hand. It established that Duante hadn't defaced the cans. It also established that at some time that night Harry Cooper had come into contact with the paint on the bins.

When Huxton Cooper had died on base, and the army had covered up the crimes of the Third Platoon, Harry had taken Huxton's letter as a confession of suicide. He'd begun to track Mirembe. Maybe if she'd stayed in D.C., Harry wouldn't have gone any further. But once she moved to Denver, Duante's fate was sealed. A life for a life. A son for a son.

Fathers and sons. With John and Kelly Broda's example before her, Cat had still missed the relevant clues. Emiliano's yearning for a son should have peeled the blinkers from her eyes. She hadn't done her job, it appeared, either at work or at home. So maybe her job would need to change. Maybe *she* would need to change.

Unlike Areesha, she couldn't go home to the safety of her husband's arms. Her safety had been demolished by Emiliano's betrayal. She thought of going home with Inaya, but she could see that Inaya, too, needed the comfort of her family. A man had blown out his brains in her presence, unable to reckon with his disastrous actions. Tania Davis was crying on the street outside Areesha's house, while Inaya sat tight-lipped and stoic in the back of an ambulance.

Tomorrow or the next day, the three women would regroup. They would meet at Cyrine's and settle in for her gentle mothering with hot cups of coffee and the world's best *kanafeh*. Tonight, Cat was on her own, but tomorrow things would be better. She'd buy a few toiletries and check in at the Motel 6. Motels didn't scare her even if they were in the seedy part of town, and after all, she had her gun.

She started to turn away, headed back to her car.

Jaime Webb stopped in front of her, blocking her escape.

"Jaime, *mi chiquito,* it's time to get some rest. I'm going home to catch some sleep."

"But you aren't, are you, boss?" Jaime gathered her up against his big body in a hug that swept her off her feet. "Something's wrong, do you think I can't tell? And I'm not going to rest until you tell me what it is."

Tears burned her eyes. He was a fine young man. But she couldn't share her sorrows with him. She told him as much.

"That's all right," he said comfortably. "I told my ma I was bringing you home. She made her best lasagna for you. Cannoli too. There's no way you can turn that down."

"My car—"

"A friend of mine will pick it up. So are you coming or what?"

Much to her amazement, Cat found that she was.

They were going their separate ways when a familiar figure approached Areesha's house. Curious neighbors and passersby were hanging around outside the cordon. Families of all backgrounds had come together to find out what had happened to David and Areesha Adams. They called out support from the boundary of the tape. In another hour or two, casseroles and baked goods would be piled up on Areesha's steps. But for now, a slender and supple figure edged as close as she could, her long curls dancing in the breeze.

Altagracia, or Luna Clyde.

She caught sight of Cat and let out a piercing whistle. Jaime all but dragged Cat right to Areesha's steps, the crowd parting to allow their passage.

Cat introduced her to the others. They spoke in hushed voices. In the distance, a flash went off, taking a picture that would soon go viral because Areesha reached out to wrap Catalina in a hug, and Jaime and Luna joined in.

Rumors had been flying thick and fast, as Luna now informed them.

"We now know neither shooting was about targeting us. But two innocent members of our communities were still gunned down by police. The protest will be on the steps of the Capitol building tomorrow, after our vigil for Mateo and Duante. I wanted you to hear that from me." Luna eyed Jaime Webb. "We want you all to be there. To stand with us, side by side."

While Cat pondered the wisdom of this, Areesha smiled wryly at David. He had kept hold of their boys, but his eyes followed his wife. He returned her smile when she said, "It seems we've lived to fight another day."

44

In the afternoon, Seif found Inaya at the small Blackwater mosque. His brothers had insisted on accompanying him, their normal boisterous manner subdued by the recent turn of events. Seif had been involved in a situation that could have gone south, and he hadn't been wearing his vest. If they'd lost him, the arguments they were ready to resurrect wouldn't have meant a damn. They wouldn't have had the chance to make peace, and were deeply affected by that knowledge.

When Seif had gotten home, they'd been waiting for him, and so had Lily. The boys had invited her in, and she rose from a seat in the great room as soon as she saw him. She didn't run to him as he expected, and when he looked at the chain around her neck, his ring was no longer there.

"They said a Community Response officer was taken hostage, and that someone was shot. I heard it on the news. I thought it was you." Her voice was even, the worry was in her eyes. "But you're all right?" Her eyes slipped over his body.

"I wasn't hurt."

"Good, good." She nodded. "I saw you with that detective on your team."

He tried to blank out the memory and failed. He'd stormed the house, found Inaya unharmed, and cradled her in his arms. Later, he'd taken wipes from an EMT, and cleaned the blood and other matter from Inaya's face and hair. He hadn't known the cameras were on.

"It's over between us for good, isn't it? Even if you don't move on with someone else."

He walked the few steps he needed to pull her into his arms. The kiss to the top of her head was his final farewell. "It was never right with us—I think you know that now. But I am sorry—you deserve a man who will give you the world."

"Is that what you'll be giving her?" She pulled back to look into his eyes. And for once, he didn't try to hide his inner self from her.

"If she lets me." He wouldn't say more. Not to Lily. Not when it would hurt her.

She nodded, her stunning legs flashing as she moved to the door. His mouth quirked. This was the Lily he had loved, in her short, stylish skirts. The Lily he hoped wouldn't change, because nothing about her needed to. Nothing about her was wrong.

"You made me a better man, Lily. I'll always remember that."

She touched her fingers to her lips in a kiss, and then she was gone.

The boys came into the room looking sheepish.

"Bro, we didn't know where to look—those legs!"

He laughed, the sound hoarse and unexpected.

"You could have died today," Mik said with great humility.

"I wasn't in any danger," he told them. "My detective, on the other hand—"

"Your woman, you mean," Alireza teased.

"She's angry at me right now."

"You'll make it work. You always do."

"Do I?" His gaze moved from Alireza to Mik. "It feels like I'm screwing it up. Everything I wanted for you."

The twins hauled him into one of their three-cornered hugs.

"You didn't know we'd turn out to be so pigheaded."

"*Astaghfirullah,*" he said, joking. "Never use that word."

Mikhail dug his elbow into Seif's ribs. "Funny, bro. No. We just wanted to say, maybe we won't always listen, maybe now and then we'll have to do things our own way, but that doesn't mean you don't matter. No one matters more than you."

"Yeah?" He hugged them harder.

"Yeah." They hugged him back.

"Maybe you should go to Palestine—you have the right of return. Maybe you *should* find the answers for yourselves."

Alireza's smile blinded him. He took their hands in his.

"Then say a prayer of thanks. And another one of hope."

At the mosque, the twins caught sight of Noor and Nadia, and peeled off to chat them up. Seif took the opportunity to speak to Haseeb Rahman, giving him a detailed description of the hostage-taking and of Harry Cooper's death.

"Your daughter is too brave for her own good, sir. She takes too many chances."

Rahman's response surprised him.

"She told me you gave her your vest."

He felt the hot color come up under his skin.

"I didn't want her in the house. She left me no other choice."

"I believe you, Waqas."

He offered nothing else, and uncomfortably, Seif raised the issue of the interview.

"I'm sorry if my manner was too harsh, but I needed to know what you knew. I was hoping you had the answers."

"My son, we may disagree on politics, but you said nothing to offend me."

Seif swallowed over a lump in his throat.

My son.

He hadn't heard those words addressed to him in years.

"Thank you, sir."

Sunober Rahman came up to claim her husband, turning a suspicious glare on Seif. She must have seen the footage.

"You put my daughter at risk," she snapped. "That man could have killed her."

Instead of apologizing like he should have, for some stupid reason Seif said, "I can't control Inaya. Nor would I want to."

Rahman murmured to his wife, leading her away, a smile tugging at his lips.

What had he said, Seif wondered, to provoke that little smile?

Restlessly, he searched the crowd for Inaya. She was probably on her way to a debrief with Cat and Areesha. He didn't expect to be invited along, but he wanted to catch her first. Say a private word or two, things he'd been too terrified to utter when the gunshot had gone off.

In that moment, he had turned to the God he'd disavowed, Arabic searing his throat, filling up his lungs and mouth. It had come to him whole as if it had never been purged.

Forgive me, forgive me, he'd begged. *God, don't punish me like this!*

Inaya had gotten Areesha's sons to safety and offered herself in their place. He hated the sheer recklessness of it, even knowing he'd have done the same.

She was safe. That's what he had to remind himself. She was safe in the here and now.

He detached her from the group of women who surrounded her, like a shark running down his prey. Without utmost circumspection, he asked her to join him outside.

When she did, his gaze dwelled on the smudges under her eyes. She hadn't slept.

"You were crazy to risk yourself like that." His voice was rough.

"I thought I could stop him."

"You did," he said firmly. "We got Cooper in the end."

"He didn't have to die. If I hadn't been so hard on him—"

"He snuffed out Duante's life. Don't feel sorry for him."

"I can't help it. What he did—" She wiped a stray tendril of hair from her face, no doubt remembering the slick spatter of blood. "If I'd just moved faster—"

"You'll have a lifetime of regrets if you start to think like that. Besides—" He indicated the mosque. "—don't you believe that a man's time is written?"

They were at the mosque, so he couldn't draw her into his arms like he wanted to. He couldn't kiss her, take her hand, touch her hair. He had to content himself with a burning look.

She arched a brow. "Playing me at my own game, Lieutenant?"

"At any game you like." He nudged her. "Are you angry with me about your father?"

"Not anymore. I know my father wanted justice for the Third Platoon's actions."

"Does he ever talk to you about Afghanistan?"

A frown pleated her brow. He wanted to smooth it away, but he caught the stern interest of Inaya's mother from the corner of his eye. Hell and damnation. He wanted to go slow, but this was far too slow.

"Rarely," she answered him. "Afghanistan is the memory of a wound for my father."

Like Palestine was for Seif.

"You should talk to him," Seif said. "I have the feeling there's more he could share."

"What about you? Are you keeping secrets too?"

Seif took a deep breath. "Some. But none that could hurt you."

The frown cleared from her brow. She smiled up at him, and again that punch of feeling caught him by surprise.

"The Egan video went viral."

Inaya had been the one to release it. "Yes. John Broda came through."

"What's your next move?"

"I'll need some time off to head up to Chicago to see that Marcus's family gets justice."

"That's not a safe place for you."

"John will watch out for me now."

"No. I'll take you there myself."

She looked appalled. "I can't travel with you!"

"As colleagues, nothing more." He cleared his throat. "Have you thought about that? If we take this where we both want it to go, I'll have to move you off my team."

Her gaze turned inward. He could see that she hadn't thought that far ahead.

"The work is important to me," she said slowly. "Are you asking me to choose?"

"Would you choose me, Inaya?"

She turned it around on him.

"Would you choose *me*?"

He'd known they would end up here. He just didn't know if he was ready.

Inaya and Areesha met up with Willie Reynolds and Raze just before the vigil in the bright heat of day. The communities who represented Mateo and Duante had blocked off both sides of the wide path between the State Capitol building and the courthouse. Police in full riot gear stood on the opposite side. They hadn't advanced, and on the other side, no one was crowding the barriers.

"We painted this for them," Raze told her.

From the mile-high step of the capitol, Inaya gazed down at the street.

Raze and Willie had re-created Duante's painting of the six women activists. At the end, they had added on Duante and Mateo, Duante with a paintbrush in his hand, Mateo strumming a guitar. A slogan circled their heads:

LOVE AND TRUTH WILL PREVAIL

Inaya thought of Duante and Raze, of Duante and Mirry. She thought of Kelly and Mateo, of John Broda's love for his son. And she thought of Maddy Hicks and Harry Cooper, how their love had become twisted up inside them until all it could do was destroy.

She remembered Seif's beautiful dark eyes and the distance he had traveled to find his way to her. Love and truth *would* prevail. She took Areesha's hand in hers, raising up their arms.

This was the good fight. And even though she wore a badge, she wouldn't give it up.

The strident note of a horn shattered the peace of the vigil.

In an instant, the barriers came down.

ACKNOWLEDGMENTS

Thank you to my dear friends Catherine, Danielle, Hector, Nettie, Alison, and everyone at Minotaur, who works so hard to help me tell these stories. You showed me so much kindness and patience when I needed it—I wouldn't be at this place without you. And thank you to my readers and fellow writers, for all the kindness and support you extend to writers in dark places.

Thank you to my loving family of Khans, Hashemis, Ahmeds, Raos, and Shaikhs. This first year without Dad was hard, but you never let me struggle alone—I hope I've done the same for you. Casim, you are a treasure I hold close to my heart. Thank you for shouldering so much, I'm so proud of the man you've become. My darling Ayeshie, you think you weren't there, but you were, at every step and in every heartbeat, planting fields of tulips. Irfan and Kashif—life keeps showing me how impossible it would be to do without you, so don't you dare go anywhere. You are two of the finest men I know, the best possible reflection of Dad. Summer, my angel, thank you for letting me be as sad in England as I needed to be.

Thank you to my sisters, whose prayers keep me afloat. Nozzie, Uzmi, Saima and Farah, Farah and Hema, Fereshteh, Firoozeh, and Haseeba, there are no words to describe how you make all of this possible for me. You listen, you love, and you stand in for me when it's needed. I love you, now and always.

Auntie Aira, Uncle Munir, Yasmin, Semina, and Blondie—did you know that memories have the weight of love? Some of the best moments of my life were at Chandni Chowk and Morningside Park. For table tennis, card games, donuts, and fresh glasses of milk, I will love you all forever.

Thank you, UJ, the best writing partner in the world. Thank you for listening and making me laugh. For reading impossible words and dreaming impossible dreams. Most of all, thank you for praying beside me at my father's *janazah*. I will never forget that.

My deepest thanks also to former US Marine and SWAT Technician Jonas Apala, and to former Marines William and Danielle Wright, for so generously answering my questions about your service. I know those memories are painful at the best of times and I'm so grateful for your honesty and insight. Thank you to Lieutenant Colonel Soraya Moghadam of the Canadian Armed Forces, for so clearly illuminating the realities of life on base. You're a natural storyteller and what you have to say has so much value. Thank you to my wonderful niece, Noor Shaikh, and to the very kind Majid Moghadam for your help with the architectural details of Seif's house. Thank you, Kashie, for finding me experts on every subject under the sun, including poisons, antique revolvers, and the brain scans of addicts. I made use of the brain scans, but haven't gotten to the poisons yet.

Thank you to my husband, Nader, for everything you do and everything you are. In this past year, the first and last thing you did on every visit home was take me to visit Dad's grave. In a year of change and loss, you have been my constant.

Lastly, I want to acknowledge the strength of my mother. She was the light of my father's eyes, and our harbor in every storm. Thank you, Mum, for keeping us together when we needed it, and for telling me to keep writing. All these stories exist because of you and Dad.

Special note: Our beloved Uncle Munir passed away during the end stages of this book. May God reunite him with his dearest friend, my father, in the perfect tranquility of Paradise. And may He grant us all *sabr* to bear this loss.